# Dagger and Scythe

## The Ichorian Epics: Book 2

Emilie Knight

Illustration and Design: David Schmelling

Printed in Canada

First Printing: October 1st, 2019

ISBN: 978-1-9990914-0-8

This book is dedicated to Dagger and Scythe themselves. To the reader, they may be fiction, but to me they have been surprisingly patient waiting for their story to be written.

They may not be so forgiving next time.

# Chapter 1

Maniodes stood in front of the fireplace in his office chambers, facing Scythe and Dagger. The fireplace was beautifully crafted from black marble, not showing a single seam. The rest of the furniture looked archaic in comparison. A single large desk and chair, both made of wrought iron and littered with parchment and quills, stood in the corner. In another corner a bench that would have been comfortable if it hadn't been made of the same iron sat. That bench was not meant for pleasant exchanges.

The short crop of his dark-blue hair glinted when the firelight hit it. It had been styled differently yesterday. Scythe knew even gods had their vanities, and she wanted to compliment him on the change, but his demeanor was overwhelming. He stood a towering eight feet as he studied Dagger and Scythe. He wasn't just angry this time; he was livid at the chaos they had caused. Scythe stayed quiet while staring at the ash on Maniodes's boots.

Beside her, Dagger was equally quiet.

Maniodes sighed, seeming to be frustrated by his own train of thought. "You were given one victim of your choice, but you decided to torch the entire village.

It will be a wondrous story, true, but you left a child alive! The Incruentus Ferrum are supposed to be subtle."

His voice scared the warmth from the fire, or so it seemed to Scythe.

"It was not intended, sire," Dagger said. "We got…carried away."

Scythe had to bite her cheek to stop from laughing. She could still see Dagger stalking around the pile of bodies in the main square, relishing his work.

"Something funny, Scythe?" Maniodes asked, turning on her.

She had stifled the laugh but not the smile. She swallowed her nerves and looked up at the god. There wasn't any point in lying now.

"We got excited," she explained.

"Of course you did; that's the problem. First, you ransack that wedding, leaving no survivors. Then you, Dagger, kill a king on his ship and everyone saw you. It doesn't matter if panic ensues. You *have* to stay hidden. You are meant to cause mischief that the living can't explain, not mayhem and chaos they can fight against. Keeping them cautious keeps them safe, and it reminds them there is a higher power."

"What's the point in causing mischief if we can't enjoy it?" Dagger questioned. "And what's the point, anyway? The living cause enough chaos with war and murder. Whatever we do, it's a small percentage of what they do to themselves."

"The purpose is to be subtle and cause terror. What's more threatening—the hunter with the axe that you can see, or the monster in the shadows that stalks you? And the *point* is to frighten them in ways they can't explain easily."

Dagger didn't reply; Scythe remained quiet as well. They were lucky they could discuss things with their ruler at all, but even they knew when to shut up.

"I have an idea," Maniodes said.

Scythe hoped it didn't involve being trapped in the river Acheron again.

"You two will marry each other."

"What?!" Dagger exclaimed.

Scythe's breath locked in her chest. She had finally gained freedom in death, and now she was going to be bound to a man nonetheless.

"That's ridiculous," Dagger said, gingerly overstepping his bounds.

"You two have worked together before, regardless of my say-so. And that's more than most mortals get in arranged marriages," Maniodes said civilly.

"But a marriage as a punishment?" Dagger asked.

"Call it an experiment. Conventional punishments haven't worked on either of you, and I don't want to rip away your lives. You two will guard each other. If one of you takes a step out of bounds, then both of you will go grey and rejoin the dead in the fields."

"Guarding each other I understand, even forcing us to live together, but why the full marriage?" Dagger asked again.

"God of mischief," Maniodes shrugged. "You two work well together anyway. Forcing the marriage should remind you who is in charge."

Scythe stared at Maniodes, the insult tasting bitter. They'd had a silent understanding of her rogue behavior so long as she followed the basic rules. Forcing this upon her was almost as bad as what her father had tried to pull.

Maniodes turned to Scythe. She didn't bother hiding her anger. He knew her story. It was why he chose her to become an Incruentus Ferrum. He guarded his expression well. She couldn't tell if he was saddened by her rage, emboldened by his victory, or if he even gave a shit.

"Come, stand here." Maniodes indicated for them to move closer.

Dagger stepped forward, but Scythe stayed put, nails biting into her palms.

"Scythe."

The cold tone of a father talking down to a child, while also threatening to kill that child, compelled her to move. She hated herself and Maniodes for it, but she couldn't become one of those mindless, stumbling shades. She took her place beside Dagger but couldn't look at him.

"Raise your left hand," Maniodes ordered.

Scythe did so and held it palm-down just over waist height.

"Dagger, your right."

Dagger raised his hand and held Scythe's from below. Their fingers wove together naturally. She forced herself to not let go. Dagger hadn't wanted this, either. He'd even protested against it.

"Shit, I don't have a ribbon," Maniodes admitted, looking at their joined hands. "Hold on."

He unclipped a chain hanging from his belt. Using that instead of the customary ribbon, the god laid it over Scythe's hand, wrapped it under Dagger's, then over again.

Once the chain encircled their wrists Maniodes spoke again.

"I won't bother with fancy words. Dagger, do you take this woman as your wife?"

Dagger cleared his throat, then said, "Yes."

"Scythe, do you take this man as your husband?"

If she said no she'd be dead. Swallowing her pride, she said, "Yes."

"Good. Now, if either of you disobey my order again, I will strip the consciousness from you both. You are to watch and guide each other. Understood?"

"Yes," Dagger said.

Scythe nodded.

"Should things go well and you learn to control yourselves, I could grant an annulment," Maniodes said. "Now go. I don't care where, neither of you will receive any work for a while."

# Chapter 2

Dagger watched as Scythe stormed out of Maniodes's castle, nearly knocking over a skeletal guard. The guard was more for show since there was nothing close to threatening down there. Maniodes was the son of Nyx, the goddess of death, so no one had ever opposed him. The only inhabitants in Skiachora besides Maniodes were the Incruentus Ferrum and the grey husks of the dead. The living, above in Ichorisis, knew of the land of the dead, of course, but not the details. No matter how rich or poor, or which city-state the person lived in, they all ended up down there. Every single human was left as a grey shadow of his or her former self.

Scythe continued down the gravel path past the dead trees. She shoved the heavily spiked gate open, hardly aware of the clang as it rebounded. Dagger caught the gate before it could swing back into his face.

The Valley of Shades stretched out under him. The dead shambled as grey shells, each alone in a hoard reaching into the millions. Their bodies were buried during the funeral but the ghosts resembled their owners as perfectly as when they died, except for the color having been drained from them. None of them cared. Dagger doubted they even knew where they were. The Acheron River split the grey valley in two, its smaller tendrils of water branching from it.

The Acheron River rose from under Maniodes's castle, split through Skiachora, then entered the land of the living: Ichorisis. Everyone born up there, ended up down here, no matter how cruel or virtuous their life.

"Scythe, wait!"

"Do not give me orders!" She rounded on him midway down the stairs. The stone steps branched around The Acheron River as it rose from under the castle.

"That isn't what I intended," Dagger said, finally catching up to her.

Her red eyes glared at him with rage; he could almost feel the heat boring into him. The marriage wasn't his bloody idea, but she looked personally offended.

"Listen, we might as well make the best of it," he said.

"Are you serious?"

"I am," he said bluntly. "I understand you're pissed—"

"You have no idea why I'm *pissed*."

"So some time apart to cool down is a good idea for us both. Maniodes wanted us to keep an eye on each other, and I have no intention of becoming one of those lifeless grey husks down there." Dagger pointed down to the Valley of Shades to emphasize his point.

"So, if you break one of his rules again we're both fucked."

"Well, what do you propose?" Scythe asked, crossing her arms, sarcasm dripping from her voice.

"I found some ruins in the mountains we could stay in. I've been working on making it homier as a project. That's what married couples do anyway, right? They at least live together?"

"A happy little couple living together. You'd probably want to go now and commence the husbandly duties with your new wife?"

He couldn't deny he liked hearing the venom fall from her voice. Not so much when it was aimed at him, but he could let that go. She was a powerful individual when angry, and he didn't need it directed his way.

"This sham of a wedding wasn't my idea, and I know we've flirted, but I'm not going to force you to consummate anything," he said.

The heat dulled in Scythe's eyes. The anger didn't disappear completely, but some was replaced with unease. That stunned him, she had never once looked uncomfortable before. Scythe never backed away from anything. He could only assume it was because of this forced marriage. It struck a hidden nerve in her.

"I'm serious," Dagger said. He knew Scythe was cautious for a reason. This woman had fascinated him from the moment he woke up as an Incruentus Ferrum. He wanted her to trust him at least, and up until now she always had.

"Not until it's on my terms," she finally said.

"Of course, my lady, but could the wedding chain be involved somehow?" He held the chain Maniodes used, half-smiling.

Scythe scoffed, but a grin took over. "Like when we first met?"

"Technically, the second time. The first time ended with a knife hilt-deep in my neck. I'd rather avoid that next time."

"No guarantees. Send a bat to my place with directions, and I'll meet you there tomorrow night. I'm not promising anything, but I might as well scout the place out."

# Chapter 3

The scythe swung uselessly through the dead as she walked towards her cave. It sliced through the shades as if they were fog, only to have them reform right behind her. They didn't protect, they didn't even seem to care as Scythe sliced their transparent stomachs open.

Her mind wouldn't stop whirling as she and Dagger talked on the stairs. He left her be after that, as he'd promised, opening the dead tree planted at the foot of the steps to travel back to the surface with his blade.

As she walked now, her thoughts rested on Dagger again, remembering how they met vividly. She admired his bold conviction right away, but his directness had frightened her. Not that she admitted that aloud.

Maniodes had allowed her one victim in the crowded city of Stymphalia. She loved it when she was able to choose. When there was a designated victim the job was still fun, but starting with a blank slate increased the thrill of the hunt. She had spent three nights stalking the streets of Stymphalia like a wraith. Several opportunities presented themselves. A prostitute working a corner alone, a drunkard stumbling home, even a well-dressed businessman, basically just waiting to be robbed. Scythe took her time; she wanted whoever she chose to feel death's presence.

Eventually, she made her choice. She had been tracking a man who worked as a cobbler, and found his family. They were a happy little family: husband, wife, and three children. Not only would she end one man's life, but she'd ruin several others.

One night the cobbler left home for an evening stroll. Scythe followed close behind well into the night. There were no stars or moon. The oppressive clouds wouldn't allow it. Scythe let him feel her stalking him as he hurried home.

She raised her scythe, ready to swing in front of him. He would see the blade before his head flew. Before she could do more than twitch, a glint of metal caught her eye as a different blade flew from above.

The flying knife struck deep into the cobbler's neck. It poked out the other side of his throat, crimson with gore. He fell, clutching his neck, and died gurgling in his own blood.

She slowly lowered her weapon, dumbfounded. She knelt next to the dead man and yanked out the knife. It was a gorgeous blade. The handle was made of corded black leather and the blade itself, Damascus steel, had a beautiful pattern of hundreds of small waves that danced across the blade. The gore made the knife look alive.

The man leapt down from the merchants' stall, Scythe knew instantly that he was an Incruentus Ferrum like herself. He stood about a head taller than her, with black hair cropped below his ears. A clever smirk was on his lips, but he didn't brag about the kill.

He bowed a bit and said, "My lady."

Scythe wanted to stick the pretty blade in his neck.

"Nice aim," she said instead. "What do they call you?"

"Dagger, and you must be Scythe?"

Obviously, she thought smugly. She gripped her weapon harder.

"You know me?" she asked, keeping her voice smooth.

"Our names are fairly easy to guess," Dagger shrugged, "and the others spoke of you. You're one of the oldest." He was clearly new.

"You looking for some pointers?"

"I'd be grateful," he said. "Maybe we could do a few jobs together?"

"First tip, then," Scythe said, stepping closer.

She stuck the blade in his neck. He stumbled, clutching the merchants' stall, but kept his feet. He glared at her, astonished, breathing around the steel in his throat.

"Do not take my kill," she hissed

She left him there, a sour yet satisfying taste in her mouth.

They hadn't met again until the circus job a month later.

Maniodes probably heard about their first encounter and forced them together, not wanting too much bad blood between his soldiers. At first, Dagger wasn't overjoyed about doing the circus job with her either, but he eventually forgave her for stabbing him. Not that she actually apologized, and he never took her kill again. They even joked about it now.

The circus job had gone perfectly; it was even fun. They had to kill the ringleader of a traveling circus and an acrobat. She had suggested they design a story with their deaths, something to cause more mischief and scandal. Dagger had come up with the elaborate story that they were lovers caught in a murder-suicide pact. They arranged the bodies accordingly and watched as they were found. The living scattered like ants in the panic. It had been hilarious.

They thought so alike, Scythe hadn't realized she might have been leading him on. People were attracted to each other all the time, and she knew Dagger admired her when they first met, but she didn't know how she felt.

They had worked together on other occasions over the years, building an odd friendship. He'd join her on a few solo jobs, and she'd tag along on his when bored.

She swung her blade through the neck of a long dead king by her cave home. His grey head didn't role. A wisp of fog wafted around the cut as his neck reformed. After unlocking the iron wood door set in a depression of stone she leaned her weapon on the wall close at hand. She continued pacing. Her little cave didn't provide much room to move around, but it was safe. The lock on the door was bolted again, and Maniodes probably didn't even know where this place was. He'd never visited before, even though it was part of Skiachora. Maniodes hardly ever left his castle to explore the fields of the dead at his doorstep. Her cave was relatively safe from him, tucked away in the rock at the opposite end of the fields and the river.

Dagger had visited once before, though he hadn't come inside. She hadn't even seen him. He left a single rose wrapped in thorns outside her door after they completed the circus kills together.

Scythe kept telling herself that just because they were married, it didn't mean things had to change, but her nerves wouldn't calm down, and she wasn't entirely sure why. No, that was a lie, she didn't know why she was so nervous around Dagger all of a sudden, but he hadn't done anything. Maniodes fucked things up by forcing them together. It was just like what her father tried to pull, selling her off to be someone else's problem.

She sat in a chair next to the fire with her hands clenched. She stared at them until they stopped visibly shaking, but it still felt like her bones were vibrating. She didn't want to associate her father and Maniodes to Dagger. He had been nothing but kind, even enticing, which was fine at a distance. She would hold onto that old friendship. This marriage didn't have to affect anything.

# Chapter 4

Dagger's castle was more like a large ruined estate in Ichorisis. It was certainly based on grand castles, but on a much smaller scale. It was probably once home to a rich, noble family who relished the ancient architecture.

It was built into the side of a mountain, with a single path winding its way over the rock where Scythe and Dagger now stood in the front courtyard. The east side of the estate ended at the point where a cliff plummeted hundreds of feet. The west end was guarded by the mountain wall itself. It was easily defended by the landscape alone.

The stone and mortar was old and cracked, waiting for that one final breath of wind to topple it over. The few towers were in the same state. Bats flew about, little more than small shadows making the stars wink. There had to be dozens living on those towers, perfect for messages. They could use them the living did with carrier pigeons or ravens.

Scythe saw there were vines climbing up the walls. The vines covered so much of one corner all that could be seen was foliage and moss. It was as if the plant was trying to protect its friends, not realizing the harm it caused. Scythe could see herself growing mushrooms in its damp shade.

From this side, the stone may have been somewhat intact, but during the walk up, Scythe saw that on the north side an entire section had crumbled away. Rooms and hallways had been exposed to the elements for decades. She couldn't wait to explore them.

"I love it. You just found this place by accident?" Scythe asked.

"Yes," Dagger replied. "There's a graveyard nearby. I've been digging up bones to fix the furniture. Should I carry you over the threshold, dear wife? I believe that's a common tradition with the living."

The joy at the sight of her potential new home hardened into trepidation again. By his tone she knew he was joking, but it was different now. They were officially married, and that tainted the fun from before. Their natural flirtations had been an ongoing gag since they'd met, and that had never changed, until now.

Scythe took a breath, telling herself to calm down. Dagger hadn't changed much, given their so-called new relationship. If anything, he'd been nothing but kind. He even left her alone until the bat arrived with directions to his castle.

She decided to hold onto their old fun. Marriage could be nothing more than a title.

"There's no need, dear husband. This lady's legs can walk on their own." She left Dagger's side and approached the main doors.

She could feel Dagger's eyes following her. She had to admit she didn't mind, as long as he kept a distance. He was an attractive man. He always had a tricky smile, but it was never cocky. He always appeared to be having fun, and it was usually at some living person's expense. His black eyes seemed cold, but they were never that way to her. His smile changed when he looked at her too. She knew what those changes meant, and she had always played it off or shied away. If things had gone differently in her mortal life maybe they could have built something.

The main door suited the rest of the estate. The wood was worm-eaten and soft from rot. The metallic shriek it gave sent a shiver down her spine.

The main hall was huge, with a staircase wound along the wall, the steps started on the left and climbed to the second floor entrance on her right. It was made of the same stone as the walls, as if it were cut from the rock itself.

"Feel free to explore all you want," Dagger said, standing beside her again. "I'd join you, but I have business to take care of in the cellar."

"Business?" Scythe asked.

"It's nothing important. Call it a guilty pleasure." He shrugged.

"Alright, is there a kitchen anywhere?"

"Yes, I can show you."

"I'll find it. I'll see if I can make some tea from the leaves outside. Care to join me in the courtyard later?"

Their bodies may be dead, so they didn't need food, but tea was always relaxing.

Surprise lit up his black eyes. "I'd like that. There's a garden balcony on the second floor. Maybe we could meet there?"

"Sure, just give me a few hours." Scythe smiled back at him and began to climb the cracked staircase to explore.

The rest of the estate was just as glorious. It was easy to find the exposed rooms on the northern side; all she had to do was follow the draft. She passed the balcony Dagger mentioned. The first bedroom she found had been a child's. There was a single small bed with curtains draped over the four posters. The once-pretty fabric dissolved at her touch. The mildew from the ruined bed wasn't pleasant, but the draft from the open wall helped. Whether it had been natural erosion or broken in a fight, she didn't know. The floor fell away, revealing the open sky and forest below. A fall from this height would easily kill a living being. Scythe marveled at the sight of the pine forest below the cliff.

Moving tentatively, Scythe peered around the corner through the open wall. The fall might not kill her, but it wouldn't be pleasant. Her bones could still break. To the left there was an office with books on the floor and a desk broken in half. Below, she could make out the floor of another corridor.

This was leagues better than her cave back in Skiachora. The cave was well-furnished and warm, but this estate was beautiful.

She found the kitchen easily enough, along with an abandoned parlor where Dagger had started fixing the furniture. He'd used strips of leather to bind one chair together. Human feet replaced the ones on the broken couch.

The kitchen itself was small but cozy. Taking the heavy iron kettle to the pump just outside, she filled it with water. Once there was a steady fire burning under the kettle, Scythe went back to the courtyard. She always enjoyed tending to plants and watching them grow.

Scythe picked several leaves from the belladonna plant and headed back to the kitchen. Once the tea was steeping, she left it to look for Dagger.

It took a moment to find the proper passageway, but she finally found the cellar door. The door was in better shape than the main entrance, being protected from the elements. The black hinges were thick as they ran along the surface of the wood. The creak it made while opening sounded like a child's scream.

The stairs led down to a more complex set of hallways and rooms. One of which was full of shelves and dusty wine bottles. The kegs were big enough for two grown men to fit inside. Cobwebs covered the kegs, and dust coated the inside of her throat.

Examining the faded label on one bottle, a scream crept up from the corridor. Scythe put the bottle back and followed the sound. Another staircase led deeper into the bedrock.

What she found was even more exciting than the wall-less bedroom. This mini, ruined castle had its own dungeon, and the corridor opened into an elaborate chamber.

There was a large bed of coals in the corner. Iron pokers waited in the glowing warmth. Various instruments lined the walls on shelves and hooks—some for which she couldn't even guess the purpose. Chains decorated the walls, and a table with leather straps sat in the center.

There was a shirtless man strapped to this table. Dagger stood over the man, watching his stomach rise and fall in pain. As Scythe got closer she could see what Dagger was so focused on.

There was a black spot growing in the skin of the man's midsection. It looked sunken in at the center, then stretched out into inches of black tendrils in his veins. There was a thick line rising over his chest and up his neck, it ended just under his jaw, marking the path of whatever he had swallowed. His eyes and teeth were clenched in pain, but he didn't scream again.

"What do you think?" Dagger asked.

"I've never seen this before. What did you give him?" Scythe marveled.

"My own mix," he said. "I don't know what to call it."

He poked at the depression in the man's stomach, and the man screamed.

"So, watching shirtless men writhe in pain is your guilty pleasure?" she asked, eyeing him.

Offence crossed his eyes, but when he looked up and saw Scythe was joking, he laughed. “Experiments and their reactions are,” he explained with a half-smile. “I wouldn’t have been able to see this if he was clothed.”

“Well, he may have to stay here. I don’t think our guest is feeling well enough for tea. I came to let you know it’s done. I’ll meet you on the balcony. By the way, do you need his fingers?”

Confused, Dagger replied, “No, just his stomach.”

Scythe picked a meaty cleaver from the wall of assorted knives. The dying man screamed as she brought it down hard on his first two fingers. She wiped the cleaver clean, replaced it where it hung, then gathered up the fingers.

Leaving Dagger with the shirtless man, she went back to the kitchen and found the tea had steeped well. After locating a tray and mismatched goblets, she took them upstairs.

The balcony Scythe had passed previously was lined with windows and a glass door. Most of the glass panes were broken, and spider webs glinted in the open spaces.

The door, not centered in its hinges, led to the wide stone platform overlooking the cliff and the forest below. Scythe set the tray down on the wooden table, which was surprisingly still whole. The legs were sturdy, but most of the wooden tabletop had been eaten away by rot. Dagger must have replaced parts of it. He had fixed the chairs as well, similar to the ones in the parlor below. She hadn't known how handy he was. She wondered if he had been a craftsman in his former life.

Scythe sat, enjoying the silence. There hadn't been sugar or cream in the kitchen, and there were hardly any useful utensils. She used one of the fingers from the dying man to stir her tea, ensuring most of the leaves had dissolved.

After a few moments, Scythe heard the door creak open. Dagger took the other chair and poured his own tea. He picked up the other finger and looked to her quizzically.

"There weren't many spoons," she shrugged.

Dagger chuckled and stirred the tea as she had.

"So that man below," Scythe began, "was he sanctioned as a victim by Maniodes?"

"Technically, yes. He was a baker in a small village in the east. There was meant to be a single death, but nothing more. At the same time, I needed a new lab rat. A man going missing causes a similar confusion."

"But it's not what Maniodes had in mind?"

"No one saw me. The experiment ended shortly after you left us, anyway. I didn't break any of the rules, only stretched them."

"Do you think torturing the man counts as crossing the boundaries, though? You know, 'going too far'?" Scythe made air quotes, imitating Maniodes.

"You going to report me?" he asked, setting down his tea.

Scythe wondered if Maniodes would spare her if she ratted on Dagger. The god might force only Dagger to go grey, killing him permanently. She didn't want to kill Dagger, though. They'd worked well together in the past.

"No, I'm not. You found a loophole and took advantage. It's not like I've never done that before."

"I remember the man in the tree. What you did with that tree was art," Dagger commented, relaxing again.

Scythe remembered that tree well. The man hadn't been a job—that's what really got her in trouble. She had been enjoying the night by herself in some city, she couldn't remember which. While exploring the alleys, a man had approached her, assuming she was a prostitute. It was a simple misunderstanding, and she had been having a good night. She played along, luring him to a nearby park before disemboweling him. She relished in the shock on his face as his intestines spilled onto the cobblestones. Taking off his limbs was easy enough with her scythe. She then decorated a nearby sapling with him. She stuck his head among the branches, his face still contorted in terror. She then wove his intestines in and out of the lower branches. It had been a great night until Pitch ratted her out.

"Thank you." She hadn't known he'd seen it. "How did you find it?"

"I was with Maniodes when he went to see it, after Pitch told on you."

"That little pustule. I had to spend three days in the river because of him."

Maniodes had sentenced her to be tied at the bottom of The Acheron riverbed. As she lay there, souls floated past her, glowing green. For three full days she writhed against the water in her lungs, unable to breathe even though her body went through the motions.

Scythe had been more careful ever since, making sure no evidence led back to her.

Until the village she and Dagger had burned together.

"So, you're alright with this arrangement?" Dagger changed the subject, watching her. "Our so-called marriage?"

"Might as well make do with an odd situation. At least you're handsome."

"I was being serious."

"So was I." Scythe felt good admitting that.

"Thank you," he said, sounding surprised. "You're quite attractive yourself, my lady."

"Call me *lady* all you want. I'm not calling you *lord* the way other pale housewives do."

"I wasn't expecting you to."

"Keep those expectations low, and we'll be fine."

Dagger chuckled again. Scythe joined him this time. Their odd friendship hadn't changed. She breathed a sigh of relief over the tea.

# Chapter 5

The rest of the week was pleasant, though boring, in Dagger's opinion. Scythe had chosen her own room down the hall from his own. He was surprised she had even decided to stay. He helped her move her belongings from the cave she'd lived in, too. Her cave had been well-furnished but not well-organized. It had obviously been a good home to her, but he was glad to see her happy and comfortable in the new estate. The move hadn't taken much time, only a day since she left most of the furniture behind. Most of the things they moved were clothing, jewelry, and weapons. The woman clearly had a passion for violence and oddities, but she had a flair for fashion as well. Each day, Scythe seemed to have a different dress, yet few shoes.

It reminded him a bit of his younger sister. She had enjoyed new dresses as well but in a simpler style. Dagger remembered being dragged to several shops with his sister and mother before his death. They weren't the wealthiest family in the city, but they were well-off.

Thinking of his sister pained him. She would be gaining the entire family fortune now that he was dead. His heart went out to her, being alone with so much responsibility. She was probably running their home and fortune now anyway, given their mother's condition.

He remembered when she was eleven, she had broken a vase by accident. She was excited about something, he couldn't remember, and her swinging hand had knocked it over. Tryphania, their mother, was in another room, heard the crash, and came to investigate. There was no time for the two of them to hide the evidence, so they waited for their mother's wrath. She was never cruel, but her illness had started to take hold, causing spells of confusion that irritated her. Dagger never blamed her for being irritated. The woman was losing her mind, and she couldn't do anything about it. Though at thirteen, he didn't truly understand it yet. When their mother came and saw the broken pottery, Dagger had expected his sister to lie and blame him, like most little sisters do, but she told the truth immediately. Even later in life, his sister had never changed. She was always level-headed, and nothing seemed to bother her. They were always a bit different, where she was calm facing their mother, he was always afraid of getting in trouble

Dagger forcibly turned those thoughts away. He could do nothing for them now. His worry didn't matter. Turning back to his current project, he finished securing the skeleton hand to the leg of the chair. Once the human hand was in place, Dagger turned the chair upright, making sure it was finally level. His studies while alive never really let him practice his skill. Once dead, though, he had plenty of time.

He couldn't feel much of the cold weather anymore either, but he still had lit a fire against the night regardless. The strong winds caused the only disturbance. Drafts filled the estate, and some sections howled like the damned if the wind hit them just right.

There was a sharp tapping at the window, and it wasn't the usual glass rattling in the panes. Turning toward the high arched windows, Dagger saw a bat in the leftmost one. Tossing his tool belt onto the chair, he strode over and opened a small section of the window. The bar on the outside had been Scythe's idea, a place the little creatures could rest when delivering messages.

The bat now hung upside down on the bar, no doubt exhausted from the windstorm. A small scroll was tied to its hind leg. Grateful it hadn't blown away, Dagger untied the parchment.

Before reading it, he set the scroll aside and gently picked up the bat. It was skittish and battered against his hand but calmed when he set it down on the inside ledge. He left the window open for the bat to leave once properly rested.

He picked up the scroll and unfurled it. There were two pieces of parchment with Maniodes's handwriting scrawled across it. There was no formal greeting, only business.

"The two of you have been rather quiet these past few days. I hope you're enjoying married life."

Dagger could imagine the snakelike smile on the god's lips as he wrote it.

"Either way, there is a job I'd like carried out. There is going to be a wedding at Kaliasma tomorrow night. I want you both there, and you are allowed one victim each. You cannot pick the groom, though. This is to be a kind of punishment for him for cheating his business partners. I know it will be difficult to go completely unseen at a wedding but be discreet."

"Finally," Dagger sighed.

He and Scythe had kept busy, but the boredom was making him restless. Dagger left the parlor to look for Scythe.

He found her quickly enough, in the kitchen cleaning off the skin and meat from a couple of human legs they'd dug up last night for materials. She used a curved razor to strip the meat from the bone. Her red hair was tied back to keep it out of her work. The leather apron covered the sleeveless black silk dress appropriately. Her feet were bare on the cold stone floor.

The woman they dug up had only been dead a couple of days, but the meat was too far gone for Dagger's tastes. He preferred it fresher, but Scythe convinced him she could turn it into a good stew. He was willing to try it.

Once the bone was clear, Scythe would set it aside with the others. Later, they would take turns cleaning and reinforcing the bones for the furniture.

"You going to come in or keep staring?" Scythe asked, looking up from the leg.

Dagger tore his eyes away from her own legs. The dress she wore ended just below her knees.

"A message just came," he said holding the note up.

"Is it an assignment?" she asked, eagerly taking off the gore-covered gloves.

"It is." He handed over the note. As Scythe read it, Dagger stole a glance at her ankle again.

"By the gods, it's about time." She untied the apron and laid it aside. "I've never been to an actual wedding before—too crowded."

"What about our own?" Dagger asked. He wasn't offended; theirs hadn't exactly been an enjoyable ceremony. Weddings had been a regular part of his life, though.

"You know what I mean. This is going to be fun."

"No doubt. We should start packing now. It takes a full day to walk there," he said.

"Let's leave early and scout the place out, come up with something grand. People wouldn't expect anything less at a wedding." Fire lit in her eyes.

Dagger helped her put the extra meat in the cold box under the kitchen. He had been looking forward to her stew, but it would have to wait.

"Probably nothing too grand, since we are on probation," he cautioned.

"You're right. A small fire could get out of hand."

He hadn't mentioned a fire at all. She was probably following her own train of thought.

Dagger held the door open from the kitchen cellar for Scythe. She smiled in thanks as she passed by.

"Do you have something formal for the event?" Scythe asked as they walked upstairs.

"I must have something nice stashed away," he replied. At the moment he was wearing a simple brown workman's tunic and trousers with a rip in one knee.

"If not, we could get something in the city," Scythe thought out loud.

"We don't have any money. Maniodes doesn't exactly pay us for this work."

"Coin is just a formality. You think I *bought* this dress?"

"Actually, I thought you made it," he admitted.

"Really?" she asked, glancing down at it.

"Dresses usually go to the ankle. They do not come that short."

"Well, I did alter that bit." It must have been easy, too. She hadn't removed much, just a few inches at her ankle. A normal dress always ran the length of her entire body, but Scythe seemed to like the freedom of a slightly shorter hem. Having the ankle exposed gained looks, like she was being inappropriate, but she didn't have to worry about stepping on the dress.

When they reached the corridor with their chambers, Scythe veered off into her room.

Dagger continued to his own, closer to the bat rookeries, and began packing for the trip. He hung his belt of tools on a sturdy coat rack next to his knives and cloak. The rack was the newest addition to the room, being his own creation of bleached wood. When he'd found the small castle, he'd picked the master bedroom. It was dusty, but he didn't mind—the room was dry, and no mold had set in. There was a wardrobe to one side of a cold fireplace. A couple of chairs, once tall and majestic pieces, had been draped in red cloth but now were a faded pink, with several rips in the fabric. He intended to replace the fabric with finely stitched human leather, but he hadn't had the time.

The trip couldn't be more than two or three days, so he packed an extra tunic and trousers. Then he turned to the formal clothes. There was only one pair of clean trousers, and mostly plain tunics, even less than he'd expected. He tossed the trousers on the bed and rolled the grey tunic into his pack.

"Ready?" Scythe's voice surprised him. She waited in the doorway by the coat rack.

"Almost," he said, grabbing the trousers again.

"What are you wearing to the wedding?" She had changed into riding trousers for the trip. No doubt she had packed away something special for the ceremony.

"Just these and a tunic," he held up the trousers and shrugged. "Keeping it simple."

"Can I see?" she asked, stepping closer.

"Why?" he asked. He knew how to dress himself for an occasion.

"Partly curiosity, partly to see if we match. We're going as a couple, so we need to look the part."

She actually was taking their marriage somewhat seriously even if she was joking. She usually kept her distance, but she was standing inside his chambers for the first time. Dagger took out the tunic and handed it to her. Scythe held it out at arm's length toward him, probably visualizing him in it.

"What do you think?" he asked.

"Good, but boring."

"Well, it's the fanciest one I have, so—" he cut himself off, his annoyance rising.

"It's nice, but do you have a vest?"

"Um, I think so." Dagger turned back to his wardrobe, which was missing part of its left legs, making it tilt so the clothing fit awkwardly.

Scythe was suddenly by his side, examining the clothing. He stepped aside, letting her pick through his options. His annoyance died. She was trying to help, and she knew what she was doing when it came to fashion.

"This one," she pulled out a black vest that had been tucked away, forgotten.

Scythe lay the grey tunic on the bed with the vest on top. It was a simple paring but could easily be used for formal occasions. The vest was stitched down the middle to hold it closed, and the silver embroidery was accented by the grey.

"Not boring anymore?" he asked jokingly.

"No, it suits you." She gave a half-smile. "Keeping it simple."

That smile made her look devious, but the kindness in her eyes was genuine. He liked that smile on her.

"Alright then." He gathered the outfit and packed it away. "Are you ready?"

"I am, but I was going to stop at the kitchen for some food."

"Good idea. I could take your pack to the main gate and meet you there." He hoisted his own pack onto his shoulder.

"Sure, it's by my door," she said. "I'll meet you outside."

"Great." He picked up his belt of daggers and his cloak, following her out of the room.

The wind still tore at his hair as he leaned against the stone column holding up the rusted gate. He had checked for the bat before leaving, but it had gone. Only then did he realize he should have sent a note back to Maniodes. A short one would have been fine, just something to let him know they received the orders. The god might not like being overlooked, but it was too late now.

Dagger didn't have to wait long for Scythe. It only took her a few moments to gather food. Being dead, they didn't have to eat, but snacks were always welcome. It was probably more of a habit from their mortal lives. He wondered how long Scythe had been an Incruentus Ferrum. He had never asked.

Watching her stride across the courtyard as she left the estate made him wonder about other things. Her red hair was tied back against the wind, and her red eyes shone in the moonlight, even from this distance. Her riding trousers hid her skin from him, but her black blouse did wonders for her figure.

Her weapon of choice was equally impressive. The long black staff was a foot taller than she was. Dagger had seen the staff up close and knew it wasn't smooth. A single line spiraled down the length of it for grip as well as decoration. The silver blade at its top curved behind her like a sigil for a queen.

He wanted her. He pushed away from the column, but kept his hands in his pockets, hoping she wouldn't notice. Luckily, he'd strapped on his own belt of daggers. There were more than enough knives to cover his waist.

"Good to go?" he asked as she reached him.

"Aye." She set the scythe against the stone and picked up her own pack.

He was about to offer to carry it, but she'd already slipped it on. He studied the weapon as she adjusted the pack, focusing on the curve of the blade. The silver was freshly polished.

"You like her?" she asked, half-smiling again, playing with the point of the blade.

"Indeed, I do." He kept his voice smooth. "Shall I open the tree paths?"

He turned to the dead tree, flipping his choice dagger into his hand. He was about to drive the blade into the tree to open the path until Scythe's voice stopped him.

"I actually feel like walking," she said. "I know the trees are faster, but Kaliasma isn't that far away."

Dagger straightened, momentarily surprised. The paths the Incruentus Ferrum were able to open were mostly used to move between jobs quickly. Dagger had always seen them as the best perk of being dead. Scythe was right, though; Kaliasma wasn't too far, and a walk would be nice.

"Good idea," he said, then added a little sarcasm into his next thought. "It could help us bond as husband and wife."

Scythe rolled her eyes, but the grin stayed. She started walking down the road away from their new estate, calling, "Well, come on then, *dear husband*."

# Chapter 6

They had several hours before the sun rose and many more to the city. Dagger and Scythe traveled the well-worn paths through the pine trees alone, chatting about general nonsense. No one alive bothered to travel at this time of night. While they talked, Scythe noticed in midsentence she'd called the estate "home" without noticing it. She hadn't intended to, but that made the slip more powerful for her. Her own childhood had never been safe, and the cave in Skiachora was comfortable, but it was a *cave*. Dagger provided walls to call home and never asked pressing questions. She appreciated him for that.

After a couple of hours, the sky in the east changed from deep indigo to several shades of red. They still had a long walk ahead of them.

"We should stop for the day," Dagger suggested.

"I know of a place not far from here we can go," Scythe offered.

"Really? Where?"

"If we keep to this road there will be a fork. We take the left instead of the right and keep going for about ten minutes."

"Alright then," he said, trusting her.

It felt good to have a man trust her word.

The sky continued to stain red as they took the left fork. The trees eventually dispersed, revealing a rocky graveyard spread over the next two hills. The tombs were old and cracked in the center; some were so worn Scythe couldn't make out the words. The farther the headstones spread, the newer they looked. There were several mausoleums throughout the area. The small homes for the dead provided the perfect shelter for sleep.

"How did you know this was here?" Dagger asked, walking among the graves.

"I found it by accident." It had been decades ago. Fifty, maybe sixty years, she wasn't entirely sure. There were fewer graves then, by the hundreds.

"Scythe?"

"Hm?" She turned to Dagger, avoiding a headstone.

"How long have you been dead?" He watched her carefully, as if the question might offend her.

"I'm not sure, but I think it's been about one hundred years," she replied, shrugging. "Eight or nine decades at least."

"Really?! Ichorisis must have been a lot different back then. It would be fascinating to watch things change over time," Dagger said.

"Not much has changed, actually," Scythe countered, "but a century might not be long enough to notice. I do remember Chalcis was a fair-sized town. It wasn't a full-fledged city yet."

"Do you remember Kaliasma, by chance?" Dagger asked.

"It hasn't changed much, Pretty boring except for that fire seventy years ago."

"King Tholus's Blaze! You were there during that?" he asked excitedly.

"I just watched from the cliffs nearby. I didn't know that fire had its own name," Scythe said.

"King Tholus nearly burnt all of the Low End, basically half of the city, thinking it would purify it," Dagger explained. "He wasn't exactly sane to start with. So, how old were you when you died?"

"Nineteen, I think. I could have been twenty."

His questions were getting more personal. Based on his line of thought, he was probably going to ask how she died. That one, she was not going to answer.

To her surprise, Dagger didn't ask.

"We could camp inside here," he said, approaching one of the mausoleums.

The stone was crafted well, with hardly any cracks. Plenty of moss covered it, though. In a few more years, the moss would consume the entire structure.

Dagger climbed the single step onto its platform and took out one of his knives. The lock on the door didn't last long with his knife hilt bashing against it.

He tossed the lock aside and opened the door inward. There wasn't much space inside, maybe four or five feet between the coffins sitting on thick shelves.

"Cozy," Dagger commented, dropping his pack in the left corner.

Scythe couldn't make her feet move. She'd stayed in mausoleums before but never with someone. They had never slept close at all. She liked Dagger, even trusted him to an extent, but her past life had tainted certain things. She always felt him looking, but he gave her space. Would he do the same in this tiny room? She could go to another mausoleum, but she wanted to see what he would do this close. She could always leave if he tried anything. She wasn't as defenseless as before.

"You alright?" Dagger asked, spreading out his bedroll.

She must have paused longer than she intended. "Fine," she replied.

Setting her pack in the corner across from Dagger's, she set up her own bedding. The only light pouring into the small space came from the tiny window in the door.

Dagger noticed as well and covered it by hanging his cloak on a nail stuck in the door. It became pleasantly dark inside. Color drained from Scythe's vision, replaced by shades of grey and black.

"It's only a few hours to the city from here, but we shouldn't sleep too long. Parties usually get going at night, and we should scout the place out first," Dagger said casually as he stretched out on his bedroll. He tucked his hands under his head and examined the ceiling.

"Mm." Scythe lay down with her back to a coffin, facing Dagger. She left as much space as she could between them. She didn't want her back to him. Tonight wouldn't be very comfortable.

Dagger glanced toward her; confusion shifted in his gaze.

"You alright?" he asked, looking more concerned.

"I'm fine." She couldn't close her eyes while he was looking at her. If he was focused on her, she wanted to see what he was doing. She couldn't look him in the eye, either. Which was new to her. She hated feeling this bloody awkward. She had to remind herself that Dagger hadn't done anything, that helped a bit, but her past kept interfering and confusing her.

Dagger turned onto his side, facing her. There was still a foot of space between them, but it was too close for her liking. She cursed herself for being foolish. They had been close before but Maniodes had fucked it up.

"Do I intimidate you?" His voice was soft with concern.

Scythe didn't know how to reply. She wanted to lie, to herself as much as Dagger, but they had promised each other honesty and respect. He promised he wouldn't touch her, and he hadn't.

"Not exactly," she finally gave.

"How so, then? You've seen what I can do to people, but you've never shied from that. You and I have danced around the edges of flirtation before."

"It's not personal."

"Is it because I'm a man in general, then? Or because there's an actual marriage now?"

It seemed vague, but it struck home.

"Scythe, were you attacked by a man when you were alive?"

"No, I wasn't, thankfully. Well, attacked, yes, but not in the way you're thinking. A woman living in the poor end of the city was an easy target, but I was never raped. This…mistrust still led to my death, though." The words wanted to stick in her throat, but she forced them out.

"Ah." He stayed quiet, then said, "You can trust me in that regard. I won't touch you. We can even lay your weapon between us like a barrier."

"It's alright. You just stay on your blanket, and I'll stay on mine." She was grateful he was willing to keep a distance. He hadn't changed in that regard. The relief surprised her, but she was able to relax. "You're actually gentlemanly about the whole thing, thank you. Very few men can lie next to a woman and leave her be."

"My little sister was attacked in a similar way," he admitted. "I saw how it changed her."

"I'm sorry that happened to her. Is she still alive?" Scythe asked.

"Yes, thankfully," he said.

"How long have you been a Ferrum?" she asked, changing the subject onto him.

"Only about ten years."

"Aw, you're just a little baby, then." Scythe laughed, lightening the mood.

Dagger cracked a grin too. “I’m far from having a baby’s innocence. I’ll admit I’m impressed you’ve been a Ferrum for a century. Most usually choose to become grey again.”

“I think you and I have a certain thirst for this life. That’s why we’re so good at it.”

“Other than getting caught,” he countered.

“Maniodes can’t force us to marry twice.” She joined his laughter.

After the good humor faded, Dagger said, “Sleep well, Scythe. We should be up again just before the moon appears.”

“Yes, sleep well, Dagger.” Scythe was able to close her eyes and relax into sleep fairly quickly.

# Chapter 7

It had taken them an hour to explore the city using the address Maniodes provided. The reception area was impossible to mistake once they found it. They managed to sneak in using alleyways and servants' passages. Scythe relished in the secrecy provided by being an Incruentus Ferrum. They weren't invisible, but the living naturally disregarded and ignored them. This occurrence never had an official name, but Scythe always regarded it as the "shadow trick." She'd even heard some of the other Ferrum using the title she had coined.

Dagger and Scythe strode into the courtyard without worry of being stopped. They stuck to the shadows, scouting out the gardens, and found several useful nooks for hiding places.

The gardens of the wedding reception were decorated beautifully to human standards. Banners hung on the columns, showing the crests of the two families. The biggest banner hung over the bride and groom, showing the combination of the two sigils. Streamers were woven between low tree branches and the beams of the gazebos where the tables were placed. Lanterns lit the area, along with the light of the crescent moon. The colors alone were striking enough to almost hurt Scythe's eyes. The reds, blues, yellows, greens, and purples were a stark contrast to the grey dust from their own estate. Scythe wasn't entirely sure if she liked the difference. The color brought life, but it looked so gaudy when overdone.

Before the guests arrived, Dagger and Scythe changed into their formal attire. She had to use a broom closet, but Scythe had chosen a simple dress she could easily get in and out of. It was a simple long piece of black satin with a red sash to tie off the waist. Taking her scythe back from leaning it on the wall, she shortened it. It didn't take any effort; all she had to do was think of the weapon shrinking. The staff of the scythe shortened and thinned in her hands. The blade kept its crescent shape, but it shrank in proportion to the handle. Maniodes might be a thorn in her side, but he had granted her this trick after fifty years of service. Scythe maneuvered the sash to hold the small version of her weapon onto her back. She was glad she didn't have to conceal it; with their power to go unnoticed, no one would see it until she wanted them to.

Guests were beginning to pour into the garden behind the bride and groom. The air was filled with shouting, laughter, and overall joy as they took their seats. Scythe spotted Dagger in the shadow of a pillar. He was dressed well in the vest and grey tunic. His belt of knives was not quite concealed by his long cloak. His hair was brushed and hung to his jaw, accenting it well. He was watching the crowd with a hunter's eye.

He turned to her when she approached. The hunter instantly changed to a gentleman.

"You look beautiful," he said, then looked away as if surprising himself.

"You look handsome in that vest as well," Scythe grinned as she stood next to him.

He surveyed the crowd again. Scythe turned to them too. The feast had begun with piles of pork, steak, and vegetables dipped in a thousand sauces. This couple was certainly wealthy to afford all of this extravagance.

The couple in question sat at the center of the head table. The bride was a young brunette girl whose smile took over half of her face. She wore the customary light-blue dress, and her hair had small flowers of the same shade woven into the curls. The groom didn't look as excited. He was calm in his formal doublet, but most of the jubilance seemed to pass around him. Scythe wondered how much of his stolen money financed this glorious wedding and if his business partners were here.

"Who did you have in mind?" Dagger asked, getting right to business.

"We're only allowed two, so we should make it count," she speculated.

Before Dagger could say anything else, Scythe scurried to the nearest table. No one noticed her as she plucked a goblet filled with red wine from between a fat nobleman and a lad who could have been his son.

She swiped another from the end of the table. She giggled at their confusion over the missing drinks.

Scythe joined Dagger again and handed him one of the goblets.

"Usually, the man gets the woman drinks," he said.

"Does he? Why? Oh, doesn't matter. I've never been to anything this fancy."

"Even with one hundred years of mischief under your belt?" He sipped the wine.

"I usually avoid crowds. Have you been to a wedding like this?"

"A couple, but nothing this big. I—" he cut himself off, nearly choking.

He stared into the crowd, looking dumbfounded and confused.

"Dagger?"

"Hold on." He handed her the goblet hastily and walked off.

Scythe watched him stay at the edge of the gathering, weaving between the servants. He kept watching a spot that looked to be at the other side of the garden, but it was too difficult to tell with all of the people. He kept moving to get a better view, then froze to stare. There was a good distance between them, but Scythe could see the sadness in his expression.

He stood there for several moments, watching someone. Eventually, he bowed his head and trudged back to Scythe. At a closer look, the shame was unmistakable. Dagger took his goblet and leaned back against the pillar away from the crowd. He upended the goblet, draining it in one swallow. It was a habit, just like eating—alcohol couldn't affect them anymore.

"Dagger, what is it?" Scythe touched his arm.

He didn't answer right away, but eventually replied. "Far end of the garden, second table from the right. There's a black-haired woman."

Scythe looked where he indicated and saw whom he meant instantly. She was a tall woman, bordering on middle age. Her dark hair was tied back with several braids and hung down the back of her yellow dress.

"A previous lover of yours? We could kill her if you want."

"No!"

He rounded on her, and she took a step back, all sense of concern gone. He'd never been mad at her before, and she hated that she'd retreated. For a brief moment, her father stood before her. His eyes were on fire with anger, but she wouldn't let him frighten her.

"Obviously, she bothered you in the past somehow. What's wrong with a little revenge?"

"That woman is not to be harmed, and this whole event will be kept quiet. We'll pick our two, hide the bodies, then leave," Dagger demanded.

"You do not get to give me orders," Scythe countered.

"Consider it a stern request then."

Scythe's hands balled into fists at Dagger's anger. "And if I don't follow your *request*? Just because some broad here you knew—"

"She will not be touched!"

Dagger stalked forward, emphasizing his point. Scythe reached behind her and gripped her weapon. She swung it around to rest the blade against his throat. Dagger glared at her over the curved steel. Scythe extended the handle, gaining more distance from him. She matched his gaze, refusing to feel small.

"If you hurt her, I'll go straight to Maniodes," he threatened, his voice more than harsh.

"Then I'll tell him about your experiments in the basement," she threatened back.

"Then we both go grey."

She noted Dagger's hand then. It had moved closer to his belt of knives. She had distance on him and strength with her weapon, but he had speed. She had seen him strike down a bird in flight with a precise throw.

The look in his eyes told her he wasn't lying. He was willing to let his consciousness be stripped away for that woman.

"Why?" she demanded.

"She's important to me, and I'd rather she be left out of this life."

"Why is she important?" Jealously played on across her skin. She pushed it back before it could take over, but she couldn't deny it was there, like a clinging insect. It had been a long time since she felt anything like this, if ever.

"I'd rather not say. Maniodes said it was safer for her and myself. You don't have to be so hostile. You've kept quiet about your previous life so far."

"Only about my death. Nothing of importance happened before that anyway."

"This is the same," he admitted. "Will you please lower your blade?"

The flame of his temper had faded, but she fell her walls creep back up. He had turned on her quick enough. He might do it again.

"You stay away from me tonight," she said, shortening the weapon. She lowered it away from his throat but still held it toward him.

"Alright, but you'll leave that woman alone," Dagger stated.

"Fine."

"And you'll hide the body of your victim? I don't want this night ruined for her."

Since that woman was having so much fucking fun, Scythe wasn't allowed to.

"We have to get on Maniodes's good side again anyway. He wanted us to be discreet."

Dagger was right on that account. She wanted to punch him.

"Fine," she said again, turning on her heel.

"Pick a low-key victim!" he called to her back as she stalked off. "Scythe!"

"Fine!" She nearly chucked her scythe at him.

She left him standing by the pillar. She found a table that had been mostly abandoned except for scraps of chicken and dirty plates. She wove her weapon onto her back again and sat at the bench.

Sitting with her back to the table, Scythe scanned the crowd for anyone who suited her fancy. She felt violent tonight. Dagger was right about Maniodes wanting them to be discreet, so she forced herself to sit and control the urges to set the banners on fire.

She held the anger in this time, but she couldn't quite figure out why it was there in the first place. For nearly a century she relished in her freedom to hurt whomever she wanted. Now Dagger was reining that in for that woman. She wanted to kill her out of spite, but the jealousy before crept back. She beat it down, though not before she realized it was because Dagger was protecting that woman.

Scythe looked toward the pretty bride and groom. They were chatting happily together. She imagined blood blooming over the bride's pale-blue gown. One quick swipe of her scythe, and the bride's head would roll. She would hide the body, just like Dagger asked, but the bride would not go unnoticed.

As the night carried on and everyone grew more intoxicated, they'd hardly notice she was missing, though. Scythe could use the groom, too. She could knock him unconscious and hide him somewhere. The crowd would just assume they had left to consummate their marriage. The bride wouldn't be found until much later. Maybe even several days later, if Scythe picked a good spot to stash her. She could even frame the groom.

She thought about how to lure the bride away. Scythe's sight drifted to the center of the gardens.

Almost everyone was dancing around each other; several just bumbled around. Everyone was having fun while she was stuck on the sides.

The woman in the yellow dress drifted by in the dance with dark hair flowing behind her. Scythe tracked her movements. The woman wasn't as intoxicated, but her face was flushed, and she couldn't seem to stop smiling. Scythe honestly considered killing her out of spite and stashing the body where even the dogs couldn't find her for months. As the woman turned, holding the side of her dress, Scythe caught sight of her eyes. They were black and glistened in the firelight. She had a strong jaw too. Her face was almost square, but still pretty.

The realization of who she must be struck Scythe instantly. The woman was older, but she had the same features as Dagger. She was his sister. The woman was technically her own sister-in-law.

The confusion in her gut surprised her, as much as the jealousy had. Why had she assumed the woman was an ex-lover? She didn't have anything to be jealous of in the first place. She and Dagger may have an odd friendship, but she had no hold over him, regardless of the forced marriage. That's probably what confused things; the marriage.

His defensiveness made sense, if that was the case. Their resemblance was hard to ignore once noticed. Scythe had to be sure, though. Staying at the table for now, she surveyed the crowd for Dagger.

She spotted him chatting with a young blond and blue-haired girl who couldn't stop giggling. She kept touching Dagger's arm, and he wasn't pulling away. Logic stated he was just hunting; he had picked an easy victim.

Anger welled up again and nearly boiled over. The girl wouldn't stop touching his arm, and he was letting her. She knew flirtation was the easiest way to make people drop their guard. She'd probably use it herself tonight, just to get it over with. She wondered how Dagger would react at seeing her flirt with another man. She wasn't used to this new emotion. She hated it.

As she watched, Dagger leaned down and whispered into the girl's ear. Her grin turned mischievous, and she nodded. He took her hand and led her from the crowd.

Scythe practically sprang from the bench, seizing her chance. She had tracked the woman in the yellow dress again and found her standing with a group of other ladies, talking.

"Excuse me?" No one had noticed her approach, and several of them jumped.

The woman turned from a tall, dark-skinned woman to Scythe, surprised that she was the one being spoken to. Scythe buried her anger for the moment and applied her mask of innocence.

"Yes?" The woman's eyes darted from Scythe's dress to her red eyes.

Scythe knew she was an odd sight to a proper lady, maybe even offensive. No one wore black to a wedding, apparently. She didn't care.

"I'm sorry to bother you," Scythe said, "but you look a bit like someone I met a few years back, I was wondering if you were related."

"Do you know his name?" The woman was cautious, but willing to help. She probably felt safe with the large crowd surrounding them.

"He never told me at the time, unfortunately. I'm Skie," she lied.

"I'm Karteria. What did this man look like?"

Karteria was growing stiff and a little nervous.

"He must have been in his twenties back then. His hair was black and hung to his shoulders. His eyes were dark, like yours, and he had a square jaw. I know it's a shot in the dark."

Karteria's arms rose as she hugged herself. The joy was dead alright; she was outright depressed.

"That man sounds like he could be my brother," she said. "He passed away almost ten years ago now."

Scythe slid her expression from innocent curiosity to sadness and understanding. She let the moment hang in silence.

"I'm so sorry. I didn't mean to bring that up."

"It's alright, you didn't know," Karteria said.

"May I ask how he passed?" Scythe asked.

"It was an accident, nothing more."

Karteria turned and left. She kept her head down as she made for an alcove alone. Apparently, she was still bothered by her brother's death even after a decade.

Scythe was about to leave, rather satisfied, when one of the other women stopped her.

"Wait."

Scythe turned to the dark-skinned woman.

"You're not from here, are you?"

"Not from this city, no," Scythe replied, playing into her lie. "I'm a relative of the groom. Why do you ask?"

"I'm just surprised you haven't heard of Karteria's brother's death. Almost everyone in this city knows."

"Why? What happened?"

"Their mother hasn't been well for years. She's prone to bouts of hallucinations, claiming demons are everywhere. She killed her own son during an episode. The only reason she wasn't arrested is because of her illness. She believes her son is still alive," the woman shared openly, the alcohol making her chatty.

By the gods, no wonder Dagger wanted to keep that quiet. "Thank you," Scythe said and left the group before they could say anything else.

Another rare emotion grew in the back of her throat: guilt. One hundred years of being a guiltless killer, and she'd had no problems. Now he was making her feel new things she wasn't used too. She wanted to be mad at him. If he'd explained the situation more clearly, she wouldn't have cornered his sister like that. But whatever explanation he could have given would have raised more questions. Questions he probably didn't want to answer.

He had left her alone in regard to her own past life, and she had dug her way into his.

Three young men sat at her table now. The stench of ale wafted from them like a cape in the wind. Scythe wasn't in the mood to kill anyone now; she wanted to get it over with. Maybe the murder would help her think.

They hadn't noticed her until she set a hand on the thigh of the young man next to her. She smiled sweetly at him. He stared down his blade of a nose, stunned. He had been bragging about a horse race, but now he was silent. Her hand was very high on his leg.

"You want to escape for a little while?" she asked slowly.

He swallowed, clearly taken aback by this woman's forward approach. Excitement lit in his eyes. He nodded, still unable to speak.

Scythe stood and took his hand. She wondered if Dagger was watching now. She hoped he wasn't. She had done enough for one night; she just wanted the night to end.

She led him to the broom closet where she'd stashed her pack. He was already groping at her as she closed the door.

Scythe didn't bother with any foreplay. He was kissing her neck as she gripped her weapon and shoved him off. Before he could protest, Scythe swung and dug the blade into his skull. He hit the wall with a satisfying thud. Using the momentum of his fall, she wrenched the weapon free from the bone. Glad that the job was finally done.

Scythe picked up her pack and left, closing the door behind her. She left the wedding and snuck out of the city. She figured when Dagger wondered where she had gone, he would probably check the graveyard.

There were still several hours of moonlight left. The graveyard was blessedly empty, and the mausoleum still stood open. Scythe climbed onto the base of a tall statue to wait for Dagger. The stonework depicted a girl holding a long bone with the empty hand extended in welcome. The statue of Nyx stood almost seven feet high. She wondered if the living knew the goddess of death chose to look like a child.

Scythe kept her weapon at max length and set it against the statue base next to her as she watched the stars. She didn't have to wait long for Dagger.

She heard the bushes rustling and saw him appear from the tree line. He hadn't bothered with the road as she had. The vest and cloak were disheveled. Apparently, he'd come straight from the city through the woods.

Scythe watched as he searched the graveyard and spotted her. His hands balled into fists, and he forced a breath. He didn't break eye contact as he stalked around the headstones toward her.

"You could have at least told me you'd left," he said as he caught up to her, "or a note would have been nice."

"I knew you'd look here," she shrugged.

"I'm that predictable, I suppose?"

"In some ways," she paused, keeping eye contact.

Dagger caught the pause. "Scythe, what did you do?"

"I confronted your sister." Guilt clawed at her throat again.

His jaw worked in anger. It took him a moment to repeat: "What did you do?"

"I didn't touch her," Scythe assured him, "but after I left you by the pillar I noticed the family resemblance and had to be sure."

"You left her alone after that, right?" His jaw was tense.

"Yes, she actually left the group."

"Good." He still wasn't delighted but clearly forced himself to accept it.

"And then another woman told me how you died."

He froze and looked away, running a hand through his hair. He didn't say anything. She had expected him to yell. She would have preferred that to this silence.

Eventually he said, "You know how to get back from here?"

"Yes."

"Good."

Dagger turned and disappeared into the tree line.

# Chapter 8

Scythe left her pack in the mausoleum, intending to come back for it later. She hadn't bothered changing out of the formal dress. She walked through the forest, scythe in hand, and tried to enjoy the cool weather.

She couldn't stop thinking about Dagger's disappointment. She could have handled anger and accusations. Instead, he'd grown sullen and stalked off.

It had been the exact opposite of her father. When he grew angry, he'd let everyone know. Their one-room house had become a patchwork of different-colored wood because of how many holes he'd punched through it. It wasn't just the walls he hit, either. When that man grew angry at the slightest insult, he'd break whatever he could get his hands on. Including his wife and daughter. Back then, she couldn't fight back but let the blows land until he grew tired. Today, she could do something about it; she could handle that rage from others.

When Maniodes chose her to become an Incruentus Ferrum, she'd chosen the scythe. It was tall and intimidating. It made her feel safe.

Dagger was not going to hurt her, though. She knew that much about him. He was a hunter of the living, but he'd never hit a woman out of anger. Tonight was proof of that. He'd just walked away.

Scythe had no idea what to do now. She'd go back to their estate—she'd have to eventually—but she didn't know what to say once she saw him again. An apology was obvious, but in her century of being a Ferrum, she'd refused to apologize for anything. Even to Maniodes himself.

She had dug into Dagger's death when he'd given her space about hers, but this was different.

A light caught her attention as she stepped around a small pool of water. It was a strong, constant light that beckoned an investigation. Scythe seized at the distraction.

Upon closer inspection, she found that the light came from a small cottage. The little house sat nestled among the trees with its own fair-sized barn and a road that led north to the city. The lantern was framed by an open window. Scythe walked right up to the window, not worrying about being seen. She leaned on the staff of her weapon and took in the happy scene before her.

A grizzled man sat beside the lantern at a handmade table, repairing a farming tool with glue. There were other tools scattered around the table waiting to be worked on. The man clearly took care of his effects. In the corner of the cottage by the warm fireplace, a woman with red hair sat in a rocking chair working on a needlepoint project. A bitter taste rose in Scythe's throat then. The woman held a small resemblance of her own mother.

Something else caught her attention in the firelight. There was a large bruise wrapped around her forearm. It was just starting to turn yellow, but given the size, it had to be an ugly purple at one point. Scythe's gaze snapped back to the man working on the tools. The only thing that could have made a bruise like that was his hands. She had seen enough of them on her own, as well as her mothers.

There was only one other door inside, probably leading to a bedroom. There were no toys anywhere to be seen, and everything was in its proper place. The couple had no children.

They did have a horse. Scythe had heard the creature's neigh cut through the night air from the barn.

Scythe approached the front door. She swung the door open, breaking the lock, and paused, letting them take in the scene of a strange woman on their doorstep with long, red hair in a black silk dress carrying a six-foot scythe.

The woman jumped to her feet, dropping her needlework, clutching her chest. The man stood as well but was more composed. He'd kept hold of a trowel to confront the stranger.

"What in the bloody name of Nyx do you want?" he demanded.

"Well, that's not a pleasant way to greet a guest," Scythe commented.

"They don't normally barge in."

Scythe flipped her weapon upside down and thrust with the base of the staff. She connected with his skull between his eyes, causing a satisfying crack. The man tumbled to the floor, unconscious from the blow. The woman gave an even more satisfying shriek.

"Bind him," Scythe ordered the woman, as a queen would a slave.

"I-I…please, d-don't hurt us. P-please leave us be." Tears streamed from the woman's eyes.

Scythe spun the weapon again and brought the blade to the woman's throat. The woman had screamed as Scythe moved but fell silent at the touch of the cold blade.

"I am not in the mood for your weeping and begging. Bind him."

The woman gave a tiny nod. Scythe removed the blade, and the woman picked a length of rope that hung on the wall.

"Please—"

"Don't talk," Scythe ordered. "Hold the rope out from the center."

The woman did as she was told, whimpering as Scythe cut the rope in half with the end of her blade. The need to hurt was singing in her veins and she loved it. Given the night she just had she deserved a little fun. This woman could provide half of it.

"Now, half again."

Once the rope was in four pieces, the woman bound her husband's wrists, crying the entire time.

After the woman cinched the rope around his ankles, Scythe rendered her unconscious as well. Scythe then set her weapon aside and tied up the woman in the same manner.

She left to get the horse.

# Chapter 9

Skiachora was as bleak as ever. Dagger picked his way past the dead. He couldn't remember it, but he had been a wandering grey shade after his mother killed him.

Most people were angry at their killers, but Dagger wasn't. His mother had been sick for years and steadily grew worse. Her hallucinations usually led to her screaming at blank walls or locking herself in the cellar, claiming demons were coming to eat her. His father had always been able to calm her, but she quickly spiraled into madness after his death.

His father was here. Dagger found him by accident while walking blindly along one of the Acheron's streams. He couldn't notice his son, but Dagger had taken some comfort in seeing him. He had been attacked in the streets at night coming home from an outing. Dagger never learned who killed him, but it was probably just a robbery gone horribly wrong.

His mother had never recovered from her grief, and her illness deepened. He and his sister started studying to be scholars, as their father had. Karteria never enjoyed the tutoring business, but it would be easy for her to get into, because of their father. Mother helped when she could, and she was always good with remembering dates. The illness had never taken that away.

During the last few months of Dagger's life, his mother had to be chained to the bed sometimes because of her ravings. The physicians kept her asleep most of the time with tonics, but there was nothing else they could do.

One afternoon in the fall she had woken up perfectly lucid, and the maids helped her sit up. She was confused but calm and asked to see her children. The servants immediately came to Dagger in the library. He dropped the tome he had been studying and rushed up to see her. The brief moments of lucidity never lasted long.

He found her at the window seat watching the birds. She turned and beamed as the door closed behind him. She stood, a little shaky, and opened her arms.

He embraced her frail form gently.

"How are you feeling, Mother?" he asked softly.

"Well enough, dear," she answered, patting his cheek. "Come sit."

He guided her to the window seat and sat with her.

"How have your studies been going?" she inquired.

"Just fine."

They chatted pleasantly for a long time. He had missed their conversations. They talked for hours and had a servant bring them dinner. After eating, they sat at the window again. Then his mother grew quiet and still.

He touched her arm gently. "Mother?"

She didn't answer; she only stared out the window at nothing.

"Mother?" he urged again.

Her hand flew up and hit the window flat against the glass.

She whispered, "Demon."

He sighed as dread filled his chest.

"I'll get the physician," he told her deaf ears. He patted her arm and stood.

She shrieked.

Dread changed into terror. Turning back, he saw her wide eyes staring at him.

"What are you?!" she screamed.

She didn't recognize him. His heart raced in panic. The physicians couldn't be far; they would have heard the scream. He knelt in front of her and took her hands.

"It's me, Mother," he pleaded. "Your son, please remember me."

She screamed and shoved him away. He fell back as she ran over him to the table of leftover food. He scrambled to his feet, then saw her grip a knife.

"Mother, don't," he called. She could hurt herself like this; she had before.

She turned on him.

"Stay away from me!" she screamed. "Monster. Demon!"

"I'm your son," he insisted. He couldn't stand seeing her like this.

He stepped closer, preparing to take the knife away. She held it with both shaking hands.

She slashed at him.

"I'm not a demon," he yelled back.

She lunged at him. He tried to catch her arm, but suddenly she was too close, and the knife was inside him.

She ran from him to cower by her bed, whispering. "Die monster, die, die, die, demon, die."

Her force had broken a rib, but he hardly felt that. The knife was buried hilt-deep, with hot blood pulsing down his chest and stomach.

He couldn't breathe. The pain was intense; he couldn't move. He crumbled to the floor, gasping for air around the pain, but blood bubbled past his lips. All his strength was replaced by sharp agony. He could almost envision his heart trying to beat around the sharp metal and finally giving up. He slumped to the floor, cold and numb.

It took considerable effort for Dagger to push the memory away, and even then it lingered in the back of his mind. He remembered the moment Maniodes had awakened him from death too. It felt as if only a moment had passed after seeing his mother cowering by the bed. It was like going to sleep and waking the next morning. He couldn't remember Nyx coming to him, but none of the other Incruentus Ferrum could either. One moment he was bleeding out on his mother's rug, the next he was kneeling in front of Maniodes on his throne.

He had never been very pious in his life, but the god didn't seem to care about that detail. Dagger had thought he was going to be punished in some horrid way, but Maniodes offered him another life. A life to deal out the god's demands and apply order amongst the living. An order through death.

Dagger had been appalled at first; he had never taken a life. A small thought stuck in his mind before he refused though. His life had been a boring slog of studies to follow in his father's footsteps. He could forge his own life with this dead one. The god of the underworld was offering him power and a new kind of life so he agreed whole heartedly.

He entered Maniodes's castle now. It was a beautiful and domineering structure. It sat on an immense rock foundation that floated above the reverse waterfall that fed The Acheron. The only entrance was the split staircase to the Skiachora fields. He walked past the cracked walls up to the god's chambers. He'd always admired this place and its foreboding feel. He hoped his own little estate could mirror it someday. He had even grown excited for the quirky yet threatening feel Scythe was pouring into the estate. Now, he wasn't so sure.

Crossing into one of the many corridors toward the god's office tower, Dagger spotted a small figure coming his way. Dagger waited at the intersection of hallways for the boy. He was about twelve and adorable by normal standards. He had a short crop of blond hair, dark-blue eyes, and olive tones skin. If he hadn't died so early he would have grown into a handsome young man. He always seemed to have the mindset of a child, though. He'd been an Incruentus Ferrum longer than Dagger, and time had matured him a fair amount, but he was still a child at heart.

The only love this boy would have received, though, would have been from his mother, if she hadn't died giving birth to him. He never talked much about his father, but he loved to brag about torturing small animals.

Dagger wasn't sure why Maniodes would choose such a young boy to be his steward. The boy didn't have much bloodlust for human life, probably because of his young age. It had never set in, so it made him easier to control. Maybe Maniodes took pity on him because the boy didn't have a mother, either. It didn't matter what Maniodes's reasons were. The god needed a new steward, and the farm boy was probably the first grey soul he happened to notice.

"Evening, Pitch," Dagger greeted as the boy approached.

Pitch was concentrating on not spilling the jug of wine he was carrying. He jumped a bit at Dagger's sudden appearance but managed not to spill a drop.

"Evening, Dagger. How's Scythe?" Pitch's smile lit up his blue eyes. You couldn't see the raging madman under the innocence unless you knew he was there.

"She's fine," he said, using her own words from the wedding.

Pitch walked past him toward Maniodes's tower, and Dagger followed.

"Did Maniodes give you any jobs yet, little man?" Dagger asked as they walked.

"No," Pitch replied with a childish pout. "The most I get to do is fetch wine."

They came to a set of stairs leading up around a stone pillar and began to climb.

"How was the wedding job?" Pitch asked. "That was my idea, you know."

"It went well," he said, wishing Pitch hadn't brought it up. "Wait, *you* planned that?"

"Aye, he was thinking of a quiet job you two could do. To stay out of too much trouble. I thought attacking the groom indirectly would be a challenge for you both. He was worried it would be too big and exciting, and you'd botch it. He wanted to test you together, so he liked the idea. I'm glad it worked because it looks good for me too, you know?"

"Well, I'm glad it worked out for you, little man," he said, managing to control his bitterness. It *had* been a challenge for them, even without Scythe interrogating his sister. Dagger wondered if Maniodes had picked the kid for his mind.

The landing at the top of the stairs was narrow. The door set into the wall only a few feet from them was made of solid, dark wood and stood nine feet high. The gods could choose how to appear at any moment, and the god of the underworld loved the ridiculously tall size.

A sentry stood by the door. He wasn't a Ferrum but a simple skeleton in chain mail armor that Maniodes put together. It stood silently watching the entrance, but Dagger knew once it moved, the bones rattling inside the metal armor made a fair amount of noise. Pitch walked right in with the wine, having that right as a steward. Dagger was supposed to wait for the sentry to announce him, but he didn't bother. He stopped the door from closing on him and followed behind Pitch.

The god of the underworld sat at a large desk made of cast iron. It fit the eight-foot-tall god comfortably; it rose to Dagger's chest. He hated how small it made him feel.

Maniodes looked up from whatever he was writing. He kept his eyes still, but everyone knew he didn't like being interrupted. Dagger's foul mood wasn't exactly letting him be cautious.

"My Lord." Dagger bowed, then waited with his hands behind his back, fiddling with a knife. He didn't intend to attack the god, but he found the knife calming.

"Dagger."

Maniodes turned to finish his letter. Dagger waited to be acknowledge.

Pitch had stayed still the entire encounter, watching the two surprised. He probably hadn't expected Dagger to sneak in behind him. Before

Maniodes could get angry, Pitch stood on a stool to refill the goblet on the desk.

Dagger watched the kid stand just behind the god, no doubt feeling awkward.

When Maniodes finally finished writing, he set the raven quill aside and regarded Dagger. The god grinned over his folded hands on the desk. It wasn't a malicious grin, but his eyes told Dagger to be careful.

"Report?"

"It went well. I chose a girl, and Scythe chose her victim. A man, I believe. I didn't learn his name but I saw them walk off together."

Maniodes showed mock surprise. "How did that feel? Seeing your wife off with another man."

"It was for work, nothing more."

"Are you sure? The woman can lure men easily."

"Yes."

The surprise melted as Maniodes took him more seriously. "And you only killed two?"

"You would know that. Nyx *is* the one who brings the souls."

Pitch held the jug of wine closer to his chest, as if it would protect him. Maniodes's eyes darkened.

"Where is she now, Dagger?" he demanded.

"I don't know, my lord," he admitted. "We parted after the wedding."

"Already a falling-out in married life? You're supposed to be watching her, and she you."

Dagger spun the knife faster and didn't reply.

"Find her."

Maniodes began writing a new document.

Dagger turned sharply, paranoid now about Scythe. He stopped short lest he barrel over the new arrival behind him, which would not have ended well.

Nyx, the goddess of death, stood behind him, watching him with her black irises and white pupils. Her childlike form was barely taller than Pitch, but her stance conveyed power. Dagger had no way of knowing how long she had been there patiently waiting, the thigh bone she held like a scepter before her.

Dagger corrected himself and knelt before the Goddess of Death. "Your Grace."

Maniodes and Pitch were behind Dagger now. He heard the desk chair scrape backward and Pitch set the jug down. Both knelt to the goddess. Dagger actually felt a little better knowing they had just noticed her too.

Given Nyx's childlike appearance, Maniodes still towered above her even while on his knees.

"Greetings, Mother," Maniodes said.

"We need to talk," Nyx said, disregarding Dagger.

In this case he didn't mind being overlooked.

"Of course. Pitch, Dagger, give us the room."

Dagger had to clench his teeth to stop from snickering. Maniodes was perfectly chaste and civil when his mother was around. Dagger stood and caught sight of Pitch picking up the jug. Pitch hurried over to Dagger's side, and Dagger held the door open for him.

"Dagger."

He stopped and looked back to Maniodes.

"You find Scythe, and you control her."

Dagger's anger bubbled up again. He gave a small bow in acknowledgement and left.

"Dagger?"

"What?!"

It was Pitch who stopped him this time, on the landing outside the office. He hadn't intended to snap, but he just wanted to get home.

Pitch took a step back as Dagger rounded on him. He saw the little madman in the kid's eyes.

"I hope things do work out between you and Scythe." Pitch's voice was more stern than comforting.

Dagger's anger deflated instantly, replaced by a bit of guilt. "I do too," he answered honestly.

Pitch nodded a farewell, then disappeared down a hidden passage by the sentry. The servant's passageways were another perk for the kid. Dagger would probably get lost in them.

Dagger only made it down about twenty steps before Pitch came bounding down behind him. He grabbed Dagger's hand, pulling him back up the stairs.

"Dagger, wait! You have to come," he said, wide-eyed and scared.

"What, why?"

"Just come!"

Pitch dragged him up the stairs again, past the sentry, and into the servant's passage. The skeleton did nothing to stop them.

Pitch pulled Dagger along a few strides then stopped at a random section of corridor. The wine jug sat on the ground, marking the spot.

"Pitch, what—"

"Quiet! Listen."

He pointed to a spot on the stone wall and Dagger noticed a small crack.

He stooped and set his ear to the crack. The words were muffled, but he could hear Nyx and Maniodes talking.

"—difficult to control," Nyx's mature voice made it easy to forget her childlike form.

"I know, but normal people don't usually take kindly to killing," Maniodes said.

"There are other options. A pack of dogs, or a larger enforcement of sentries."

"Good ideas, but mindless dogs could become harder to control."

"Not if they're trained well."

Maniodes didn't reply.

Again, Dagger had to stop himself from laughing. The mighty god of Skiachora was being scolded by his mother.

"I like the Incruentus Ferrum operation," Nyx admitted. "They get the job done, dealing out caution. It reminds the humans there is a higher power. The acts of violence, however, give the Ferrum a sense of power over the living. That leads to burned villages and hundreds of innocents dead, and it's getting worse. Their bloodlust is growing."

"Those two have been dealt with," Maniodes said, trying to defend himself.

"By *marrying* them to each other." Nyx was not amused by the idea.

"It's given results so far. Regular punishments haven't worked on either of them."

"Either way, the rest of them might become just as dangerous. I want you to disband them all."

Dagger's dead heart hit the floor. The shock and fear was clear on Pitch's face too. The goddess wanted them all officially dead.

"Give me some time," Maniodes asked. "Let me prove to the other Ferrum that I can control Dagger and Scythe. That should calm the rest down, show them who's in power."

"It *should*?"

"It will."

Silence.

Pitch trembled beside him.

"Alright," Nyx said. "I know you're fond of them. You have one turn of the moon. If either of those two step out of line, they are all disbanded."

"Yes, Mother."

The silence was more final this time. Dagger prayed neither of the deities would appear and catch them.

"Pitch," Dagger kept his voice low. He knelt before the boy to look him in the eye. "Can you keep this secret?"

The madman was gone now. Pitch was just a scared kid, trembling under Dagger's hands. He didn't reply right away.

"You *can't* let Maniodes know we heard this," Dagger said, trying to control his own panic for Pitch's sake.

"I can stay quiet," Pitch whispered.

"Can you stay calm?"

"I think so."

"You have to, Pitch. I'm glad you brought me here, but Maniodes *can't know.*"

"I can keep it secret," Pitch said, stronger now and a little annoyed at being pressed.

It was the best Dagger would get. He would have to trust the boy.

Dagger stood, letting go of Pitch.

"What are you going to do?" Pitch asked.

"I have no idea. Play along with Maniodes's demands, I suppose."

He hated how those words sounded, but he had the fate of the entire Incruentus Ferrum to consider now.

He left Pitch in the narrow corridor. Just as he was about to leave the fold in the wall and sneak down the stairs, the office door opened.

Dagger's heart jumped to his throat as Maniodes peered around the door to the sentry standing outside. Dagger managed to stay silent and sneak behind the fold, where Maniodes wouldn't be able to see him.

"Dagger should still be in the castle. Run down to the front courtyard and cut him off before he leaves," Maniodes said to the sentry. "Bring him back here. I need to talk to him."

Dagger heard the door close. Confusion matched the sudden fear in his heart. He'd thought Maniodes wouldn't want to tell them about Nyx's demand. He'd only been an Incruentus Ferrum for a decade—maybe he didn't know the god as well as he thought.

Dagger peeked around the corner slowly. The sentry was still there, looking right at him. He and Pitch had run right past the guard on the way into the hidden corridor, so of course it knew where he had gone. The sentry hadn't given Dagger away to Maniodes immediately. It stood there waiting and watching Dagger.

"I'll go in ten minutes," Dagger whispered to it. That way the timing made it look like the sentry did its job.

He waited uncomfortably for several long moments behind the fold in the wall. He had no way of knowing the exact time, but at one point the sentry nodded to him. Dagger hoped that meant enough time had passed to make Maniodes believe the sentry really had gone. Dagger cleared his throat, stepped out from the hidden corridor, and knocked on the tall door.

"Come," Maniodes's voice called.

Dagger opened the door and entered the office again. He buried his fear of being caught and kept his expression neutral. Maniodes was back at his desk writing.

"You called for me again?" Dagger asked.

Maniodes put down the quill and rubbed his temple. Dagger wondered if the gods could get headaches. He had never heard of one falling ill. At the moment, though, it looked like he had a throbbing migraine.

"Yes, there has been a new turn of events. Nyx and I talked," Maniodes started.

"Yes," was all Dagger could say to fill the silence that followed.

Maniodes sighed, then said, "I didn't want things to get this far. I know there's only about thirty of you, but you're the only intelligent creatures I have any connection with. Phaos created his living beings to fill Ichorisis. I get the leftovers down here with the dead."

Dagger remained quiet this time, watching in wonder as the god admitted something oddly personal. Perhaps he had been wrong about him.

"Nyx has demanded that if you and Scythe step out of line, all of the Incruentus Ferrum will be killed," Maniodes finished.

Dagger stammered for a moment, allowing the knowledge to surprise him for the 'first time.'

"If that is her will, then Scythe and I will be extra cautious," Dagger said, regaining his composure. "Thank you for telling me, my lord. I should go and find Scythe."

"Yes," Maniodes said, turning back to his letter. "Find her and inform her of the situation."

Dagger bowed and left the room. He had to look for Scythe. If she had killed anyone, they were all dead.

# Chapter 10

Scythe straightened her dress while leaving the cellar. She considered going to her chambers to change and wait for Dagger to return home when he practically ran in through the crooked main door.

"Perfect timing," she said, hardly able to contain her excitement.

"Scythe, we have to talk."

"Later. Come with me, I got you a present." She took his hand and led him back to the cellar.

"Wait, what?" he asked, caught off guard.

He had assumed she was mad at him. She led him down the stairs to the first cell door on the left. Unlocking it, she brought him inside the small space to his gift. The man and woman from the cabin were chained to the wall opposite the door. Scythe let go of Dagger's hand and gestured toward their guests like she was displaying a new fine wine.

Dagger took in the scene, wide-eyed. She could see the ideas surfacing in his mind on what they could do.

"I thought we could torment them together," Scythe explained, hardly able to contain her excitement.

"Scythe, this is great," he said, grinning. His demeanor changed as he remembered something. "But they *can't* die."

"Well, obviously. Maniodes would kill us."

"Not just us anymore. Everyone." His dark, wide eyes weren't eager anymore.

"What are you talking about?" Scythe asked.

"I overheard Maniodes and Nyx talking. She wants all of the Incruentus Ferrum dead."

"How did you hear that?!"

"Pitch found a crack in the wall of Maniodes's office. I had gone to give the report of the wedding. Then Maniodes kicked Pitch and me out when Nyx got there," Dagger explained.

"Fuck, I always forget the reports."

"I know, but then Maniodes summoned me again, and told me about the new penalty of everyone's deaths if we fuck up."

"So all of the Ferrum could end up grey because of us?" The idea did not fit well in her mind.

"Yes."

"Fuck!"

After a moment of hesitation, Dagger said, "I think we could be okay."

"Really, how?" Scythe couldn't control the sarcasm. The news had broken her good mood.

"It will be another challenge. As long as these two don't die, Nyx and Maniodes won't find out."

"So, we have to let them go?"

"You make it sound like I'm denying you ice cream." He was smiling again.

"I was looking forward to doing this with you," Scythe said. "I've never tortured anyone with another Ferrum before. None of the others enjoy it the way we do."

Dagger took a step closer to Scythe. In the small cell, they were already fairly close. He was looking at her hungrily again. Usually he tried to hide it, and she tried to ignore it. Scythe had never noticed him look at other women this way. Not even with the blond girl at the wedding. This look in his eyes was meant for her alone. She could feel the lack of space between them, but for once she didn't step away.

"I won't deny you anything," he said.

He plucked a knife from his belt. Keeping his dark eyes on Scythe he laid the edge of the blade against the man's sternum. The man had fallen from the horse into the mud, so she'd removed his tunic. The first half-inch of steel sunk into his flesh. Thick blood welled up from the wound and dripped down to his stomach.

The man only grunted against the pain, probably trying to not give them the satisfaction. His wife, on the other hand, screamed into her gag. Dagger would get his satisfaction, Scythe knew. The knife followed the line of blood and he took his time cutting down to the man's midsection. The man was screaming with his wife by the end.

"That wasn't fatal," Dagger stated.

Scythe kept her red eyes on Dagger's and plucked a knife from his belt. Her hand lingered a second longer than necessary. Dagger's smirk turned more carnal.

Scythe rested the blade against the man's right pectoral and dragged it down as Dagger had. She angled her cut, so it crossed Dagger's and ended at the man's left hip.

The man screamed again, woman kept crying.

Scythe could feel a heat growing inside her. It was different from the usual excitement of blood. Dagger was making this happen.

"Let's get some chairs," Dagger said through heavy breath.

After some maneuvering, Dagger and Scythe had their two guests tied up in the experiments chamber. They tied their guests facing each other and the real fun began. After a full week of playing nice, Scythe was ready to bend the rules. The wedding had been a disaster, but this would make up for it.

The same hunter's look was in Dagger's eyes as back in the burning village. There was something different this time when his eyes landed on Scythe. Every time they did, the warmth inside Scythe grew. She still couldn't decide if she liked it, but she wanted to experiment.

"Where do you want to start?" Dagger asked, coming up beside her.

"We'll have to keep things shallow and avoid main arteries." Scythe leaned into him. "I have an idea."

Scythe untied the woman's right wrist. The woman started babbling, but Scythe tuned it out.

"Hold this." Scythe held the woman's hand out at full length.

Dagger took the hand, keeping the arm outstretched. The woman pleaded louder. The man was yammering as well.

She leaned closer than necessary to Dagger and removed another knife, purposefully choosing one at his back. He stood a little taller as she did.

Knife in hand, Scythe started below the woman's elbow. Cutting smoothly, she spiraled a single line from the elbow halfway down her forearm, stopping at her wrist. The scream was fantastic. Crimson covered the woman's arm and dripped to the stone below.

Scythe made one more incision from where she started. She connected the beginning of the bloody spiral to the line beneath it. Using that end, Scythe lifted the skin. Sinews and veins stretched between the skin and meat, a deep, reddish-purple.

She felt Dagger's hand touch her waist. He kept his grip on the woman's wrist but wrapped his other arm around Scythe as if they were dancing.

She listened to his breath at her ear as she unwound the woman's flesh. The screams were loud enough to crack the air. Scythe peeled the flesh away in one long strip, painting her hands crimson. When she reached the end at the wrist she gave a quick tug, breaking the strip free.

Scythe twirled the flesh between her fingers as Dagger tied the woman's arm down again. As Dagger straightened, Scythe caught his head with the strip, wrapping it around the back of his neck. Given his height, it was easier to pull him closer. She wanted the challenge.

Dagger obliged, hardly letting the flesh stretch. Their lips met. Dagger's arms wound around Scythe, locking her to him. Scythe let go of the strip and buried one hand in his hair, the other wrapped around his shoulders.

She knew this was right. She wasn't afraid as Dagger pressed her back against the wall and kissed deeper. She felt heat radiating off him. The warmth inside her grew so intense it felt as if she was burning. She loved it.

Eventually, Dagger pulled away to breathe. Scythe was glad to be against the wall, supported by him, given how lightheaded she was. Judging by his glassy gaze, she could see he the same.

The strip of flesh still hung around his neck, getting blood on his vest. Scythe noticed the streak of crimson under his ear. In the spur of the moment, she'd forgotten her hands were covered in it. He didn't seem to mind or even notice.

"I guess I don't frighten you anymore?" His voice was husky, almost low enough to be a growl. He kissed her again, running his hands down her waist.

Suddenly and without welcome, her father flooded her thoughts. Her father, along with the brute he'd brought home. That man had stared at her in the same hungry and lustful manner. This was different. Dagger was different. While that man had looked at her like he was studying a slab of beef, Dagger appeared to be admiring fine art.

Scythe's arms slid from Dagger's back to hang at her sides. She wanted to scream at herself that this was okay. She knew Dagger, and he knew her. More images of her father and that brute filled her mind, killing the fire Dagger had ignited.

"Dagger, wait."

He had finally relinquished her lips and had begun kissing her neck.

It felt good and warm, but the passion was dead inside her.

"Stop," she said more sternly.

He finally did but still held onto her arm. She didn't know why. He probably didn't mean anything by it. He was gripping the same spot on her upper arm as the brute did to take her away. Fear jumped to her throat.

"Why?" he asked, his eyes slightly glazed over. "You seemed to be enjoying it."

His lips met hers again.

Scythe could only see the brute and her father.

She pushed Dagger's chest. Catching him off guard, he stumbled back and nearly tripped on the captured woman's foot.

He stared at her with clear eyes now. They were hurt and confused.

"Why?" he spat.

She darted from the room before he could finish the question.

"Scythe!" he called after her.

She practically ran, but the brute and her father followed her.

Once on the balcony, Scythe saw the moon was angled into a smile. The night was warm, and the stars danced in the sky. She couldn't help comparing it to the night the man had come. The moon had been the same then, too, and although it was beautiful, it always reminded her of that night. She shoved those thoughts aside, refusing to let them ruin her again.

The door behind her creaked open. Turning, she saw Dagger, his hair still tussled.

"I would like to ask you something," Dagger said seriously.

"Alright," she said after a pause in her pacing.

"You won't like answering it."

"Just bloody ask!" she demanded, not appreciating the tension.

"Tell me how you died. Back in the graveyard you were nervous about sleeping next to me," he said. "You said you weren't raped, but something bad happened, and I can only imagine that the next option would be death."

"I don't want to talk about that," Scythe protested.

"It's only fair. Marriages are built on trust. I trusted you, Scythe, and you dug into my past."

“They’re built on business arrangements for men who want to sell off their daughters.”

“This one doesn’t have to be.” He paused. “Is that what happened? Were you sold?”

“Enough!” Scythe spun her weapon to full length and held it for comfort. “I am not sharing that.”

Dagger sighed frustrated. “Fine, I’ll leave you alone.” He turned and left the balcony.

# Chapter 11

Dagger paced around the torture chamber. The woman's raw arm glistened crimson and gold in the fire he'd stoked in the brazier. She gave a whimper every time Dagger got too close. He was very tempted to gag her, but that wouldn't stop the small cries. The man watched Dagger pace. He would have seemed brave if not for the tremble in his hands.

Dagger cursed to himself again as he reviewed the events. They had practically been dancing in the passion. He could feel the anticipation radiating off of her like the sun where he touched her. She had flirted and played along before, but that was different.

He remembered her wrapping the string of flesh around his neck to pull him close. Growling now, he ripped it away and threw it against the wall of hanging tools. It caught on the jagged edge of a saw blade.

The woman screamed again as if she still felt the flesh hanging on the saw. Dagger's fingers itched to stick a knife into her throat.

"Lady trouble?"

The knife flew but not at the woman's neck. It buried itself into the man's leg shortly after he'd spoken. His scream made the woman cry again.

Dagger chastised himself for coming down here. He didn't need these creatures criticizing him. He wanted to slaughter them both. He wanted to feel their blood course through his fingers. Dagger wrenched the blade free from the man's leg and walked to the door.

He paused just outside the archway, thinking. He'd come down here to relax, but that had failed miserably. He didn't want to run into Scythe upstairs.

His captives were married; maybe they could actually help with something.

Dagger turned on his heel, plucked a stool from the corner, and sat in front of the man. He angled himself directly between the man and his wife.

The man sat up, his back pressed against the chair as if trying to phase through it. He stared wide-eyed at Dagger, and Dagger couldn't help but smile now.

"No more witty remarks?" Dagger goaded him, keeping his voice calm.

The man shook his head, though it was hardly more than a twitch.

"You're right, actually," Dagger said. "What did you make of that situation?"

The man stammered, no doubt terrified at being addressed.

"Oh, come on, the knife hit your leg, not your tongue."

"I-I'm not sure," he stammered. "Maybe she gained a conscience?"

Dagger chuckled, and the man flinched again.

"Scythe's bloodlust is the strongest I've seen. Peeling flesh off an arm doesn't bother her. I've seen her rifle through a man's intestines while he squirmed," Dagger said.

"Something frightened her, something she thought of."

The man's mouth hadn't moved.

Dagger turned, stunned that the woman had spoken coherent words. She was still trembling and couldn't even look him in the eye, but he gave her credit for speaking.

"That's nonsense," Dagger replied. "She's never afraid of anything."

For a moment the woman couldn't reply, now that he was looking at her. Finally, she said, "She changed her mind about something."

That was true at least, Dagger realized. One moment she used the strip of skin to pull him close, the next she shoved him away. When he confronted her about it she had changed. She wasn't confused or scared, but tense and defensive. Maybe the frightened woman had a point.

"What should I do?" Dagger found himself asking.

"Go to bed with your own hand for company," the man growled.

Dagger flipped the knife in his fingers to point at the man. "Any more wit from you and your wife gets a new hole."

The man shut up.

Dagger turned back to the woman, waiting for a legitimate answer.

She could only stammer, “I-I don’t know.”

“You must have some idea,” Dagger insisted. “What would you want, if a man came on to you too strongly?”

Her eyes flickered to her husband, then back to Dagger. She sobbed, saying, “I’d want to be left alone.”

It was a fair answer. Dagger stood, sheathing his blade. The woman cowered in her chair, but he left her alone as he left the chamber.

He’d leave Scythe be, as the woman suggested. It was along the same line of thoughts he’d had, but it felt good to have someone unknowingly agree.

His blood hadn’t completely cooled from its former boiling point, but it was cool enough. He even made it upstairs to his bed without running into Scythe, so that had helped. There was nothing more he could do tonight anyway.

# Chapter 12

The night was cool as the moon rose on the next night. Scythe stood on the second-floor balcony watching the bats fly, a goblet of wine in her hand. She hadn't spoken to Dagger since last night. She didn't want to explain the conflict inside her, but she knew they had to smooth things over somehow. In all their time together, she had never pushed him away before. She had also never kissed him. Something new had bloomed in her dead heart when she shouted at him: guilt. She tried to stamp it out. She had nothing to feel guilty for. Yet Dagger had looked so downtrodden and angry when he left.

The scrape of broken glass underfoot caught her attention. Turning quickly, she saw Dagger at the doorway.

He kept his expression neutral while he asked, "May I join you?"

"It's your home," Scythe shrugged, turning back to the bats. She scolded herself for the new guilt.

Dagger came up next to her and looked out over the forest. He stayed quiet, probably unsure what to say himself.

Scythe hated this. They'd never fought like that before. They had always known what the other was thinking when they worked together. This fucking marriage was ruining everything,

She asked Dagger, "So, what did you do last night after…?" She wasn't sure how to end the question politely.

He looked at her, confused, raising an eyebrow. Scythe hoped Dagger sensed this was her way of smoothing things over.

"Talked with our guests in the cellar for a while," he said. "Then just went to bed. What about you?"

His tone wasn't sarcastic in any way. Maybe her non-apology was working.

"I stayed in the garden for a while," Scythe admitted. "Then went to bed too."

Dagger just nodded, running a hand through his hair.

"You called this place your home yesterday," he said. "I was hoping you could see it as your own, eventually."

"I do," she answered honestly. She hated how small her voice sounded, but it was true.

"I'm glad." His voice was soft.

Scythe stole a glance at him and caught him looking, too. There was a small smile on his lips. Scythe let in an easy breath for once; they were alright.

"Do you want to talk about last night?" Dagger asked tentatively.

"Nope."

"Okay then."

"There is one thing we should discuss, though," she said.

"What's that?"

"What are we going to do about Maniodes and Nyx?"

Dagger contemplated for a moment.

"We'll have to stay quiet about it for now," he said. "If they find out I listened in on them, he will kill us. Pitch too, probably. And I don't know if he informed Nyx that he told us. She didn't forbid him from telling us. We should just lay low."

"So we play along?" she asked, disappointed.

"For now, yes," he shrugged. He wasn't happy about it either.

"I'm tired of him using us," Scythe admitted. "Not just you and me, but all of the Ferrum. For him we're just an easily replaceable tool to dish out mischief."

"Be careful," Dagger chuckled. "If he hears that, he'll disband us. I don't entirely think that's true anyway. When he told me about Nyx's new order, he seemed worried about us. He's not the best leader, but he's trying."

"There's no peace of mind for us," she pressed. "I'm tired of being controlled."

"What do you suggest we do, then?" he asked with no small hint of sarcasm. "Storm the castle?"

"Maybe not, but we could take him down."

Dagger stayed quiet but watched her, trying to determine whether or not she was serious.

"We could be king and queen of Skiachora."

"You're serious?" he asked.

"Yes, I'm tired of his dictatorship."

"I wouldn't call him a dictator. He just doesn't manage the place well."

"But imagine if *we* did. The Ferrum would be safe. We know how they think. We could even give the sentries their own voices. Maniodes created them but refuses to let them talk. He probably wishes he gave us the same restrictions. He wants us to be lapdogs."

Dagger leaned on the balcony railing and focused on the forest below. Scythe let him gather his thoughts.

"Why not go after Nyx?" he asked. "She's the one who ordered our deaths. Maniodes actually stood up for us."

"Only because of his pride," Scythe countered. "Nyx has never had a problem with us before, but Maniodes is always mistreating us. You remember why he forced Halberd to go grey?"

"I remember," he said, "but he was always a bit of an ass. The joke he said was in bad taste of Nyx anyway."

"Yes, but that's not a good enough reason to kill someone."

"You and I use much smaller reasons," he countered.

"Only against humans, and it's our *job*. What if we could change her mind? Even get her on our side about deposing Maniodes?"

"I highly doubt she'll be willing to depose her son," he said.

"She could be if we convince her it's the right choice," she argued.

"How, Scythe?"

"I don't fucking know yet; that's the point of a plan. Obviously, you're not interested."

"I didn't say that," he said. His black eyes held warm mischief again. "I respect Nyx, and she might be misguided about us. Maniodes, on the other hand, is not a good leader for us."

"And I like Nyx," Scythe added. "Call it a petty reason, but she always seemed to respect us. I think we can change her mind about killing us. We also have easier access to Maniodes, in a way. We have no idea where Nyx even goes when she's not collecting souls. Maniodes's throne is an easier goal."

"Relatively speaking, he is still a god," Dagger said. After a few moments he added, "The first thing I would do is get rid of his giant desk." A smile playing at his lips.

Scythe rolled her eyes. The desk was gaudy, but it wasn't her priority.

"I'm in," he said, surprising her. "I'm sick of how inconsistent he is. One moment he's willing to kill us, the next he's vying for us. Talking to him is like walking on eggshells."

"King and Queen of Skiachora," Scythe purred.

"Now, daydreaming is one thing," Dagger said, still serious. "How do we go about taking down a god?"

Scythe had no idea, but she wondered if myths and history could provide hints. "I don't know. Nyx just created them. I've never heard any story of one god destroying another," she admitted.

"True, but there must be *some* way," Dagger said as he paced, thinking.

"We could examine the stories more. Ask around, do some research," Scythe suggested.

"Yes." Dagger pointed at her, excited. "The library in Maniodes's castle."

Scythe had completely forgotten about that library. It held all knowledge of men and gods, and much more.

"That's perfect," Scythe agreed, "but how do we get in without being noticed?"

"We're going to be noticed regardless. His sentries are everywhere, and he spends his free time in there. The point is to be discreet about what we're looking for."

"So we waltz in, telling Maniodes we want to spend the day with him? While trying to find out how to kill him?" Scythe asked, raising a dubious eyebrow.

"I don't think we can kill him. I don't think they can die." Dagger started pacing again.

Scythe finished her wine, then stopped Dagger from pacing by catching his arm.

"Let's not rush into the first half-baked idea we have. The first thing we should do today is make sure our guests are fed."

"Shit, I forgot about them."

"They were alive when I checked on them about an hour ago."

Dagger breathed a sigh of relief and held her hand. "We're really going to do this. You and me, King and Queen of the underworld."

# Chapter 13

After wrapping the woman's arm in linens, they forced stew down their guests' throats. Scythe decided to clean out their small library. Dagger hadn't gone in there much but knew it was a mess. It was in the section of their castle that was missing a wall. Most of the books and scrolls had crumbled away or turned to mold long ago. Scythe had been determined to save what she could and wanted to convert one of the guest rooms into a new library. She was going to keep an eye out for any kind of old folktale books or scrolls documenting the creation of their world. Anything related to the gods and their myths that might help pinpoint a weak spot. Dagger didn't think the chances were likely, and he let her know this, but she could search all she wanted.

Dagger always found that letting his mind rest while doing physical labor helped him think.

After fixing the wardrobe in his bedchamber, he still didn't have any ideas. Leaving that project with a new foot on its base, he went to find Scythe. She was in the library, sorting through thin scrolls at the desk.

The library was larger than most of the rooms and once housed hundreds of texts. At one time it was probably one of the grandest chambers, with its vaulted ceiling and expensive carpets. The entire north wall was gone now, exposing the rest of the room. That wall had been covered with shelves housing books, just like the others. Dagger wasn't one for reading idly, but even he felt a little sad knowing so much was lost in those texts. The books on the west and east walls close to the opening had nearly rotted away. Thankfully, the ones on the back wall were relatively fine. Most were covered in a film of mildew, but they could be saved. The only furniture left in the room was the desk and a couple of chairs that at one time had probably been comfortable.

Scythe stood at the desk with books open, glancing through the scrolls.

"Find anything useful?" Dagger asked, leaning on the surface next to her.

"No, this is just boring records of what it used to cost to run this place," Scythe sighed.

Dagger glanced over the numbers but was more interested in how Scythe's red hair fell around her neck and moved in the breeze as she read.

He controlled the impulse to brush her hair aside and kiss her neck. She had seemed fine since their attempts at passion before. He was worried about making the first move after their last encounter.

Something grazed past his head, catching his hair painfully. A bat trying to get their attention landed on the back of a ripped chair and screeched at them.

"There's a parchment on its leg," Dagger said, rubbing the back of his head.

"Another job already?" Scythe laid the parchment down, looking at the bat.

"I've never heard you disregard a job before," he said, raising an eyebrow.

"Taking down a god will be time-consuming enough," Scythe shrugged.

He had expected her to avoid eye contact, but her gaze met his as they spoke. It was like their fight hadn't happened. She seemed happy again, but it could be an act.

Dagger untied the message, and the bat flew off through the open wall.

"What is it?" Scythe asked.

"A list of three names and a city, Chalcis," Dagger replied, "and um…"

"What?" She came closer to read the note herself.

"He only wants me to do it," Dagger confessed, handing her the message.

"Why?" She demanded after reading the clear instructions at the bottom. "Did you tell him anything about the wedding?"

"No," he said, taken aback. "The wedding job went fine."

"But did you say anything about our fight?"

"No, why would I? That's just spiteful," he accused back.

"That's the point. I wasn't there, so I don't know if you said anything out of anger to make him think we couldn't work together anymore."

"Why would I do that?" He followed her logic but didn't appreciate being accused of something so petty. Scythe froze but kept the eye contact. Her hands balled into fists, and her red eyes darkened.

Regret quickly followed the spiteful comment. "I did not say anything against you to Maniodes." he said to be clear.

"Okay, good." Scythe looked down at the note again.

Dagger couldn't tell if she was guilty or embarrassed at accusing him, or sad she couldn't partake in the assignment, or bothered by his comment. She was damn impossible to read sometimes.

"You could come," he said, trying to lighten the awkwardness. "I have to be the one to kill them, but there's nothing here about not letting you in the city."

"That's probably one of his unspoken rules, though," she said. "He clearly wants you to carry this out alone. Besides, someone has to make sure the guests don't die. You don't think he knows about them, do you?"

"I don't think so. He would have confronted us immediately."

"You're right; he'd come right for us."

"It should only be a couple of night once in Chalcis," Dagger said. "I could ask around as research, actually. Talk to the locals about myths. See if their libraries have anything. The temples might have some hidden knowledge."

"I could go to Skiachora," Scythe realized, brightening at the idea. "I could go to his library and sniff around. He might even approve of that. He could keep an eye on me himself."

"Searching for his downfall right beneath his nose. I like how devious you think." When it wasn't directed at him.

Scythe handed the list of names back to him. "You should prepare for the journey. It takes a day and a half to ride there. Unless you know of a dead tree close by as a short cut?"

"I don't know of any so I'll ride, at least we've got a horse now," he said, referring to the stallion Scythe had used to kidnap their guests.

"I suppose I should play the dutiful wife and prepare food for your journey?" Her voice had become bland, but he caught a glint of anger.

"There's no need," he said.

# Chapter 14

After seeing Dagger off on the assignment, Scythe visited their guests. She tried to bury the resentment, but it crawled just under her skin like an insect. There was no reason for Maniodes to keep her on the sidelines. He wanted them to play nice, but keeping her out of the game only frustrated her. At least she could release some of it before she left for Skiachora.

The man and woman were sitting in their own filth, but they were awake this time. The woman moaned in fear as Scythe entered the room. The man was braver.

"What do you want?" he demanded.

Scythe let his question hang unanswered while she picked up a hefty iron rod. She set it against the brazier, but the fire had burned out. She left the man yelling after her as she fetched wood from the kitchen. Once she had a steady fire going, the rod cooked under the coals.

"If you want money, it's back at the house," the man offered. "We don't have much but you can take whatever you want."

"M-my necklace was my grandmother's. You can have it," the woman said.

Scythe just laughed. The pendent was just a protective charm stamped on cheap metal hanging on thin twine. The bauble wasn't worth a damn thing.

Scythe stirred the coals and took up the iron rod. The tip glowed a blazing-hot, pristine white. She took her time, wondering where to place the fiery tool. The woman had dissolved into tears and was babbling again. The man was quiet but couldn't look away. The woman was missing a good chunk of her arm, and the man only had a few cuts on his chest. There was a new wound on his leg though. Scythe decided it seemed only fair that he should share in the fun. She brought the rod close to the man's cheek. Its white glow reflected back at her in his green eyes.

"No. Wait, no please. Wait!"

Scythe laid the iron rod lightly against his cheek. The woman and her man screamed as the smell of cooking flesh filled the air. Scythe peeled the iron rod away, watching the man's melted skin stretch as the rod dulled to a reddish hue. The man was left with a bloody, melted gash stretching from his ear to his mouth. There was even a small hole where Scythe could see the man's tooth through his flesh.

Scythe saw her father's face as the man burned.

He breathed hard, fighting the pain, trying not to scream again. With his gasping, a flap of skin moved through the hole in his face like a leaf in the breeze.

Scythe stuck the rod in the fire. Neither the man nor the woman tried to bargain with her. The woman kept crying, and the man even had tears streaking down his face; salt probably didn't feel good in his new wound. Scythe wanted to carry on, but held herself back. If Nyx came to gather their souls, she and Dagger would be caught. Scythe could almost feel the presence of Nyx in the room. It was as if the goddess of death was standing over her, with her bone, waiting for Scythe to make a mistake.

The bone.

Nyx always carried that as an instrument of her work. Each god had some item sacred to them, the way the Incruentus Ferrum chose a weapon. Scythe was as tied to her weapon as Dagger was to his. She didn't know if those items could hurt their owners. If her scythe was broken in half, nothing would happen to her physically. On the other hand, the gods guarded their items carefully.

Before Ichorisis was created, there was only Nyx and her bone. She grew lonely. Somehow, she had fashioned a shield and a sword from the nothingness of the universe. From the sword, she had brought forth Phaos, the god who created Ichorisis for the living. Then from the shield, Nyx drew Maniodes, the god who created Skiachora for the dead.

If each god had a sacred object they cherished and guarded, what would happen if the deity was separated from it?

Scythe wanted to tell Dagger the idea but didn't trust writing anything in a note. Written messages could be intercepted. Scythe left the fire blazing with the rod sticking out of it. Her guests would assume she was coming back soon, and she wanted to mislead them. Torturing the mind was just as important as the body.

Scythe took her weapon to the dead tree in the courtyard. It was once a grand oak, but now it stood bleached white on dry roots. She gripped the staff of her scythe and brought the end of it down on the base of the tree. Where the roots gripped the ground, her weapon acted like a key. A crack appeared in the tree and spread up the trunk, stopping where the branches began to stretch. The crack widened, moving the trunk out of the way and creating an opening wide enough for a person to walk through. The ground beneath the tree hardened into a staircase leading deeper into the earth.

Scythe began her descent into the underworld. She heard the dead wood creak as the opening closed behind her. It was dark, but she wasn't bothered by it. The earthy scent was pleasant.

After a few long moments a soft grey light illuminated the bottom. The light grew as she approached and stepped into Skiachora. The stairs ended and a crack opened as it had above, only this time through a tree beside The Acheron River. The river's water appeared to plummet over the cliff into nothing below, but upon closer inspection the water was rising from that nothingness. Scythe exited the tree on the left bank and quickly climbed the stairs to Maniodes's castle.

As usual, the castle was mostly empty except for a few skeletons standing guard here and there. Others patrolled the corridors, bones rattling under their armor. Scythe wondered what they were patrolling for; no one threatening ever came down here. Except for her now, she supposed.

It took her longer then she would have liked to find the grand library in the maze of cracked corridors. After finally finding the open archway leading into it, she froze. The library took up an entire hollow tower, hundreds of feet tall, its walls lined with books. Scythe was able to see straight to the top. There were walkways at intervals where the other floors should be. The only way to reach the landings above was a narrow spiral staircase that started in the center of the main floor and stretched upward. There were walkways branching from the stairs to the landings; looking at them from the bottom, they resembled a spider web.

She wasn't alone in the room. There were two others sitting in random chairs, reading by lamplight. Both of them were Ferrum, but she couldn't remember their names. She made a note to herself to learn them properly. A good queen should know over whom she ruled.

What made Scythe pause was the vastness of the library. She had no idea where to start.

Refusing to be deterred, she started at the beginning. Scythe scanned the titles and covers of the books on the first floor. Many of them were bard's tales of the time before written history. Something here might help.

One of the other Ferrum looked up as she past him. He did nothing more than get distracted from the tome in his lap. It was basically a warning. If she acted odd, people would take notice and remember details. So she acted casual, like she was just killing time until her husband returned home.

She paused. She had thought of Dagger as her husband without realizing it. She hadn't shied away from the thought, but the actions.

She hoped his travels were going smoothly.

Scythe spent the next couple of hours browsing through the plethora of information. Finally, she realized the books were in chronological order, but by the date they were written and not the events they depicted. The older texts were housed at the bottom and the newer ones rose to the top.

She looked at the ceiling again, wondering if the ones at the top were part of the present time. If the very top wasn't present-day knowledge, that meant the future ended at the roof. Scythe looked back down, not liking that concept. She hoped she was wrong.

After several more hours, she hadn't made much progress. She had seated herself in a comfy purple chair on the second landing. She had a good view of the entrance and the banister that led to her floor. No one could sneak up on her.

She set the book of another bard's *Theogony* on the table and rubbed her eyes. She had spent hours in this library and only narrowed her search down to the first three floors. She hadn't found anything useful yet. She didn't want to give up and leave empty-handed. Glancing down to the main floor, she noticed one of the others had left.

The dark-skinned man, with a short crop of black hair, who noticed her before was still below. He didn't have a weapon with him, so Scythe couldn't guess his name. He must have felt Scythe watching him. He glanced up and met her eye.

Scythe instantly scolded herself for drawing his attention. She smiled kindly at him and picked up her book again, hoping he would dismiss the gesture.

She heard the staircase creak slightly, followed by footsteps rising.

"Excuse me?"

Scythe took a breath to stifle the annoyance and looked up. The man now stood just outside her circle of chairs with his hands clasped behind his back. He was an older man, perhaps in his thirties, and his skin looked like ebony in the fire light.

"You are Scythe, yes?" he asked, gesturing to the weapon leaning over her chair.

"I am, and you are?"

Once the initial annoyance was gone, Scythe was actually grateful for the distraction.

"I'm Axe. May I join you?"

"Of course."

Axe took the chair next to her own. "I couldn't help but notice you are looking rather bored after being here for nearly four hours."

"It's been four hours?!" she admitted. "No wonder I'm tired, but you've been here just as long."

"I spend most of my free time here. Whole nights go by, and I hardly notice," Axe chuckled. "Our lord has even granted me rooms close by."

"How gracious of him," Scythe said, holding in the toxicity. "I couldn't help but notice you don't carry your weapon with you."

"It's back in my chamber. I don't carry it around that often anymore, only when working."

His eyes darkened. Scythe wondered if he didn't enjoy the assignments anymore. A good number of the Ferrum grew tired of their now-dead lives, and some outright couldn't handle it. Those were the ones who chose to die again and go grey. If Axe was so depressed by this lifestyle, why hadn't he made the same choice? She wanted to ask but knew it would be rude.

"How is Dagger?" he asked. "I realize this is a personal question, but please forgive my curiosity. Usually, newlyweds are inseparable."

Axe sounded genuinely concerned, like a father wanting to see that his daughter was safe. They'd only spoken for a few moments, and she already knew Axe's heart was too soft for their line of work.

"Everything is fine," she replied. "He received a job, and it will take him a couple of days to complete. So, I thought I'd spend some time here."

"Don't you usually do jobs together? That village burning the two of you pulled off is practically legendary."

There was a hint of resentment at mentioning the village, like he didn't approve.

"Dagger was assigned to this job alone." She left out the detail that she had actually been banished from it.

"Ah," Axe replied.

"May I ask you a personal question?"

Axe paused before answering, so she expected him to refuse. "It's only fair," he shrugged. "I was a bit direct with mine."

"You don't seem to enjoy the work of a Ferrum anymore. Why is that?"

Axe looked down at his hands in his lap, most likely regretting that he'd let her ask a question.

Given a moment, he confessed. "I did enjoy it for a time, until I was sent after a little girl. Twelve years old with blond hair down to her waist. She was a stranger to me, but she reminded me of my daughter. I didn't want to kill her, but defying a direct order leads to death for us. I wondered if Maniodes knew of my daughter and picked that child as a test. I took her life. I've left my axe in my chambers ever since, only using it on new jobs. I don't even want new jobs; it's like something in me has changed. I can't explain it, but it's like my mentality has gone back to its old self. I'm rather happy about that. So I spend my free time in this library. It's a nice reprieve."

“If you don’t like the work, then why not go grey? Many have. There’s no shame in it.”

“I don’t want to die again,” he said, meeting her eye. “If Maniodes were to learn that I don’t want to kill anymore, he would decommission me instantly. Then I would lose out on all of this knowledge, and I would never see my daughter grow. I visit her sometimes in secret. This life may be dark, and I may not like it, but it is a life.”

# Chapter 15

Scythe lay in bed watching the light change from indigo to daylight as the sun rose. She had left the library after the awkward conversation with Axe. They tried to have a normal chat after his confession, but it was stilted. As she took her leave, Axe asked her to keep their conversation private; he didn't want Maniodes learning about his disinterest in being a Ferrum. Scythe gave her word that she wouldn't tell a soul.

It seemed only right to promise Axe that he could trust her. She was about to be his queen; he had to trust her. What she didn't understand was why he didn't want to kill anymore. Their job was about more than just killing random humans. It kept the remaining humans cautious, which kept them safe—sometimes even from themselves. Humans hardly seemed entirely rational at times, and she had been studying them for a century now.

Her own parents had never been good to her, and now here was a father who just wanted to see his daughter again. She knew that's how a father should act. Axe was being rational toward his living family, but that shouldn't have mattered to him now. Axe was dead, and the Incruentus Ferrum should have come first.

Scythe couldn't understand Axe, but she didn't have to yet. She'd worry about that once she was queen. What she needed now were allies. Axe was perfect because he practically lived in that library. He could help her, and then she'd decide what to do about his lack of bloodlust. He wasn't exactly an effective Incruentus Ferrum without it.

She would have to go back to the library tomorrow night. She discovered how the tower was organized, but no other useful clues. She'd start on bard's tales tomorrow as well. Focusing on one branch of myths might help narrow the search. Bards were always colorful in their words and tended to exaggerate, but each story held a grain of truth. It would be a more entertaining read before moving on to philosophers.

When the sky was an icy blue, Scythe was finally able to doze off with that plan in mind.

As the sun set on his second night of riding to Chalcis, Dagger found the sky stained red. It reminded him of Scythe's hair, and he took a moment to watch the colors fade from the sky. As the night continued to darken, he saddled the horse and set off for the city. The road was well taken care of on this stretch. It made his horse's movements much easier, not having to worry about random holes. He'd forgotten how it felt to simply ride a horse. Ever since he'd woken as a Ferrum, he'd traveled using the dead trees they could open as pathways between any two points. It was very fast and convenient, but taking his time was important too. Maniodes had wanted them to be more discreet and think about their actions; what better time to do that than while riding through the night toward a job. It gave him plenty of time to think of a proper strategy in finding the victims.

Continuing west, Dagger spotted two other figures on horses in the gloom in front of him. He pulled his reins and slowed his own horse, staying a good distance from them. As long as he didn't get too close, he could rely on the shadow trick. If he tried to pass on the narrow road, a horse might stumble or sway into him, and the spell would break.

The moon rose, and as the sky darkened to black, the two ahead of him turned off the road for the night. There were small ditches on either side of it, and Dagger watched as the first horse with the taller rider avoided the ditch easily. The second horse wasn't so lucky. Its hind leg sunk into a hidden snake hole. Dagger cringed with the horse when its leg snapped. The horse screamed and panicked, falling to its side. The rider shrieked in the chaos but managed to get out of the way before the horse could crush her.

"Marella!" The first figure jumped off his horse and helped the woman to her feet.

"I'm alright," she said, dusting off her riding dress.

The horse kept screaming, its leg stuck in the snake hole. It would never walk right again, and that's if they got help quickly. The other horse was growing nervous, and the two people just stood there and watched, seeming unsure of what to do.

Dagger knew well enough he should leave them alone. He could pass right by, and they wouldn't notice. The creature's strangled, pain-filled screams wouldn't stop until it was dead, and the two were clearly at a loss.

Dagger nudged his horse closer, though it was growing skittish as well. "Hello, there!"

The two looked up at his call. The bearded man with black and grey stepped in front of the young woman, who kept her arms crossed. Both were rightfully nervous.

Dagger dismounted and tied the reins onto a bush by the road. He knew he looked threatening, especially with his belt of knives, so he kept his distance, with his hands clear for them to see.

"May I help?" Dagger asked, gesturing to the fallen horse.

"Oh! Yes, I'm not sure what help can be done, though," the man said.

Dagger approached the fallen horse and knelt where the creature could see him. "Hush, quiet now, you're alright."

He stroked the horse's neck, feeling the strong tendons jump and twitch. Its coat was a beautiful white with grey spots down its back. It calmed after a time, but it was still in pain. Blood soaked the ground and sank into the snake's den. The hoof was buried, and the bone jutted through the pale flesh.

Dagger reached behind him and unsheathed his chosen weapon. Keeping it out of the horse's sight he angled the blade close to its ear. One swift motion ended the horse's pain.

Once it was done, Dagger stood and cleaned the blood with a handkerchief.

"Thank you, sir," the man said, moving closer. "I knew it had to be done, but…"

"Have you ever killed anything?" Dagger asked. Judging by the man's well-made and clean attire, he wasn't a warrior.

"I haven't," he admitted sounding a bit embarrassed. "I'm a stonemason."

"No shame in that; it's good, honest work." Dagger stowed his knife away.

"Maybe, but that horse was expensive. No point dwelling on it. Will you help me lift him to salvage the supplies?"

"Of course."

They shifted the horse's corpse enough to get the saddlebags from under it. The man tied them to his own horse, and the woman stayed close by him. She seemed familiar, but Dagger couldn't place why.

"You two should find a different clearing to camp in. You and your wife don't want to be around when the wolves come for the easy meat," Dagger suggested.

The man turned back to him, confused, then turned to the woman. She started laughing, and the man cracked a grin as well.

"This is my daughter, Marella. My name is Thomas," he corrected.

The woman did seem very young compared to the man, but there had been odder parings. Father and daughter made more sense.

"My mistake," Dagger said, a little embarrassed. "My name is Jason."

He wasn't about to give his real name.

"Thank you again for the help," Thomas said. "You could share the night with us if you like. It would be safer to travel as a group anyway. You seem to be going the same way."

"Thank you, but I must pass. The road to the western cities is a long one, without the mountains in the way, and I'm in a hurry." Another lie.

"That is a long journey. Well, if you happen to stop in Chalcis and need a place to stay, ask for me in the market district. It's the least I could offer for your help."

Dagger cringed inwardly. These two lived in Chalcis. Now he would have to worry about running into them on the road again. Once the shadow trick was broken, it couldn't be recast on that person.

"Thank you for the offer," Dagger gave a small nod and took his leave.

"What business do you have in the west?" Marella interjected before Dagger could mount up again.

"Marella, don't bother the poor man," Thomas scolded.

Marella ignored her father as she waited for Dagger's answer. She appeared angry, as if she were trying to accuse him of something. He was tempted to just leave, but curiosity stayed him.

"Visiting a friend I haven't seen in a few years," he said. "And you? Where do you travel from, if Chalcis is your home?"

"The city southeast of here: Kaliasma. Returning home from my sister's funeral."

"Marella!" Thomas bellowed.

She shut up then and stared at Dagger. He didn't like what that look held.

"I'm sorry for your loss," he forced himself to say kindly.

"I'm sorry to bother you with this, sir…" Thomas started.

"She was murdered at her friend's wedding," Marella interrupted again.

"Enough!" Thomas cried again, rounding on his daughter. He was on edge now, no doubt from having his other daughter's death brought up.

The realization of why Marella was familiar struck like a spear. She had the same shaped nose and eyes as the blond girl he'd chosen at the wedding in Kaliasma. He had killed her sister. She recognized him from that wedding. She must have been there and noticed her sister talking to a strange man before she was murdered. The shadow trick had its limits when a loved one was already keeping an eye on someone else.

He wasn't allowed to kill these two to cover his tracks. If Maniodes learned he had been noticed, all would be lost.

"I understand you are grieving, ma'am, but I don't appreciate what your eyes are accusing," Dagger said.

"She accuses nothing, sir," Thomas insisted. "It was a mistake."

"Her throat was cut in a back alley!" Marella shouted.

"Stop bothering a random stranger with your—"

"I saw him there," Marella said to her father.

Thomas didn't respond, torn between trusting his daughter and not causing trouble. Dagger saw his hands begin to shake. If this man realized he was in the presence of the one who murdered his daughter, it wouldn't end well for any of them.

"I've never been to Kaliasma," Dagger claimed, trying to calm them. Though he had been born there.

"Where were you the other night?" Marella accused with fire in her eyes.

"Back in my home in the mountains, east of here."

"Convenient that no one can back up your alibi right now."

"My wife can. She's home now, and we spent the whole night together."

"Marella, you can't just accuse the first man you see," Thomas said, coming back to himself.

"I saw him!" she shouted again, growing more frustrated.

"You were drinking that night; you said so yourself."

"That doesn't matter!"

"Forgive her, sir," Thomas said, turning to Dagger. Dagger could see the tears he was holding back in the moonlight. "I think it would be best if you leave. Just mind your business, and we'll mind ours."

"Father—"

"Enough, Marella."

"I think parting would be best," Dagger said gratefully. "I am sorry for the loss of your daughter."

"Thank you," Thomas managed to say.

Dagger turned his back on the two and mounted his horse again. He could hear Marella's raised voice and Thomas arguing until he was out of earshot.

"Fuck," Dagger cursed under his breath.

# Chapter 16

The ride to Chalcis would have been pleasant if it hadn't been for that meeting and the rain byt the end of the trip. The horse's hooves sunk into the mud, slowing Dagger's progress even more. He might not feel cold as he once did, but the wind and rain were not pleasant. The roads had degraded, which made the mud worse. When he reached the city gates he was ready to stab something, though he took care to avoid more travelers.

The city of Chalcis wasn't spectacular, having grown from a farming village centuries ago. It was spread over miles of flat, fertile land, making it the perfect trading hub, especially so close to the sea. The walls surrounding the city were well-crafted stone at least one hundred feet high. Dagger wondered if Thomas, the grieving stonemason, had helped in the construction.

Chalcis's main gate was just closing for the night when Dagger arrived. He'd planned it that way, so he'd have a full night to find the people on his list.

The city itself was clean by most standards. The buildings were made of white brick with terra-cotta roof tiles. Each street looked the same, which would make navigating difficult. The victims' locations were provided by Maniodes, but Dagger didn't know what the people looked like. How Maniodes even got that information, he didn't know.

He left his horse in a large public stable with a note. If this horse was gone when he returned, he'd steal another one. The list of victims only held three names, but he would have to get information on them somehow. Problem was, most people slept at night.

He left the stables and began exploring the city.

The first person on the list was a man named Basil Paavo, with an address on Lapis Street, which wasn't hard to find. All of the main roads and side streets were marked with signs on buildings at each corner. Lapis Street ended up being part of a housing district that was nearly empty at this hour. The only people outside were the homeless, trying to stay out of sight.

For the second person, Dagger had only a single name: Nereus. Fortunately, this location was a gambling den called the Checkered Card. He found it after an hour. It was a lively place at this hour, but the barkeep said he hadn't seen Nereus. Apparently, Nereus was well known here but not well liked. Dagger considered waiting for him but changed his mind. He wanted to keep moving.

The third name was Sappho, also known as Sapphire, on Gem Street. This street was not as well kept as the others. Wet filth lined the roads and even the rotting vegetables were ignored by the rats. Dagger noted two brothels on this road and given the victim's name, she was probably a prostitute. She turned out to be the easiest one to find.

Several women were working the streets tonight. Dagger picked a spot under a burning torch, as he could be seen leaning against the wall. He let the shadow trick slip away and only had to wait a few minutes before a woman approached him.

"Hi, handsome." The smell of roses wafting off her was strong enough to gag on.

"Sapphire?" he asked.

The woman scoffed, she didn't even try to bargain with him. "That whore's on the other end of the street," she said. "Just look for the blue scarf."

With that, she turned to look for a more willing customer.

Dagger walked the length of Gem Street and spotted a dark-haired woman on the corner. She didn't look as enthused as the rose-scented woman, but he spotted the blue scarf.

She noticed him as he approached and, to her credit, stood her ground. Prostitution was never a safe profession.

"Sapphire?" he asked when he caught up to her.

"Mhm, and you?" She wasn't as welcoming as the last woman. Dagger wondered how much business Sapphire actually got.

"Jason," he said. "I was wondering if you'd grace me with your presence tonight."

"That's a fancy way of putting it. How much coin you got?"

Dagger revealed a silver coin but didn't hand it to her. It was the only one he had, and probably the equivalent of a month's wages. Her eyes lit up.

"What is it you'd like?" Her voice changed from standoffish to erotic.

*Oh, now you're friendly*, Dagger thought. "It's not much, but I'd prefer to stay outside," he said, keeping the coin in her sights.

"Alright, just lead the way." Sapphire linked her arm around Dagger's, pressing her breast to it. He pocketed the coin and led her off of Gem Street. They found a relatively clean alley, and Dagger stopped Sapphire in the center.

She paused then, taking a step back. He didn't blame her for being cautious.

"Coin first," she demanded.

Dagger fished the coin out of his pocket again and handed it to her. She didn't try to run but she did try to bend it. When she realized it was pure silver, she looked up at him with a mix of fear and awe.

"What exactly do you want to do for this much?" she asked.

Dagger unsheathed his blade and buried it into Sapphire's breast. Crimson stained her pretty blue scarf. Dagger lowered her to the ground and waited for the light to die in her eyes. Once it did, he removed the knife, took the coin back, and cleaned the blood from his blade with her dress.

He wasn't concerned with hiding the body. Their job was meant to cause fear in the living, so he wanted it found. He wondered though if this target was meant to make other prostitutes more cautious.

Once that job was done, Dagger walked back to the Checkered Card for Nereus. It was still full during the small hours of the night. Dagger took a stool at the bar and searched the floor.

"You still looking for Nereus?" the barkeep asked Dagger.

"I am; is he here?"

"Aye, he's there." The barkeep kept his hand low and pointed to the corner. Obviously, he didn't want to be seen ratting out one of his own patrons.

Dagger followed his gesture, but there was a table of five men gambling.

"Which one?" Dagger asked.

"His back is to the corner, blond hair." He kept his voice low as to not be overheard.

Dagger looked at the man in the corner seat. His hair was shaggy and probably hadn't been washed in weeks. Dagger ordered an ale from the barkeep to pass the time and kept an eye on Nereus.

"I'd stay away from him," the barkeep said as he served Dagger. "He's not a pleasant man on a good day."

Dagger thanked him, paid, and waited. It would have been possible for him to assassinate Nereus unnoticed in this crowd as long as he didn't touch anyone to break the shadow trick, but the barkeep had already seen him. He'd use that as a last resort if the barkeep ever left the room, but it wasn't as entertaining as a hunt.

Nereus played cards for a couple of hours. Eventually, his group ended its last game, with Nereus not looking happy. The cards clearly weren't in his favor tonight. Most of his group left through the front door, but Nereus and another man snuck into a hallway in the back. Dagger finished off his ale and followed.

The two men slipped out of a back door into an alley. The opportunity was perfect. They were alone, and the shadows were thick enough to hide in. Dagger didn't even have to kill the other man to cover his tracks. He could throw a knife into the other man's leg, forcing him down, then cut Nereus's throat.

Dagger picked a throwing knife and aimed with his keen eye. With one quick throw, the blade flew from his fingers to the back of the other man's knee. The man collapsed, clutching his leg. He gave a single loud curse instead of screaming when the soft tendons were punctured. The man would never walk properly again, but Dagger gave him credit for handling the pain.

Nereus stood beside his downed friend, stunned. He looked back down the alley, but his eyes passed over Dagger standing just a few strides away in the shadow. Nor did he see Dagger take out his chosen weapon and advance.

Nereus bolted down the alley, leaving his friend swearing after him.

Dagger hadn't expected the man to run. He chased his target as Nereus veered down the street and down another alley. The thrill of the chase burned in Dagger's veins. He felt like a wolf hunting down a deer. His quiet city life never provided this kind of thrill.

Nereus darted down another corner with Dagger close behind. Nereus was already tiring, and Dagger hoped the man could hear him at his heels.

This new alley ended at a solid white mud-brick wall, and Dagger laughed. Nereus turned again, unexpectedly. In his excitement, Dagger had missed a door set into the wall. Nereus wrenched the door open and disappeared inside.

"No!" Dagger reached the door, but it was locked.

He resisted the urge to kick the door down right away. Nereus knew he was coming, but Dagger didn't know if there were more people behind this door.

Dagger waited a moment and listened. The air was silent, and he couldn't hear movements inside. He might only have ten years of being an Incruentus Ferrum, but he'd never let his prey escape.

Dagger took a step back and kicked, causing shrapnel from the lock to scatter into the room.

Crates were stored inside, creating perfect hiding places. Dagger stayed by the broken door, guarding it. Piles of lumber stacked up the walls made a pleasant woodsy scent. It was a nice reprieve from the shit and vomit smells of the alley. There was a raised walkway around the perimeter so those above could watch the workers below. There didn't appear to be any other doors on this level, but Dagger would have to be careful not to lose his prey.

•

He kept his chosen weapon in one hand and placed a few more throwing knives between the fingers of the other. Keeping his senses sharp, Dagger entered the warehouse.

He saw the shadow peek around a stack of boxes on the walkway above him. The smallest sound of a click followed by the twang of a taught string being let go reached his ears before the bolt did. Two inches of steel punched into his right shoulder. Dagger cursed; the man hadn't had a crossbow before. This place must have been a well-stocked hiding place with weapons at the ready.

The force of it made him stagger, gritting his teeth against the pain. He took a step back and Dagger threw the knives into the corner where he had seen the shadow.

There was a satisfying choking sound, and Dagger saw the man stagger from the corner, clutching his neck. Dagger hurried to the ladder that led up to that walkway and climbed up, deciding to leave the bolt in his shoulder, he'd heal relatively quickly once it was out. The scared bastard couldn't kill him anyway, even if the bolt had pierced his heart.

He found Nereus clutching his neck. The crossbow on the floor was a new design that was able to keep two bolts notched. He managed to get the weapon up and fire the last bolt into Dagger's stomach. Nereus dropped the now-useless weapon and tried to rise as death approached.

Dagger left the bolts in him as he knelt over Nereus. One of his knives had landed in Nereus's arm, while the other had opened his neck at the side.

"Fucking Salus couldn't wait to be paid, eh?" Nereus managed to choke out.

"Salus didn't send me," Dagger replied. He didn't know who Salus was, probably one of the other gamblers back at the Card.

"What the fuck are you?" Nereus spat blood. His eyes darted from Dagger's face to the bolts in his shoulder and stomach.

"It's not important."

"I'll pay you," Nereus was growing pale. "Help me out of here, and I'll forget this."

"You couldn't even pay Salus, apparently," Dagger said.

Nereus coughed up more blood. He was struggling to breathe as his life poured through his fingers. "I can get the coin…"

"I don't need it," Dagger shrugged.

Nereus slumped to the ground, and the second name on the list was eliminated.

# Chapter 17

Scythe slumped lower in the high-backed chair, letting the scroll curl back into its tube. She was getting nowhere. After caring for their guests again, Scythe had come right back to the library for research. All of the stories she found were the same. Nyx creating Phaos and Maniodes. Phaos creating Ichorisis, then Maniodes creating Skiachora. The fights between the two brothers was interesting, but neither of them actually defeated the other. Their war had come to a stalemate when Maniodes created Hamia and the Blood Warrior line.

Scythe vaguely remembered hearing about the Blood Warriors during her life, but couldn't recall any details except that the last living one had gone mad and had to be hunted down. Though he couldn't do more then send thin spikes of blood a few feet from his veins. It was said the power weakened over generations. She felt sad for them, actually. They were once respected and honored.

Moving on in the myths, they carried the stories of the gods meeting with humans and the trouble that caused. It even led to when Nyx forbade either of her sons from procreating with humans again.

The last demigod had been a child of Phaos known as Furos. It turned out to be an abomination that ripped its way out of its mother in three days and caused enough chaos with its uncontrollable storms to nearly drown all of the northern city-states. Phaos couldn't control his monstrous son, so Nyx had to kill him.

Scythe wished Dagger was in the library with her. At least she'd have someone to talk to. Axe hadn't come to the library all night, and she wondered if he was avoiding her. Pitch had come to say hello but couldn't stay because of his duties.

Scythe got up and set the scroll back where she found it. It was another ancient text about their origins. It referred to Maniodes's shield a lot, and Phaos's sword, but there was nothing useful about destroying or controlling it. Maybe this tactic was useless. She turned back to the thick book that held the death of Phaos's son at Nyx's hand. Maybe widening the scope to the defeat of any divine being might help. It was worth a try, but even that had been putting her to sleep.

Scythe took her usual spot on the second-floor balcony where she could see the entrance. The sound of footsteps reached her before she could start reading. The shape of the tower and its hollowness made every small sound seem grand. She glanced up to the archway expecting to see Pitch or Axe.

Maniodes strode in and took the extra-large chair by the fireplace. Pitch followed, and Maniodes gave him an order. Pitch scurried off to fulfill whatever it was while Maniodes waited, watching the fire burn.

He hadn't noticed Scythe on the second floor. She had to greet him; this was his house, and it would be rude not to. In her century of bloody service, she had never felt so anxious. The god she was trying to take down was in the same room as her research. Her and Dagger might have joked about it before, but now it was actually happening.

Scythe managed a breath and set the book down. Her weapon leaned against the chair at full length. She shortened it and tied it to her waist to seem less threatening. Not that the god of the underworld would feel threatened in his own home, but having her scythe looming over her might cause a questionable image in a place of learning. Her nerves crackled like the logs in the fire. She started her descent down the spiral stairs to greet the god.

The sound of her steps was enough to bring Maniodes's attention out of his own thoughts. His expression didn't hold any malice, but he looked surprised when he spotted her.

"My Lord," Scythe gave a deep curtsy when she reached him.

"Hello, Scythe," Maniodes said. "I thought you'd be in Chalcis with Dagger."

*I wish I was*, she thought.

"The letter said only Dagger was to carry out the job," she said. Which he well knew; he wrote the damn thing. "So I thought I'd spend some time here."

"A wise choice," Maniodes said. "I'd rather you here than out causing trouble. I'd let you stay in that regard, but I'm meeting Phaos."

"I'll leave you alone then, my lord," she said gratefully.

She curtsied again and turned to leave, but Maniodes stopped her.

"What were you reading anyway? I've never seen you use this library."

"Just the old tales, my lord. I had just finished with the last son of Phaos," she explained. If she tried to lie completely, she'd botch it.

"Ah." Maniodes sneered at the mention of Furos. "The one that had us both forbidden to feel a human woman's love again."

Maniodes looked to the fire in thought, probably of his own lost lovers. He appeared concerned about something.

"You may go, Scythe." He waved at her dismissively, not looking away from the fire.

She didn't bother with another farewell curtsy. She hated them.

# Chapter 18

Dagger admired the temple of the spider goddess. No one knew her name or where she fit into Nyx's family tree, but she was usually worshipped in smaller towns. Her main attendance and imagery were those of spiders, but people associated her with small animals and livestock too. Having grown from a small farming village, Chalcis clearly still loved the nearly forgotten goddess. Chalcis wasn't a monarchy like most city-states in Ichorisis but chose to be a democracy. It had its flaws, of course, but the fact that the people chose to spend their hard-earned gold toward this temple proved their love for her.

The temple was huge and made entirely of white marble with black-and-grey veins crossing all over the surface. These veins were fitting for the goddess, resembling a giant network of webs. The main structure was surrounded by almost a hundred columns made of the same material. The columns supported the peaked roof, which was made of terracotta tiles like the rest of the city. There was no door on the temple's entrance. A single, tall archway stood open on the west side. Everyone was welcome to enter at any time and provide sacrifices and worship.

There were crypts below the temple that held the late husbands of the goddess. She was an ancient deity that supposedly often took human lovers. Those chosen by her were placed here, though there hadn't been a new addition in a few years.

Dagger wasn't sure about the credibility of this myth. This goddess supposedly took a random man from each generation as a lover, yet no one noticed him go missing? She also didn't even have a name. Dagger wondered if she was one of Phaos's daughters, although this religion seemed older. This temple alone seemed as old as Nyx.

Dagger cast the questioning thoughts aside. The sun was rising, and Basil Paavo would have to wait. Dagger entered the temple. The statue before him was just as breathtaking as the temple itself. A stone woman stood at the back without any facial features. There were windows cut into the marble, so she was illuminated by the rising sun. She stood as a silhouette with both arms outstretched in welcome, but eight spider legs sprouted from her back. The bottom two touched the floor. The top two touched the walls above her, as if she were about to climb.

Other than the statue and the alter at her feet, the room was empty. There was a cut in the floor by one wall that opened to the crypts. Dagger descended the stairs and was greeted by several stone coffins, each with the spider painted on the surface. Statues of these men lined the walls, but none were as grand as their goddess. A tarantula the size of a small cat was carved to cling to each of the statues right shoulders. The detail in the men's faces was incredible, no two looked alike. The detail in the tarantulas was just as impressive. It looked as if Dagger could feel the fur if he ran a hand over them.

"Don't move," a female voice warned behind him. Dagger heard the creak of a crossbow being hefted.

"Cross?" Dagger turned to face the other visitor. He knew that voice, and all sense of threat vanished.

A woman stood with a huge crossbow drawn and aimed at his heart. Her green dress was ragged at the hem as if it had been too long for her. It ended in tatters around her ankles where she had ripped it. Its color matched her dark-green hair, but her most striking feature were her eyes. They were bright orange, like a tabby cat.

Cross relaxed her crossbow and smiled.

"Where have you been, Dagger? I haven't seen you in months," she said slinging the weapon across her back.

"Here and there," he confessed. "Lately, I've been lying low at home. I'm kind of on probation."

"Right. 'Probation.' " Cross made air quotes. "How is married life, anyway?"

Dagger was taken aback. The Incruentus Ferrum wasn't a huge organization, but he hadn't expected word to spread this quickly.

"How did you know marriage was part of the punishment?" he asked.

"Oh, come on, you and Scythe are the most vicious among us. Did you really think it was going to stay quiet?" she scoffed, but smiled.

"Pitch told everyone, didn't he?"

"Actually, he only told me and a few others. The rest spread like wildfire."

Embarrassment took hold then. He knew he and Scythe were well-known, but he didn't appreciate the attention. People always gossiped for entertainment, but he never wanted to be the subject of it.

Being king of the underworld would make that worse. Dagger didn't know if he could handle that. He preferred to work from the shadows.

"Hey, be honest," Cross said, sitting on top of one of the coffins. "Was the marriage your idea, and you hinted at it to Maniodes?"

"No, why?"

"Because everyone knows how much you two have been eyeing each other. That village-burning you pulled off was spectacular."

"Okay that was my idea, but Scythe jumped on it instantly." This was something else he'd have to deal with as king. People reading too much into his actions and making the wrong assumptions.

"Alright, relax," Cross said, probably reacting to his agitation. After a moment she asked softly, "Is everything alright between you two? I know marriage changes everything."

"Everything is fine," he said. "Have you been married?"

"I was," Cross admitted. "He's buried here. He was the last one added to this collection. Over there."

Cross pointed to the coffin closest to the entrance. It was the same as all the others, but the stone looked a little cleaner.

"He died after me, fifty years ago. You know, I still don't believe he ever met this spider goddess."

Cross's jubilance had faded. Even after all this time, she still missed her husband. Dagger felt guilty at having brought it up.

"It must have been a good union, since you still visit him." He didn't know what else to say.

"He beat me every day."

Dagger almost choked, her words forcing him into an awkward silence.

"Don't feel bad," Cross said, looking back to him. "I've accepted it and moved on."

"Good for you," he said. "I'm glad for that, but why visit him then?"

"Honestly, I don't know. Every day I woke up with new bruises, and I was terrified when he'd come to me at night. I hate him, but I always visit when I travel this way."

Cross fell quiet then and gazed at her husband's coffin. Her eyes bored through the stone, seeing the memories beneath it.

"Can I admit something else?" Cross asked, sounding hopeful.

"Of course, but why tell me?"

"Because it felt good to admit what that man did to me. And I trust you," Cross shrugged.

"Of course you can tell me." He sat next to her.

Cross took a moment to gather her thoughts. Her words at first were slow and nervous, but as she continued she grew calm.

"He stopped hurting me when I got pregnant. He still got angry at the smallest thing, but he broke furniture, not me. He was…tender with me. And I know he didn't change overnight; he just didn't want to hurt his son. He always assumed it was a boy. If it had been a girl, I think I would have taken her and run. It was a boy though, my little bundle."

Her eyes were soft, watching the memory of her son float by.

"He tried to be kinder to me, but I had served my purpose in giving him a son. He started beating me again, but he never hurt our boy. I still hated my husband, but a boy needs his father, so I stayed." She shook her head. "My son died in his first year."

Dagger wanted to say something, but he didn't want to interrupt Cross. He stayed quiet, leaning forward with his elbows on his knees.

"My husband grew so angry he nearly killed me," her hand drifted up and caressed her neck. "The only reason he didn't was because he needed a new son."

"I threw myself into the river at the bottom of a cliff shortly after. It was the only way to escape that."

Cross fell silent, wringing her hands over a bolt she had plucked from her quiver.

"I have a loved one in Skiachora as well: my father," Dagger said. "He was killed in a robbery, and I visit him sometimes. Have you found your son there?"

Cross shook her head. "Maniodes forbade me to look for him."

"You have a right to visit your son," Dagger argued, shocked that Maniodes would refuse her.

"He thinks if I find my son I'll never leave his side. I probably wouldn't, come to think of it. There's no convincing him, though. He's denied my request to go grey twice."

The rage was enough to cause Dagger's hands to shake. That pompous ass of a god had denied a mother her child.

Cross was one of their elite and one of the few to choose a long-range weapon. Her jobs were carried out with cold precision, and she never missed a target. Maniodes would lose an efficient weapon, but given her situation, it shouldn't matter.

They had been sent on a mission together once. Maniodes wanted five people killed in Stymphalia in a single night, so he sent two of his weapons. Cross had seemed almost obsessed with catching her targets, as if the thought of missing one would cause her physical pain. Dagger had asked once why she had been so obsessed with that mission. He always took care of every victim just like her, but he took his time and enjoyed the moment. Cross had said she couldn't help it. When she was given a target, she had to dispatch it quickly and cleanly.

"You could try missing a target," he suggested. "Show him you're distracted and losing your skill. Once he sees you as less valuable, he'll let you either see your son or go grey."

"I've thought about that, but I can't," Cross said quietly.

"It'd be easy, just miss a target or two."

"My father taught me archery," she said after a pause. "When I got a crossbow, I loved the challenge and learning curve it gave me. My father was proud too, because I mastered both. Every time I miss my target, I feel like I'm failing him. I know I'm not, but I feel closer to my father whenever I fire. I know he wouldn't appreciate me killing people, but there's a certain thrill in that, you know?"

She looked at Dagger, as if hoping he'd understand. He knew the bloodlust she felt. He nodded for her to go on.

"Every time I fire and a person falls, I see him." Cross gestured to her husband's coffin. "I imagine him choking on the blood as the bolt sticks in his neck. I don't want to lose that feeling."

He'd seen when working with her that Cross was stubborn. Trying to change her mind would be useless.

"Alright, so no fooling Maniodes." Dagger let the argument drop.

Cross stood and approached her husband's coffin, looking down at it over folded arms.

"Cross?"

She looked back toward him.

"Why did you choose to become an Incruentus Ferrum?"

"To gloat over him." Cross kicked her husband's coffin. "For spite, I think. My life wasn't kind, so I thought life-in-death would be. It's not."

"You're one of the happiest people I know," he said, approaching her. "Is that all an act?"

"No, no it isn't." Her eyes seemed to plead for understanding. "I am happy, but that need to be with my son has never left. I am happy on the surface, but deeper it's…cold. I'm sorry if that doesn't make sense."

"It's fine," Dagger said, staying by her. "If things were to change, say if Maniodes wasn't in charge, would you still go grey?"

"If seeing my son wasn't enough, yes." There was no hesitation in her voice.

He wasn't sure how to respond, so he let the moment hang.

"Cross?" he said then.

She looked up from her husband's coffin.

"Can I talk to you about Scythe?" he asked.

"Of course," she said surprised. "*Are* you two alright?"

"I don't know," he confessed. "Things seemed to be fine. A little on edge, getting used to the whole idea of this, but we were managing."

"So what's the problem?" she asked.

"Well, at one point things were…getting exciting." He looked up from his hands to see that she understood.

She nodded for him to go on.

"But then she pushed me away."

Cross took a moment to think, then said slowly, "When you say 'exciting,' do you mean for both of you or just you?"

"Both of us," he insisted. "She was passionate, seemed to pause, then panicked."

Cross sighed. "Scythe and I haven't really talked much. She usually keeps to herself. The only thing I can think of is you frightened her, or reminded her of something frightening. I was always afraid of my husband, but he never let me push him off. Do you know anything about her mortal life?"

"She never talks about it. I know her father was never kind. Don't tell her we talked, okay? This doesn't leave the crypt," he said.

"Of course, I'll keep it secret. My only thoughts are she must have been attacked by her father. Maybe even raped." Her eyes darkened at the thought.

"She told me that didn't happen, actually," he clarified.

"What, did you ask her?" Cross asked, taken aback.

"Well, yes. She looked uneasy when we spent the night together in a mausoleum. I wanted to know she was okay. I was subtle about it," he defended.

"That's good, I suppose," Cross said, "but she could have been lying."

He hadn't considered that. Given her actions, it made sense.

"She seemed fine the next day. We had a whole conversation, and she was normal," he added.

"She could have been acting, though." Cross grew quiet, as if not wanting to prove him wrong. "I always had to act like I was fine."

Dagger sighed. "Well, what do I do?'

"Give her space to think," Cross said. "See where things grow naturally, then go from there. Just don't push her into anything she's uncomfortable with."

# Chapter 19

Dagger and Cross shared opposite corners of the crypt for the day. Neither of them spoke much after dealing with the emotions from the last conversation. Cross had seemed to sleep well, but Dagger was restless.

Pitch had run straight to him when he needed help, and now Cross confided her past to him. Both of them needed something from him, a kind of security. If he took over Skiachora, it would get worse. Comfort after a conversation was one thing, but once he was their king their expectations would rise.

Scythe hadn't seemed to recognize this. They were both tired of being overlooked, but Scythe wanted to cause anarchy. She was reckless to begin with, so what kind of queen would she be?

They weren't the only ones being overlooked by Maniodes, either. He wondered if there were others like Cross and Pitch. Would doing something as extreme as becoming king help them?

He would listen to the others, like Cross, and take their well-being into account. They would work together to find a compromise. With a request like Cross's though, she would choose death again in a heartbeat. Seeing her dead grey child wouldn't stop her from wanting that. It would make her want to be with her son even more.

Cross was still curled up asleep next to her crossbow when Dagger left. Being unable to sleep much the previous day let him wake up early to finish his job. The sun was only half set when he strode out of the spider goddess's temple. The sky was a beautiful crimson as before, but Dagger had to shield his eyes from the light.

The streets were more active at sunset, and Chalcis's people traveled home after a productive day or left their homes to explore the city's night life. Dagger avoided a horse drawing a white carriage as he crossed the cobblestone street. At the next corner, he turned toward Lapis Street, where Basil Paavo lived. He had no other leads. Dagger hoped the first person he asked directions for was kind, was in no mood to argue.

The power of being hidden in plain sight was useful in a crowd, but it didn't make him invisible or any less solid. As he turned the corner there was a gap in the buildings, allowing the last of the sun to surprise him. Shielding his eyes from its rays, he turned the last corner onto Lapis and barreled over another person.

"Shit, I'm—" he was about to apologize when the shade let him see whom he'd knocked over. Marella sat on the ground with a small blue hat askew.

"You!" She shouted, more surprised at seeing him than being almost run down, it seemed.

"I'm sorry," he said, trying to act casual. "The sun hit my eyes and I wasn't looking where I was going. Are you hurt?"

He reached out a hand to help her up, but she refused it. She got to her feet, brushing her blue skirts aside angrily. Her eyes bored into him with rage hot enough to burn.

"I thought you were going over the western mountains, Mr. Jason," she accused.

Dagger's hand itched for his knife, but he stayed the urge to fix this problem the easy way.

"I had to take a detour," he said.

Marella crossed her arms. "Chalcis is a long detour. Why not stop at the mountain border? Or the town just below it. That was closer."

"My horse was growing sick," he lied. "I thought a larger city would have an animal physician."

"There happens to be a good one in that town; she's a good friend of mine. I would refer you to her, but she might end up dead."

Dagger had to give the woman credit for bravery. Not many would confront someone they thought was a killer. He called it bravery, but stupidity was just as likely.

"Look," he sighed. "I'm sorry for knocking you over, but I am tired of your accusations."

He ignored whatever she was about to say and walked past her. She wasn't having it. Marella grabbed his arm as he passed. He stopped more out of shock than from the physical force of it.

"You murdered my sister, you fucking piece of—"

Dagger cut off her words with a hand to her throat and pinned her back to the wall. He let up enough to allow her to breathe and leaned in. The fear showed behind the bravery now.

"You stay away from me," he said smoothly, making sure she heard every word. "Or you'll end up like your precious sister."

He let her go, and she coughed. Marella stayed quiet, finally feeling the threat. He turned his back and left.

"Guard!"

Dagger turned back at her shout, knife in hand. He couldn't remember when he'd unsheathed it.

Marella had shouted to a man in green city armor on the other side of the street. Dagger hadn't realized he was there.

"Arrest that man for murder," she pointed at Dagger, breaking the shadow trick for the guard. "He threatened me as well."

The guard saw Dagger and shouted for him to stay put as the guard hurried across the street. Instead, Dagger ducked into the nearest alley. The sun had set now, casting perfect shadows into an alcove that held a door. It was only a stride away from the alley's entrance, but Dagger stepped into it, pulling his cloak around him. He waited.

The guard appeared in the entrance, and saw nothing but an empty alley. The shadow trick wasn't completely broken, like it was for Marella, because

Dagger hadn't revealed himself directly to the guard. The guard glanced right over Dagger's shadow and saw nothing.

Marella appeared at the guard's side. Dagger quickly hid behind the stone and listened. If she took one step into the alley she'd see him.

"Lady Paavo, yes?" the guard asked Marella.

"Yes," she acknowledged, sounding distracted.

Dagger cursed silently. Marella was probably related to his victim—again! He wondered if Maniodes had known this when he assigned the job, to make it more difficult for him.

"Do you remember what the man looked like?" the guard asked.

"He's tall with black hair, black eyes as well. He was just here."

Dagger saw her foot stop just before his hiding place.

"Let me walk you home, my lady," the guard offered. "It's growing late."

"But—"

"We'll find that man, I promise."

The guard sounded sincere. Dagger almost felt bad that he would fail in the promise. Luckily, Dagger's features were too generic to be of any use to the guard.

"But where the fuck did he go?!"

"There are many places to hide in a city this big. He will be found and questioned."

"You don't need to question him. I outright saw him."

Marella's words faded in the distance, but her anger didn't.

Dagger waited a full fifteen minutes in the shadows. He would have to be careful around that guard now. If he was in a large-enough crowd, the guard would probably overlook him. if they crossed paths alone in the street, Dagger couldn't be sure he would be dismissed.

The sky was pleasantly dark when Dagger peeked out of the alley. The street wasn't completely empty, but no one paid him any mind when he left the alley.

A different guard was kind enough to point him in the right direction. Dagger had made up a story that Basil was a friend of his and Dagger wanted to surprise him. The guard was happy to help describe what the Paavo house looked like. Dagger followed the guard's directions to the opposite end of Lapis Street.

The Paavo house was grand. It towered three stories of white walls with a long courtyard. There was a tall stone fence ringing the property as well.

Scythe stood against the stone wall. Dagger paused, surprised but grateful for the sight. He approached her, finally enjoying the night. Scythe looked up at the sound of his footsteps and smiled. It seemed genuine.

"What are you doing here? I'm glad, given the night I've had so far," he said. "How did you find me? And how did you find the Paavos' house so fast? I couldn't find it yesterday."

"I knew you were in Chalcis," she shrugged. "Then I used your list of victims to narrow it down. I heard people talking about two murders last night. It wasn't this man's, so I knew you'd be here eventually."

"So, when you got bored with the research you came to visit?" He was only half-joking. Dagger wanted to talk more about their failed passions in the experiments chamber, but he followed Cross's advice and didn't.

"Well, I did get bored, but that's not why I left the library," she explained. "Maniodes almost caught me."

"What?!"

"He doesn't know why I was really there," she said quickly. "He walked in while I was reading, then ordered me to leave so he could meet with Phaos. I told him I was just reading old stories while I waited for you to come home," she said.

"So he didn't suspect a thing?" he asked.

"He thought it was odd that I was there in the first place, but no, he didn't suspect anything."

"Thank the gods," Dagger sighed.

"Whom we're trying to overthrow," Scythe added.

That raised a laugh out of Dagger, which he was thankful for. Pretty soon, people might be thanking or cursing their names in the same manner.

"It is too risky, though," Scythe said, bringing down the mood. "If he finds out what we're trying to do, we're dead. Looking for ideas right in front of him draws too much attention."

"You're right, but there's no other option."

"There might be," Scythe said.

Dagger waited for her to go on.

"I met someone in the library when I first went there. His name is Axe, and he's fed up with Maniodes's way of doing things too."

"How so?"

Before Scythe could answer, Dagger spotted the guard who was looking for him leave the Paavo house. The two of them stood by the gate that opened the courtyard to the street, and the guard was heading straight for them.

"Hold on," Dagger cut her off.

"What?"

Dagger took Scythe's arm and hurried down the street, around the corner of the stone wall. Just as they were out of sight, the guard opened the gate and stepped through. Dagger leaned around the stone, watching as the guard walked away from their hiding place.

"Who was that?" Scythe whispered, though she didn't have to. She had peeked around Dagger's shoulder to watch the guard as well.

"A woman pointed me out to him," Dagger explained. "Apparently, the girl I killed at the wedding was the sister of a woman who lives here. That woman saw me talking to her sister before she died and made the connection that I did it."

"And she lives here? What, do you have to kill her father now?"

"No, I think it's her uncle or grandfather. I met her father on the road too, and he has a different name. Come on, let's get this over with."

"Don't be so glum," Scythe said. "It will be a challenge. More fun that way."

"Not if our lives are on the line. When that woman's relative dies again, she'll suspect me."

"But as long as she doesn't *see* you we're fine," she argued.

"I suppose."

"You worry too much." Scythe stroked his arm. Heat trailed after her fingers like she was stoking a fire in him.

"Come on," she said, taking his hand. "I already know a way in."

Dagger followed Scythe to a smaller gate in the back of the property used by the servants.

"These are usually locked," Dagger said.

"I stuck a rock in the way to keep it from closing behind the last person," she said, opening the gate.

"You wouldn't happen to know which one is Basil, would you?" Dagger asked hopefully as they walked up the path to the house. "I still don't know what he looks like."

"I don't either," Scythe admitted.

"That's alright," he said. "More of a challenge."

Scythe's smile was wicked.

The servant's door to the house was unlocked as well. Dagger went first, keeping an eye out for Marella. The kitchen they entered through was empty, but voices could be heard down the corridor. Dagger and Scythe passed through the kitchen and saw an archway on the left side of the corridor that opened to a parlor. A young serving girl holding an empty tray hurried past them back to the kitchens. The girl didn't notice either of them as they kept close to the wall.

Dagger moved to peer inside the archway. The voices were louder now, joined by the tapping of utensils on plates. The Paavo family was enjoying a late dinner, it seemed.

"Wait." Scythe caught Dagger before he could peek around the corner. "Let me look. That woman you mentioned won't see me."

Dagger hadn't thought of that and cursed himself. The two of them switched positions so Scythe was closer to the archway. She peered inside, and Dagger couldn't help but touch the small of her back as he waited. Scythe turned back at him briefly, a little surprised. He let go. He wanted to kiss her, hell he wanted more, but he forced himself to focus on the task at hand. He did note that she didn't look angry anymore.

"What do you see?" he asked.

"There's four people eating," she answered, "two men and two women."

"Is one of the women in a blue dress?"

"The younger one is."

"That's Marella, the woman who knows me. One of the men is probably her father, Thomas."

"She's sitting with her back to us," Scythe said. "The man she's facing, then, might be her father, so he's facing us."

"Does he have a beard with graying hair? He's a stonemason, so his arms looked strong."

Scythe regarded him again, distracted. "Were you admiring a man's biceps?"

"Not as much as I'm admiring your backside right now. It was just a feature I noticed."

Scythe turned back into the dining room. "That is Thomas, then; the other man doesn't have a beard. You know, now that you mention it, Thomas's arms are impressive, along with those broad shoulders."

She was playing as they had before. He had to step lightly. Leaning this close to her, he noticed the scent of blood and jasmine. It made it harder to focus on the job.

"You getting bored of me already?" he asked.

"Don't be jealous, dear. You're the one who brought up the man's biceps." That lustful gleam was back.

"Keep in mind," he leaned in closer, his lips at her ear. "If we weren't on probation, Thomas would be dead for drawing your eye."

"You *are* jealous."

"And you *wouldn't* slaughter any woman who drew my eye?"

"I probably would," Scythe admitted.

She was flirting again. He risked touching the small of her back.

The scrape of chairs distracted them. The family had finished dinner and were about to come this way.

"Back to the kitchen," Scythe whispered.

Dagger let Scythe go, and they hurried back.

As Dagger watched from the kitchen, mostly hidden behind the door, Marella and a tall woman with pinned-up blond hair left the dining room and disappeared into the parlor. Once they were out of sight, Dagger and Scythe crept to the dining room archway again. Scythe watched the conversation between the men as Dagger kept watch outside as before. He listened to the conversation between the men, waiting for his moment.

"Thank you again for letting us stay." That voice was Thomas; Dagger was sure of it.

"It's the least I could offer, brother," the other voice said. "I can't imagine your pain."

Thomas was silent for a long time and the other man, presumably Basil, let him have that moment.

"I can't even pass by her room." Thomas's voice was thick.

"I understand why," Basil said softly, "but you have Marella. You need to hold onto that."

"I know." Thomas heaved a breath, "but she's just so angry all the time. It can't be healthy."

"People grieve differently."

"I suppose."

There was another moment of silence between them.

Only being able to watch Scythe's reaction to their words, Dagger noted how soft her eyes were. She was a creature who caused the living this pain, but she respected it.

"Do you believe her?" the other man asked. "Do you think the man who took your daughter is here?"

Thomas took his time before answering again, probably trying to get his thoughts in order.

"Marella has never been a good liar," he said. "I do believe her, Basil. And if it was the man we met on the road, I would gladly hang for murder if it meant avenging my daughter."

Dagger had never regretted taking a life before; he didn't think he had the capacity. He'd never met their families however, and he was about to make it worse.

"Get some rest, Thomas," Basil said. "I wish I could say you'll feel better in the morning. Given enough time, that will be true again. For Marella, too."

"Go hide in the kitchen," Scythe said then. "Thomas just stood up."

Dagger didn't want to leave, but he did. Scythe stayed by the arch. He watched from afar as Scythe stayed still and Thomas left for the parlor.

Shortly after Thomas had gone, Basil entered the corridor. Scythe stood right next to him, yet Basil didn't see her. Dagger left the kitchens and approached the man. As long as neither Dagger nor Scythe drew the attention of Basil, they would be safe.

Basil had the same hair color as his brother, but nearly everything else was different. He was clean-shaven, with a pointed nose, and was dressed in a clean doublet. Given the size of his estate, he was certainly a wealthy man, but Thomas didn't seem to share in that wealth. Where Thomas's hands were rough with stonework, Basil's were soft and manicured.

Basil left the corridor and followed his family. Dagger and Scythe trailed a good distance behind him. Dagger paused at each entrance and doorway so Scythe could scout ahead for Thomas or Marella. Both of them had gone to bed, it seemed. The woman who had left with Marella was nowhere to be seen either. Dagger could only assume she was Basil's wife. She was about to be his widow.

On the second floor, Basil stopped at a dark wood door and opened it. Dagger caught sight of bookshelves and a desk before Basil closed it again. Neither of them had been quick enough to sneak in behind him without being noticed. Pitch probably could have dodged his way in.

"Did you see anyone else inside?" Dagger asked Scythe, who was in front of him.

"No one," she said. "It's a private office."

"Good." Opening the door to enter would draw attention and, in turn, break the spell for everyone inside.

Dagger opened the office door, letting Scythe in behind him. Basil stood by the fireplace with a book in his hand, probably about to sit and enjoy it before bed. He looked up, catching Dagger's eye as the spell was broken. Basil also noticed Scythe as she leaned against the door to keep it closed.

"Who in the bloody name of Nyx are you people?" he demanded.

Dagger let the cold-blooded thrill wash over him, but it was different this time: diluted. Basil was about to either shout or make another demand, but Dagger cut him off with a quick punch to the throat.

The book nearly fell into the fireplace as Basil hit the floor, gasping. He had a hand on his throat, choking in air. Dagger hadn't hit him hard enough to kill him that way, but it was enough to stop any more screams. Just to be sure, he took out a black handkerchief and stuffed it into Basil's mouth.

Basil swung at Dagger, but Dagger avoided it easily. This man was a merchant not a warrior. Still, Basil struggled. Dagger took his head and bashed it onto the wood-paneled floor. Again, not to kill but incapacitate. Basil fell limp, but his eyes were still aware and scared. Dagger tied off the gag and stood, grabbing a handful of Basil's hair and wrenching him to his knees.

Dagger unsheathed his weapon and pressed it to Basil's soft throat. The other residents probably heard the noise. They'd have to be quick.

Basil let a single muffled plea escape, then fell silent, waiting. In that instant, Dagger thought of Thomas again, along with Marella. Thomas was grief-stricken as it was, and Marella was dealing with her own anger. There was the other woman as well, Basil's wife.

Dagger's hand was steady as always, but he couldn't make it move.

Dagger looked to Scythe leaning against the door. She was watching him with a wild gleam in her eye. She was waiting to see that first rush of blood. He couldn't blame her for that; he wanted it too. He still couldn't move. This man had to die because of them. They had to complete the job for the sakes of all of the Incruentus Ferrum.

Finally, his hand moved. He took the blade away from Basil's throat. Flipping the dagger into the air he caught it by the blade. He held the hilt out to Scythe, unsure of the expression on his own face.

He forced a smile through heavy-lidded eyes. He hoped it was close enough to the playfulness in the corridor below.

"My lady?" he asked.

Scythe beamed at the invitation. She practically skipped over to them and plucked the dagger from his hand.

"Do you think Maniodes would mind?" she asked, hesitant but excited.

"As long as the job is done, and we're not seen, I think we'll be fine."

Dagger kept hold of Basil's hair, arching his head back. Scythe took her place beside Dagger. She didn't hesitate and cut deep. Blood sprayed, painting a nice leather chair in droplets, then pulsed down Basil's doublet. His eyes rolled white, and Dagger let him drop to the floor.

Dagger knelt and pulled his handkerchief free from Basil's mouth. There hadn't been enough time for Basil to cough blood onto it. Standing back up he took the blade from Scythe and then cleaned it.

"We should go," he said, pocketing the blade and cloth. "You lead, like before."

Scythe retraced Basil's steps back to the first floor and to the kitchens. They hadn't crossed paths with a single soul, but as they stepped outside, a sharp scream woke the night. The scream forced Dagger to stop and look back at the house.

"Are you alright, Dagger?" Scythe asked.

Dagger didn't bother replying. She would be able to see the lie. He couldn't organize his thoughts properly to know what to say anyway.

To his surprise, Scythe took his hand and squeezed it. He wasn't sure why.

He looked back at the house. Shadows crossing behind a window caught his eye. That window no doubt opened to the second-floor office, and the body had been found. A figure appeared in the window. Her hands were up to her face, and her shoulders shook. Her hair was down, but Dagger recognized the shade of it. He hoped Marella hadn't been the one to find her uncle, but she was there nonetheless.

Either because of the horrid sight or the feeling that she was being watched, Marella turned to face the window. She froze as she saw him. He and Scythe hadn't bothered to hide in a shadow, and the moonlight was strong. Even so, there was no way Marella could identify the figure she saw on her uncle's property. He knew who she suspected, regardless.

"We have to go." Dagger squeezed Scythe's hand and quickly led her back to Lapis Street. He prayed his horse would still be at the stables.

"Wait." Dagger pulled Scythe to a halt, remembering her waiting for him back at the house. "How did you get here so fast? I had to ride for a day and a half, and it did not take you that long. Is there a dead tree nearby?"

"There's a dead willow about a league east of here. Pitch told me about it, so I was able to go directly there from Skiachora."

"Thank the bloody gods," Dagger sighed, hurrying off again. They could leave the damn horse behind and make straight for the tree. Once in Skiachora again they could make a tunnel back to the dead oak in their own home.

"What's the rush, Dagger?" Scythe asked.

"I just need to get home," he said. "I'll explain more tomorrow night."

As they rounded the last corner, with the city gates in sight, the last thing Dagger needed caught his attention. He heard running footsteps behind, trying to catch up to him.

Dagger ducked into an alley, dragging Scythe behind.

"What?"

"Shh," he hissed.

There wasn't time to hide. Marella came barreling around the corner. She wasn't even dressed for the cold night. She had a thin robe over her nightgown and slippers on her feet. Her face was flushed with the run as well as rage.

"I knew it," she said. "I fucking knew it."

"Marella, what are you doing out like this?" Dagger said, thinking fast. "I thought that guard walked you home. Well, clearly he did, given the nightgown."

"Don't you act all innocent," she nearly screamed, stalking forward. "You murdered Uncle Basil!"

"What? I've been on this end of the city all night."

"He's been with me all night," Scythe said next to him.

"And who are you? Some whore he picked up for an alibi?"

"I'm his wife," Scythe said, getting closer to Marella.

Dagger kept hold of Scythe's hand to hold her back. He couldn't let Scythe get too close lest she kill Marella.

Marella's eyes blazed at this new fact. "The wife who is supposed to be back home in the eastern mountains?" she accused.

"Fuck," Dagger cursed. His cover had been destroyed.

"You've got balls, girl," Scythe said, laughing at Marella. "Not many would chase down a killer in their nightie."

Scythe might be complimenting her, but Dagger saw her hand drift to her weapon tied to her waist.

"He murdered my sister," Marella growled. "You're married to a monster!"

"He suits me just fine. We've both done much worse."

Scythe's casual tone infuriated Marella even more. He had no idea why Scythe was antagonizing Marella, but it had to stop. If Scythe killed Marella they were all dead.

Dagger pulled Scythe back and forced himself between the women. "Listen, Marella—"

He hadn't exactly planned what he would say to calm her down, but it didn't matter. He only saw the glint of a kitchen knife before it was buried into his chest. Marella missed his heart, but she also missed a rib. The blade had slid through and punctured his lung. It was instantly harder to breathe.

"That's for my sister," Marella wrenched the knife free and made to stab again, probably in the name of her uncle.

Dagger's frustration snapped, and he defended himself. As Marella swung down a second time he grabbed her wrist, ripped the knife free, and plunged it into her own neck. Red filled his vision.

"No, Dagger!"

Scythe's scream broke Dagger out of the red haze. His hand still held the handle of Marella's knife while the steel protruded from her flesh. She could only stare at him, wide-eyed and properly scared now. Blood poured from her lips and through his fingers.

"No!" Dagger pulled the knife free causing more blood to spray.

Marella collapsed, and Dagger guided her to the ground. He clasped a hand over the wound to try and stop the bleeding. Marella choked and gurgled as the life drained past his fingers. The rage and fear faded from her eyes. Everything faded from her eyes.

"Fuck!"

"Dagger." Scythe knelt beside him.

He could feel the air rushing through the hole Marella had left in his lung as he tried and failed to control his panic. He couldn't look away from her face. He'd never wished another person to be alive as he did now. Even with his own father, he'd accepted that fate.

The ground beneath them shook. The sound of breaking stone drew their gaze to the alley behind them. The earth cracked open, revealing a staircase down to Skiachora.

# Chapter 20

In all of her time, Scythe had only been summoned like this once before. When Maniodes was angry he usually sent a sentry or a bat. The only other time he'd cracked open a doorway like this was after she raided that village with Dagger.

Dagger stood facing the staircase. Scythe stood as well and took his hand. His face was calm, but his hand spoke otherwise. It kept trying to clench into a fist, even while enveloping her hand.

"You should leave," Dagger said. His voice gurgled as his blood spilled out of place around his lung. Other than that, he sounded steady. "Don't go back to our estate, just hide. You weren't involved in this, but he won't care."

"I'm involved as much as you are."

Dagger finally met Scythe's eyes, and she saw the faint waver.

"Maybe we can convince him to be lenient?" Scythe suggested.

Dagger chuckled nervously at the idea. A stream of blood fell from the corner of his mouth. Scythe didn't believe they could convince Maniodes of anything either.

The staircase led through the earth into the cold darkness. Dagger swallowed more blood and started to descend. Scythe kept hold of his hand, keeping pace next to him. The alleyway closed, locking them in darkness. The descent was long, and for every step, Scythe's heart beat twice as fast. The only comfort she had was Dagger's nervous breathing beside her.

She'd finally found a man who cared for her after one hundred years. A man who thought and felt the same way she did. She had never actively looked for a man, and she had made a promise to herself that in death she wouldn't need one. She was actually glad that promise had been broken.

Scythe stopped walking and pulled Dagger to a halt. He turned back, confused but grateful. The exit had closed above them so there was no hope of escape, but they could prolong the inevitable.

Scythe was on the stair just above Dagger's, making them almost the same height. She wrapped her arms around his shoulders, holding him close. She pressed her lips to his, tasting his blood. He buried one hand in her hair while the other caressed up her back. It felt like they stood there for an eternity, but that was still too short.

When they finally pulled apart, Scythe had to take a moment to gather her breath and thoughts again. Dagger spat blood and stayed quiet as well.

"We'll both be dead at the end of this," Scythe finally breathed.

"I'll convince him otherwise," Dagger said, echoing her earlier words.

She smiled at the thought, resting her forehead against his.

"We should keep going," Dagger said.

Scythe wanted nothing more than to stay, but she nodded. She took Dagger's arm again and they continued down.

A soft grey light appeared below them. They stepped from the last stair through the dead tree into Skiachora, onto the gravel and dirt. Maniodes's castle loomed above them as before. Dagger spat more blood as they entered it.

The main entrance was totally empty; even the sentries were gone. She found them quickly enough when they entered the throne room. Hundreds of skeletons in armor lined the walls, as if waiting for them.

Pitch stood anxiously in the corner behind the throne, and Axe was there as well to watch the proceedings. Maniodes himself was seated on his black marble throne, waiting for them. His dark-blue hair was ruffled, as if his frustration at them couldn't be contained. His iron shield was strapped to his back.

The Goddess of Death stood in front of them below the dais. Her raven hair fell to her waist, and her black-and-white eyes studied them. The human bone was held out before her, no doubt containing the souls of Marella and her uncle.

Dagger and Scythe knelt before the goddess, heads bowed. The feeling of Nyx watching them crawled down Scythe's back. Maniodes may have towered over the childlike form his mother took, but she held all of the power. Her word was the final say.

She could almost cut the tension in the air with her scythe.

"I gave you one task," Maniodes started, disappointed. "To watch each other to make sure this didn't happen again. To keep order, not cause havoc."

Scythe clasped her hands together in front of her to keep them steady. Dagger appeared as calm as ever, watching the floor at Nyx's feet.

"In all honesty, I expected you, Scythe, to go against my orders," Maniodes said.

It was Scythe's fault, whether or not she held the blade. She antagonized Marella into attacking, and she'd given away Dagger's lie. Not that she knew what he had said to the woman, but she should have stayed quiet to let Dagger try to calm her.

"Spare Scythe," Dagger pleaded. He looked up at Maniodes. "This wasn't her fault. *I* killed Marella, and *I* hadn't been careful enough at the wedding."

"What does the wedding have to do with this?" Maniodes asked, surprised.

"You know her name," Nyx overrode Maniodes. Her voice was smooth and unnerving.

"Yes, Your Grace," Dagger said, answering Nyx first. "I met her and her father, Thomas, on the road to

Chalcis. The man on the list, Basil Paavo, had been her uncle and his brother."

"And the wedding?" Nyx asked.

"The girl I chose there was Marella's sister. Marella saw us talking, but she did not see me take her sister's life," Dagger explained.

"Do you know the sister's name?" Nyx asked.

Dagger thought for a moment then answered. "No, Your Grace."

"It was Maya," Nyx supplied.

Dagger lowered his gaze again to the floor, keeping his expression still.

"You've left me no choice, Dagger," Maniodes sighed. "Not only did you kill someone I did not command, you let that same girl see you previously."

"Just leave Scythe be," Dagger pleaded.

"She failed her test as well, actually."

"What test?" Scythe demanded, letting the tension snap.

Maniodes's blue eyes bored into Scythe at her question. She couldn't maintain the eye contact, so she looked down to her hands again.

"The three names were for Dagger only, so you could practice self-restraint. I had high hopes after meeting you in the library."

"But I offered her the knife," Dagger protested. "If we had known—"

"The point is not to know," Maniodes roared.

"He is right, Dagger," Nyx said gently. "I was there for Basil, and Scythe was eager to take his life. She did pause though."

Maniodes looked ready to deal out their sentence, but that last comment made him stop.

"She asked Dagger if you would mind," Nyx said, clarifying for Maniodes.

"And I convinced her it was fine. The job was done, and we hadn't been seen at the time," Dagger said. "I didn't think the technicality of who killed him mattered."

"Regardless," Maniodes said, "you both went beyond my orders again. And you, Dagger, obviously weren't careful enough at the wedding."

Maniodes stood from his throne and descended the dais. Nyx stayed where she was, so Maniodes had to curve around her.

"Just spare Scythe," Dagger pleaded.

"You're both tied to this. I am sorry to lose you two. You are my most ruthless."

The god towered above them and raised a hand over Dagger's head. Scythe didn't want to watch, but she couldn't tear her eyes away. Dagger had been following Maniodes's hand, but now he looked to Scythe. His black eyes held a mix of sorrow and gratitude, but he smiled at her.

Scythe quickly reached over and took Dagger's hand in both of hers. His sorrow deepened, but his smile grew.

"Wait," Nyx commanded.

Maniodes stopped before he could draw Dagger's consciousness from him. Scythe finally relinquished a breath she hadn't realized she'd been holding. Dagger blinked, dazed but still alive.

Maniodes turned back to Nyx, confused. "Why wait? This is what you wanted."

"He's learning," Nyx said.

Maniodes stammered at the sudden shift. Scythe kept her eyes on Nyx, praying she had heard the goddess right.

"He learned Marella and Thomas's names. Names of people he didn't have to kill," Nyx clarified.

"Where did you learn their names?" she asked him studying his reaction. "They weren't designated victims."

Dagger paused, seemingly surprised, then said, "I met them on the road to the city. Their horse had fallen and broken its leg. They had no means of helping it, so I had to put it down. They introduced themselves after."

"Did you know they were related to Basil?"

"No, Your Grace."

"So, they were just strangers on the road, and you wanted to help their horse?"

"Yes." Dagger glanced at Scythe for a second, clearly uneasy at Nyx's questions.

Nyx crossed her arms and said, "Well, he's starting to respect the living. Leave them be for now, Maniodes."

"But you wanted them disbanded before," Maniodes argued; Scythe knew he referred to all of the Incruentus Ferrum.

"I did, but if they can learn, then they can control themselves. I hope Scythe can learn that as well, though with something more direct than an injured horse." Nyx strode forward, forcing Maniodes to step aside. She stopped in front of Dagger. While on his knees, they were the same height. Scythe had never seen the goddess this close before. The black around her white irises was unnerving.

"You will be given one more chance, which is far more then you deserve," Nyx said to Dagger.

"Thank you, Your Grace," Dagger breathed.

"But you will suffer punishment for Marella's life. Three days in the chains."

Dagger didn't reply; he only bowed his head in thanks.

Nyx turned to Scythe. Her white pupils shot through Scythe like ice picks.

"You do need to practice more self-restraint," Nyx said.

"I will, Your Grace."

Nyx rounded on Maniodes next. The stress was making Scythe almost giddy. She had to bite her tongue to stop from laughing at the sight of the four-foot Nyx intimidating an eight-foot god.

"And you," she said to her son, "should make your intentions more clear. You gave no indication that Scythe couldn't kill until now. They're meant to cause mischief and mystery for the living, not be your playthings."

Nyx was defending her. She was defending Scythe against her own son. Even Axe, behind the sentries, looked stunned.

Maniodes could only stammer rather than protest. Eventually, he just nodded.

Nyx disappeared then. No flash, no flourish. She was just gone.

Scythe could finally breathe properly again. Dagger was panting a bit too, but more blood stained his tunic. Where Scythe could hardly contain her joy, Dagger seemed more composed. It was understandable; he was about to be stuck in the chains for three days.

"Guards!" Maniodes barked. "Take him below."

Two skeletons parted from the ranks and approached Dagger, bones rattling menacingly.

Scythe stood as Dagger did when Maniodes left the throne room. Pitch risked a glance back at Dagger and Scythe before hurrying after his master.

Scythe realized then that she still held Dagger's hand. The sentries stood on either side of him but seemed to be waiting for them to say their good-byes. The walking corpses had more heart than their master.

"Go home," Dagger said, drawing Scythe's attention.

"No, I'll stay until the chains are in."

"I'd rather you not see that," Dagger protested. "I wouldn't mind a visit later, though."

Scythe wrapped her arms around him again. Dagger held her against him and stroked her hair. He was actually the one comforting her while he was the one about to be impaled.

Scythe forced steel into her spine and pulled away, looking up to his eyes. They were soft and loving, but she saw the plea behind them, asking her to go.

Scythe planted one more kiss, then, staying close, she whispered, “I’ll visit you later.”

# Chapter 21

Scythe strode from the dead oak tree in her own courtyard. She had stayed long enough to watch the sentries escort Dagger out of the throne room. She could do nothing for him but cast another encouraging smile. She hated doing nothing. That's all she had done as Maniodes and Nyx dealt out her husband's punishment. She had been too scared and stunned to protest. She had done nothing for Dagger to protect him.

Scythe detoured toward the vines along the west side of the courtyard. She extended her weapon to full length and sliced through the vines crawling up the castle. It felt good. She screamed and sliced again. Her vision turned crimson with anger and emerald with foliage. She screamed and sliced until her arms hurt and her voice cracked. Eventually, there was nothing left to cut. Scythe stalked inside, leaving the garden in shreds.

Scythe went straight for the cellar and strode up to their captured guests. She wanted to rip them apart; she wanted them to scream with her. She wanted them to feel as helpless as she had.

It was just like before with her father. She couldn't do anything against him. She could only let him hurt her again and again. A man in power, abusing that power and hurting those below him.

Scythe wanted to tear the couple apart. Every inch of her body screamed for it, but Nyx had advised self-restraint.

Both guests were still alive, so she locked them in separate cells. The man had been quiet the entire time, waiting for more torture. The woman screamed after her as Scythe locked the cell door. Scythe stood there, enjoying those screams as one would enjoy birdsong.

Before the night was out, Scythe went back to Skiachora. The first sentry she saw stood at the iron gate at the top of the floating stairs. There was no way of knowing if this was one of the two that took Dagger away; they all looked the same, but they all shared the same mind. It didn't matter which one you gave an order to or which one carried it out. They all remembered the actions as if they had done it themselves.

Maniodes would refuse her request, so she walked right up to the sentry.

"Take me to Dagger," she demanded.

The skull looked at her through empty sockets as if thinking, though it didn't have any brains. If it didn't move soon, Scythe would shatter it to pieces and find another. Eventually, it hefted its rusty spear and started walking back to the castle. Scythe followed close behind.

The sentry took her below the castle. Cracks ran through the foundation, but the castle always held strong. The sentry let her down through the cracked corridors to an open chamber that held Dagger in the center.

The chamber was large enough that the walls and ceiling were cast in shadow. Chains sprouted from those shadows, all meeting in the middle and embedded in the rock at Dagger's feet. His arms were outstretched by three chains in one arm and four in the other. He stood straight regardless of the obvious pain he was in.

To get closer to him, Scythe moved around a chain that punched through his chest and stepped over another pinning his foot.

Dagger spat blood and said, "Hello again, my lady."

Scythe got as close as the chains would allow. "I'm sorry about this."

"It was my own fault." His voice was ragged.

"But I gave away your lie to that girl. I made her angry," Scythe argued.

"Marella followed me with a knife. She already had the intention of killing me." Dagger tried to shrug, but the rattling chains stopped him. He grunted and squeezed his eyes shut against the pain. "There was no talking her down. How are our guests?"

He kept his voice as low and casual as possible.

A sentry stood nearby and would report to Maniodes if anything odd happened. Scythe didn't know how they reported since they didn't have tongues. Maybe they could write.

"They're alright," Scythe replied. "Having the time of their lives."

"I'm glad," he said, gritting his teeth.

"Dagger," Scythe reached through the web of iron and cupped his cheek. He didn't hunch over from the pain, but he leaned into her hand. It was the only thing that didn't hurt him.

"I'll be alright, but you have to lay low," he said earnestly. "Nyx may have spared us, but their ears are perked our way."

"I'll be careful," she reassured him. "I'll do some reading in the library."

His eye glinted.

"Scythe," he started. "I do appreciate the visit…but I'd rather there not be another until these are gone."

He didn't want her seeing him in this pain. He stood straight with a cringe now and then, but soon he wouldn't be able to manage it. He was strong but several chains piercing through your body would even bring Maniodes to his knees.

Scythe nodded but didn't remove her hand immediately. With a sigh she said, "I'll come back when they are taken out."

"Until then, my lady." Dagger gave a slow nod and a smile.

Scythe let her hand drop and turned to leave. She wished she could do more for him, which surprised her a bit. She actually felt guilty for leaving him there, but he wanted her to. She remembered the mausoleum they shared, and how uneasy she had been then. She wanted to go back there with him.

She walked past the sentry, remembering the way on her own. When she reached the main floor, she made for the library. She was determined to find a way to take down Maniodes quickly. With the shield as her only lead, she might as well steal the damn thing and destroy it just to see what would happen. She wanted so badly to break something instead of read, but they had to be sure before they took action. She couldn't afford to be reckless.

It only took her a moment this time to find the hollow library. It was warm and inviting as always. Scythe even saw Axe through the archway, head bowed in concentration over a text he was reading. As she was about to greet Axe, Scythe strode through the archway and spotted Maniodes.

He looked up at her entrance, surprised. Apparently, he'd come here to clear his head after the throne room. His shield leaned on the chair next to him beside the lit fireplace. It was a beautiful piece of work. Four feet in diameter, the rounded iron and steel depicted a dragon's skull.

Scythe's blood started to boil again. She imagined herself grabbing the shield and bashing the mighty god's brains in with it. He didn't look pleased to see her either. Before anything could happen, Scythe turned her back on him and stormed out.

# Chapter 22

Scythe paced around the parlor in their own small castle, restless but unsure what to do. There were hours before the sun rose. She had hoped researching would calm her, but she wasn't about to do it with Maniodes looming over her shoulder. So, she was stuck at home to wait out the night.

A fluttering noise caught her attention, breaking her out of her thoughts of wreaking havoc on something, anything. A bat hung onto the little bar at the window. Scythe opened the glass window and plucked the message tied to its claw. Once free of its burden, it flew away. The message was small, just a single sentence scrawled on the parchment.

"I'm at your front door—Axe."

Confusion washed away her anger. She was on the same floor as the main entrance, but she hadn't heard a damn thing. There was a huge iron knocker shaped like a raven's skull on the front door. How had she not heard that?

She threw open the tall entry door, expecting it to be empty. Axe stood on the front step. The initial surprise at the door opening so suddenly faded to relief.

"I'm glad that bat found you," he said. "I was here for fifteen minutes before running back to Skiachora for it. You're quite lucky to have a dead tree in your yard."

"What are you doing here?" she asked, confused, not intending to be rude.

"I heard Maniodes talking about you after they took Dagger," he said. "May I come in?"

"Yes! Yes," Scythe stepped aside, letting Axe through, then shut the door behind.

He took in the estate entrance. Scythe never had guests back in her cave home, but it was never a proper place to receive them anyway. Standing in the entrance felt rude and awkward, though.

"Let's go sit," she said hurriedly and led Axe to the parlor.

"Is that human leather?" he asked when he saw the couch.

"Yes," she said, proudly. "I tanned it myself, and Dagger helped me stitch it together on the frame."

Axe's gaze drifted around the parlor, no doubt absorbing the fact that the furniture was fixed with more leather and bone. His eyes widened with awe and slight repulsion.

"We didn't kill any unnecessary people to make these," she said to reassure him. He probably wouldn't think too kindly of killing people for fancy décor. "We just dug up fresh graves."

"Ah, well, good," he said, examining Dagger's latest project in the corner.

It was a high-backed dining chair. The back of it was made from interlocking ribs, resembling a ribcage but on a flat surface.

"It *is* rather beautiful," Axe admitted, distracted.

"Thank you." She was eager to let Dagger know Axe liked his work. She took a seat on the couch. "So what did Maniodes say?"

Axe snapped back into reality and took a seat on the couch next to Scythe.

"After the sentries took Dagger, I went to the library," Axe explained. "Maniodes came in an hour later, but he didn't seem to notice me. He sat at the fire in his usual chair. He looked tired too. He didn't pick a book like he usually does, but just stared into the fire. Pitch came in and handed him a goblet of something. He spoke then, more to himself than Pitch, I think. He thought you were going to do something rash, even spiteful. Pitch suggested giving you a job to keep you occupied. Maniodes agreed. I suppose the only one he really listens to is the little fellow. He said he'd pick something that 'reminded you of your place.' His words, not mine."

Scythe didn't bother hiding her frustration and rolled her eyes. Pretty soon, her place would change.

"So what happened after I popped in?" Scythe asked.

"I don't blame you for walking away; it was the best action. He muttered something, but I didn't catch what. Pitch looked taken aback but stayed quiet. He's afraid for Dagger too, you know."

"Maniodes?"

"Pitch. I've talked to the boy often. He idolizes Dagger and even tried asking Maniodes if he could lighten the sentence. He asked if it could last one day, but Maniodes refused. Maniodes said Nyx's word was the final say, and that it was for Dagger's own good."

"How does having a dozen chains webbing through your organs help anything?!" Scythe snapped.

"His words." Axe held his hands up in peace.

Scythe stood and started pacing, muttering. "His fucking good, my ass. We'll see which place I belong in."

Scythe wasn't sure how long she had been walking, but sitting still wasn't helping the rage. Axe waited on the couch with his hands pressed together.

"Scythe," Axe stood and took her arm. "You have to calm down."

Her hand inched into a fist.

Axe let go of her arm, realizing that touching her wasn't the best approach. "I understand you're angry, and I'm worried about Dagger in those chains too, but he'll be fine. I'm worried about you."

Her fist tightened.

"Nyx might not be there to defend you next time, and Maniodes won't hesitate in forcing you to go grey. He was going to do it this time. If you step out of line, you're both gone. I like you two. I don't want to see either of you as walking husks."

"We just met," Scythe said, forcing her hands to relax.

"I've known Dagger for a while. And, yes, I only met you officially yesterday, but I've heard much about you. Mostly from Dagger, actually. You two make beauty out of the grotesque. That dining chair is the perfect example."

The rage melted away. Axe looked embarrassed at his confession but held strong to it. If she and Dagger managed to take Skiachora, they were guaranteed at least one ally.

Maybe he could help. He knew every inch of the library, he must have read almost every text. She wanted to run the idea by Dagger, but he was indisposed for three nights.

"Axe, can I trust you?" she asked.

"I've already entrusted you with enough information to lead to my own death," he said. "Yes, you can trust me."

"Dagger and I are going to take Skiachora from Maniodes," she confided quickly.

Axe opened his mouth to reply, but no words escaped at first. Finally, he said, "You're trying to kill a god?"

"Kill, banish, capture, anything to take him out of power."

"You know how ridiculous that sounds, don't you?" he scoffed.

"You've seen how Maniodes runs the place. You know how he treats us, all of us. I don't think he even knows how the sentries work," she defended.

Scythe thought of the two who took Dagger away. They had waited until he was ready.

Axe cupped a hand around the back of his neck and looked away, thinking.

"You told me about your daughter, and you came here to tell me what Maniodes said. If he knew you were here for that reason, we'd both be in danger."

"I won't be your spy," he said. "I came to help a friend. That was all."

"I appreciate that, and I'm not asking you to spy," Scythe said softly.

Axe waited with a dubious look for her to continue.

"Maniodes was created by his shield; he's tied to it. I have been researching to see if there is a way to use it against him."

"That's why you were in the library," Axe said, stunned. "Reading the old myths and trying to find a way to destroy it."

"Yes, exactly."

Scythe waited for him to gather his thoughts. Axe sat again and gazed at the dining chair of ribs.

"You want me to research for you," he said.

"Well, not *for* me, exactly. I'll be there to help, but you must know that library perfectly. Do you know anything that could narrow down the search?" Scythe asked.

"Maybe, I…" he was still trying to absorb the initial shock.

Scythe sat beside him. "Axe, listen."

He turned to her. His gaze was different now, like he was seeing her in a different light.

"If you don't want to help, I won't hold it against you. You have seen how he treats his people. And I'd like to confide one more thing."

"What?" He sighed at the burden.

"If Dagger or I disobey him again, Nyx wants all of us disbanded."

"All of the Incruentus Ferrum?" he asked, stunned.

"Yes."

Axe stood again in his agitation, "Why?!"

"Because, apparently, we're all too hard to control," Scythe explained.

"Isn't this proving his point then?" Axe stated. "You want to overthrow a god."

"So you're fine with living under his shadow and sneaking behind his back?" Scythe said. "You've seen how easily he dismissed us. If he's willing to take out all of the Ferrum now, because Nyx wanted him to, then he will be willing in the future. Maybe he'll grow bored of us after we've served his purpose. You can't even let him know you don't want to kill anymore. He'll just force you to go grey because you're useless to him. Axe, you came here to warn me about him. What if you didn't have to sneak around your leaders and could talk to them as an equal?"

"So you and Dagger would take that role?" he said. "I'd put my neck on the line to put you in power?"

"If you help us, you can stay a Ferrum and visit your daughter. We could think of a new position for you. One where you're not obliged to take a life again."

He was considering the idea.

"If I agree, you'll let me see my little girl?" he asked.

"If she can keep a secret, you can even reveal yourself to her. How old is she again?"

"She's five," he admitted.

"Maybe wait until she's older to tell her, but you can visit."

Axe nodded. No toddler would be able to keep quiet about papa coming back from the dead.

"I'll help you," Axe agreed, "but not while he's in there."

"I had to leave the first time he came in too. How often does he visit the library?" she asked.

Axe thought for a second. "Three, maybe four times a week. Never on a Friday, though."

"Alright, we'll focus our search on the days he's not present then. Once Dagger is free, he can join us. Are you able to take books out of the library?" Scythe asked.

"I can take one or two to my chambers, but he doesn't want them leaving Skiachora."

"Maybe we could stash some important ones in my cave there. He never bothered to visit that place, so I don't think he knows where it is," Scythe contemplated.

"That could work." Axe took a seat again. "I think the sentries could help us too. You're right about them; I don't think they're as dumb as they seem."

"Maybe they could spy on him for us," Scythe suggested.

"Perhaps, but we should hold off on approaching them until we're sure."

"Yes. Do you think Maniodes is still in the library? I'd love to get some work done rather than sit around."

"You should stay here, I think. I'll go and see what I can find in the old poets, but you should lay low for a few days."

"Fine," she sighed. "And you'll stay quiet about what you're searching for?"

"Of course. If he found out, I'd never see my daughter again."

Scythe might not have felt a father's love herself, but she saw it in Axe's eyes.

# Chapter 23

She hardly slept that day after seeing Axe back through the tree. Eventually, she fell into a restless doze that she wanted to continue as the sun set, but Dagger wouldn't leave her thoughts. He was bound up in chains while she lay comfortable in bed. She got up, not bothering to set the sheets right, and went to the balcony with some tea.

There hadn't been many dried leaves stored. She wanted to get more, but she had torn up the garden in a rage last night. She resolved to spend the night cleaning it out to see what she could salvage.

While working outside, she realized there was no chive plant. She had told Dagger she couldn't remember anything from her past life, but that wasn't the whole truth. She had blocked out most of it, but sometimes memories would leak through like pus from a wound.

There had been a tiny patch of chives growing beside her family's doorstep. Mother took care of it as a hobby. There was never enough to sell, but now and then what food they could afford was seasoned well. Scythe saw a woman with her own red hair in mind, kneeling by the little plant, brushing off dust from the leaves. It was a strong image, closer to a hallucination, but Scythe couldn't see the woman's face, even though she knew it was her mother.

Kneeling in the dirt, hands full of dead plants, Scythe felt nothing. This woman had been mother in name only. She'd probably given that tiny herb more love then her own daughter.

Dagger loved his mother, even missed her, regardless of the fact that she killed him. Scythe wished she couldn't understand that love, but she did, the same way she recognized a father's love in Axe last night. She had seen it and grown up with it, just not from her own family. She couldn't force up any specific memories, but she knew there had been a family next to hers. They had been just as poor, but they got along better. Scythe would watch them through the windows.

Scythe pushed the thoughts away. There was no need for them. She wasn't going to plant chives; there was no need. She and Dagger didn't have to eat anyway, so why season the food?

The faceless woman grew into her thoughts again. Scythe stabbed the spade into the earth, forcing her back down.

The sight of the bat was a relief. It hovered around the main door, looking for a way in until Scythe approached. It landed in her hands, allowing her to untie the parchment. It gave a welcoming screech and let Scythe scratch behind its ears before flying off.

The note from Maniodes was simple. A single woman's name with an address in the Low End of Kaliasma.

It ended with a warning though, saying, "I am tired of giving you chances, Scythe. I've been sticking up for all of you, and that alone should demand respect. If you can't keep your bloodlust in check, then you will leave me no choice."

This had to be the job Axe warned her about. She was curious to see how it *put her in her place.*

Scythe cleaned out the garden and packed quickly. She was tempted to use a tree as a shortcut through Skiachora but didn't know of any dead trees near Kaliasma. She thought about asking Pitch, but she didn't want to risk running into Maniodes. So, she walked.

She let her mind wander to try to relax. Dagger in his chains would surface in her thoughts most often. Now and then, the faceless woman would appear, and Scythe would have to beat her back again.

She walked through the night and well into the morning. She avoided the main road that she used with Dagger before. She cut through the forest heading straight for the city and made good time. She spent the rest of the day in the crypts below the city. The walk and her thoughts had exhausted her.

As the moon rose, Scythe followed the directions on the parchment and found the house. It was more of a hovel than a proper house. The room she needed was part of a larger complex but belowground. There were stairs cut into the stone leading down to the door.

Her target was inside alone. Scythe saw her through the single window next to the door. All Scythe could see of her was her skinny form lying on a bed with one arm outside of the blankets. That arm was battered purple and yellow.

Scythe felt bile rise in her throat. If she had eaten anything, it would have ended up on the cobblestones. She had seen that pattern of bruises enough times on her own body.

Her fingers were stiff, but Scythe forced herself to open the door to the little room. It wasn't locked. There was a small oven in the corner next to a rickety table. Shelves lined the walls with regular home equipment, but that was all. A single candle, stuck to a narrow end table beside the sleeping woman, provided the only light. The woman didn't stir until Scythe closed the door loud enough to break the shadow spell.

Apparently, the woman hadn't been sleeping. She had been crying. She sat up in bed, swinging her legs over the side. The thin, white slip barely covered anything on her. The same bruises patterned her legs, more so on her thighs. Her brown hair hung around her face like a veil. She wasn't afraid.

"Who are you?" she asked confused. Her voice was kind but cracked.

"My name is Scythe," she answered truthfully.

"Did my husband send you?" Her hands clenched at her slip, trembling.

"No."

She calmed. "Are you here to rob us?"

"No."

"So why?" she asked, surprisingly calm.

"I have to kill you." There was no point in lying.

"You *have* to?"

"I don't *want* to," Scythe admitted. To her shock, she really didn't.

The woman grew quiet as if considering the idea. She still wasn't afraid; she just looked tired.

Scythe sat beside her, causing the bed to creak violently. Her weapon was small, and she gripped it in her lap. The woman glanced at it, curious.

"What's your name?" Scythe asked. The name had been on the note, but she wanted to hear it from the woman herself.

"Astraea."

"I can make it quick," Scythe said. "You won't even feel it."

"Make it obvious," Astraea said. "I'd rather not die, but I can't stay here, and I can't leave. I don't want him thinking I escaped through suicide out of spite either. I want him mad. I want him mad at someone he can never find." Life lit in her eyes: life and anger. "If he thinks it was suicide then he's just mad at me for a short time. If it wasn't me, and he can't find who did it, then he's mad forever. I hope it haunts him."

Astrara's need for even a small revenge was contagious. The bile left Scythe's throat, and she loosened her grip on her weapon. Maniodes couldn't have known of Astraea's ideals.

"I can do that," Scythe agreed.

"Thank you," Astraea took Scythe's hand and squeezed it. She looked to their hands, confused and distracted. "You're cold."

"It's a small side effect of being dead." She hadn't mean to say that. Why did she admit that?

Astraea met her eye again. "What are you? Will I be like you when I die?"

Scythe didn't want to tell her about the depressing grey husk she would become.

"You can if you're chosen," she said.

"What do you do? Just kill random people?"

"Maniodes sends us after targets, yes."

Astraea's eyes widened at the god's name.

"You're a goddess then?" she asked in a whisper.

"No, I'm his servant," Scythe clarified, hating the words.

"That's fascinating. I don't think I could do that," Astraea said. "Kill people."

"You won't have to." Scythe squeezed her hand.

"I don't have to do anything anymore, I suppose," Astraea said. "You'll make it quick?"

"Yes, I'm sorry." She surprised herself again by how truthful that was.

"Don't apologize," Astraea smiled. "Can I stand while you do it? I'd rather die on my feet."

"Of course." Scythe helped her stand, cringing as Astraea's knees popped. She couldn't be more than thirty, but she moved as if she was eighty.

Astraea stood with her head high, her body painted in her husband's 'love.'

"Thank you, Scythe," she said sweetly.

# Chapter 24

"Anything special to report?" Maniodes asked from his throne.

"No, my lord, the job went as planned," Scythe said, standing below him. "You would know. I'm sure Nyx was there."

Maniodes drummed his fingers on the arm of the black stone. "You would do well to watch your tongue."

Scythe kept her gaze down and her mouth shut. She wanted to snap, but the practice was doing her some good.

"Did anyone see you?" he asked.

"The victim did. I revealed myself to her, but we were alone. We talked." Scythe shrugged. She didn't bother mentioning how she stayed to watch Astraea's portly husband return home. His scream was music as she watched him stumble back out of the room, vomiting.

"About what?" That had caught his attention.

"She had questions about what I am. She also wanted her husband to know it was murder, which is why I made a show of it, taking her head off but leaving it in that hovel. I had planned to cut her wrists and make it look like a suicide."

"She was willing?" he asked, surprised.

"Yes, my lord."

"Much like yourself back then," he commented.

"Not in the way you assume," she countered, meeting his eye. "Neither of us wanted death, but it was the only escape."

Maniodes nodded but didn't understand. "Do you think she'd make a good Incruentus Ferrum?"

"No," Scythe said truthfully. "She was too kindhearted."

"Mm." Maniodes ran the side of his finger across his lips as if in thought, but Scythe knew he didn't care.

"I've been thinking about Dagger," he said, rolling his fingers together. "How he pleaded to me to spare you, and the look in your eyes when I was about to take his borrowed life. It was quite touching, but I was surprised. I didn't know an arranged marriage would actually grow into anything. You should be grateful; few are so lucky."

He stood. "We're done here. I let you get away with a lot, Scythe, especially with how you speak to me. Nonetheless you will not disrespect me or Nyx, understand?"

It was like he was scolding a child for speaking its mind. She wanted to point out that she meant no disrespect to Nyx. She visibly swallowed her pride.

"Yes, my lord," she said but didn't apologize.

"Tread carefully, Scythe. I really don't want to lose either of you."

*You have an odd way of showing that*, she thought, gripping her large scythe harder.

Scythe left the throne room, feeling Maniodes's cold eyes on her back. She kept hold of her weapon, the weight of it providing some comfort. At the main entrance, her anger hadn't cooled and she nearly used the weapon.

"Hey, Scythe?"

The little voice made her spin and raise the weapon instinctively. Pitch stood behind her, looking apprehensive at the raised scythe but not backing away. Scythe lowered it and forced a breath.

"What do you want?" she asked.

"I was wondering how you were feeling?" he asked, looking away then: embarrassed.

Scythe could only watch the boy, confused for a moment. He had been dead for about twenty years, twice as long as Dagger, but she hardly knew him. They hadn't spoken much until Dagger came into their lives. She couldn't understand why the kid would come to her now.

"What do you mean?" she asked.

He paused and stared back at her, annoyed now. "Dagger's been taken away, and I thought you'd be stressed lately. Sorry if I'm showing too much compassion."

Dagger actually had brought them together. Scythe hadn't seen that coming. The kid was worried about him and just wanted to talk.

"He's being let out today," Scythe said, trying to mend the annoyance. "You should come over to visit him."

Pitch blinked, surprised at the invitation. "I'd like to, but I don't know if I can. Maniodes has me doing a lot of messenger work lately. Can I send a bat to you when I can come?"

"Sure," she said, shrugging.

"Alright," he beamed. "Thank you. Um…actually, I was wondering how the job really went too."

Again, a surprise, but Scythe played along. "It went fine. You were there during the report."

"I know." He started picking at a fingernail. "But I wondered how you felt after the job. The girl was like you. I thought she would help."

"Help with what?" she asked.

"Nothing," he said, focusing on his fingers. "I just wondered if it would be like when Dagger changed after meeting Marella's family. Maniodes told me about that."

"Dagger hasn't changed," Scythe promptly said. The moment she said those words she realized it wasn't quite true. He hadn't been able to kill Basil. That had never happened before.

Did Pitch expect the same thing to happen to her?

"Why do you ask?" she asked Pitch.

"Just curious, really," he said, examining the piece of nail he'd ripped off. "I should go. Maniodes is waiting for me."

He looked up then, flicking the nail away, and smiled at her. He looked as innocent as always.

"I'll send a bat when I can come visit," he said, taking the stairs behind him up two at a time.

Then he was gone around the curve in the stone. Scythe stood there for a moment, trying to make sense of the boy. She'd never seen him pick nervously at his fingers before while talking. Pitch had a spine of steel, he could even maintain eye contact with Maniodes on his bad days.

Scythe brushed the thoughts from her mind. Pitch was probably just worried about Dagger. They hadn't known each other personally for very long; maybe the kid did have the habit of picking his fingernails.

# Chapter 25

Scythe stormed through the cracked corridor back to the chamber that held Dagger. He was finally being released. She already had ointments and linen for bandages back home. If Maniodes insisted that he stay in Skiachora to heal, Scythe would probably stab him. Not that she could reach any higher than his elbow, but there were more sensitive places she could reach.

She forced her temper down. There was no point in thinking like that. It did nothing but make her angrier.

She didn't need a sentry to lead her as before. She was good with directions and remembered the way. Having spent a century exploring Ichorisis, she knew almost every back road through the thickest forests.

A skeleton waited in the corridor before she could enter the chamber. Its bones rattled as the heavy axe with the long handle thudded against the ground, blocking her path.

She halted, tempted to slash it to bits. Instead, she demanded, "What are you doing?"

The sentry held out a note between its fleshless fingers.

Scythe took it and opened it, reading quickly.

"Dagger asked us to stall you until the chains were removed," it read.

"That bastard," she cursed.

She went to walk around the sentry, but it stopped her. It didn't use the axe but just its arm clad in chain mail. She looked up to its empty eye sockets, and it shook its head slowly. Scythe was taken aback again by how aware it was.

"Can you understand me?" she asked him.

He nodded.

"Will you let me pass?"

He shook his head.

Scythe sighed in frustration. "Dagger needs me."

She went to shove around him, but he held her back. He didn't show one shred of violence, even with the imposing axe.

A scream ripped through the corridor behind the sentry, followed by the sound of rattling chains. The scream washed through Scythe like a wave, and she shoved her way past the sentry. He didn't stop her this time.

Dagger held himself on his knees and trembling arms. Seeping red wounds covered his body where the chains had been. They were out of sight now, hidden by the shadows. Another sentry, shorter than the first, stood by Dagger, holding his effects.

Scythe hurried over to Dagger and knelt beside him. He looked up at her touch. The relief in his eyes left him looking dazed, as if he was wondering when the chains would come back.

"Hi." His voice wavered with his delirium, but that was fading. Scythe could see the sharpness coming back in his gaze.

"Hey," she said tucking sweat-soaked hair behind his ear. "How do you feel?"

She knew it was a dumb question, but she didn't know what else to say.

"Feels great to be off my feet," he admitted, "and other than the fact that my entire body is screaming, I'm fine. What's this?"

Dagger couldn't quite control his fingers, but he managed to turn over the note Scythe had dropped. It was the note the sentry used to stall her. The sentry had followed her inside without her noticing.

"You couldn't have been more discreet?" Dagger asked the skeletal figure, with more sarcasm than anger.

The sentry just shrugged, unable to answer another way.

Dagger snickered despite the pain he was in. He cut himself off with a cringe as the movement caught up with him.

The shorter sentry stepped forward and held out Dagger's cloak and belt of knives. Scythe took them and draped the cloak over Dagger. He flinched but smiled in gratitude.

"Let's go home," he said softly.

"Can you stand?"

"I think so, yes."

He was able to, but the cloak nearly fell off him. Scythe was about to get it, but the taller sentry caught it first.

"Thank you, Chip," Dagger said as he gingerly slipped his arm into the sleeve the sentry held for him.

"Chip?" she asked, wondering if the blood loss was making him dizzy or if the pain had driven him mad. She helped him into the other sleeve and adjusted it to cover him.

"The tall one has a chip in his jaw." Dagger indicated on his own face.

Looking closer Scythe saw the notch in the bone on its left side below the teeth. The sentry nodded in acknowledgement, as if appreciating the name.

"I've been calling the other one Shorty." Dagger nodded to the other guard.

This one gave no indication whether or not he liked the name, only glancing between Dagger and Scythe.

Dagger grunted and hunched over. Scythe took his arm gently and lifted it over her shoulders while slipping her other arm around his waist.

"My dear wife, I missed you too, but now isn't exactly the best time," he said, commenting on her closeness.

"Enough joking," she said, but couldn't stop the half-grin. "Let's get you home."

"It's either joke or scream."

The dazed jubilance was gone. He was as sharp as ever.

Chip stepped closer and supported Dagger's other side. Dagger's eyes softened again as he let them support him. Seeing he was no longer needed, Shorty nodded to them and left. Dagger managed to shout his thanks to Shorty's back, causing Shorty to turn and nod again.

It took some time, but Scythe and Chip managed to get Dagger home. Scythe opened the dead tree to their estate and held the main door as Chip helped Dagger limp inside. Chip even helped lead him up to his chambers and set him on the bed.

The sentries were aware and alive. Scythe watched, stunned, as Chip made a writing gesture in the air.

"There's parchment on the desk," she answered his silent question, "but the ink has run out."

Chip turned to the desk anyway, pulling a long piece of charcoal from behind his breastplate. The skeleton's spine gave a faint click as he bent over the desk, writing for a few moments.

Scythe kept a hand on Dagger's shoulder, helping him sit up, but watched Chip. Dagger watched as well. The trembling had calmed as he sat, but his body still twitched now and then as if searching for the chains.

Eventually, Chip tucked the charcoal back and turned to them with the new note. Scythe took and held it up so Dagger could read it too.

"If either of you need anything, or to hide anything, my leader knows we can trust you."

"Isn't Maniodes your leader?" Scythe asked, dubious of the sudden information.

Chip shook his head.

"They have their own kind of hierarchy," Dagger clarified. "A central leader who reports to Maniodes but is separate from him. He's always been kept hidden."

Chip lowered the note once they'd read it.

"Why is he kept hidden?"

Chip just looked to the floor as in embarrassment and didn't write anything else.

"Don't hound him, Scythe. I've been poking at him about it the past few days," Dagger said.

Chip looked up to Dagger and, although he couldn't talk, Scythe felt the appreciation roll off of him.

Scythe caught herself assuming Chip was a male. The skeleton was only made of noisy bone, and there was no indication of gender.

"Chip," she said getting its attention. "Are you male or female?"

Chip tilted his skull, either surprised by her question or trying to remember the answer. Chip turned back to the desk and wrote on the back of the original note, then held it out to them.

"I was male, and Shorty was female."

"Oh, oops," Dagger laughed. "I thought you were both male. Let Shorty know I'm sorry about the assumption." He went to chuckle but cringed again.

"Okay, you need to lie down," Scythe said to Dagger. "Thank you, Chip, and we'll keep your offer in mind."

Chip left the note on the desk and bowed deeply to her and Dagger before seeing himself out. Scythe had never seen any sentry bow to Maniodes before.

"Can they be trusted?" Scythe asked, easing Dagger down against the pillows.

"Those two stayed with me the entire time, for the three days straight. Talking to them was the only reprieve I had. It was wonderful, because there was no sense of time down there. The chains made it feel much longer than just three days. A century could have passed for all I knew. Are you sure this is a good idea? I'm going to get blood all over the sheets."

"Don't worry, I can clean them later."

Dagger finally relaxed and let Scythe bind his wounds. Scythe used the ointments to keep each one clean, but she honestly didn't know if it would help. Neither of them had to eat or drink anything, and alcohol didn't affect them. Potions to ease any physical pain probably wouldn't have any effect either, and that made her wonder about the ointments. Incruentus Ferrum healed quickly and cleanly, so he had that advantage. With fifteen holes punched through his body and organs, healing might take him a week regardless.

"Scythe," Dagger was quiet. His eyes had closed a while ago, and she thought he'd fallen asleep.

"Yes?" Scythe paused in binding the wound on his thigh.

"Maniodes came to me at one point. I think he was trying to goad me into an argument, but I kept quiet. I'd probably would have just screamed if I had opened my mouth. I don't remember most of what he said, but he seemed angry at us. Angry that we were happy. It was like he *resented* us."

Scythe started to fidget with the linen she held. It felt like her throat had clogged up with nervousness.

"I don't know what he was getting on about, but it got me thinking about us. I know we were forced into this marriage and we've had our fun before, but nothing serious came up before."

"He said something similar to me," she admitted, which felt good. The ball of tension eased but didn't loosen completely. "After I gave my last report, after he took you away, he commented on being impressed by our working marriage. He was surprised by how you pleaded for my life and my expression then."

Dagger shifted in the pillows, watching her intently. She didn't like how nervous she felt.

"He kept talking over the comment though, so I didn't answer. Then I started wondering *why* I didn't answer. Then I started thinking about pushing you away in the cellar. I've only ever used flirtation as a tool. When I met you, it was different. You didn't want anything from me. Well, no, that's wrong. I knew you wanted me, but you never forced anything. Then when you did start…pursuing, it was because I let you. And it felt right. Dagger, it felt good, and I wasn't used to that. My mind wouldn't let me have that moment, though, because I started thinking of my father and what he tried to do. That's what scared me."

Scythe stopped there, unsure how to continue. Her thoughts were whirling around too much.

"It's rather daunting, isn't it?" Dagger said. "Are you…happy at least?"

"I am," she admitted right away. She shifted on the bed to sit closer to his side. "I don't want you thinking I'm not happy with you. I don't know why I didn't answer Maniodes, but I know how it felt when they took you away. I wanted to tear that place apart. And when he was standing over you, it was like I couldn't breathe."

"That's how scared I was when I thought you were going to be punished for my mistakes," Dagger said. "When he was standing there, I could only look at you. I wanted you and our memories to be the last thing I saw."

Scythe stroked Dagger's hair and left her hand on his cheek. He leaned into it, closing his eyes. All sense of anxiety was gone, and she was surprised how much easier it was to breathe.

"I don't think either of us are used to this," he said, opening his eyes. "We've always played around the edges."

"I am sorry I pushed you away," Scythe confessed.

"It's alright, I realized I had frightened you somehow," Dagger said.

"It wasn't really you. I'd like to explain, but I don't know how."

"Don't worry about that now. I'm not going anywhere." He took her hand.

Scythe leaned down and kissed him. It did cause him to flinch and grunt in pain. She was about to pull away, but Dagger cupped the back of her head and held her still. His other hand trailed along her side. She wanted to touch him too, but didn't want to hurt him again.

She broke the kiss off despite his protest but stayed close.

"I think I know why I'm not used to this yet," Scythe said. "My father tainted a lot of things for me. I'd like to tell you about it."

Intrigue lit in his eyes, but he kept quiet, letting her finish.

"Later though, when you've rested, and I can gather my thoughts about it more."

"Come now," he said half-grinning, "you can't work me up halfway, then leave me hanging."

"I've worked you up far more than that and left you more than just *hanging,*" she grinned right back. Her hand trailed down his stomach.

He laughed in agreement and didn't argue. He could barely keep his eyes open.

Scythe kissed his forehead as he drifted off to sleep.

# Chapter 26

Dagger lay in bed for two straight nights. He wasn't just sleeping; he was unconscious. Scythe knew there was nothing to be done, and he couldn't die anyway, but she stayed close.

While Dagger healed, Scythe took the time to really examine their guests. The man was fine and kept begging to be let out, but the woman was quiet. She was conscious, sitting in the corner of her stone cell, cradling her arm. The stink was rancid. The pus oozing from the raw muscle was thick and yellowish. Scythe cursed while using the rest of the ointment on her. She resolved to cauterize it. The woman wasn't too feverish, so there was still a chance.

Scythe contemplated letting them go to die of exposure, but they might survive. If that happened, Maniodes would eventually learn about them. Even if they died out there, Scythe didn't know if they would say anything to Nyx. If they told her where they had been held, then she and Dagger would be found out. She couldn't risk it.

Scythe lit the brazier and strapped the woman to her chair again. She wept and begged, but Scythe ignored her. Scythe found a butcher's cleaver among the collection Dagger kept here and heated the side. It took a few tries and a lot of screams, but Scythe managed to burn away most of the infected flesh.

After she sent a bat to Axe asking, as vaguely as possible, if he'd found anything useful. After a full day went by with no reply, she grew paranoid. She was torn between going to find him and keeping an eye on Dagger. Dagger hadn't moved an inch, and his wounds were fine, so she decided to make a quick run to find Axe.

The castle was nearly empty as always, except for a few guards. All of them bowed their head as she passed, and she greeted each one. It was odd and uncomfortable having so much subtle attention, but she would have to get used to it.

The library was empty, and Scythe didn't know where Axe's chambers were. She cursed and headed back to Dagger, glad she could stay with him but worried about Axe. Images of Maniodes torturing Axe ran through her thoughts. Only two options were open to him if that happened: talk or don't. Both could doom them all.

Scythe controlled her paranoia until she got back home and ripped a random vine from the wall.

She headed back upstairs to Dagger's chamber.

Scythe froze as she entered the room. Bloodstains marked where Dagger had been, but he was gone. The agitation at not finding Axe almost made her panic now. Her hands shook with a confused mix of worry and anger. Scythe took a breath and left the room.

She checked her own because it was close. He wasn't there, and she hadn't entirely expected him to be. The dread started to rise again when she couldn't find him in the garden, parlor, or on the balcony.

She practically raced down the stairs to the kitchen, reminding herself to check the library, along with the dozens of other empty rooms. The kitchen door rebounded off the back wall as she strode through.

The noise caught Dagger's attention. He was leaning on the counter, eating out of a pouch of peanuts he'd stashed away.

"A little violent with the door, don't you think?" He popped another peanut into his mouth.

"I didn't know where you went! I searched the entire fucking place." It felt like she was boiling over.

"I knew you'd find me eventually," he said. "Are you okay?"

"I'm bloody glorious." She shrugged it off. "What about you?"

She took the arm not holding the pouch and unwound the linen on his bicep. The chain there had been thick and left a hole large enough to see clean through. The circle was raw and deep, but the meat inside had stitched together. It must still hurt, but at least he was able to move.

"How are you standing?" She took a step back for a different look. He wasn't trembling anymore.

"I'm sore, but I'll manage," he shrugged eating another peanut.

"There were over a dozen punctures, most through your organs."

"They healed first. I can finally breathe without tasting blood."

He demonstrated with a grin, which slipped when he took in her expression.

"Scythe, what's wrong?" He set the pouch down.

"I told Axe what we're doing, and now I can't find him."

Hi jaw worked to speak but nothing escaped until he said, "Why would you tell him?"

"He came to me behind Maniodes's back after you were taken." Scythe described what they had talked about and that Axe didn't trust Maniodes anymore.

The shock in Dagger's eyes changed to concern and disappointment. Scythe's fist shook at her sides as the frustration boiled over.

"You were in chains, and Axe was willing to help us. So, I went out on a limb," she said in defense.

"That's a precarious limb, Scythe," Dagger argued. "You should have told me. It's not a bad idea, but the risk—"

"I know the fucking risk."

"Then why did you take it? There's no deadline for us to take over. Taking our time was our advantage. It could have waited three days. It's a good idea. Axe practically lives in that library."

"It doesn't matter now. We have to find him. He might be at home, but I don't know where he lives."

"Or he's singing our names to the high heavens," Dagger sighed, running a hand through his hair.

"Look, I know it was rash—"

"This could kill us, Scythe. We *just* avoided that."

"Then let's go find him," Scythe said, sharper the she intended to.

"And run into Maniodes while we're down there? Things are sensitive right now. What do you suggest we tell him?"

"The sentries could help us avoid him. Do you have any other fucking ideas?"

Dagger took a breath again but didn't reply. He didn't look happy.

"Will you follow my lead while we're down there?" he asked.

"Fine. Just get dressed; I'll meet you outside." Scythe hurried off to get her weapon.

Dagger met her by the dead tree, adjusting his coat over his shoulders. Guilt washed most of the panic away, seeing him flinch then drop his left arm.

"Are you okay?" she asked. "I should have helped with your wounds."

"I'm alright. I can dress myself. It felt good to stretch anyway." He flashed a grin, but it didn't touch his eyes.

He took out his main dagger and stabbed it into the roots of the tree. It split open.

There was already an awful taste in her mouth, and she didn't need Dagger angry at her too. She didn't want to antagonize him either. She stayed quiet.

"Do you have any idea where he might be?" Dagger asked as they began the descent.

Maybe he wasn't as angry as she thought. His annoyance was justified, but he was talking to her normally.

"He lives by the library, but I don't know where. He visits his daughter in secret; maybe he's with her?"

"Maybe, but we don't know where or who she is. Let's focus on his home. If he lives in that castle, then Pitch probably knows where. He knows that castle better than Maniodes, I think."

The stairs took them to the base of Maniodes's castle. The sentries nodded to them again as they passed.

"Do you know where Pitch might be?" Scythe asked as they walked.

"I know where he sleeps, but it's close to Maniodes's main chambers, so we'll need to be cautious," he replied. "Maybe a sentry could scout ahead for us."

They passed a couple of sentries on patrol, and more on the higher levels. Dagger went straight to what Scythe thought was a random door.

He tried the door, but it was locked. He cursed and knocked, calling, "Pitch, you there? I need to ask you something."

No answer.

Scythe wrung her hands over her weapon.

"Shit, kid probably scampered off somewhere. It is Friday," Dagger said dismissively.

"Is it?" Scythe didn't realize the day until now.

"Yes, it's his day off," Dagger shrugged.

"Maniodes might not be here then. In the castle, I mean. Axe said he never visits the library on Fridays," Scythe explained.

"Really? That's the place he goes to relax when it's not his own chambers," Dagger speculated. "What's so special about Fridays?"

Scythe shrugged. "Let's find a sentry."

"Right."

It didn't take them long to find a couple patrolling a corridor. There was no indication of name or gender, but they were still eager to help. They each held a boney fist over where their heart would have been and bowed when Dagger stopped them in the corridor.

"Do you two have names?" Dagger asked it.

The guards nodded.

"Is there any way you can tell it to me?"

They both shook their heads and shrugged.

"I should have brought something to write with."

Always the kind man with the formalities. Scythe just wanted to get to the point.

"Do you know where Pitch might have gone?" Dagger asked. "Or Axe? We were looking for him first."

The skeletons tilted their head as if listening or thinking. Scythe started fidgeting with a piece of lace from her dress, but Dagger was as patient as ever.

The skeletons turned back to them after a moment and beckoned them to follow. One of them led Dagger and Scythe down several dusty corridors. The rattling of the bones was almost infuriating, but Scythe controlled her temper. The damn noise couldn't stop. Scythe eventually realized they were heading for the library again. The sentry passed the turn, though, and kept going. They were led to a tower with a set of stairs rising along its edge. The sentry stopped partway up on a landing with a door.

Another skeleton waited for them there. This one was taller than the first. Scythe was about to ask where they were when the second skeleton handed Dagger a message.

Dagger's face lit up instantly at reading it.

"We're at Axe's chamber, and Pitch is playing in the garden. He's fine."

Relief flooded through Scythe. "Thank you both."

They both bowed as Chip had and left them on the landing.

Scythe beat Dagger to the door, almost banging on it rather than simply knocking.

"Axe, are you there? It's Scythe."

A moment of silence stretched. She was about to pound on the door again, but the rattling of a lock distracted her. The door opened, revealing Axe, looking delighted.

"Evening, Scythe," he said. "Good to see you, Dagger. How do you feel?"

"Fine, thank you. I was wondering if we could talk."

"Of course, of course, come in. I'm glad you're here. I've found something fascinating."

Axe held the door open wider, and Scythe stepped inside with Dagger close behind.

Axe's home was almost circular, having to fit inside the tower, but it was spacious. Curtains hung around the bed for more privacy, and books covered nearly every surface. Scythe wondered if they were all Axe's own collection, since he couldn't take many from the library. Half-melted candles lit the room; several of them sat on the mantel over the fireplace. There was a portrait of a young black-haired girl with dark skin hung above the mantel: Axe's daughter. There were a couple of high-backed chairs by the fire with more books stacked on the seats.

"My apologies for the mess," Axe said, moving the books to the desk. "Please sit."

Dagger did. He leaned back with a sigh, looking paler than usual, and he moved gingerly. Scythe was about to ask if he was really alright, but he caught her eye. His jaw was set, but he grinned at her. It was kind but pained. Scythe didn't bother asking and laid a hand over his shoulder.

"Did you get my letter?" Scythe asked, turning to Axe.

"I did," he said pulling out the chair from the desk and sitting beside them. "I had every intention of replying, but I was so close to finishing a translation I'd put it off."

"It's been a full day since I sent that bloody bat," Scythe accused, letting her frustration bleed through.

"Has it?" Axe's surprise was honest. He stroked a hand over his neck, embarrassed. "I'd lost track of the time. I burned the note, lest Maniodes find it. Not that it was incriminating, but just in case. You must have been worried."

"We thought Maniodes had you," Dagger said, sitting up more.

"I'm fairly safe here, especially today. Maniodes isn't in the castle. He isn't even in Skiachora," Axe said.

"Where does he go?" Scythe asked, curious.

"I don't know. Probably wandering around Ichorisis, I expect. It does get rather dismal down here. Or he visits Phaos," Axe speculated.

"So what did you find?" Scythe asked, taking the last chair.

Axe lit up with excitement. "You were right to focus on the items of the gods. I started with Maniodes's shield and expanded from there. I found this."

Axe plucked a huge old tome from the desk and opened it to a marked page. As he handed it to Scythe, Dagger leaned closer to see.

There was a beautifully detailed image of a breastplate drawn on the left-hand section. The right held script in a foreign language. Scythe could hardly recognize most of the runes that made up the words.

"How does this help?" Dagger asked. "What does it say?"

"This language is old, ancient even. I think it was one of the first books added to that library by a forgotten bard. It was tucked away in a dusty corner. I know of this language, but I couldn't read it right away so I brought it here to translate," Axe explained practically bouncing in his seat.

"So, what does it say?" Dagger asked more sternly.

"It's a dead language that speaks of Lumeon, the third son of Nyx, and brother to Maniodes and Phaos. Also how he was imprisoned."

Dagger's eyes widened. Scythe looked back to the text. She couldn't understand any of it, but she wanted to drink in the information.

"Are you sure?" Dagger asked. "How can we trust this source?"

"Well, the bard has been dead for centuries, maybe a millennia, so we can't ask him," Axe replied, joyous about sharing the discovery. "I have been studying this language extensively during my time here in Skiachora. It's complex, but there's a trick to the placement of the verb because it's at the end of the sentence, no matter the context."

"Axe, I don't mean to be rude, but I don't care how the sentences are structured," Dagger admitted.

"Most aren't," Axe shrugged, unfazed, "but learning that trick helped me translate it. Once I learned Lumeon's name, I was able to find it again and again. He was nearly erased from the histories, but he still exists in the ancient texts."

Axe retrieved another book from his desk. This one was smaller but just as old.

"This one described him standing alongside Phaos and Maniodes as they created the world. Phaos created Ichorisis, and Maniodes created Skiachora, but Lumeon created the sea. Then Lumeon wanted to create his own race of beings like Phaos had. Maniodes was content with managing the dead and Phaos had the living, but Lumeon didn't have that connection with anything. Nyx wouldn't let him create anything other than the sea creatures that we know of today. He wasn't allowed to make anything intelligent. Now, I think it's because Phaos's first men were young, she wanted to see how they turned out. Along with how quick the dead would rise for Maniodes. There's nothing to prove that idea, though.

"Lumeon obviously didn't see this as fair and created his own race anyway. It nearly wiped out all of Phaos's men."

"What did he make?" Scythe asked, fascinated.

"I haven't found that out yet. I don't think they even got their own name. The translations only say 'sea beast.' Now, the war between the humans and the sea beasts almost killed all of the living.

"That was when Nyx stepped in and destroyed *all* of Lumeon's beasts. Their souls weren't even allowed access to Skiachora, either. Lumeon was furious and vowed to create another, stronger race that could supposedly counter death and Nyx herself.

"Nyx did not take any chances with him. She took the armor she originally crafted for him and sealed it inside a driftwood box. His essence and power were trapped inside. Nyx hid this box, ashamed of what her own son would do. Phaos and Maniodes don't even know where their brother is."

Dagger and Scythe sat in silence for a moment, absorbing the tale. Scythe couldn't look away from the armor drawn in the book. It was simple and old-fashioned, but it looked durable. The metal of the breastplate was hammered out, and thick leather straps with more metal worked into them draped over the shoulders. There were wide strips of metal and leather that hung like a shirt to cover the god's thighs. It was simple, but given its history, daunting.

"And no one knows," Dagger said, stunned. "No one except Nyx, Maniodes, and Phaos."

"People knew once perhaps," Axe said. "They even supposedly knew what Skiachora was and their fates down here, but I think that was stripped away. This bard had to come to know this information of Lumeon somehow. Lumeon has passed beyond legend and even myth. He's been forgotten from existence."

Dagger leaned back in his seat and ran a hand through his hair.

"We could seal Maniodes away like Lumeon. We just need his shield and a box," Scythe speculated.

"It won't be that easy," Axe said. "He guards that shield constantly. It hangs above his bed as he sleeps."

"Why a *driftwood* box?" Dagger asked, distracted. "Seems like an odd detail."

"I'd thought that was rather specific too, but I couldn't find any indication why," Axe said.

"Driftwood comes from the ocean," Scythe said. "It's basically any type of wood, but it's created that way by the waves. Lumeon is associated with the ocean; he created it. Maybe that's why."

"That's likely, but I want to be absolutely sure before we try to steal the essence of Maniodes himself," Dagger said.

"I'll keep researching the topic," Axe offered. "Even if I find a type of tree or wood connected to Phaos, which would at least confirm the idea."

"That's good but there's another problem," Dagger pointed out. "Nyx would prosecute us if we seal away her son."

"Maybe not," Scythe speculated. "What if we get her on our side?"

"How, for the love of Skiachora, would we get her to *help* us banish her son?" Dagger asked cynically.

She wanted to snap right back, but she held her tongue. Based on the way he was holding himself, Dagger was still in pain.

"Do you think the goddess of death has ever had a friend?" Scythe asked. She was able to contain most of the sarcasm, but some still bled through. "She was willing to seal away one of her own children. If we show her how incompetent Maniodes is, she might be willing to help us. Even seal him away herself."

"But Lumeon was violent. He almost killed humanity. Maniodes is practically his opposite," Dagger said.

He had a fair point. Maniodes was incompetent, but he was hardly maniacal. Another idea came to her.

"What does Maniodes do on Fridays?" Scythe asked.

Neither of them bothered to answer.

"It must be something he's trying to hide. Nobody knows where he goes. Even Pitch, who helps plan out his days and suggests jobs for us. He's hiding something. Maybe we could find out what that is and use it against him."

"While in the meantime befriending Nyx before we blindside Maniodes." There was no sarcasm in Dagger's voice. They finally had a direction.

"Exactly," Scythe added.

# Chapter 27

Scythe locked the door to the estate behind them. They had left Axe to his research some time ago. It took them longer to reach home than usual because of the stairs between the dead trees. Dagger had slowed down. When they left the tree, the moonlight showed his leg to be bleeding again. No doubt the other wounds were as well.

Now Dagger leaned on the wall beside the door with his eyes closed.

"Let's get you to the parlor," Scythe said, taking his arm. He let her lead him. "You can sleep on the couch. I'd rather you not attempt the stairs like this."

He grunted as he lowered himself to the couch but didn't lie down. He gripped the edge of it, leaning forward.

"An eventful night." His voice was rough but steady.

Scythe sat next to him. "You should lie down. I'll get the bandages to patch you up again."

She went to stand, but Dagger caught her arm.

"There's one more thing I'd like to hear before I pass out again," he said.

"Whatever it is, I'm sure it can wait."

"It's been waiting since you dug up my death. You promised to tell me yours."

"You want to hear that *now*?" Her heart started to seize at the thought.

"It's a night for discoveries." He didn't let go of her arm.

"I will tell you, but not until you've healed more. You can barely walk," Scythe protested.

"The promise was after I had rested," he said. "I've rested enough."

"Clearly, you haven't."

"Regardless, I would hear that story now. It's not like it can affect my health."

"By the gods, you're stubborn," Scythe cursed. She was tempted not to tell him out of spite.

Dagger's eyes softened at her harsh tone. "I'll admit I'm not in the best mood, but this has been hanging over us since that wedding. I'd rather it not anymore."

She didn't want it there either. Now did seem like as good a time as any. She might as well get it over with.

"Alright," she said, "but let me get the bandages to patch you up while I talk."

"Alright," he agreed.

It only took her a few minutes to come back with the linen strips and start removing the spoiled ones.

"I can hardly remember my old home anymore. I think I blocked most of it out. I remember dying perfectly though," she started begrudgingly.

He settled back while she cleaned his wounds again. She was uncomfortable sharing her death, but she forced herself too. This was one of the few things Dagger ever demanded of her, and she had dug into his death. She tried holding back the resentment as she spoke.

"I lived in a city with my mother and father. I don't remember the city's name, but I don't think it exists anymore. We lived in a tiny one-room house beside an apothecary in the poorest corner. Father worked with the blacksmith but made hardly any wages. Mother helped the family who owned the apothecary; they paid her now and then, but it was never enough. Feasts for us counted as a slice of bread for each of us; cheese was a luxury.

"Father and Mother were always bitter with each other. He blamed her for not having a son who could work better. Mother would snap back that him never worked hard enough to provide for them anyway. They both also blamed me for not being more useful. Most of that talk started when I was six. As I grew older I taught myself to pickpocket and sold everything I could get. It got harder to rob people as I got older because I wasn't small anymore, so I picked up odd jobs around the district for coin.

"That couldn't have been an easy childhood," Dagger said sympathetically.

"No, it bloody wasn't. After a long day at a hot dye shop, I came home and found that my parents weren't arguing for once. They stopped talking entirely as I entered the room. I asked if there was something wrong. Which was a stupid, loaded question. Something was always wrong.

"Father said there wasn't, and that they had found a way to make a lot of money fast. He was calm as he spoke. I was used to anger, so him being calm frightened me. Mother didn't say anything; she just shivered and looked away. Father nodded to the corner of the room behind me. There was a man standing there I hadn't noticed as I walked in.

"'This man is going to take care of you,' he said. 'You will work for him, and he'll pay us handsomely.' "

Dagger frowned, probably sensing where the story was going.

"The new man kept looking at me like I was a horse he wanted to purchase. Only he was undressing me in his mind. It made my skin crawl. I asked him what kind of work I would be doing.

"He didn't say at first, only, 'Something I'm sure you will be very good at and earn a hefty price too.'

"I demanded to know what the job was, knowing father might hit me. The new man was taken aback too. Living that poor you had to stand up for yourself.

"He said it was a brothel. They were selling me to a whorehouse. I turned to mother, but she wouldn't meet my eye. I knelt by her, begging her not to let it happen, to understand. I knew she would. I begged her not to let them take me. You know what she said? She said he would take care of me. Those words felt like a knife through my heart.

"The brute grabbed my arm and hauled me up. Father stood aside as the new man tried to take me away. I fought, though, and broke free from his hand.

"I bolted. I had no idea where to go, so I just ran. I heard them yelling after me, but I didn't stop. I ran the length of the city before collapsing in an alley. When the sun set, I knew what to do and I knew where to do it. It took me about an hour to sneak into the astronomy tower and creep up to the top level. Then I jumped.

"The wind felt wonderful. I remember hitting the ground and not dying instantly. I lay there with pooling blood, shattered bones, and smashed organs. The next thing I knew Maniodes was waking me up. I don't remember seeing Nyx."

Dagger stayed quiet for a long time. She didn't want him to reply anyway. It hadn't been good by any means. If he said the generic 'sorry' like humans did at funerals, she would probably leave him.

"I would have killed them," he said instead. "The man who tried to buy you, and your father. Your mother too, actually, because she didn't do anything to protect her daughter."

Scythe paused in rebinding his arm. Her nerves were on end as it was; that comment was the charge before the lightning.

"They're dead now, of course. Given that you've been a Ferrum for nearly a century," he said.

"I did."

"Sorry?" Dagger leaned closer.

"I did kill them. After I was chosen, I hunted down the owner of the brothel. I nailed him to the wall of his establishment and burned it down. I made sure all of the women and girls were gone before I set it on fire. I don't know what happened to them after.

"When I went home, mother and father were there. She fainted at seeing me, and father fell to his knees and begged me for mercy. I took both of their heads."

"Imagining you standing over them, beautiful and terrifying: it's a good image."

Scythe didn't reply.

"Have you ever found them in Skiachora?" Dagger asked.

"No."

"I found my father down there," he admitted.

"How did he die?" she asked, grabbing at the change in topic.

"Killed while he was being robbed."

"And your mother?"

"She's still alive, not well, but alive." His eyes darkened with the reflection.

"The woman back at the wedding told me she was hallucinating about demons."

"Yes, she panicked after dinner and thought I was one. A knife through my heart was all it took."

"Is that why you chose daggers?" she asked.

"Aye, why did you choose the scythe?"

"Security," she answered. "No one would take advantage of a woman with a weapon that big."

"It is daunting," he said. "Although messy. Daggers are more precise."

Scythe didn't bother replying. They'd probably end up comparing weapons for hours. They had before in a playful way. Now she wasn't in the mood.

She tied off the last strip on his shoulder rougher then she needed to, but Dagger didn't react.

"I'm glad you told me," he said softly.

"It was only fair." Scythe couldn't meet his eyes despite the kind words.

The silence stretched between them. Scythe packed away the clean bandages and gathered the maroon-stained ones. She stood with the soiled linens, intending to burn them in the kitchen oven. There was no point in trying to clean them of that much blood.

"Scythe." Dagger stood as well and caught her free hand.

She ripped it out of his grip like he was on fire. She stopped though, several strides away from him.

The surprise and hurt in his eyes made her want to slap him. She hadn't been able to hold back the resentment.

"I'm sorry I forced you to share that," he said.

"You didn't twist my arm." The gods knew her father had, many times.

"I might as well have," he said, looking solemn. "Do you feel better at least, having talked about it?"

"No."

"I don't want this hanging over us either," he sighed.

"What the fuck did you expect? Did you think I'd enjoy telling you how my father beat me, how I murdered him and my mother? You had the happy life with parents who loved you. Did you really think people from the other end of the spectrum were going to have a fun time talking about it? You were the only one in my life who hadn't forced me into anything until now."

The rage was boiling over again. His sorry expression wasn't helping either. It just made her feel guilty at being angry, which made her angrier.

"I am sorry I betrayed that," he said, "but it had to be said."

"Well, I'm glad you're happy." She swept her arms wide in a mock bow, then turned on her heel.

# Chapter 28

Dagger took his time making his way back up to bed. He had woken up only hours ago feeling great. As they talked to Axe, a dull ache had begun to rise from the unexpected movements. Then once they were back home, the wounds were screaming at him.

Talking to Scythe and hearing her story had distracted him for the moment, but he had been bitter with her beforehand. He hadn't intended to, but he wasn't in his right mind. Still, Scythe didn't deserve that.

She hadn't been on the balcony or in her chambers as he passed. He decided to leave her be, assuming that's what she wanted. She had lived her entire life and death that way. It was what she was accustomed to.

The bloodstains were still on the sheets, but Dagger didn't care. He crawled into bed and fell asleep almost instantly.

Scythe still wasn't around when he woke up. Judging by the drastically changed length of the candles, he'd been unconscious again for nearly twenty-four hours. He didn't want to spend the entire night in bed, but knew he should take it easy. His body wouldn't let him do otherwise.

He went to the cellar and cracked open an old wine bottle. The result was sour but pleasant. Taking his pouch of peanuts, he went to relax on the balcony. The disappointment at the sight of it empty didn't surprise him.

Something Scythe had said hadn't left him. She had described them as living on opposite ends of a spectrum. He hadn't realized the extent until last night. His family hadn't been as wealthy as royalty, but they were well-off. He had a home with two floors, while Scythe had a single-room shack. He had parents who loved him, while hers disowned and tried to sell her. He had his sister to relate to, while Scythe had no one.

He was grateful that Scythe had confided in him about her death, but the moment was bitter. She hadn't done it willingly. He didn't know how to make it up to her, either. She already knew his death. She didn't know the details, though. It wasn't much of an option, but it was the only card he had to play.

Dagger ran a hand through his hair and set down the empty goblet. His wounds ached again, but they weren't screaming. He stood to find Scythe. Luckily, he didn't have to look far.

She stood in the broken-glass doorway. Surprise crossed her face at the timing of him turning around before she looked away, embarrassed.

He was about to suggest they talk properly, but she beat him to it.

"The woman is sick."

At first Dagger had no idea what she was referring to, then remembered the guests they had kidnapped and tortured. Listening to screams of pain and feeling the gentle softness of exposed organs might clear his mind at the moment, but he had to stay focused. He wondered if Scythe had the same idea of the torture and that was why she had been down there.

"How badly?" he asked.

"The raw skin of her arm is infected," Scythe replied in a monotone. "I cauterized it days ago, but it's still rotting."

"Sonofabitch." Dagger stepped around Scythe and headed for the cellar.

"She's not in there," Scythe stopped him. "I put her in one of the servant's rooms."

She gestured for him to follow, and he did, quietly. The room she stopped at was in the empty servant's quarters. There was only a single bed inside.

The woman was on the bed, unconscious and tied down. The sickly-sweet stench of infection permeated the air. Dagger sat by the woman's side and gently unwrapped a section of the linens. The skin around the burnt meat was swollen and red. The scab itself oozed pus thick and green.

"We should cut off her arm," Scythe said leaning against the doorframe with her arms crossed. "I was going to just do it, but I thought I should let you know."

The passive sarcasm was almost as thick as the pus.

"I appreciate it," he said, letting her be angry.

"Keep an eye on her. I'll get something to start a fire in to cauterize the stump." She walked off without a second glance.

"Let me help you with the brazier," he called after her.

"I carried a full-grown woman up here. I'll be fine." Scythe didn't even slow down.

Dagger sat on the edge of the bed beside the woman.

"Is being passive-aggressive normal?" he asked her.

Of course, there was no reply. At least she was breathing.

Scythe returned with the iron brazier, kindling, and a cleaver. She met his gaze as she handed him the cleaver, but kept her eyes guarded.

"Start hacking," she said, turning back to the brazier. She struck the flint together and started the small fire.

Dagger stayed guarded himself and addressed the woman again. There was no headboard so Scythe had to use the feet of the bed as anchors for the ropes. The rope was just long enough to prevent the woman's arms from going numb, but short enough to stop her from untying herself.

Unfortunately, the infected arm was on the side against the wall, away from Dagger. He shifted her body as much as he could and straightened her arm at the shoulder. The elbow stopped at the wall, leaving the arm bent, but it would do. He took aim.

She woke as the cleaver met bone. Dagger felt the crack of the bone vibrate through the handle rather than hearing it over her scream. He hadn't gone all the way through. The awkward angle, along with his injuries, slowed him. Scythe hadn't gagged the woman, and she bucked as she screamed.

"Don't move!" he shouted.

The screams cut off with a choke, but she stopped squirming. Tears and snot poured down her face as the blood poured from her arm.

Dagger gave one more swing of the blade and the meat gave. He tossed the rotted arm aside, held a bunch of the bedclothes to her stump, and handed the cleaver back to Scythe.

Scythe buried it in the flames. The woman screamed and bucked again, but he held her down. It took only minutes for the blade to glow, but the sheets had soaked through with a deeper red.

Scythe handed him back the blade, hilt first. Dagger pulled the sopping sheets away and pressed the flat of the hot blade to the stump. Burning flesh mixed with the noxious infected air, creating a nauseating effect.

Once a warm scab was left where her arm had been, Dagger stood. The woman curled onto her side, crying. It was the best they could do.

"We should move her to a clean bed," Dagger suggested.

"There's one next door."

She helped him untie the woman, who tried to squirm away from him. He lifted her tenderly and followed Scythe to the other room. This one was identical to the last.

Dagger set the woman down on the bed. "Can you get the ropes?" he asked Scythe.

"I already brought them." She had them in hand.

"Ah, good… thank you."

They tied her to the bed as before, listening to her whimper. They left her there to rest, locking the door with Scythe's key ring.

Scythe walked away. He called after her, but she didn't stop or even glance his way. He let her go, deciding to go to the cellar for something to go with the wine.

The man down there was screaming for his wife. His curses grew more colorful and vulgar as Dagger sat against the door, trying to enjoy the tart wine and the screams.

He wasn't sure how much time had passed, but the man had stopped yelling a while ago. The restlessness was driving him mad. He left the cellar to find Scythe.

He found her kneeling in the garden. Only then did he notice the mess it was in. Plants were torn up by the roots, and half of the vines were gone.

He knelt in the soil next to her. She didn't look up. She kept watching her hand, the one she had held against her body in the servant's quarters. His breath caught when he realized what she was examining.

Blisters lined her thumb and index finger, and the skin was a tight red.

"Scythe, what happened?" he asked gently.

"When I was heating up the cleaver the handle wasn't long enough." Her voice was dry.

Dagger took her hand to see the damage more closely. She let him but still didn't look up.

"You should have balanced it on the brazier's edge," he said. "Just held the end for balance."

Scythe shook her head. "Letting go like that meant I would have had to grab it properly again before handing it to you. It would have taken time that woman didn't have."

The blisters would heal, but the flames raising them had to be excruciating. Yet she hadn't let go.

Scythe took her hand back, cradling it in her lap.

"Did you do all this?" he asked referring to the torn-up garden.

She nodded.

"Why?"

"I couldn't kill our guests or save you from the chains."

That last part left him feeling like he'd been punched in the chest. His three days of imprisonment had tormented her as much as him.

"I'd like to plant chives," she said almost too quietly to hear.

"We can do that," he said, not sure why she wanted chives in particular.

"Why didn't you kill Basil?" she asked, finally looking at him. "I saw you hesitate before handing me the knife."

"I wanted to," he admitted. "I wanted to feel his blood pulse through my fingers. But I kept thinking about Thomas."

"About his family."

"Yes." He didn't know what else to say but let slip, "You never had a family."

No sarcasm, just silence. She looked away again.

"Scythe, I can't have this hanging over us too," he admitted.

"I don't want it there either," she said. "I don't care about sharing it now. It's just brought up a lot of things I'd rather forget."

"If you want, I'll tell you of my death," he said. "Tell you exactly what happened. Then we're even."

Scythe shook her head. "That just seems petty on my part."

"It's not petty," he insisted. "I want you to trust me. And I *want* to tell you. I've never told anyone."

Scythe stayed quiet.

Dagger sighed and ran a hand through his hair, unsure how to carry on. He figured his first option was the only one still available, so he took the chance.

"My mother was strict but kind," he started. He told Scythe about the occasional hallucinations his mother would have, and how they got worse after his father died. He described how she was lucid now and then, but it was fading, and of their dinner together. He stopped at the moment when his mother pointed the knife at him, remembering the cold metal turn to fire inside him. He didn't know how to put it into words, but Scythe let him take his time. She listened quietly, and Dagger saw she was coming out of her shell again.

Scythe still didn't say anything when he finished. There was really nothing to say. He was grateful when she took his hand again.

"We should get a salve for those blisters," he said, changing the topic.

"I don't think they work on us. We heal quickly anyway," Scythe replied, shrugging. "How are your wounds?"

"They're alright, better than yesterday."

Scythe just nodded. "Do you want to get some wine?"

"Gods, yes." He didn't care that they couldn't get drunk.

The moonlight glinted off the goblets on the balcony's crooked table. Scythe had just finished trading a tale of how she tormented a town by killing their Earl, who was an official victim, and riding around the town with his body tied to a horse. The townspeople had been terrified but violent. She eventually left them with half a dozen arrows stuck in her.

"That might have been a grand sight," Dagger said. "You as a night wraith, not the arrows."

"That part was funny too. I looked like a damn porcupine."

It felt good to laugh. Even the holes in his chest didn't protest as much anymore. Scythe took a sip of wine after the laughter died down. He couldn't help but admire her neckline as she swallowed, and how her blood red hair sat on her shoulder. She caught him looking and smiled sweetly.

He tried to push away the thoughts of her neck, but they protested. He had to focus; there was one more topic he wanted to discuss.

"So how do we get Nyx on our side?" he asked.

Scythe contemplated the question. "It will be hard to try anything that won't seem odd or suspicious."

"My thoughts exactly," he said. "Maybe we could start small. Wait for another victim to be chosen. When we take the life, we call to her and thank her for giving us a second chance."

"It's good to start with, but then what?" Scythe asked. "Asking her over for dinner would seem strange. Does anyone actually include her in anything? I know Maniodes and Phaos have brotherly visits, but does anyone invite Nyx over for a chat?"

"Probably not," he agreed, "but what if we do something a bit bigger? Offer her a sacrifice, maybe. The harvest moon is rising; it's almost time for Nukternios. They're in her honor all across Ichorisis, so it wouldn't seem out of place."

"A small sacrifice isn't enough to make her an ally, but honoring her is a good idea," Scythe considered. "It would catch her attention."

They both fell silent for a moment. His eyes kept drifting to Scythe's neckline.

Scythe sat up suddenly, breaking his gaze.

"What if we throw a ball for Nyx on Nukternios?" Her eyes were wide with excitement.

"That's a little *too* big, don't you think?" he countered. "It would draw too much attention to us."

"Not if we play our cards right." Scythe stood, hardly able to contain her excitement. "We invite all of the Incruentus Ferrum. Nyx would be the guest of honor, of course, the night is meant to celebrate her. We'd have to invite Maniodes and Phaos too. If they weren't included, they'd sense something was wrong. Even the sentries could come, just for the fun of it!"

It was drastic but could work.

"People throw festivals for Nukternios anyway. A ball wouldn't seem that out of place."

"Exactly, and as long as you, me, and Axe lay low, no one will notice anything strange about what we're actually doing. You trust Axe, right?"

That last thought broke her excitement. They hadn't addressed that yet.

The man seemed a little overeager about new discoveries, but he was smart about it. He did the research in his rooms alone. If Scythe or himself had found that old text, neither of them could have translated it. Dagger had seen the portrait of Axe's daughter as well. Axe wanted to live anyway he could for her.

"I trust him," Dagger said, "but the next time we want to recruit someone we *talk* first."

Scythe paused before stating, "Fair enough."

"Besides, I do have someone in mind who could help us spy on Maniodes," Dagger said.

"And who's that?" Scythe took her seat again.

"Pitch is Maniodes's right-hand man. He could inform us of his actions," he suggested.

"Pitch? He's twelve," she countered.

"Yes, but in Ferrum years he's at least another twenty on top of that."

"Dagger, I don't know."

"Just hear me out. Pitch actively helps Maniodes make his schedules. All Pitch would have to do is send us a message whenever he can. He's a mature kid; he can handle it."

"He's excitable, though. What if he can't keep his head down enough and tips Maniodes off?" Scythe asked.

"He understands the pressure of the situation. As soon as he heard Nyx and Maniodes talking, he ran to me for help. He's terrified of dying, just like us."

Scythe thought for a moment, wine in hand again. "The sentries can't get close enough to him," she said, weighing the options, "and it's too dangerous for Axe as it is."

"The sentries could still help," Dagger suggested. "We let them know Pitch is involved, and they'll keep an eye on him for us."

"Well, I don't see how either of us could get that close to Maniodes."

"We'll have to be clear to Pitch about the caution. As you said, the kid *is* excitable," he admitted.

"If he can stay calm, it would be perfect."

"So you agree that Pitch should be on board?" Dagger asked. "I see no reason to delay talking to him about it."

"Yes, but we'll have to explicitly emphasize the caution," she said. "You know, speaking of Pitch, he mentioned something weird before."

"Like what?" Dagger asked, confused.

"He wondered if I felt any different after killing that girl in the hovel, the way you changed at the Paavos's house," Scythe explained.

"I haven't changed," he defended.

"But you couldn't kill Basil, you had me do it."

He fell silent then. He still hadn't figured out why he couldn't kill Basil at the time. He just kept thinking of the man's family, and what the deaths were doing to Marella. Maybe he had changed, but he didn't like the idea. It felt like his edge was turning dull. At the same time, though, he just hadn't wanted to hurt that family anymore.

"Did Pitch mention anything else?" Dagger asked.

"No, he just kept picking at his fingernails." Scythe shrugged, sipping her wine.

"Wait, really?" he insisted.

Scythe eyed him. "He looked nervous. I thought it was because we haven't talked much."

"Pitch only does that when he's anxious about something," Dagger speculated, "and that's not often."

Scythe thought for a moment, then said, "You think Maniodes put him up to something?"

"No idea, and if it was a direct, but secret order, he won't tell us."

"Oh, come now, he would tell you," Scythe said.

"Not if it's from Maniodes," Dagger said.

After another pause Scythe lowered her goblet. "Do you think Maniodes has planned something else about us?"

"Maybe."

"Maybe we shouldn't recruit a twelve-year-old to denounce his god," Scythe speculated.

"No, Pitch will be fine. He'll be willing to help, I'm sure of it," Dagger said. "Even if he is hiding something, it can't be anything deadly against us. Maniodes wouldn't trust *anyone* with anything like that."

"If you're sure, he will be a good asset in our plans." Scythe gave in.

"So, it's decided. A conscious decision made by a couple together." Dagger raised his wine in a mock salute. "Much easier that way, isn't it?"

Scythe's just scoffed.

# Chapter 29

Dagger made his way back to Skiachora in the small hours of the night. Scythe had volunteered to stay and watch the sick woman. She didn't seem particularly happy about staying behind, but it was her idea. It probably had something to do with the bad joke about communication on the balcony. He had meant it as an honest jest, but it must have been too soon. He hoped she didn't think he was mocking her.

The guard at the ruined front door told him Maniodes was back, but that he had retired to his chambers. The last sentry to see Pitch reported the boy heading back to his own rooms. Dagger clapped the sentry on the shoulder, thanking him. The sentry stood a little taller at that and nodded.

They had been right about Pitch's whereabouts. The boy opened the door soon after Dagger knocked, scratching an eye.

"Hey, Dagger," he said in a voice thick with sleep, "whatcha doing?"

"I was wondering if we could talk about something, little man," Dagger replied. "Did I wake you?"

"Maniodes had me running messages back and forth from a sentry by one of the caves," Pitch shrugged.

He stepped aside to let Dagger in, closing the door behind him. Dagger had to smile at the room around him. No matter how long Pitch would be a Ferrum, he still died a child. There was an overturned box for him to step onto to reach the bed. The table had been shortened for him and was littered with detailed wooden soldiers. The pitchfork the boy had chosen leaned on the wall beside the bed.

"You keep this place fairly clean for a kid," Dagger joked, sitting on the bed. Even the chairs had been sized for Pitch's stature.

"I got tired of losing things," Pitch replied. "So, what do you want to talk about?"

Pitch sat at the toy-covered table, anxious. The look he gave reminded Dagger of a child not sure if he was going to be scolded. He didn't want to put Pitch in this situation, but they needed a person on the inside.

"I need to ask you something, little man, ask something *of you*, really," Dagger started.

"Like a favor?"

"Yes, like a favor." He couldn't help but keep his voice low. Just being in the castle again, knowing Maniodes was back, added the feeling of being watched.

"If you don't want to do it you don't have to," Dagger started. "It is dangerous."

Pitch sat patiently with his hands clasped between his knees.

"I need you to spy on Maniodes for Scythe and me," he said. "You don't really need to do anything special. When you can, send us a bat in secret with anything you think is peculiar. Better yet, send a sentry with a note; any one of them should be willing to help and can be trusted."

Pitch's eyes widened like a puppy's. "Ever since we heard Nyx and Maniodes talking, you've been planning something."

The awe in his voice was inspiring and heartbreaking.

"Can you keep this secret?" Dagger asked.

"Yes, yes. It's actually not as hard as I thought."

"Scythe and I are going to take over Skiachora," he admitted.

Pitch practically jumped out of his chair. "Like a king and queen?"

"Yes, but Pitch, listen—"

Before he could continue, Pitch hollered in joy and scrambled onto the bed beside Dagger. The kid threw his arms around Dagger in a powerful hug before pulling away. "I could be your squire!"

"Pitch, this is not a game," Dagger held him by the shoulders, making sure their eyes met. "If you get caught, we are all dead."

Pitch calmed considerably, but the excited light never left his eyes. "I understand."

"Do you?" Dagger was greatly regretting this idea.

"I've been good with the other secret," he pleaded.

"You have, but this is a little different."

"I'm not an idiot, I know that." Pitch shrugged off Dagger's hands. "All I would have to do is write a letter to you, right?"

"Yes, but if you act suspicious in any way, Maniodes will know something is wrong."

"I'll stay quiet. Most of the stuff he does is boring anyway," Pitch said.

"Alright," Dagger conceded, "but the moment you want to back out, I won't hold it against you."

"I won't back out or get scared," Pitch insisted.

"And you can stay calm around Maniodes?"

"Yes, I promise."

Dagger believed he would try his hardest. He might even find out there was nothing useful in Maniodes's schedule, but he still wanted to know what Maniodes was doing on certain days.

"There is one day I'd like you to focus on," Dagger said.

"What's that?"

"Try to find a clue about what he does on Fridays. Where does he go?"

"Oh, that's easy. He told me once that he wanders Ichorisis, testing mortals on hospitality and stuff," Pitch said.

"That may be true, but I'd like to be certain," Dagger insisted. "Maybe try to keep an eye out for a letter or something he says when he returns."

"Okay. This is exciting!" Pitch clapped his hands and bounced on the bed.

"It's not supposed to be exciting!"

Pitch flinched at his tone.

He hated scaring the poor kid, but it had to be done.

"This isn't a game," Dagger said slowly. "If he finds out you're spying for us, we're all dead."

The pressure sunk in then. Fear crept into Pitch's eyes, and he held his hands in his lap again, picking at a nail.

"I will protect you, Pitch," Dagger said, taking the boy's hands in his own. They were small and rough. Dagger had expected them to be soft, like a normal child's skin, but Pitch was being raised on a farm before he died. "The moment you feel something wrong, you tell me."

Pitch swallowed and nodded.

"I'll be careful," Pitch reassured him. "And Nyx said she'd protect me too."

Dagger was taken aback for a moment. They hadn't spoken of Nyx.

"Well, good." He didn't know what else to say in that regard. "Wait, she told you this specifically? That's great, but why."

Pitch's excitement faded to nervousness, suddenly. He looked down and started picking at his nails again. It was definitely the look of a boy who had said too much.

"Pitch," Dagger said gently. "Did Nyx ask something of you?"

The conversation he'd had with Scythe was still fresh in his mind. She had said Pitch was acting strange, and now he was trying to hide something.

Pitch looked up, then away again. Finally, he said, "I'm not supposed to say. I think telling you is a good idea though. That way you'll know what she wants you to learn. I don't see why things have to be so secret, anyway."

"Nyx has some plan, which needs to stay quiet, right?"

"She said Maniodes wouldn't like it. She said it would be stronger if you and Scythe learn about it yourselves. But, I don't see how you can learn anything if you don't know what it is," Pitch argued.

He wasn't picking at his nails anymore, and he met Dagger's eye then. The trust the boy showed was innocent and genuine.

"'Cause Nyx said—"

"Pitch, hold on."

Pitch stopped talking and just looked at him, confusion clear in his eyes.

"If Nyx asked something of you and wanted you to keep it secret, you should. I'd love to know what you and Nyx are doing, but we need to trust her. She wanted you to do something in secret, so you shouldn't betray that trust," Dagger said.

"We're betraying Maniodes," Pitch said as if Dagger had forgotten the simple fact.

"I know, but Nyx is different. Maniodes doesn't think much of us, except as his weapons. I thought we were the same to Nyx, but maybe we're not."

Pitch said Nyx told him to keep this secret between them. So Maniodes probably didn't even know what it was, and that meant he probably wouldn't approve. Pitch wanted to tell him, whatever it was, so maybe it wasn't too bad. Maybe Nyx was looking out for all of the Incruentus Ferrum in a way. Then what was the point of the order to disband them? Was that just a tactic she used on Maniodes to have him do her bidding while thinking it was his own idea?

The thoughts of who was playing against whom was too convoluted for him to think of right now. He was never one for politics anyway. He'd discuss it with Scythe later, and maybe they could come up with a decent theory together. One thing was certain: Nyx was planning something for him and Scythe. Something less certain, but fairly likely, was that Maniodes wasn't involved.

"I should head back," Dagger said, standing. "You just keep your head down, okay? Do whatever it is Nyx wants you to. She's a step above Maniodes, so we'll have to be careful around her."

"I will, Dagger," Pitch said, smiling then added, "You and Scythe just think of your previous jobs, okay?"

"Alright," he said, not understanding but trusting the little man.

# Chapter 30

Scythe left the servant's quarters, wiping blood off her hands. She had to check on the woman often, and this time there was blood on the stump. She still had a fever. Scythe cleaned the blood from around the stumps edges and tied a tourniquet above where Dagger had cut.

Scythe tucked the bloodstained cloth into a hidden pocket in her dress. She always made sure her dresses had pockets. She turned into a corridor that eventually led to the main entrance. The garden still needed some tidying, so she headed there, wishing she had gone with Dagger to talk to Pitch.

Nyx appeared in the corridor. Scythe nearly tripped on the hem of her dress at the sudden stop. Regaining her composure and trying to control the panic, Scythe knelt in front of the goddess.

"Don't worry about that," Nyx said before Scythe could give any greeting. "This is your home. Stand."

Scythe did and looked Nyx in the eye. It was unnerving, but she had to ask. "Am I going to die?" Ice filled her veins.

"No, I'm not here for your soul," Nyx reassured her. "I'm here on business."

Scythe's thoughts ran wild about the two guests trapped in her home. If the woman woke up and gave so much as a single wail, they would be found. Her blood was cold but Scythe kept her face calm.

"What business, Your Grace?" she asked.

"I was hoping to talk to you and Dagger. Where is he?" Nyx said instead of replying.

"He's in Skiachora at the moment."

"Is he? Why?"

"He's spending the day with Pitch. The boy looks up to him like a brother." Scythe hated herself for mentioning Pitch, but lies needed consistency and a small bit of truth if they were to be believed. She hoped Nyx wouldn't look into Dagger's whereabouts.

"I'm surprised by you Ferrum sometimes," Nyx admitted, seemingly distracted. "When Maniodes first made you, I didn't think you would have proper emotions, but you do. You're one of his first, yes?"

"I am, Your Grace."

"And Dagger is the youngest?"

"I think Axe is, actually."

Scythe had no idea where Nyx was going with this tangent. It made her more uneasy.

"You make a good pairing," Nyx admitted. "Violent, but you work together well."

The surprise struck sharply. "Thank you. Um, would you like to sit in the parlor? I could make tea or get wine if you like." Anything to get Nyx away from the now-armless woman tied to the bed. "We could wait for Dagger if need be."

She offered the hospitality, but her heart probably couldn't take the tension. This opportunity would be perfect, though. Show a little hospitality and offer some food, and the guest warms up to the host.

"I cannot stay, but thank you," Nyx said. "I came to give you a job. I'd like the both of you to hunt down a crime lord in Stymphalia."

"Why this crime lord in particular?" She bit her tongue at questioning the goddess.

Nyx didn't seem to mind.

"He's growing cocky, along with his subordinates. They need to be put in their places."

"He must be important if you came here yourself, Your Grace," Scythe said. "I mean no offense, but why didn't Maniodes give us this job?"

"Don't worry about that," Nyx explained. "If he causes a fuss about the two of you carrying out this job, you can tell him it was on my orders."

Scythe's initial thought was that Nyx was willing to back up her and Dagger. Why would the goddess want to destroy them in one moment, grant them a second chance, even coming to them directly as if on equal footing? The equal footing was an illusion, of course. Scythe couldn't oppose Nyx's order. Nyx could be setting them up. She and Dagger would kill this crime lord, and Nyx could abandon them to Maniodes's wrath. Nyx could be setting this up to eliminate all of the Incruentus Ferrum with one move. If that were the case, their game was over.

Scythe couldn't deny the order.

"I'm honored you would come to us, Your Grace." Scythe said, swallowing her pride and paranoia.

"Don't let it go to your head," Nyx said. "I had thought about contacting Cross because of her marksmanship."

Scythe knew of the archer. Her orange eyes were piercing but friendly. She was a friend of Dagger's as well; he spoke highly of her.

"Then why us?" Scythe asked.

"This job is a complex one. He is to be the only one assassinated, and an arrow can stray. It would be easier to do it up close, but getting close to him will not be easy."

"Where is this man in Stymphalia?" Scythe followed Nyx's logic but still believed this to be either a test or their doom.

"He runs a gambling den and a fighting ring called The Den. His name is Limaros; you'll recognize him by his dark-green hair and beard," Nyx explained. "It shouldn't take too long to get to Stymphalia, but I'd like this done in a fortnight."

Scythe curtsied. "It will be done."

Scythe paced around Dagger's room. It was almost morning, but he still hadn't returned from talking to Pitch. Images of him in those chains kept flashing through her thoughts.

Axe had sent a bat with a note saying he hadn't found much about sealing away a god's essence. What he did find was a lovely tidbit about an ancient city, dead more than a thousand years, which had once traded spices for opium. Axe reassured her in the note he was still looking and that she should burn the parchment.

Of course she would burn the bloody parchment, but not before she tore it in half with her fidgeting.

Nyx's sudden visit had terrified her. Scythe held her own in the conversation, so that was useful. She had to tell Dagger what happened, and he wasn't fucking here.

She couldn't wait in the bedchamber anymore. Axe's note was a crumpled mess in her hand as she made her way downstairs and outside to wait by the dead tree.

The black sky had started to turn indigo by the time the tree opened, and Dagger stepped through. He smiled when he saw her, his hands in his pockets casually. The smile dropped when he took in her expression.

"What happened?" he asked.

"Nyx stopped by and gave us a job." Her voice was sharp enough to cut.

"She came here herself?" he asked, stunned.

She explained what they talked about and the job. Once she got it all out of her system, her hands finally stopped tearing at Axe's note.

Dagger ran a hand through his hair. "She didn't notice the guests?"

"We were right next to the woman, and I had her bloodstained bandages in my pocket," Scythe exclaimed.

"Thank the gods. We could use this, though," Dagger nodded. "Thanking her before we kill this crime lord would look humble and grateful: definite points for us."

# Chapter 31

The journey to Stymphalia didn't take as long as Nyx had predicted. Scythe knew of a dead pine tree only about a mile from the city walls. They traveled light and planned to stay in the city's crypts during the day. Although Scythe wanted to rent a room in a proper inn, Dagger insisted on waiting until they had enough coin for it.

During the walk, after the pine tree closed, they discussed plans for the ball. Who would cook, where they would get the food, how much wine they'd need, how the invitations should be sent, and so on. Dagger was quite good at planning these events due to his previous life. He admitted he never overly enjoyed such events, too many people in one place, but he learned how they were planned.

Scythe was willing, even eager, to cook most of the food. There were only thirty Incruentus Ferrum in existence, and the three gods to cook for. They would have to think of something for the skeleton sentries, as they couldn't consume anything.

The biggest dilemma was music. Every good ball had musicians to fill the air. Scythe suggested hiring several people, but they would have to be human.

Almost none of the Ferrum were musically inclined that she knew of. Their skills were held elsewhere. Dagger wasn't opposed to the idea, but there was the matter of coin again. The sentries would terrify the human anyway.

Stymphalia rose around them on its three hills. The city's architecture was crisp and angled due to the many terraces the streets were built on. The economy ran smoothly through its business and people. It had its slums, just like any other city this large, but even they were patrolled well. The general population was perfectly safe from itself.

The sally port, a discrete gate set into the wall only large enough for a single person. It was lit from inside, the shadow of a single man clung to the wall from the lantern light. She had used this entrance many times before, making sure the guard was different each time. She'd have to get closer to see the soldier.

She and Dagger didn't approach the gate directly but stayed close to the wall's shadow. Closer up, Scythe saw the guard on duty was a young man. He stood vigilant at his post. His patchy dark-yellow beard probably matched the hair hidden beneath the helmet.

"We could jump him," Dagger suggested quietly behind her. "Get him close enough to the bars then throw his head against them. Steal the keys."

"I don't think we need to," Scythe said, putting a hand on Dagger's chest. "Wait here a moment."

She let the lantern light fall on her and waved shyly to catch the young man's attention. "Hello."

He blinked, surprised by her sudden appearance. "What are you doing here, miss?"

He stepped forward, willing to help, but kept out of arm's reach from the bars. Young, maybe new to the job, but not dumb.

"My friend and I left the city to enjoy some time in the forest," Scythe held the bars and leaned a hip on them casually. The young man's eyes wandered from her face to her waist. She let his imagination come up with its own ideas on what that time in the forest entailed. "We took longer than intended, and the gates were closed when we got back. Would you mind letting us in?"

"I—" He had to clear his throat before continuing. "I'm really not supposed to open this gate for anyone, miss."

"I understand, and I don't want you to get in trouble, but it's so cold tonight." She crossed her arms under her breasts. "You could search us for weapons, if you like. Though this dress isn't the best to hide anything in."

The black velvet was perfectly tailored to her form. It had a small hidden pocket that held her weapon shrunk down to the size of a fork. The pocket was hidden in such a way that if the young man did take the chance he still wouldn't find it.

The man took in a breath and kept his eyes straight.

"What were you and your friend doing in the forest?" he asked taking his job seriously. Scythe started to admire him a little for that. He wasn't jumping at her flirtations. Her plan was working, though.

"Well, we…" She looked away, pretending to be shy. "It was a little naughty. Please, don't tell my father."

"Do you live nearby?" he asked.

"Down a street just off Skell Square."

"By the eastern market place?"

"Yes, it's not far. You could escort us."

"I can't leave my post," the young man said, unable to hide the small disappointment. "Where is your friend?"

"He's here," Scythe took Dagger's arm and pulled him into the guard's view before he could protest. "I know he looks intimidating, but he's really a sweetheart. He loves crab cakes."

Dagger smiled awkwardly at the guard, trying to look innocent. Luckily, his cloak was closed, hiding his knife belt.

The young guard looked torn between two decisions. He looked Dagger up and down, then sighed, reaching for the key at his belt.

"Stay quiet about this and go straight home," he said opening the small gate. "If the captain finds out about this, he'd hang me."

"Thank you so much." Scythe pecked him on the cheek when he opened the door, lighting up his eyes again. "Don't worry; this will be our secret."

They left the young guard at his post seeming a bit dazed. Scythe hoped he wouldn't get in trouble with his captain. As long as he stayed quiet, he'd be fine.

"Just for the record, I don't like crab cakes," Dagger admitted once they were on the street, "and I don't like you flirting with other men."

"Relax. It was the easiest way to get in." She took Dagger's arm and walked along the cobblestones closer to him.

"My idea was just as easy; might have been quicker too," he argued.

"It didn't take that long," she countered. "Not everything needs to be done in violence."

"Says the woman who decorated a tree with a man's extremities."

"That was just for fun, but I can be discreet if need be. Now let's find The Den and Limaros."

"You've been to this city often enough. Do you remember where it is?' he asked.

"I do," she said. "This way."

She led him along several streets and up terraces, admiring the city. Half of the way up the eastern hill, tucked away was an establishment at least three stories high. Laughter and music filled the night air through the open windows. A beautifully carved sign above the door showed a bear coming out of a cave, but no name.

"Seems sophisticated for a gambling den with fighting pits," Dagger commented.

"Gambling isn't illegal here, like in some other city-states, but the pits are. So they're housed in the levels belowground," Scythe explained.

"How do you know that?" he asked, surprised.

Scythe shrugged. "I like dice games, so I've been here often enough. Maybe we could earn some money for the ball?"

"Might as well try; we do have a fortnight to find Limaros," Dagger said.

The realization of how long they actually had sunk in then. Scythe hadn't paid attention to that detail because excitement at the new job, combined with the panic of having Nyx in her home.

She stopped Dagger from entering The Den.

He turned back, confused and curious.

"Why would she give us a full two weeks?" she speculated out loud. "The most Maniodes has ever given me was five days. Most of the time there isn't a deadline anyway."

Dagger realized the oddity too, but he didn't look as confused.

"It could be to force us to take our time," he suggested. "They could be trying to teach us something again."

It made sense. The biggest thing Nyx had said before was to practice self-restraint. Maybe this was an opportunity to do just that. It could also be a ploy to destroy them, in which case there was nothing they could do.

"You're probably right," she said.

Dagger took her hand again. "Come on, let's go scout out the place."

The Den had a set of grand double doors opening to the first floor. It opened up to a large room with a long central hearth. To combat the smoke from the hearth, the wood had been cut away from the second and third floors. The hearth was banked with warm coals for the moment to keep the space warm while not risking too much exposed flames. The open space above helped with the fumes.

The first floor held tables for games of Chase Me and The Devil's Number. The second level held tables for dice games. The third seemed emptier, but colorful tapestries hung between the doors and columns.

The establishment was full of patrons laughing, drinking, shouting, and cursing. Scythe breathed in the scent of smoke, musk, ale, and too many unwashed bodies packed together. She loved it.

Dagger seemed to enjoy it too, though his eyes were still wide while drinking in the sight.

"I take it those stairs lead to the fighting pits?" Dagger indicated to the archway leading to the stairs. They were guarded by a tall brute with a dark-green beard that completely hid his neck.

Most of the patrons had similar Stymphalian dark-green-and-yellow hair. That wasn't the only shade in the establishment, of course. The Den received patronage from all over Ichorisis.

"We'll probably need a password or invitation to get in," Scythe said. "Last time it was a password, but it's been a couple of years. We could cause a distraction."

She broke off, giggling.

Dagger turned toward her, confusion knitting his brow. She wasn't entirely sane, but she rarely broke off into laughing fits.

"Sorry," she said, regaining her composure. "I just imagined one of the sentries walking headless through here, juggling a couple of skulls."

"Why would it be headless?" he asked, curious now. "Wouldn't it just fall over if it lost its head?"

Scythe shook her head. "They can remove any limb and be fine, even their heads. If one skeleton lost an arm, for some reason, it would be able to find it, no matter where it was. I don't know how they do that, but it's hilarious watching them hopping around on one leg. Though I suppose it would be harder if it lost its head, and the body had to wander around on its own. Juggling would be very hard as well."

"How do you know this?" he asked, astonished.

"I might have stolen a bone or two to see what they'd do," Scythe shrugged. "Come on, we should look around. Either one of us can cause a distraction if need be."

They walked through the crowds. The hearth's smoke and ale weren't the only thick scents in the air. Pockets of wildwood drifted just as lazily as the smoke did. Almost all of the patrons were men. Most of the women were either serving girls or prostitutes. Scythe was one of the few ladies in the establishment who was a guest.

"Why don't I get us some drinks?" Dagger suggested, having to lean closer to be heard.

"Alright, I'll meet you on the second floor by that table." Scythe pointed to a dice table above.

"I'd rather not lose you in this haze," he said, referring to the wildwood. No doubt he had noticed the lack of female patrons as well.

She found it rather endearing, even though there was no reason for him to be concerned.

"I can take care of myself, dear," she said. "See if the barkeep has anything fiery."

Scythe patted his arm, then wove through the bodies to the second floor. From the railing she could see Dagger at the bar, awaiting his turn. The barkeep was working hard and seemed to be peeved by it.

With her power of going unnoticed, Scythe sided up to a dice table to watch the game. She had a couple of coins she wanted to make grow. The thrill of the game rattled in her bones as the dice did in their cup. She watched a few rounds before jumping in.

From what Scythe could see, the dice weren't loaded. Paying attention to the dealer's hands proved he hadn't practiced any sleight-of-hand, either. She took a single silver coin from her pocket and flashed it into the dealer's eye letting the shadow trick slip away. The light caught his attention, and she joined the game. She let the other men at the table notice her as well.

Most of the men sneered at her. A woman was ruining their game. She smiled right back, perfectly kind. The man beside her, however, couldn't keep the sneer on his face. In fact, he could barely lift his eyes from her cleavage.

Dagger still hadn't returned from the bar. Scythe guessed he was chatting up the barkeep for info. She won the first round, calling four fives from the dice, tripling her winnings.

"What's your name, sweetheart?" the man beside her asked.

The man's brown hair was tied back in a bun at the base of his neck. Given the size of the bun the hair probably draped past his shoulders without it. The reek of ale wafted from his breath, but he didn't sway or slur. His eyes were still clear as well. A man who could hold his liquor.

"My name is my business," Scythe said, watching the dice roll. "I don't care about your business."

"That's alright," he said, slipping a hand over her knee. "Names aren't important."

She met his blue eyes with her red ones, not saying a word. She wanted to stab him either in those eyes or his groin; she hadn't decided. The groin would probably kill him. She breathed slowly, forcing herself not to make that decision. The breathing did seem to help with her temper. It wasn't completely dulled, but it was manageable.

The man faltered at her crimson gaze. Red eyes were rare, especially in Stymphalia. It didn't deter him, though. He took it as advancement and raised his hand higher.

"I already paid for a room upstairs," he said. "Care to join me?"

"Remove your hand before you lose it." Scythe kept her voice smooth, not wanting to cause a scene yet.

Another man cleared his throat behind them. Dagger stood there holding two copper goblets. The look in his black eyes matched Scythe's murderous impulses.

"Don't worry, you'll get your turn, mate." The man gave Scythe's thigh a squeeze and turned back to her.

"She's my wife." His voice was as black as his eyes.

Dagger handed Scythe one of the goblets, probably to free up a hand for a knife.

"Wait, what? What kind of a man brings his wife *here*?"

"A good man with a wife who has a taste for gambling. Now remove your hand before I remove the fingers for you," Scythe replied for Dagger.

The man took her threat more seriously with Dagger standing over him. He removed the hand and held it up for them to see.

Scythe gripped his first two fingers and bent them back. The crack of bone was hidden in the clatter of the dice; his scream wasn't.

"You fucking bitch!"

"I didn't remove them." Scythe kept hold of her drink and stood with Dagger. She took her winnings and left the man hollering while clutching his deformed hand to his chest. Everyone around him watched with a mix of curiosity and annoyance. Violence was common. Dagger and Scythe slipped through the crowd to a relatively quiet corner.

"I'd say that was extreme," Dagger said, "but I wanted to do worse."

"So did I," Scythe admitted. "Did you find out anything useful from the barkeep? You were there a while."

"He was dismissive, actually. Almost rude about it, but I think he was being overworked. He did say he'd never met Limaros himself, but that he often visits the levels below. He wouldn't say what was down there, of course."

Scythe took a swig from her goblet. This liquor painted fire down her throat. "We could just sneak in past the bodyguard."

"I'd thought that same thing, but he takes up almost the entire archway. One accidental brush against him, and we're caught," Dagger protested. "Is there a back entrance to the pits?"

"Most likely," Scythe speculated. "Probably several for a quick escape if need be, but I wouldn't know where to look."

Dagger swirled his drink thinking. His eyes wouldn't meet hers for the moment, and they looked troubled.

"What are you thinking?" she asked bluntly.

"Well, there may be another way to get information from the barkeep," he paused before continuing. "You could talk to him."

"You mean flirt with him?"

"It worked on the guard," Dagger shrugged innocently.

"You *just* said you don't want me doing that," her voice rose higher than needed, "and you wanted to kill the last man."

"He was touching you," Dagger defended, dropping the innocent act. "If the barkeep tried that I'll do more than break a few fingers. A man drops his guard around a beautiful woman. He talks to impress her, shares secrets or opens doors without really intending to."

Scythe sighed, knowing full well what he was talking about. She wasn't innocent in that tactic, but she never liked to do it. If it didn't lead to the victim bloody on the floor, it left her feeling dirty. She hadn't liked tricking the guard, but it was easy, and he was sweet. It would work on the barkeep too.

"Fine, but if he does try to touch anything, I'm breaking your fingers too."

"Now, that's a little extreme."

They made their way back to the first floor. The bar was a fine, dark wood polished by hands and cups. The barkeep was a thin man with a shaved head and bronzed skin. The stubble only told of a dark shade rather than a specific color. His eyebrows were constantly knit together as he focused on the orders being thrown at him.

Scythe took a seat at the last stool on the end. Dagger positioned himself close behind her, leaning on a column. She appreciated the feel of his presence.

She waited for there to be a lull in the orders. When the barkeep finally leaned on the back counter to mop sweat from his forehead, she took her chance.

"Excuse me?" Scythe leaned forward on the bar, catching his attention.

"What can I get you, miss?" He looked exhausted, but his voice hid it well.

She didn't know the name of the liquor that Dagger had gotten so she said. "Some fiery whiskey."

He just nodded and refilled her goblet from a short bottle with the image of a horse stamped into the glass. She tasted it, and the fire erupted as before.

"So, you been working here long?" she said, striking up a conversation.

"Yeah," he huffed, "couple of years."

More patrons came to the bar for more ale. Scythe let him refill their tankards.

"I was wondering if you could help me find someone?" she asked him when he was free again.

"Who's that?" He met her eye. They didn't stray either. She was leaning over the bar practically shoving her cleavage in his face, and he hadn't stolen a peek.

"The owner of the place, Limaros. He has green hair and beard but given how common that is here, that's probably not too helpful. Sorry."

The barkeep rolled his eyes, all sense of kindness vanished.

"You're the second person tonight looking for him. I'll tell you what I told him. I was hired through an agent of his and never met the man."

"You don't know what your own boss looks like?" Scythe tried to keep the rudeness out of her question, but it was ridiculous.

"It pays well, and I keep my head down. I think he has a wolf tattoo on his arm," he shrugged while helping another patron.

"You must know something." Scythe brushed a hand through her hair, showing off her collarbone. The man barely looked.

"Listen, sweetheart."

Why was everyone calling her *sweetheart* tonight?!

The barkeep gestured to her chest broadly. "I ain't interested, so buzz off."

Scythe pulled back, stunned. She picked up her drink and joined Dagger by the column.

He looked stunned too, but failed to hold in the laugh as she met him.

"You'd probably have a better time seducing him," Scythe said.

Dagger cracked up again. "I had no idea."

Scythe let him have his laugh. In all honesty, she was glad men like him were accepted in Stymphalia. If he were in Kaliasma or Potamis, he might have been prosecuted.

"What are you laughing at?" Scythe asked. "Aren't you from Kaliasma?"

"Yes, but I never cared about judging anyone for his sexual preferences. I mean, come on, I get off by cutting into people's organs," Dagger admitted.

"I do remember how you were holding me when I peeled the flesh from our guest's arm," Scythe commented.

The laughter faded, but the playful gleam and grin didn't. "And I remember the moments after. It was glorious at first."

Scythe chuckled into her goblet. When she was gaining information or access from a stranger, flirtation came easily. With Dagger it was different; it was genuine. It had been wonderful before her anxieties took over.

Dagger stepped closer behind her and wrapped his arms around her loosely. She leaned back into him. He bent to her ear and whispered. "We could use one of the rooms upstairs."

Scythe stiffened but threaded one hand through Dagger's on her stomach, the other still holding the whiskey. "I'm pretty sure they're meant for the prostitutes' uses only."

He shrugged. "We find an empty one and lock the door."

Scythe sipped the whiskey to buy time. "We should get back to business."

She heard him sigh. His hands let go of hers and both slid to her hips, holding her an inch away now.

Scythe quickly set down her whiskey and turned into his arms. She didn't like how guarded his eyes were.

She kissed him. It took a moment, but he relaxed and leaned into it.

"Let's spend the day here anyway," she suggested after pulling away. "We'll take our time scouting the place out, like Nyx wanted."

"In separate rooms?" he asked carefully.

"It would be easier to keep one room blocked off. It'll be like at the mausoleum," Scythe said.

Dagger nodded. "Seems fair."

# Chapter 32

Dagger opened the door to the landing on the third floor. It squeaked as he did, which he hadn't noticed last night. The squeak caught Scythe's attention. She stood at the banister watching the crowd and now turned to him. The noise had ruined his surprise of sneaking up on her, but he liked the imperfection of the squeaky door. This gambling den was so well taken care of he liked finding something wrong with it.

"Did you sleep well?" he asked, standing next to her.

"After eating that chicken we stole, very much so. This place was surprisingly silent during the day, actually," she replied.

"Most of the work takes place at night, obviously, especially for the whores."

Scythe gave him a curious side glance.

"Are you saying you didn't hear them all night while we were eating?" Dagger asked.

"Oh, I heard them; the one next to us sounded like a banshee." Scythe chuckled as she shook her head. "We should probably start searching around before the place picks up again. Look."

Scythe gestured over the banister.

Dagger followed her finger and saw that the archway to the mystery hall was unguarded. There was already a good number of patrons in The Den, but it wasn't a roaring crowd yet. The bartender was different as well.

"The lower levels probably aren't open yet," he speculated.

"Which means the perfect time to explore," Scythe said.

"It is the best opportunity we've had so far."

They left the third floor and approached the archway. No one noticed or stopped them. The arch led to a hallway, then down a spiral flight of stairs. The stairs ended at another set of double doors in a fair-sized, and well-lit, parlor. Dagger tugged on the handles, but they only rattled. He expected as much.

Scythe sighed, disheartened. "We'll have to wait for someone and slip in behind them."

"Not necessarily." Dagger picked a tool from his belt. It was more of a thin spike than a knife. One poke into the neck, and a victim would be drowning. The spike slid out smoothly without spraying too much blood. It wasn't his favorite, but it was useful.

"Keep an eye on the stairs," he said as he crouched by the lock.

Scythe took position by the stairs, listening. Dagger slid the thin knife into the lock and began to work. He listened for the slightest motion behind the door. It was silent, but he didn't trust it. The lock was more complex then he'd expected, and lock-picking had never been his best skill.

The silence on the other side of the door was starting to grate at him. The anticipation of expecting the door to open from the inside made the agitation worse.

The pick slipped but the lock didn't open. He was ready to kick it in at this point.

Dagger stood, pushing his hair back and trying to breathe out the frustration from his system.

"I could try," Scythe offered. Her voice was sweet. He tried not to let that grate at him too.

It was like the mechanism was mocking him. Dagger swore and stood ready to kick the door. He didn't care if it fell off the hinges; maybe that would draw out the owner of the place.

Scythe appeared by his side. She held a hand over his chest, and he lowered his foot back to the ground. He begrudgingly let her take the pick.

Scythe knelt by the lock and inserted the pick. Dagger crossed his arms, waiting and listening. He watched as Scythe's focused expression turned to frustration, then, to the surprise of them both, there was a small click and the lock finally gave.

Scythe stood and handed the pick back, smiling. She didn't say a word about her opening it instead of him. He tried not to let it irk him, but he couldn't help it.

Scythe opened the door slowly, making sure the other side was empty. The room opened up to a grand fighting ring. A huge pit stretching ten feet down to a sand floor took up most of the room. There was a railing along the edge so spectators couldn't fall in, but Dagger had no doubt several bodies got flung over that rail if someone was angry enough.

More columns and banisters of wood held up the wide ceiling. There were two other doors like theirs that led off, and two were in the pit itself. The gates in the pit were iron, and the opponents could see each other to plan what they could before facing off. It might be empty now, but the night was still young.

"We should wait here for the rest to arrive," Scythe suggested. "I'd rather not risk getting stuck outside again."

"Hopefully it doesn't take long," Dagger agreed.

They picked a corner close to the door they'd entered through and settled in to see what would happen.

The occasional shout from a lucky winner could be heard through the floorboards above them. The two of them chatted to pass the time, mostly about arrangements for the Nukternios ball.

After about an hour, dozens of people flooded in at once from all of the entryways. The men and a few women flowed around the ring, making bets and hoping for a bloody show. The boredom of waiting quickly slipped from Dagger's frame and the same could be seen in Scythe. Both had fallen quiet, but the excited gleam was there.

"Scythe," he said to catch her attention.

She had been scanning the crowd but turned to him.

"I have a plan. See the banisters on the ceiling? I could easily climb them. I'll be able to see the entire crowd from above."

"And be able to strike," she said, seeing his idea.

"Exactly. If you see anyone matching Limaros's description, signal me somehow. I'll do the same if I see him first. I'd still like to use his death as a sacrifice to Nyx, but if he's here we'll make do," he finished.

"Good idea. You climb on up. I'm going to get a closer spot by the ring," Scythe said.

"Don't jump in and join the fight," he jested.

"Come now; you know I won't," she said, practically reading his thoughts. "If anyone gets a little too handsy, he'll be going in."

Dagger laughed. "Just don't break the shadow trick, then."

"Relax, I won't," she said, swatting at his arm. "Go on and climb. Be the vulture studying his prey."

He stole a quick kiss, and she leaned into it. He left her there and approached the supporting column. It was sturdy, with a glowing lantern affixed to it.

Dagger knew Scythe was safe with the shadow trick. Part of him didn't want to leave her alone in this crowd, nonetheless, a large part of him, and he was glad it was there. She would be fine of course. She could probably slaughter this entire room, along with its toughest fighters.

The crowd was moving about like a tide. Talking to friends, yelling at rivals, and finding a clear spot by the railing. He had to wait for the people to disperse around him. Once there was an opening, he used the lamp to hoist himself up to the banister.

He noticed then that the ceiling was slightly bowl-shaped. The wood paneling was expertly done so the weight of the building above was transferred to the columns and the banisters he now clung to. The support system didn't let him get to the center of the ring, but he was just inside it above one gate.

He managed to get his feet under him and stay crouched on a beam. He waited calmly like the vulture in Scythe's mind.

He spotted her across the room. She weaved expertly between the men. Scythe paid closer attention to the green-haired men, though that was most of them. She kept glancing at their clothing and arms, looking for the wolf tattoo the barkeep mentioned.

The gate directly beneath Dagger opened. A man in a finely tailored red robe stepped onto the sand and raised his arms.

"Gentlemen!" he cried walking in a circle.

They fell silent, watching the announcer in the pit. The anticipation hung in the air like a stagnant fog.

Scythe paused and managed to get a spot against the rail to watch the show opener as well.

"Tonight, names do not matter. I know we all have our favorites. The Biter," he began to list.

The crowd roared at the name.

"The burned man: Jasus."

They roared again.

"Alexos the Quick."

An even louder roar.

"But tonight is a nameless local legend. I had heard that he died while floating in his mother's womb only days before his birth. When he was scraped out of her, he fought Nyx herself and lived. Many would call that a gift from the gods, but we know better, don't we," he sneered.

The crowd laughed along with the roar.

If that story had a drop of truth, his mother most likely died on the birthing bed. It left a bad taste in Dagger's mouth. Not that this nameless so-called legend killed his mother, no babe should be accused of that, but that he bragged about it. That mother probably died hoping her son would have a good life, and here he was beating people to death for money.

"And his opponent," the show opener raised a hand to the gate he'd come through. "Some fresh meat in our establishment, but he is by no means inexperienced. He grew up in his father's forge until he grew tired of the monotonous work. So naturally, he stole his father's finest weapons and left to survive in the wild. And survive he did. This man once throttled a bear in the dead of winter. He then tore open its flesh with his bare hands and slept inside its carcass. Now, I know men grow desperate in a blizzard, but that could not have smelled nice."

The crowd laughed. Even Scythe cracked a smile.

"Now, my friends." He walked slowly to see all of the faces. "Enough with introductions. Let's see some blood!"

The roar this time was the loudest yet, blowing away the fog of anticipation.

The red-robed show opener darted through the other gate as it opened. A tall man stepped through after him. This local legend had to stand at least seven feet tall. He could easily reach up to the ankle of a spectator and drag him screaming into the ring.

The dark-green hair and beard was thick and matted, hanging past his shoulders. Personally, Dagger would have preferred shorter hair for a fight like this. Long hair was too easy a target. He stood bare-chested, facing Dagger's way. His fists were held tightly at his sides.

The gate beneath Dagger opened again, and the opponent stepped through. The newcomer was shorter by a head but thicker. The forge he supposedly was raised on had toned his arms to almost ridiculous slabs of meat. His black hair curled close to his scalp. A better idea for this fight, but it could still be ripped out by a fistful grabbed properly.

Dagger saw Scythe react to something that caught her attention. As the two opponents sized each other up, Scythe worked her way around a person to get a better look at the local legend's side. She looked up to Dagger and noticed he was already watching her. She pointed to the man in the ring excitedly.

Dagger examined him again, but from this angle he couldn't see the man's side. There was a smudge on his left bicep that caught his attention. Dagger couldn't make out the entire shape but there was definitely a tattoo there.

Dagger caught Scythe's eye again. He pointed to the spot on his own arm and mouthed the word *wolf* to her.

She nodded.

The nameless fight made sense, then. Limaros kept his identity a secret so he could participate in the fights. If the opponent knew who he was fighting he might feel too threatened by a powerful man to fight properly. The opponent would just throw the match or be bribed to throw it.

The two didn't break into fists immediately. They circled each other, waiting for the other to make an opening.

As they changed positions, Dagger was able to see the tattoo properly. It was a simple black shape of a wolf in silhouette, howling upward. Dagger rolled his eyes. Of course, the man they needed was in the damn ring itself. He knew now what Nyx meant by this being a more complex job and having to get close to the victim.

Limaros threw the first punch at the wild man's jaw. The other man dodged the fist and rerouted his own attack at Limaros's gut. He blocked the arm and sidestepped away, almost dancing, and kicked at the wild man's back.

The wild man stumbled but caught himself. Limaros laughed then, and Dagger could see the fury growing in the opponent's eyes. Limaros was playing with him.

The opponent rushed Limaros, who didn't bother to block the attack. The man's fist connected with Limaros's jaw. His head snapped back, and spatters of blood rained onto the sand.

The crowd cheered with bloodlust.

Limaros spat blood and phlegm, still chuckling. The opponent threw another punch, but Limaros ducked, then charged and caught his opponent around the middle. He heaved the man up and threw him to the ground. After a hearty kick to the man's gut, he settled to beating the man's face inward. Blood painted Limaros's hands as well as his mouth.

It would have been over quickly if the man hadn't kneed Limaros in the groin. He then used the distraction to role Limaros off of him. His nose was broken, his lips were smashed, and his eye was quickly turning black. He'd taken a good beating, and he wasn't dazed one bit.

He rushed at Limaros, both on their feet again, and the blows continued. Fists flew, some connected, and Dagger watched as a tooth buried itself in the sand as if cowering from the brawl. He didn't know whose tooth it was.

Nyx had said they should get close to Limaros; this was as close as Dagger suspected he would get.

He picked a perfectly balanced knife from his belt.

"Nyx," he called, not bothering to raise his voice over the crowd's jeers. She would hear him. "I know you're here."

To his shock, she revealed herself. She stood in the pit. A seemingly innocent ten-year-old girl, waiting patiently for the grownups to finish their business.

He saw Scythe gasp and grip the railing tighter. She wasn't watching the fight anymore either.

Nyx watched Dagger in the banisters waiting for him to continue.

"I offer you this man's soul. Not for the joy of killing, but for the necessity of it. We would like to thank you for this personal opportunity. I would also like to give my deepest gratitude to you for sparing me when I took Marella's life. Limaros's death is now yours, Your Grace."

Limaros had his opponent trapped in a headlock. The man's face was turning from an angry red to a suffocating blue.

Dagger held his knife between two fingers and flicked his wrist. The knife left his hand and embedded itself in Limaros's neck.

Limaros coughed, and shock widened his eyes. He held his opponent for a good time as his own life leaked over his shoulder. The joyous roar turned to confusion and silence as they watched the wrong man's blood pour. None of them had seen the knife fly. The most anyone could have seen was a glint of silver.

Limaros's grip slipped, and the opponent was free. The man gasped for air and regained his feet. He spun to face Limaros but stopped at the sight of the steel in his neck.

Limaros choked and fell to his knees, clutching at the knife. He pulled it out but that just made the bleeding worse.

The opponent stood there, stunned, as Limaros died in front of him but not by his hand.

Nyx knelt beside Limaros in the bloody sand. The local fighting legend scrambled backward as he saw the real legend. She spoke to him gently and presented the bone she carried.

Limaros's wide eyes softened with acceptance. He reached out, touched the bone, and then fell limp in the sand. The blood sank into the sand before it could pool around him.

Nyx stood and looked to Scythe, then Dagger, acknowledging them both. She gave a single nod and vanished.

# Chapter 33

Scythe managed to sneak to a corner as the confusion escalated. Dagger stayed on the banister above, watching as the crowd was denied a proper kill. Accusations were thrown, more fists flew outside the ring, and Dagger had to laugh at the opponent.

The man Limaros had been fighting kept looking from his own hands to the knife to Limaros, as if trying to convince himself he didn't do it or figure out how he did. The dumbfounded wide eyes were hilarious.

The show opener came out again and tried to calm the place, but nothing worked. Eventually, the crowd dispersed, and Dagger climbed back down and met with Scythe.

The two of them left The Den in its confusion. With Scythe on his arm and a fresh kill under his belt, the night was glorious, but it was best to leave The Den as they had.

"We have to go back to Skiachora," Dagger said. "Report to Maniodes."

"I know, I just hope Nyx will be there to back us up," Scythe admitted.

"I think she will be. She almost looked proud when I thanked her."

They snuck through the city walls back to the sally port. The guard on duty wasn't the young man as before, but a man much less competent at his job. The guard was asleep in a chair and didn't stir as Scythe wove the keys off his belt. She tossed the keys back at the guard's feet when she relocked the door behind them.

Dagger opened the dead tree to Skiachora. He was beginning to feel Scythe's worry more as his own now. She had told him of her theory that Nyx was setting them up. He didn't want to believe it, but it was plausible. He had heard Nyx herself say that she wanted them all disbanded, but then she spared him. He couldn't read Nyx's motivations, and that frightened him. As they walked closer to Maniodes's castle, his anticipation rose.

Scythe's did as well; he could feel her hand tightening against his.

Maniodes wasn't in the throne room, but the sentry directed them to his office. Chip was stationed at his door and bowed to them as they approached.

"How are things here, Chip?" Scythe asked. "Is he in a good mood?"

Chip looked to the office door then shrugged, shaking his head a bit.

"He never is," she sighed.

"We'll be fine." Dagger squeezed her hand.

Chip opened the door and let them in. Maniodes sat at his desk scratching out a document, and Pitch was by the fireplace stoking the logs. Pitch paused long enough to wave, and Dagger waved back. He didn't want to draw attention to the boy in Maniodes's presence but everyone knew how close they were. A simple wave couldn't harm anything.

Maniodes set his quill down in surprise, looking up at them.

"I wasn't expecting either of you for a fortnight," he said.

The anxiety billowed out of Dagger. "Nyx told you of our job then?"

"She informed me shortly after talking to Scythe. Why are you here so early?"

"Limaros has been taken care of. We broke into his fighting ring and saw he was present in the fight itself," Dagger shrugged. "I took advantage of the situation."

"Did anyone see you?"

"No, my lord. I hung on the banister where no one couldn't reach me and threw a knife."

Maniodes nodded. "And you Scythe?"

"I scouted out the place and spotted Limaros."

"You stayed out of the way in the death then?" The surprise was obvious again.

"The room was too full from where I was to be subtle."

Dagger squeezed her hand. He hoped she took it as a warning. The sarcasm in her voice was far from subtle.

Maniodes let it pass.

"Good," he said. "Well, you might as well go on home. There might not be another job for a while."

Dagger and Scythe bowed and took their leave, casting one last wave at Pitch.

Moments later they were crossing through a courtyard, heading for the main entrance. Dagger was glad to be on his way home. He intended to write to Axe and Pitch, asking if they had found anything of use.

More than anything he wanted to cut into something. Limaros's death had been a chore with little pleasure in it.

# Chapter 34

Seven days later, summer ended, and the leaves had begun their beautiful decay. Scythe had managed to empty out their pitiful library, so rain couldn't damage what they could salvage.

The two of them joined Axe in the library in Skiachora when they could spare the time. The research of the types of wood to seal the god away made little progress.

The frustration at the stalemate irked Scythe. She could only hope Pitch would find something useful soon.

The rain turned into a storm at the end of the week, putting Dagger's plans on hold. He had wanted to gather food for the ball, but it would have to wait.

Scythe strode back to the parlor after checking on their guests. Dagger was working on his dining set to pass the time.

The woman's fever had finally broken, and she was able to keep food down. The man, on the other hand, refused to eat until he saw his wife. Scythe left him the soup, knowing he'd eat once his stomach protested enough.

The sound of the knocker on the main entrance stopped her. She had no idea who could be out in the storm. She approached the door with her weapon shortened but in hand.

Scythe opened the door an inch. Axe stood on the doorstep with his hood up against the rain.

"Axe, what are you doing out on a night like this?" she asked, surprised.

She held the door open wider for him to step through.

Axe lowered the hood and combed the rain from his hair.

"There's news on our project," he said.

"Is something wrong?" she gripped her weapon tighter.

The paranoia that Maniodes would find out always crawled just beneath her skin.

"I don't know," Axe admitted. The worry in his eyes matched her paranoia. "Pitch sent me this message for Dagger."

Axe removed a slightly damp parchment from his vest.

"He's in the dining room." Scythe tucked her weapon back into her belt and took the note from Axe. Dagger's name was scrawled on the front. The parchment was folded over with a spat of red wax holding it closed. "Pitch brought you this himself?"

The kid hardly had time to escape his chores.

"A sentry did," Axe explained.

Scythe cracked the wax and opened the note.

"Wait, shouldn't we find Dagger first?" Axe suggested.

"If it's about our project, then I'm involved," she argued.

There was nothing incriminating against her as she suspected. She skimmed the note over and beamed. She almost hollered in excitement.

"What is it?" Axe asked, curious.

"In a moment, let's find Dagger." Scythe hurried off toward another corridor.

Axe left his rain-soaked coat on a chair by the door and caught up to her. "Well, you read the information first when it was clearly meant for Dagger."

"It was meant for all of us," she argued, surprised by how peeved he sounded.

"Then what's in the note?" Axe demanded.

"I'd rather not repeat myself twice, so you and Dagger can see it at the same time. Relax, he's in here anyway," Scythe climbed a few decorative steps and entered the dining room.

It was a long, narrow room with high, broken windows facing the forest. Rain trickled inside, but the mountainside protected them from most of the downpour. A marble fireplace stood in the center of the back wall, surrounded by the windows. Dagger had managed to light a fire before the storm hit. A pile of wood was kept dry in a different corner.

The dining table was a new, solid piece of beautiful dark wood. It lay on its side while Dagger worked on it.

He had been replacing the legs of the table with human spines. He knelt by one end of it, now securing the last spine into the wood.

He hadn't noticed them enter at first. He glanced up as they got closer, grinning and not minding the interruption.

"Axe." Dagger stood, wiping his hands on a rag. "How are you? Have you found anything about sealing Maniodes?"

"I haven't yet, but I'm not convinced those resources have run dry," Axe replied. "Pitch had sent me a message and asked me to bring it to you."

"Is he okay?" Concern wiped away the pleasantries from his face.

"He's fine, for all I know. Scythe's read the note already and hasn't mentioned any harm to the boy."

"He is fine," she said, not appreciating how Axe pointed out that she'd read the note first. Dagger didn't seem to care anyway. She handed the parchment to Dagger but couldn't wait for him to finish reading.

"Maniodes has a lover!" she said excitedly.

"What?" Axe asked, dumbfounded.

"It's true," Dagger said, not looking away from the note. When he finished reading, he blinked in shock. "Pitch found a letter written by a woman that Maniodes left on his desk by mistake. There was no name for her, and she addresses him as Tyndareus. They're probably not using real names to keep her safe. This is fantastic!"

"Pitch also mentioned a thin box he keeps at his bedside," Scythe continued. "Pitch walked in on him one night looking at it, but he closed and locked it as soon as he noticed Pitch."

"What could be inside it?" Axe speculated. "More letters he's kept?"

"That, or a portrait maybe," Dagger offered. "We have to see what's inside that box."

"Could Pitch let us into his room?" Scythe asked.

"Maybe, there must be a secret entrance that he knows of. Scythe, this is it. We could use her." Dagger's excitement mirrored hers.

"You're not going to hurt her, are you?" Axe asked dubiously.

"It depends on the situation," Dagger said, his grin turning sly.

"I'd rather we didn't yet," Scythe admitted to Dagger. "She probably doesn't even know who *Tyndareus* is. So, I'd rather not terrify her yet."

Dagger thought it over and nodded. "We still need to find her."

He turned to Axe and clasped his shoulder. "I know you just got here, but we need to go."

"Now?" Axe questioned. "It's a bit rash. We should form some plan of attack first, or at least our next move."

"Research has been taking too long. We have a lead, so I'm going to take it. We've been sitting on this idea for weeks now, but the moment there's potential progress, you want to stall?"

Scythe couldn't agree more. The boredom had been itching at her for days.

"I'm not stalling, I'm just being practical." Axe argued. "We shouldn't jump on this out of impulse. We don't even know what this mystery woman looks like."

"The box Pitch found might have a clue."

Dagger dropped his hand from Axe's shoulder. Scythe could see the friendly tone leaking out of Dagger.

Axe saw it too. He was about to protest again but closed his mouth.

"Is there a problem?" Dagger asked. "If there's something on your mind, tell me. We may be leaders soon, but I'd rather listen to a proper advisor. I don't want to be a dictator and have people plotting behind my back, because that is exactly what's happening to Maniodes. I may be tired of waiting, but I will listen to your argument"

"I just think you are moving too fast," Axe admitted, having a hard time meeting Dagger's eye.

That wasn't all of it. He had sounded angry the moment Scythe opened the letter. She crossed her arms, and let him continue unhindered. She wanted to hear what he'd claim.

"You're jumping on the word of a young boy. I'm not disputing Pitch, but we should come up with a proper plan of action."

"What would you suggest then?" Dagger asked.

"The box is a great lead, but we shouldn't abandon the research and progress we've made in sealing him away," Axe said.

"The best progress we had was discovering Lumeon and his story. That was weeks ago. There's been nothing since," Scythe argued. She wanted to get to that box too, and was glad Dagger felt the same.

It could be that Axe didn't want to be outdone by Pitch, Scythe wondered.

"You can continue the research," Dagger said. "It has been a great help, and we may still need it. For now though, that path has grown cold. We know that Maniodes has a secret woman, and the box might have a clue that would lead us to her."

"As I said, I'm not disputing Pitch," Axe said.

"We even know *where* that box is," Dagger continued. "Whatever plan you want to come up with, it will end with us reaching that box."

"So why stall?" Scythe finished for Dagger.

Axe balked at the question.

"I'm only advising caution," he snapped.

"We're not running headlong at him with a battle cry," Dagger said, watching Axe's reaction. "We'll sneak our way in. He won't even know we were there. We'll have the sentries keep an eye on him for us. They will let us know when he's coming, and then we'll vanish. He won't suspect a thing."

"If you think that is best," Axe conceded begrudgingly, "but if you get caught, do not mention I was involved in any way."

"You have my word I will not," Dagger promised.

Dagger didn't sound angry but understanding. Scythe thought he'd make a good king.

Axe gave a curt nod and glanced at Scythe. He tried to hide the scowl but failed. He didn't bother to wait for any reply or similar promise from her.

"I'll see myself out then."

He turned back to the dining room archway.

"Axe!"

He paused at the step and turned back at Dagger's call.

Scythe was glad to see slight fear in his eyes.

"Do we have to worry about you going to Maniodes?" Dagger asked.

Axe balked again, but this time anger grew. "Of course not. That would condemn us all."

Axe turned on his heel and left them by the table of spines.

# Chapter 35

The cracks on the upper level of the castle weren't as prominent as those below. Here, they were as thin as spider's silk, stretching across the stone walls, starting in the corners. Scythe had never been able to figure out why the castle didn't crumble. It had stayed constant and frozen during her century.

Pitch and Chip climbed the stairs ahead of them, with Pitch leading the way. Chip had been more than willing to leave his post in the empty garden to help them. He carried a roll of parchment and charcoal in a pouch and used that to tell them Maniodes was in the library again with Phaos.

Not only was there one god to keep away from, but there were two.

"I've never been in this tower before," Scythe admitted to the others, "not this high anyway."

"I thought you would have explored the entire thing?" Dagger asked.

"This section was forbidden," she said.

"Never stopped you before," he said with a half-grin.

"Well, since it leads to the god's bedchamber, I left well enough alone."

They climbed to the top, to Maniodes's private quarters. By the time they reached the landing, Pitch was practically dancing on his toes.

"Come on, let's go!" The key ring jingled in his hand. He sounded like a giddy kid at the beach.

Scythe held back her annoyance. He was just a kid stuck with a boring job, and she couldn't blame him for being excited. She just wished he would take it more seriously.

"Relax, we're coming." Dagger ruffled Pitch's hair when he caught up.

Pitch jogged ahead again to the only doors on the landing. The double doors were tall to accommodate the god's preferred height, with thick hinges running over the wood.

Scythe knew the room was empty, and they had the sentries watching Maniodes, but her dead heart was nervous. She kept her fists clenched to control her nerves.

Dagger took a breath beside her, probably to control his own anxiety. Pitch, however, could barely stop hopping.

Scythe turned to Chip. "You'll let us know the moment he moves?"

Chip nodded and crossed his arms.

"Alright," Dagger said to Pitch. "Open the door."

Pitch plucked the correct key instantly. It was a bulky piece of iron almost as long as his hand. He inserted it into the lock at the center of the doors above his head and twisted.

Scythe had expected more resistance, a spell of some kind, but the door opened without a sound. The four of them entered Maniodes's bedchamber unhindered.

Most of the furniture was framed with iron and padded with dark-blue fabrics. The windows circled the room, looking out onto the planes of Skiachora. Scythe approached one window. It looked like a shifting grey mist wove its way over the dead fields. The shades themselves were too small to be seen properly. The river Acheron in the center provided the only light with its sickly green glow. Scythe hadn't seen the land of the dead from this height before and was taken by its beauty.

The closing door caught her attention again. Pitch locked the doors, and Chip stood in front of them with his arms crossed. Dagger was walking around the set of chairs by the fireplace. Annoyance was written all over his expression.

Scythe left the window and touched his arm.

"What's wrong?"

The strong annoyance faded when he looked at her, but something still irked him.

"This furniture is huge," he admitted. "It just makes you feel small."

Scythe hadn't noticed at first; she was used to the stature Maniodes preferred and expected the furniture to match. Dagger was right though; the scale of the chairs alone made her feel as if she were trapped in a doll's house. Like they were toys meant for Maniodes's pleasure.

"Just imagine it decorated in your bone-oriented style," Scythe suggested.

He took the idea and looked around again with a small grin, no doubt visualizing what it might look like later.

Dagger turned toward the tall bed and leaned closer to Scythe.

"We should save the bed for last, though."

Gooseflesh rose up her spine when he talked deeply like that. She stayed quiet, hoping he'd continue. He did.

"We could break it in a few times."

"Dagger, hush. There are children present," she jested.

His hand slipped around her waist.

"He probably doesn't know what we're talking about." He kissed below her ear.

"There *are* children present, and I know what you're talking about." Pitch popped into view.

Dagger straightened like a boy caught with his hands in the cookie jar, but didn't remove his hand from Scythe's waist.

"So, stop it," Pitch said.

"Sorry, kid," Dagger said. "So, where's that box?"

Pitch led them to the bedside table.

The bed alone reached up to Scythe's chest and was positioned on a dais, just like his throne below. Pitch probably needed a small ladder to climb it.

Pitch paid the bed no mind, no doubt used to it towering over him. "It's here."

He picked up a thin ebony box. It was probably an inch deep and a foot in length and width. He handed it to Dagger.

Dagger examined it, turning it over in his hands. Scythe couldn't hear anything shifting or rattling inside. There were no markings on the outside to give any indication of its contents. He shook it harder but still nothing.

Scythe held out her hand for it, and Dagger handed it over.

"You are better at picking locks," Dagger admitted.

Scythe took the box and set it back on the end table. She backed it against the wall to anchor it and took out some pins from her pocket.

The lock itself was tiny despite Maniodes's love for stature. Scythe slid the pins inside and started feeling for the tumblers. She had to be careful not to break it.

Her heart was in her throat, which tried to make her hands tremble, but she wouldn't let them. She kept her breath calm to control her hands, but her toes kept curling against her will. Given her hatred for shoes, everyone saw her tension.

Scythe felt the tumblers catch. Keeping steady, she started to turn them.

"Shit," she hissed as the pins slipped. She began again.

"Scythe," Dagger said quietly.

"Shut up."

She heard Chip's bones clicking as he moved.

"We need to go," he insisted. "He's coming."

"What?"

She kept her hands in place but turned back to the others. Chip held a parchment with the words *he's coming* written on it.

"What happened to the fucking meeting?" she hissed.

"Sometimes they don't last that long," Pitch shrugged, defensive.

Scythe turned the pins again.

"Scythe," she heard Dagger closer now.

"I've got it!"

The lock clicked open. She shoved the pins back in her pocket, but not before scratching the surface in her haste.

Scythe threw the lid of the box back as Dagger stood at her side.

The portrait was immaculate and expensive. It showed a woman with wide, dark eyes and blond hair falling past her shoulders. Streaks of lavender accented the natural blond, giving her an almost mythic quality. Her back was straight and proper but instead of a fancy dress she wore brown riding clothes.

"Maniodes's love," Dagger said to himself.

Chip's white hand snapped the box shut. He pointed to the door in urgency. The library wasn't far from this tower. If they went back the way they came, they would be seen.

"Pitch, do you know another way out?" she asked. Castles always had secret exits.

Pitch was gripping Dagger's arm with wide eyes.

"Behind the bookcase," he said.

"Find it," Dagger said to him.

Pitch left Dagger's side, and they all followed the boy to a tall ebony bookshelf. Tapestries hung on either side. Pitch shoved one aside and ducked behind it. He pressed an unmarked stone and a tall passage opened for them. Scythe ducked in behind Pitch, followed by Dagger and Chip. Chip had to crouch in order to fit, his bones continuing to click as he moved.

Pitch touched another stone and the passage closed. Before it could seal shut, Scythe heard the chamber's main doors open and close again. Maniodes was in his bedroom.

Scythe felt something tug her sleeve. Her weapon was at the ready, though she didn't remember drawing it.

Pitched looked up to her and mouthed, "He may hear us."

Dagger caught Pitch's warning too. He touched Chip's arm to get his attention. The tiny grind of Chip's neck set Scythe's teeth on edge.

Dagger held out his hands and mouthed, "Don't move," to Chip. If Chip moved too much, Maniodes might find them.

Scythe felt Pitch begin to shake beside her. She put an arm around him and held him closer.

She heard one of the chairs creak as Maniodes sat, but she didn't know in which chair. There were a few by the fireplace, but there was a thick one beside the bookcase they hid behind.

As the moments crawled by she tried to think of a plan where they could all leave. She saw Chip raise a hand slowly, but it clicked anyway. He touched Dagger, then pointed to the three of them, then down the passage.

Appalled at leaving his friend, Dagger shook his head and hissed. "No."

Chip pointed down the passage again, and his bones rattled a bit.

Scythe touched Dagger then. When he looked at her, she saw his torn concern and fear. She quickly looked to Pitch, then Dagger again. Dagger caught the hint and saw Pitch clutching at her skirts. He swallowed, then turned back to Chip.

Chip bowed his head, calm as ever, letting them go.

Dagger gripped Chip's arm again and nodded in thanks. Given that Chip didn't have any meat, Dagger's hand completely enveloped Chip's bone. Scythe said her thanks in the same silent way.

Dagger helped Pitch let go of Scythe's skirt and took his hand. The three of them hurried as silently as they could down the passage to a tight spiral staircase leading down. Scythe cast a glance back to Chip.

He risked raising a hand, causing his bones to click.

# Chapter 36

"Pitch, look at me," Dagger said gently.

They were back home in the parlor. Dagger knelt in front of Pitch, who sat on the couch. Scythe sat next to Pitch with her arm over the boy's shoulders. She could feel his trembling.

Pitch looked up from his clenched hands to Dagger.

"Are you going to be alright?" Dagger asked. "That was closer than it should have been."

"He's not going to catch us, is he?" Pitch asked.

"He won't. We left nothing behind. He won't know we were there," Dagger reassured him.

The tremble slowed but didn't stop.

"You won't hurt him, will you?" Pitch asked. "Or the girl in the picture?"

Dagger broke eye contact for a moment, then replied, "Not if we don't have to, especially with the girl. She's innocent in all this."

Pitch nodded and looked down again.

"Hey." Dagger took his hands. "Will you be okay facing him tomorrow? Or at the Nukternios ball? I need to know you can act normal around him."

"I can," Pitch said. "I've hid little things from him before."

"This isn't little."

"I know. I've just never hid anything him before. I never realized I'm actually *betraying* him."

"I shouldn't have asked this of you, Pitch," Dagger said.

"I wanted to help, though," he insisted. "I want to be your steward, not Maniodes's."

Scythe couldn't help but admire the boy's loyalty to Dagger. For Pitch, this wasn't about taking down a god but helping his older brother. She knew Dagger saw the same thing.

"But Nyx will be mad at me," Pitch said, his voice wavering.

"She'll be mad at all of us, little man," Dagger tried to reassure him.

"But she asked me to convince Maniodes to give you guys certain jobs. I'm pretty sure she doesn't want me to betray him altogether!"

"Do you want out of the mutiny? We'll take all of the heat if he ever finds out we were in there," Dagger insisted. "I won't let him hurt you, Pitch."

"I know, and no I don't want out. Nyx said she'd protect me too, if he ever got mad. Let's not tell Nyx I was in on this though, okay?"

"I promise. Nyx will never know you were involved."

Pitch nodded slowly, growing more content.

"Do you want to spend the night here?" Scythe asked Pitch, rubbing his arm. He was a brave kid, but a scared kid nonetheless.

"Yes, if it's okay," Pitch said.

"It's okay," Dagger said. "You can use one of the rooms upstairs."

"It's almost dawn anyway," Scythe said. "Sleep will do you some good."

She hugged Pitch and he smiled. The trembling stopped.

"I can't let him get caught." Dagger paced around his room as Scythe closed the door.

"He won't be," Scythe tried to reassure him.

"How do you know that?" Seeing Pitch scared set him on the edge of his own dagger. Pitch trusted him, and he had taken advantage of it for his own goals. He didn't want to snap at Scythe, but the anxiety was vibrating in his veins.

"We didn't leave any evidence." Scythe stopped his pacing and held his shoulders, forcing him to look at her. "Maniodes won't know we were there. We left the box in the same position, and I didn't break the lock."

Dagger hadn't thought of that. If she'd broken it, that would have been significant evidence. His heart leapt to his throat again at the thought.

"There's no way he could know, so Pitch is safe," she said.

"What about Chip?" Dagger snapped. "We left him there."

"He'll think of something. He'll probably stay still until Maniodes falls asleep. Then he won't be heard going down the tunnel."

"How do you know?"

"I don't, obviously," she threw up her hands with a shrug, "but we have to work with what we have, and you're kind of overreacting."

The frustration boiled over to anger.

"We were almost caught, Scythe! If we'd left when I said, it wouldn't have been that close, but you had to keep fiddling with the lock."

"Well, I'm sorry I wasn't fast enough." Her voice dripped with mockery, "but I got the lock open, and now we have a proper lead."

"We didn't have to risk it that much, though. Axe was right; we should have waited for a proper moment. Maniodes leaves the castle on a weekly basis. We should have waited until then."

"There's no point on dwelling on 'what-ifs.' Nothing bad happened," she said.

"This time," he said. "We may not be so lucky next time. Luck is always bound to run out."

"But it didn't, and Pitch is fine," she said.

"That's not the point, Scythe. I know Pitch is fine, and he got spooked. That makes sense. I put him in a position that could get him killed. That didn't happen this time, but if this coup doesn't succeed, then he'll be killed along with us. He's caught between two gods and us. He's pretending to be on Maniodes's side, while doing some kind of bidding for Nyx, while also taking down the god with us! I'm not surprised the kid is terrified, juggling all of that."

Dagger had to pause after saying most of that in one breath.

"I know you didn't want to put him in danger," Scythe agreed. The relief that she understood soothed his nerves, but not completely.

Scythe took his hand again and squeezed it. "You want to wake the guests downstairs and play with them a little?"

The laughter surprised him; it felt good. "Not now. I think sleep will do us all some good."

"Really?" Scythe asked, surprised. "Usually cutting into something cheers you up. Oh well, it has been a long day."

She kissed his cheek. "I'm off then, too. I'll see you tomorrow night."

Dagger just smiled and watched her make for the door. The grin faltered, though, at the thought of what he'd just declined. Cutting into people did calm him down. Their screams were like music most of the time. He had even bonded with Scythe over that kind of slaughter. Why had he declined her invitation?

He wasn't in the mood. It was a small thing, and it had been a long night, but this had never happened before.

He recalled Basil Paavo's house then, and Marella. Ever since their deaths, things had been different. He couldn't even kill Basil; he had wanted to, but couldn't.

"Scythe, wait," he called, turning to her.

She was about to close the door behind her but stopped, looking back at him. One brow was arched, silently asking what he wanted.

"I think there's something wrong with us," he said.

"What?" she asked, looking dumbfounded.

"I mean all of us. All of the Incruentus Ferrum." Dagger buried his hand in his hair, trying to think of the words. "Something makes us more violent."

"What are you talking about?" Scythe asked, stepping closer.

"Before you died, you told me your life was hard," Dagger said. "Your family struggled for coin, and your father was abusive, but as for violence that was about it, right? I mean you never sought out people to hurt."

"The streets were never easy. You had to be violent just to stay alive, especially as a woman growing up." Her voice was growing harder and defensive.

"But you never murdered anyone for fun, right?"

"Well, no."

"And I didn't, either," Dagger continued, the dots quickly connecting in his mind. "I was just a normal man in Kaliasma, studying history. I never wanted to rip into people's organs or stick knives in their throats."

"What are you getting at, Dagger?" Scythe asked, growing frustrated.

"We weren't violent before. I think Maniodes does something to us when he picks us. I don't know why or have proof of anything. Think of Axe too," he insisted. "You said you talked when you met, and he admitted that after the job with the little girl, he didn't want to kill anymore. It was that way for me in the Paavos's house."

Scythe's eyes lit up then in understanding.

"Pitch said something about bloodlust after my job with the woman in the hovel," she said. "He asked how I was *feeling* after killing her."

"Did you feel anything different?" he asked.

"Well...no, not after, but the woman was basically me when I was alive. Or at least who I might have ended up as." Scythe crossed her arms, and she looked away.

The initial enthusiasm he felt at the possible discovery faded. Scythe was looking very uncomfortable.

"I think," Dagger said lightly, "that job was meant to make you aware of the new violence, or bloodlust, or whatever we call it. That woman was you, and I was related to the Paavo family in a way. Not literally, of course, but I was part of a family affected by needless murder."

He stepped back and sat heavily on the end of the bed. He couldn't help but wonder if his father had been murdered by a Ferrum. There was no way of knowing unless he asked Maniodes, and he didn't entirely want to know the answer. If it was the case, then Maniodes was manipulating his subjects well before they died.

Scythe's bare foot appeared in his line of vision. He had just been staring at the floor as he thought. Looking up, he saw her hard red eyes had softened a small bit. She sat next to him on the bed.

"I think you're right," she said, "but only that he added something. He mistreats us and orders us around like the sentries, but I still chose this path. I decided to kill my parents; he didn't force me to. He didn't even mention them. I wanted them dead."

"And I wanted to burn that village with you," Dagger said, "but I don't think we would have if we weren't Ferrum."

"We'd be dead if we weren't. We wouldn't have even known each other. You were born decades after me. I hate Maniodes, but I'm not blaming him for how I am. I wouldn't be who I am without him."

"It sounds like you're defending him," Dagger said, surprised.

"I—" She sighed. "I'm not, but I made the choices that led me here, not Maniodes manipulating me from the shadows."

"Maybe you're right in that case," Dagger said, "but he still did something to us afterward. I'd like to know what."

"So would I," Scythe admitted, "but it won't change who I am."

"I don't want you to change."

Moving slowly, Dagger placed his hand over Scythe's. She looked down at their hands. He thought she would pull away, but she didn't. It almost looked like she was mourning something.

She did look up at him, but she only said, "Goodnight, Dagger."

He didn't move his hand as he replied in a dry voice. "Goodnight."

She stood and left the room.

# Chapter 37

Nukternios was in three days, and all invitations had been sent long ago. Anticipation ran through Scythe like liquid fire at the thought of it, as she went to check the captive woman's wounds. She'd been to several balls her undead lifetime but had never hosted one before. She had even discovered a solution to the music, and was excited for everyone to arrive and see it. All of the food was gathered and stored, along with the wine. All they had to do was finish the decorations, and the cemetery nearby provided plenty of material for that.

All of the Incruentus Ferrum sent back letters of thanks, stating they would be glad to attend. Even Maniodes and Nyx sent messages announcing they would be attending.

The last letter to arrive was from Phaos. It came tied to the talon of a majestic brown hawk while they were preparing decorations and discussing food ideas. It thanked them for the invitation, and Phaos said he was actually glad Nyx could have a proper celebration. He declined the invitation, though, because he always went to the citywide party in Stymphalia with his children. The letter ended with Phaos wishing them well and the hope that he hadn't insulted them.

Scythe wrote back a quick reply saying they weren't insulted and understood perfectly. Stymphalia was one of the first civilizations Phaos's precious humans had created, so it held a soft spot for him.

Truth be told, Dagger wondered aloud if it was because Phaos never seemed to approve of the Incruentus Ferrum. Their job was to mistreat his humans, even though it had been his brother's idea. At least this way, they only had to hide their secret motive from two gods rather than three.

They had sent Pitch back to Skiachora yesterday, and the kid reassured Dagger he would be fine. He put on a brave face, and Scythe trusted him to get along normally. He had been working with Maniodes for decades, after all. More than anything, she appreciated him for trying to use that experience to relieve Dagger.

They hadn't heard from Chip. Dagger didn't want to send a message back to Pitch either. If Maniodes knew they were asking about a seemingly random sentry, he might suspect something. If he had Chip, he would know they were all involved.

"Are you letting us go?" the woman broke Scythe out of her worried thoughts of Chip bringing her back to the servants room turned prison cell.

The woman's fever had broken, and the stump of her arm had scabbed over nicely. Scythe still kept her tied to the bed as she changed the bandages.

"No," Scythe replied.

There had been a few rare occasions when she'd had a conversation with a victim. Most of the time they just screamed, cursed, or cried. Scythe would laugh, relishing in their torment. Once they started talking rationally, that sapped some of the fun out of it.

"Is my husband dead?" she asked, sounding tired.

"He's in the cellar, alive."

"Thank the gods," she sighed.

"Don't." Scythe stopped with a bandage in hand and stared at the woman. "They're the ones who send us after you."

The woman flinched but couldn't cower properly. Fear was back but to Scythe's surprise, the woman asked softly, "What are you?"

"You and your husband might be alive now, but my husband and I are not."

Scythe finished up and left the woman there. She hated when her victims became rational people.

She meant to find Dagger to discuss what their next move should be. They knew what Maniodes's lover looked like. Now they just had to find her.

She crossed the archway from the corridor to the main entrance, planning to head upstairs. Lately, Dagger had been working on his bedchamber.

Scythe didn't have to go that far. Dagger was in the main entrance, beaming at an unexpected guest. Chip stood next to him with a parchment.

"Chip!" Scythe hurried over to join them, interrupting their conversation. "How did you escape?"

"He waited until Maniodes fell asleep, then crept down the passage," Dagger replied for him.

Chip nodded and indicated to the parchment he held. It said basically the same thing.

"Do you think he suspected anything?" Dagger asked Chip.

Chip shook his head.

"Good," Dagger breathed.

"See? Everything was fine," Scythe said.

"This time," he replied. He turned back to Chip. "So why come here? Is something wrong?"

Chip laid the parchment on a side table and wrote.

"I wanted to let you know I was okay. Also wondering what we should do next?"

Charcoal stained his pale finger bones after writing.

"We need to find the woman. That's what's next," Scythe said.

"Yes, and tomorrow is when Maniodes is leaving Skiachora again," Dagger said, thinking. "We'll have to follow him. There's no other way of seeing where he goes."

Scythe was all for risk and excitement, but given the recent scare, it sounded too rushed. Chip's charcoal-stained bones caught her eye again. The idea that struck then was perfect.

"Wait, what if we don't have to follow him personally?" Scythe asked.

"What do you mean? How can we not follow him?"

"Chip can stash a tiny bone in Maniodes's clothes, then track it."

Dagger's eyes lit up. "That's perfect. Chip, would you mind if we borrowed one?" He blinked then continued with, "I just realized how bizarre it is to ask you for a body part."

Chip opened his jaw as if to laugh. He even leaned his head back a bit for the imitation. Scythe wondered who Chip was in his lifetime. He was certainly a loyal friend in death.

Chip plucked off the tip of his pinky finger and handed it to Dagger. He turned back to his parchment and wrote. "Hide it carefully. He may be able to trace it back to me."

"Chip, if this puts you in danger, we can find a different way," Scythe said, concerned.

"We could follow him ourselves," Dagger suggested. "My friend, Cross, is an amazing tracker. She could help us in this."

Dagger tried to hand the piece back, but Chip closed Dagger's hand around it. Chip then made a staying motion indicating that he could keep it.

"You're sure?" Dagger pressed.

Chip wrote again then showed them.

"It's the best way of finding him when he opens a passage out of Skiachora."

"He has a point," Scythe said. "The stairways to the surface can open anywhere. We just need to think of a place."

Dagger sighed but held the bone closer.

Chip nodded in consent again.

Dagger strode through Maniodes's castle. He and Chip used the dead tree to go back to Skiachora. Now he held Chip's finger bone safely inside his cloak pocket.

Chip had to leave to fulfill his post when they reached the dead lands. He informed Dagger that Shorty had seen Pitch in Maniodes's office, writing a letter that Maniodes was dictating.

Dagger went up to the office but didn't enter. He heard Maniodes talking on the other side of the door. Shorty stood guard and nodded in acknowledgment.

Dagger tucked himself into the servant's corridor to wait for Pitch. It was perfect to see anyone leaving the office without being seen. He pulled a knife from his belt and settled in for the wait, twirling the blade through his fingers.

After an hour, the office door opened. Maniodes left the room and strode down the stairs, trailing Shorty behind him. Pitch was nowhere to be seen.

Dagger stowed the knife away and crept from the servant's passage. A hand stayed close to the knives, and he watched the stairs. He tried the door, which only rattled in its hinges. He cursed silently, not wanting to wait for Pitch to emerge, if he was even still inside.

He thought of Scythe and what she would do. She'd try to pick the lock and sneak inside, but he'd left the picks at home.

He gave a silent prayer to Nyx for her son not to come back and knocked. There was silence at first, followed by footsteps growing closer. Dagger stepped into the shadows as the door opened.

Pitch stood on the threshold, confused, allowing Dagger a sigh of relief.

"Pitch," he said, leaving the shadow.

"Hey, Dagger." Pitch beamed at the surprise.

"Hey, I've got another mission for you," he said, keeping his voice low.

"What?" The fear of almost being found out had completely left Pitch.

Dagger took Chip's bone from his pocket and handed it to the boy. "Hide this in Maniodes's pocket or boot. Somewhere he can't find it."

"Is it a bone?" Pitch asked confused. "What would this do?"

"It's part of Chip's finger. He'll be able to track it where ever Maniodes goes."

"That's perfect," Pitch said, excited again. "I know just where to put it too. He always has me polish his travel boots the night before he leaves."

"That's good, but make sure it's nowhere he can feel. If he thinks there's a rock in his boot, he'll find it."

"There are some straps on the outside," Pitch explained.

"Okay, good. I'm counting on you, little man." Dagger flashed a grin. "I have to go. I can't let him see me here. It may raise questions."

"Right, right. Bye, Dagger."

Pitch closed the door as Dagger descended the stairs again. His nerves jumped at every corner. He kept expecting Maniodes to appear with a knowing look. He had to get back home and wait for Chip to report back.

Having Pitch plant the bone left a bitter taste in his mouth. If all of this played out and he and Scythe became the leaders, he'd never put Pitch in this position again. He would never be involved in anything dangerous for Dagger's sake again.

He had to relax. All this time spent on the coup and festival planning was getting to him. He strode back into their estate to look for Scythe. He hoped she was up for some fun with their guests. The armless woman was healthy again; they could poke into her more. He wasn't overly fond of the idea at the moment given the bloodlust realization, but Scythe would enjoy it.

The first room he checked was the parlor. Scythe was inside, but all hope of relaxation disappeared. Nyx sat on the couch next to Scythe. His hand twitched to his belt. Not that a knife would do him any good against death herself.

"Dagger, good." Nyx stood as he entered.

He saw Scythe sigh in relief as Nyx turned her back to her. He had no idea how long Scythe had been forced to stall Nyx.

Dagger gained his composure and knelt to one knee. "Did you need me, Your Grace?"

"Yes," Nyx said. "I need your help. You may stand."

He did. "Help with what?"

"Your mother is dying, but she refuses to let go of life until she sees her son again."

Ice locked in his chest. Scythe's eyes widened at the news and turned to Dagger, concerned. Apparently, Nyx hadn't told her.

He couldn't breathe. After a moment, he found he could force himself, but it didn't do any good. He knew his mother would die, sooner rather than later in her condition. He remembered she would go days without eating, convinced someone had poisoned her food.

A pressure filled his hand. He flinched away from it, looking up from the floor, knife in hand now. Scythe stood next to him. Concern and kindness filled her eyes. She didn't even glance at the knife he had drawn. He put the knife back and put a hand around her waist.

Scythe stayed quiet. Nothing she could have said would have helped anyway, but he was glad she was there.

It took a while longer to regain his composure, but when he did he asked Nyx, "What can I do?"

"Just come with me to give her peace," Nyx said.

"But we're not allowed to let the living see us, let alone see our families," he said.

Dagger wasn't sure why he was protesting. It felt like he was stalling, but he didn't want to prolong the situation. Several thoughts kept buzzing in his head, and he couldn't grasp any of them.

"I know the rules," Nyx said softly. "If I wait long enough, eventually your mother will join me, with or without seeing you. She's in pain however, and this will help her let go."

"I'll do it. I'll come," he said before he could stall again. "Can Scythe come as well?"

"Yes," Nyx allowed. "I'll strengthen the spell that keeps Ferrum hidden to the living. Scythe, I would stay out of her line of sight. It might raise questions and needlessly frighten her."

"What if I broke the shadow trick for his sister though?" Scythe asked surprisingly meek for the moment. "What if she's there?"

"When did that happen?" Nyx demanded.

"In Kaliasma at the wedding," Dagger defended. "She was there, but I stayed hidden from her. I had asked the same from Scythe but… well…"

"Curiosity got the better of me," Scythe shrugged, "after Dagger asked me to leave her alone."

Nyx went to speak, confused, then sighed. "Stay behind me when we're there. I'll have to strengthen the spell more for you"

"I'll stay in the shadows," Scythe promised.

Nyx approached them. It felt like his feet were glued to the floor. Nyx held a small hand out to them.

Dagger kept hold of Scythe and reached for Nyx's with his free hand. The warmth of Nyx's hand surprised him. He had expected it to be cold, but the goddess of death was a warm.

The color from the parlor drained away suddenly. Fear seized him, but he could still see Scythe and Nyx in the blackness around them. Scythe appeared just as frightened but held steady.

The color came back just as quickly as it had gone. They stood in his mother's bedchamber. Nothing had changed since his death. The curtains were still a vibrant yellow, and the furniture was perfectly clean.

He noticed one change. The pale-yellow rug at the foot of the bed was gone. He felt the ghost of the knife his mother had buried in his chest. He had fallen on that rug. He remembered the softness of it while he watched his own blood spread. The servants probably couldn't get the stains out.

Two other figures were in the room. His sister, Karteria, sat on the bed in a simple black gown. His mother, Tryphania, lay on the bed, sleeping.

Her room hadn't changed in the ten years since his death, but she had. Her condition had sapped all her strength, leaving her thin and pale. She was in her fifties, but she looked well into her seventies.

Nyx let go of his hand and gestured to the bed. She stood aside and waited then, letting them take their time.

Dagger turned to Scythe. She squeezed his hand and smiled. The smile didn't touch her eyes, though. She looked uncomfortable.

"Dagger," Nyx's voice was soft. Their quiet moment was over.

Dagger let go of Scythe's waist. It felt like wading through mud, but he approached his mother's side and sat next to her. His sister sat on the other side and didn't take notice.

Karteria had to be thirty now. Hair just as dark as his was, tied back in a bun. Her eyes watched her mother's hand in her own as she stroked it. She looked so tired.

Dagger wanted to give some indication that he was here. To prove she wasn't alone, but Nyx stood too close, and he had promised not to.

He forced himself to swallow against the dry throat. Taking his mother's other hand, he waited for her to react.

Tryphania moaned and opened her eyes. She looked straight at him and smiled. Her dark hair was thin, and her skin was pale, though her eyes were sunken.

"There's my little man," she sighed. "Though I should probably stop calling you that."

"Hey, Ma, I really don't mind that nickname."

In truth, he had hated it in his younger years, but that didn't matter now.

"Ma?" His sister spoke up. She even sounded tired.

"Your brother came home, sweetie. I hope you made those fine cherry tarts for us."

"I do miss those," he admitted.

His sister wasn't the best at cooking, but she was great at baking sweets. The cherry tarts had been his favorite.

His sister couldn't hear him. She even glanced over his side of the bed but didn't see him. Normally, the spell would have been broken then, but whatever Nyx had done kept him hidden.

Right now, he was just another one of his mother's hallucinations that his sister couldn't see. His heart seized at the thought, choking him again.

"How have your studies been going?" his mother asked him.

He had no idea what his sister had been telling her to explain his absence. His mother refused to believe he was dead, so his sister probably had to make up stories about the life he'd never have.

"They're fine," he said, keeping it vague. "A little tough sometimes, but worth it."

"That's good, dear. The best experiences are the hard ones," she smiled lovingly at him.

"Ma?" his sister whispered.

Mother looked to her, still smiling. "Keep an eye on your brother now. You know how rowdy he gets sometimes."

She was lucid. She wasn't completely sane, but she knew what was happening to her.

"I will, Ma," His sister was crying now.

Dagger wanted to console her but stayed frozen.

"And protect your sister," his mother said to him. "Watch over each other."

"We will, Mother," Dagger said.

His mother's eyes wandered for a moment. Eventually, they focused on a point off the bed beside him.

"Who's—?" she couldn't finish the question.

Nyx stood beside him, waiting patiently with her bone.

"She's a friend, Mother, you can trust her," Dagger explained.

"Hello," Nyx said softly.

Tryphania didn't respond. He wondered if she was so drained she couldn't express herself anymore.

Nyx held the bone close to the hand Dagger held so she wouldn't have to reach far.

Dagger let her frail fingers slip from his. She gripped the bone, still smiling. He watched as her dazed gaze faded into a distance he couldn't see.

Karteria started to cry harder. She didn't shudder with heavy sobs, but quiet tears fell as she held her mother's hand.

Dagger's eyes burned. No tears fell, but they burned. He reached over and touched Karteria's shoulder heedless of Nyx beside him.

The spell broke. Karteria jumped at the sudden contact and stared at him. Confused fear quickly rose.

"It's okay," he said removing his hand and hoping she wouldn't scream. "Don't panic."

"What? How?" Her eyes darted from him to their mother. "How are you here?"

"I can't say. I can't stay, either. I'm sorry."

Hope replaced the fear, regardless of what he had said. This was a bad idea. He had to leave her alone as well as confused. He wanted to comfort her, but this would just confuse her more.

"I'm sorry," he said again, breathless.

"Don't apologize. This is amazing," she said. "Can anyone else see you?"

"No."

The light in Karteria's eyes changed at some realization. She looked to her mother then back to him.

"Are you really here?" she asked, on the verge of tears again.

"Yes. You're not hallucinating."

"Dagger."

He looked to Nyx. She was furious.

"I have to go," Dagger told Karteria

"No, wait," she pleaded. She couldn't see Nyx.

"I'll take care of Ma," he promised.

He stood and took Scythe's hand, hoping Karteria couldn't see her. Without warning Nyx gripped his wrist and the color faded again.

The parlor of their estate reappeared around them seconds later. Nyx stepped away from them and crossed her arms. The silence demanded to be filled.

Dagger quickly knelt before the goddess, keeping his head low.

"I'm not sorry," he admitted. His throat was still very dry.

Nyx's eyebrows rose at the confession.

"She was scared and alone," he said nervous but firm.

He could feel Scythe's tension beside him.

"I gave you a second chance at Marella's death, and I let you join me for a moment to help your mother," Nyx said. "Then you disobey the order to stay hidden right in front of me."

Dagger said nothing.

"Can Karteria be trusted?" Nyx asked.

Dagger looked up, shocked that Nyx knew her name. He didn't think it had been spoken when he was there. Nyx probably knew the names of every living person, now that he thought about it.

"I trust her with my life, including this dead one. Given our mother's condition, she might still think I was a hallucination anyway."

Nyx stayed quiet, thinking.

"May I ask you something, Your Grace?" He had to tread lightly.

Nyx eyed him, then said, "Yes."

"Why bring me along?" he asked. "You said yourself she would have joined you either way in the end."

"She would have. I felt the pain she was hiding from you. Normally, when they ask to see a dead loved one, I can't do anything about it. This time I could."

"Thank you, then," Dagger said, still on his knees. "Thank you for letting me say good-bye to them."

Nyx sighed, letting her arms fall. She swung her bone like a baton, watching Dagger. He kept his eyes glued to Nyx's feet.

"I will let this pass."

Dagger was able to breathe again.

"Partially because you invited me to the festival."

Her honesty caught him off guard. It sounded so human.

Nyx saw his surprise and actually looked away shyly. "The mortals invented this festival in my honor. Providing sacrifices and praising my name all throughout Ichorisis. Phaos and Maniodes have joined the festivities now and then, but I've never been specifically invited to one. Call it a petty reason, but—" she shrugged.

"It's not petty," Dagger reassured her. "People like to be thought of personally. I don't imagine you get out for many social occasions."

"No, I don't," she admitted. "You can stand, Dagger. I don't like making people feel like supplicants."

He stood, letting his admiration for the goddess grow. She was nothing like her son.

"Then I look forward to the festival," he said. "Where we can be equals, even if it's just for one night."

Dawn almost crested over the forest hills. Nyx had left them hours ago. Dagger hadn't spoken much since then. Scythe left him alone to mourn. Unease and awkwardness still holding her back. She was glad Nyx had let her join them for Dagger's sake, but she didn't know how to react properly.

Her own mother had never showed her that kind of love. She'd never had little pet names.

She saw Dagger's pain in his eyes, but she couldn't sympathize with it. When Nyx had left, neither of them had known what to do next. She asked if he wanted to talk. It felt right, though she didn't know what kind of condolences he needed. He had declined, saying he just needed to be alone for a while. So she let him go.

Scythe spent the rest of the night in the garden. She kept an eye on the dead tree, hoping Chip would appear with a report. When the sky began to lighten, she gave up waiting for Chip and went to check on Dagger.

He stood on the private balcony in his room, hands propped on the rail, shoulders hunched together. Scythe paused by the bed, picking at a fingernail and watching him. He had said he wanted to be alone, but that was some time ago. She didn't know if she should leave him be or approach him. If he still wanted to be alone, she didn't want to interrupt, but she didn't want to seem insensitive and just go to bed without saying something to him.

She sighed at her own frustration and opened the balcony door. Dagger didn't look up.

Scythe stopped next to him. He knew she was there, though he didn't react. He kept staring at the trees below them. Interrupting might have been the wrong choice. Still, she followed through because of her own worry for him.

"You want to get some sleep?" she asked.

She hated the awkwardness, but wanted to help.

He looked to her then and gave a tiny half-smile. It died quickly, hardly more than a twitch in his lips.

"In a moment," he said softly.

He wasn't angry at her interrupting. She was glad for that, but he still needed time.

"Alright." Scythe squeezed his shoulder and left him be.

Scythe changed into a nightgown and crawled into her own bed. She hoped he would be alright come the next dusk. Her ears were tuned to any small noise. She probably wasn't going to get much sleep today. She kept hearing Dagger's mother call him "little man." The realization that Dagger called Pitch that nickname didn't escape her.

Her door creaked open. Light poured in for a second, but Dagger shut it out. She felt the bed shift as he sat down. She stayed quiet, not sure what to do. He'd never come to her chamber before.

"Scythe?" His voice was so quiet she could have imagined it. "Are you awake?"

"Yes." She twisted her back to half-turn toward him.

After a long pause he asked, "Can I sleep here?"

"Of course."

She shifted closer to him while he lay down, still fully dressed. His arm snaked across her waist and he held her back to his front. He buried his face in her hair at the crook of her neck. Scythe took his hand in front of her now and curled her fingers through his. She held it closer to her face, cuddling with it.

Dagger let out a long sigh and relaxed into her.

# Chapter 38

The parlor was immaculate. Garlands of dried red-and-orange leaves flowed from every corner. Tucked neatly into the leaves was the occasional human heart. The silver chandelier in the center was finely polished, and the candlelight danced off it like dew on a spider web. Human intestines of the recently deceased sprouted from the chandelier and hung like ribbons down the walls. All of the furniture was stitched with skin and bones. The centerpieces, similar to the garlands, were set on every table in the main hall and corridors leading to the balcony and dining room.

Scythe was beautiful as ever in a close-fitting black silk dress that billowed slightly from her waist. Silver thread depicted a spider web starting at her left shoulder and spread down her form. Dagger was a little uncomfortable in the outfit she'd made him, but it fit perfectly. The black doublet embroidered with silver fit the occasion comfortably enough, but he was paranoid about spilling anything on it. She even fashioned a small bone from a cat into a brooch for him.

The other Ferrum did what they could by means of formal clothing. Axe and Lace were dressed flawlessly, but Maime probably had a harder time finding a clean tunic without a stain on it. He had managed though, just like the rest of them. Maime stood off to the side, mostly with Hammer. The men must have been blacksmiths in life because their arms were muscled like slabs of meat. Rather than choose a weapon, Maime preferred to tear his victims apart. Hammer looked similar to Maime, but he chose to fight with a giant war hammer. Dagger wasn't sure if they could have been related. Maniodes had never picked a pair like that before, but they had similar features.

They arrived in groups of two or three. Scythe greeted them in the main hall and directed them to the parlor, where Dagger waited. They were all impressed that Dagger and Scythe had put everything together by themselves, especially the decor. Dagger admitted the sentries had helped.

"I had no idea they were sentient," Lace whispered to Dagger, watching the skeletons play their instruments.

Scythe had come up with the idea of the sentries performing. Hiring a regular bard would have terrified the living person. What better way to include the voiceless sentries than to let them play. A surprising number of them volunteered too. They no doubt wanted to break away from their monotonous guard duty. They even incorporated the rattling of their bones into the music to provide a fascinating, chilly effect.

Dagger and Scythe had arranged the parlor furniture to have space in the center for dancing, and a section for the skeletons to compose. They were good too; Dagger loved their calming music of drums and string instruments that filled the air.

"How did you find out?" Lace asked. Her blond hair was braised and tied back. Tiny black gems glittered through the strands.

"They reacted when I talked to them while I was being held in the chains," Dagger explained. "And you don't have to whisper. They're not angry that we didn't know. I think they're just happy to be included now."

"They're fascinating," she said. She left Dagger to watch them play more closely. Strips of black lace hung from her wrists and swirled around as she walked. Dagger had thought choosing lace was an odd weapon, but she must like the challenge of strangling her victims with it.

He saw Axe enter but stop in the archway. Axe examined the chandelier and the intestines with wide eyes. This time he carried his namesake. It wasn't uncommon for the Ferrum to carry their weapons, of course. Scythe had hers incorporated into her dress; Dagger had his signature knife hanging at his belt. Dagger had never seen Axe's. When they had been in his chambers, it had been hidden somewhere.

Now the double-headed war axe hung on his back. Dagger was surprised by how massive and barbaric it appeared on kind, sophisticated Axe in his navy blue formal attire.

Dagger approached Axe, being sure to catch his line of sight.

"Glad you made it," Dagger greeted.

Axe held his tongue for a moment, unsure how to reply, it seemed. He looked up again and said. "Interesting design choice. I knew entrails were long, but I didn't know they could stretch that far."

"We had to stitch some together," Dagger said.

"I thought you two couldn't kill needlessly anymore. How did you get the materials?"

"There's a graveyard nearby. We just dug up the freshly dead to get the materials. But don't worry; we didn't kill anyone for the décor." Dagger patted Axe's shoulder. "Help yourself to some food. There's wine in the punch bowl."

Axe nodded but didn't meet Dagger's eye.

"Beauty in the grotesque," Axe muttered as a quiet compliment.

Axe left to join Lace by the sentries. The room was full of people now. Even Pitch was included in the adults' conversations.

Dagger went to Scythe, slipping a hand to the small of her back.

"Was Axe the last to arrive?" he asked.

"Yes, that's all of the Ferrum," she said. "Nyx and Maniodes aren't here yet." She looked worried.

"I don't know about Maniodes, but I hope Nyx comes," Dagger said.

"What if he doesn't? What if neither of them do?" Scythe asked.

A knock at the door interrupted Scythe before he could reply.

Dagger stayed close as Scythe opened the door.

Nyx stood on the threshold. Her childlike form was clothed in a regal purple gown with a corset of black ribbons. Having only seen her in a black robe, Dagger didn't know she owned anything different.

Scythe noticed the dress too. "You look ravishing, Your Grace."

"Thank you." Nyx's hands were clasped in front of her, looking rather nervous.

Dagger wondered where she stored the thigh bone she usually carried.

"Come in, come in," Scythe said excitedly.

They stepped aside, letting Nyx in. She may have looked uncomfortable in the dress, but she moved fluidly in it.

"It feels strange to actually use a door," Nyx admitted, then cleared her throat. "I thought just appearing would be rude."

"We wouldn't have begrudged you that. It's what you're used to," Dagger said. "I hope you can have fun tonight."

"I'm sure I will," Nyx smiled. It was sweet and innocent.

The three of them entered the parlor together. The conversation died immediately as everyone saw Nyx. They turned to their goddess and knelt, including the sentries who had stopped playing for a moment. Dagger and Scythe knelt beside Nyx as well.

"Rise, everyone, please," Nyx said hurriedly. "Let's celebrate the festival as equals tonight."

Everyone stood, but unease still flowed through the air.

"Shorty!" Dagger called. "Play something fun."

Shorty sat among the other musicians lounging on a couch of bone and human leather. Yellow ribbons were tied to her arms. She plucked her fingers through the lute in her lap and started a festive tune. The other skeletons quickly joined in.

The unease dispersed. Nyx even appeared to relax as the conversations started up again around them.

"I'll get us some drinks," Dagger said to Scythe and Nyx.

"Your Grace, may I ask you something?" Scythe asked as Dagger left for the punch bowl.

"Yes, and don't worry about that 'grace' business. You can use my name," Nyx said.

Scythe had never addressed the goddess by her name before, at least to her face. It felt odd, but Scythe was glad she had been given that honor.

"Nyx, I'm just curious about where you're storing the bone in your dress. I've never seen you without it."

"It's here," Nyx plucked it from a hidden pocket in the sleeve. It was the size of a small animal's bone. "It has the same power as your weapon."

Scythe hadn't known other weapons like hers. Maniodes granted the weapon with that power as a reward after fifty years of service. Other Ferrum who had worked that long usually got a similar reward, though most only last a couple of decades. She wondered if her scythe's power was inspired by Nyx's bone.

Dagger reappeared, balancing three goblets in his fingers. He handed one to Scythe and Nyx, keeping the last for himself.

"Maniodes hasn't come yet?" Nyx asked him after tasting it.

"Not yet," Dagger replied rather stiffly.

Scythe wanted to elbow him into being more discreet.

"Let's not worry too much about him tonight," Scythe suggested. "If he doesn't come, there's really no harm done."

Nyx nodded, though she looked perturbed.

"Let's have fun tonight either way," Dagger encouraged.

The night felt different after Dagger said those words. For years, Scythe had attended events like this, but she had never truly been a part of it. She was always the hunter stalking its prey in the crowd. That hunting did provide its own thrill that this festival lacked, but here was a different kind of enjoyment. Scythe could mingle with friends and join conversations she actually cared about. She was surprised by how much she was actually enjoying herself. True, the ball was to strengthen Nyx's opinion of them, but she was actually able to enjoy the night as a regular partygoer.

Later in the night the musicians played a slower ballad. Scythe stood by the fireplace with Lace and Cross. The others cleared the center of the floor, waiting for the hosts to start the waltz. Her heart seized then.

She knew about the custom, she had seen it many times, and she knew how to dance. In her early years as a Ferrum she had been clumsy, but she learned quickly. She had only ever used it as a tool, though, just like flirting with her victims.

Scythe might fit perfectly into the regal life, regardless of her upbringing in the slums, but she had never started a dance before.

Dagger caught her eye when the music slowed. He excused himself from a conversation with Axe, Maime, and another Ferrum, names Hatchet. He strode over to her.

He bowed and extended a hand to her. "My lady?"

Scythe forced herself to calm down. She wasn't used to being the center of attention, so she focused on Dagger's warm black eyes.

Setting her goblet on the mantel, she curtsied to him as deeply as the dress would allow.

"My lord," she said, taking his hand.

His warm eyes lit on fire. He led the way to the center of the floor. Dagger slipped a hand to the small of her back, while Scythe laid hers on his shoulder. Their other hands clasped together, extended. Focusing on Dagger helped calm her as they started to slide with the ballad.

Others joined them after they completed the first turn around the floor. Axe danced with Cross, who wore a beaded green gown to match her hair. Hatchet joined with one of the newest Ferrum. Lace joined the dance as well, but by herself. Lace weaved through the other dancers, gracefully enjoying the music.

Dagger pulled Scythe in closer, breaking the rule of a few inches between partners. Their bodies met.

Scythe let it happen, and she wrapped her entire arm around his neck. It brought his lips closer to hers, as well as his body. She stole a quick kiss before the ballad ended.

The musicians changed the feeling in the air from slow and romantic to quick and festive again. Mostly, everyone stayed on the floor as the steps became livelier. Dagger and Scythe left it and stood by the fireplace again.

Dagger wouldn't let go of Scythe's waist. She didn't want him to anyway.

Two loud knocks cut off the music. Everyone froze and glanced toward the main hall, where the noise had come from. The final guest had arrived.

Dagger glanced at Scythe, a knowing look in his eye. Scythe let the mischievous smile spread, hoping it looked like normal excitement.

The two of them left the parlor after Dagger asked Shorty to begin the song again. She did, but the feel wasn't right anymore.

Scythe let Dagger open the main doors. Maniodes stood on the step at the modest height of six and a half feet tall. His dark-blue hair was combed and tied behind his neck in a small tail. The navy frock suited him.

"My lord, so good of you to finally make it," Dagger said.

Dagger sounded pleasant enough, but he didn't kneel. Scythe followed his lead.

"Come in," Scythe said, sounding equally kind. "The waltz was already done, but you didn't miss much."

Maniodes stepped inside, then said, "Quite a home you've managed here."

"Thank you," Dagger said.

His gaze paused on Scythe for a moment too long. He had taken note that she hadn't addressed him as her lord yet.

Scythe kept her grin in place.

"The parlor then?" Maniodes said.

"Yes, come," was all she said.

Scythe took Dagger's arm and led both of them back into the parlor.

The Ferrum had fallen silent as Maniodes approached, but the music kept going. Nobody knelt to him the way they did to Nyx. The conversations slowly rose again as Nyx strode over to join them, breaking the tension.

"You're late," Nyx said matter-of-factly.

"I was finishing up some business. Besides, at least I came, unlike Phaos," Maniodes countered.

"You know he always goes to the festival in Stymphalia. That one is special to him," Nyx countered. "No matter. Come see how much food they've prepared. It tastes amazing."

Nyx took Maniodes's hand and led him off to the finger-food table.

Scythe let go of the breath she hadn't known she was holding. The mood had returned to normal somewhat, and Nyx was actually having fun.

As the night continued, Scythe kept an eye on the gods. The Ferrum relaxed somewhat and tried to include Maniodes into the festivities. It was rather awkward, but at the moment he was talking pleasantly enough to Cross, Hatchet, Chip, and Pitch.

When Maniodes first joined the party, he had been confused about why the sentries were there. Scythe listened as Nyx, thankfully, explained they were alive. Scythe knew Maniodes wouldn't have taken the knowledge of his negligence lightly from the Incruentus Ferrum. He didn't protest their presence once Nyx had talked to him. If anything, he looked guilty when talking to Chip and the other skeletons now and then. Apparently, Scythe learned later, he had known they were conscious individual beings, but the fact had slipped his mind after so long.

The skeletons were having a great time. Dagger had provided stacks of small parchment with quills on each table for them to write. They couldn't eat or drink anything, so Scythe had invested in hundreds of different-colored ribbons. The skeletons picked their favorites and tied them to their bones. A couple of them had even woven the longer strips through their ribcages.

As the music slowed again, Dagger and Scythe didn't have to start the waltz, but they joined anyway.

Maniodes even asked Nyx to dance. Scythe thought the sight would be bizarre, a nearly seven-foot-tall man swirling around with what looked like a ten-year-old girl. Nyx surprised them all. She agreed to the dance with her son, but they didn't join immediately. Nyx took a moment to change her form. Her childlike features aged, and she grew taller. The purple gown grew with her as she took the guise of a woman in her forties, matching Maniodes in height.

The gods joined the waltz, trying to ignore the stunned looks from the Ferrum. Nyx actually looked a little embarrassed, but they danced with the others, enjoying the night.

The skeletons didn't join the Ferrum on the waltz. They seemed to enjoy the faster music, letting their bones click along with the notes. The colorful spectrum of ribbons tied around them was a beautiful spectacle as they danced. Pitch joined in with the sentries as well. He had been watching the slow dances but when the livelier music filled the air he would weave through the skeletons. He even tied some of their ribbons onto himself.

After a couple of hours that felt like minutes, Dagger turned to Scythe in a discreet corner by the punch bowl and broken windows.

"I think we should carry on with the sacrifices," he said. "We should draw the others to the dining room."

"But the night will end then," Scythe protested.

"It has to eventually," he chuckled, "and not immediately."

He touched her waist again and guided her closer to him. When their lips met Scythe couldn't hear the music or the conversations around her. Her world only included Dagger at the moment.

Dagger pulled away but kept hold of Scythe's hand. He strode to the archway, where everyone had a clear view of them. As the music lulled to a close Dagger raised an arm to catch their attention.

"Everyone!" he called. "The night of Nukternios draws to a close, though I wish it wouldn't. If you would please follow us to the dining room, we'll commence with the night's sacrifices. Though by no means will the night be over after them. I'm sure Shorty would like to compose something else for us."

Shorty raised a fist in the air in agreement, a new red strip of fabric tied to her wrist.

Dagger turned with Scythe and led them through the main hall down the corridors. They passed centerpieces of leaves and hearts on every surface.

The dining hall was just as disturbingly immaculate as the parlor. Dried leaves in colors of maroon, orange, and brown littered the floor. The tall, broken windows let in the full moon's light and glistened on the pumpkins in the windowsills. Each pumpkin was carved with angular faces of joy, terror, and despair. The candles inside them provided the most light.

The Incruentus Ferrum, skeletons, and gods poured into the dining room. The long table with spines waited with a dozen high-backed chairs made of ribcages. The center of the table held a tall cage covered in a black cloth. From inside they could hear the occasional skitter of the animal it housed. A tall, dusty bottle of old wine stood next to the covered cage. The bottle had lost its label long ago.

As Dagger approached the cage, Scythe picked up the old wine. When mortals celebrated something important they poured their oldest wine into the earth. It was thought to be absorbed as a libation to the gods. It was pure nonsense; so much good wine was wasted that way. Their libation would be tasted by the goddess herself. Dagger waited by the cage while Scythe refilled everyone's goblet.

Once Scythe finished by filling their own goblets on the table, Dagger removed the cloth from the cage. Inside was a beautiful snowy owl. It sat calmly on the perch watching Dagger. He wondered briefly what happened to the animal's soul if Nyx took care of the human ones.

The owl was well trained when he bought it. Dagger opened the cage and it clung to his arm. He didn't have a leather glove, so the talons pierced into his flesh. It hurt but he didn't mind.

He guided it to the thick cloth Scythe had set on the table previously. It hopped down, peering at the audience with giant glistening eyes. It didn't cause a single fuss at being around so many people. A small coo escaped now and then as if it was politely asking who they all were. Dagger stroked the fine white feathers on its back. He removed a small blade from his belt.

"Dagger, wait."

He stopped with the blade an inch from the owl's breast. Nyx had stepped forward as she spoke, back in her small form.

"There's no need to kill the poor creature," she said. "I appreciate the gesture, but I don't know why humans felt so inclined to kill these beautiful birds for me. I would rather see it set free."

She still looked shy regardless of her regal stature. Almost as if she were worried about insulting him, but the concern for the owl was stronger.

"Of course, Your Grace." Dagger set down the blade immediately, glad he didn't have to soil the white feathers.

He had the owl hop back onto his arm. Approaching the nearest window with the largest hole in the glass he guided the owl outside. Feeling the cool night air, the owl flew away instantly.

"Thank you," Nyx said.

"It was my pleasure," Dagger said rolling down his sleeve, "and we can still have our libation with nothing wasted."

He picked up his goblet and held it high, his other hand wrapping around Scythe's waist naturally. She held hers aloft toward Nyx as well.

"To you, Your Grace," Scythe said.

"And for Nukternios," Dagger added.

The rest of the audience followed suit, raising their goblets in a toast.

Nyx appeared nervous but happy at the same time. She gave a small curtsy and drank with them.

After the libation, they found themselves back in the parlor with Shorty playing a sweet melody as the night drew to a close.

"That went perfectly," Scythe said to Dagger as they settled by the fire.

"It was better than perfect," he agreed. "This has to be the best night Nyx has ever had."

"Excuse me?"

Dagger turned abruptly, seeing Nyx herself waiting close by. He felt Scythe slip her hand into his. He hoped Nyx hadn't heard them lest she suspect their motivations.

"Yes, Your Grace?" he asked.

"I said you don't have to keep calling me that," Nyx playfully chastised.

"My apologies," Dagger bowed his head. "What is it you need?"

"I wish to confess something, actually, and apologize for it."

He didn't have a chance to hide his confusion. He wished he had but decided to use it. "What do you mean?"

Nyx sighed. "I need to apologize because I had wanted Maniodes to disband all of the Incruentus Ferrum."

"I'm sorry?" Scythe squeezed Dagger's hand as she spoke, playing to the surprise.

Her confusion and worry was believable. Dagger followed her lead to keep the false surprise as well.

"I thought you had all become callus and power-hungry because your bloodlust was so strong," Nyx explained. "I was wrong. I hope you can forgive me for assuming that."

Dagger could hardly believe their luck. Nyx actually felt guilty for issuing their deaths.

"It was an easy assumption to make," he said. "There is nothing to forgive, but may I ask you something about Pitch while you're here?"

"You may." Her smile faltered.

"He's been acting odd lately. He's always asking about our jobs, and how it feels afterward. It's as if he's grown restless."

Nyx watched him carefully. If his heart could beat it would be fluttering like the owl should have been. He had to step lightly here. The last thing he wanted was to get Pitch in trouble.

"We were wondering why Maniodes was still preventing him from going on missions," Scythe added quickly. "He's seemed stressed lately. We were hoping you could keep an eye on him, if you get the chance."

Dagger wanted to kiss Scythe for rescuing him out of the awkwardness.

"I know we have no right to ask anything of you," he added, "but I'm worried about the kid. I'm wondering if he's being punished for something."

"No, not at all," Nyx said, her voice rising in earnest. "Maniodes isn't harassing the boy. He must be nervous because I asked something of him. I asked him to monitor your bloodlust."

Dagger only blinked in response; he hadn't expected her to outright say her goals. Scythe squeezed his hand and played along with his confusion, saying, "What do you mean?"

"When an Incruentus Ferrum is created," Nyx explained, "Maniodes gives you a sort of lust for violence. He believes it makes controlling you a bit easier because you were already willing to kill innocent people. He didn't want his creations to worry about damaged morals or have a personal crisis. It was a good idea at first, but then a pattern started. The bloodlust grew, and the recipient became harder to control. Particularly you, Scythe."

Scythe squeezed Dagger's hand again. He grasped back, giving what silent reassurance he could.

"It's been growing in you for a hundred years, and you became more rebellious and violent. Going so far as burning an entire village."

"That was Dagger's idea," Scythe accused.

"You still jumped on the plan instantly," Dagger defended.

Nyx chuckled. "It's alright. Dagger, I think yours was increasing rapidly because of your closeness to Scythe. As for Pitch, he didn't have much to begin with, and it didn't grow."

"But Pitch has been dead longer then I have," Dagger said. "Shouldn't his be stronger than mine? Why is he different?"

"It's because of his age. He's basically stuck at being a twelve-year-old. He had some curiosity about violence but he's never acted on it strongly. That's also why he's been the best steward to Maniodes."

"So why have him monitor our bloodlust?" Scythe asked. "Why not Maniodes?"

"Maniodes is prideful in his work. I don't fault him on that; he's proud of what he's created: you. Yet, because of that, he fails to see the down-sides, other than your rebellious nature against him. Working through Pitch was subtler. He trusted Pitch's word, and the kid had good ideas for assignments. I asked Pitch to feed Maniodes certain jobs so they would go to you two.

"There was another reason, though," she continued. "As your bloodlust grew stronger and you started slaughtering the living, it reminded me of something one of my sons did."

Dagger exchanged a glance with Scythe. Nyx was talking about Lumeon.

"I won't say who, but I was not going to let that slaughter happen again," Nyx finished. "I thought it would be a stronger lesson if you came across it yourselves. But, considering you basically asked about it because of your worry for Pitch, I thought I might as well tell you. It seemed to have worked either way. You two are following the ground rules again, though this décor is rather questionable."

"We didn't kill anyone to set this up," Dagger quickly said. "We dug up fresh graves."

"It's still odd, but beautiful in its own way. You *are* leaving the living alone anyway."

"I hope we live up to your true expectations," Scythe added, "to rectify that assumption."

"I'm sure you will," Nyx said. "I wish you both the best happiness. If you need any personal help, write a note addressed to me and burn it. The letter will appear to me almost instantly."

Nyx curtsied to them. They quickly replied in kind. Nyx left them then to join Maniodes by the sentries again. Scythe took Dagger's arm and guided him to watch the fire. He watched her curiously as she leaned toward him and whispered sadly, "We're going to ruin this night for her when the time comes."

After a couple of hours the estate was mostly empty again. The Incruentus Ferrum started to trickle away, in groups of two or three, and the sentries followed suit. Nyx had even given Scythe a hug before she decided to vanish. Now all that was left was to clean the used plates and reorganize everything. Scythe was tempted to leave the mess for the next night, but she hated seeing her home in the aftermath of the celebrations. Dagger hadn't given much complaint at helping clean either. She was glad about that.

They decided to leave the decorations for the next night, so they focused on the cutlery, goblets, and plates. They chatted about nothing in particular, but it was nice. Scythe couldn't stop thinking about their dance. Every time there was a lull in the conversation Dagger would just smile at her, and their eyes would linger a second too long.

While she gathered used plates from the parlor, Dagger came up behind her. She was leaning over the table and felt his hand stroke her lower back, then stay there. Straightening she took in his scent of blood and musk, and his black eyes filled her vision.

"May I admit something?" his voice was deeper than normal.

"Of course, dear husband," she said leaning into him.

"Ever since our waltz," his hand moved lower, "I've been wanting to rip this dress off of you."

"How dare you," she said kissing his cheek. "I worked hard on this dress."

At one point later, as she walked past him to take a handful of goblets to the kitchen, he pinched her ass. She just laughed and swatted his hand away playfully. Before, she would have shied away, she knew, but things were better now.

Coming up from the kitchens to gather more plates, Dagger stopped her in the corridor.

"I'll be gentle," he said pulling her toward him and planting his lips on hers.

Scythe kissed him in reply. She didn't know how to put what she felt into words as their embrace deepened.

She broke off the second kiss to breathe, but he clearly wanted more. She slipped from his grasp but kept hold of his hands.

The rest of the mess could be dealt with later. For now, the fire inside her was burning away all reason. Dagger had lit that fire. She wanted to thank him for it.

In the main entrance, Dagger untied the red ribbon around her waist and let it fall to the dusty floor. While climbing the cracked stairs Scythe took off his belt of knives and his doublet. By the time they reached Dagger's bedchambers, Scythe was down to a short, black undergarment, and Dagger only had his trousers left. Scythe was already undoing them as Dagger closed the door, not looking away from her eyes.

# Chapter 39

Several quiet nights passed after Nukternios, with Dagger and Scythe mostly enjoying the pleasures of a proper honeymoon. Scythe couldn't deny to herself: she was loving it. Dagger was everything she needed, and she hadn't known that before. As a new night thickened, Chip had come up through the dead tree leading two creatures. Dagger and Scythe hurried down to meet him.

Two glorious animals now stood before of them, their ivory bones gleaming in the moon's light. They stood like skeletal horses, similar to the way Chip resembled a human, but with a prominent difference. Where Chip was hollow, these creatures had thick black smoke curling into itself in their ribcages and skulls. The two largest clouds were connected around the spine of its neck by thin tendrils of the same smoke. More tendrils sprouted from the ribcage and spread along the back and down their legs. The tendrils faded away as they reached the hooves  and tail of the beasts.

"What are they?" Dagger asked in awe.

"Night Mares," Scythe explained. "Maniodes created them during his war with Phaos thousands of years ago."

"How come I've never seen them before?" Dagger asked, touching one of the horses' skulls.

"He keeps them in the stables, but rarely uses them anymore," Scythe said.

Chip pointed to Dagger, then Scythe, and then the two mares.

"You know where Maniodes is?" Scythe asked excitedly. "The bone in his shoe actually worked?"

Chip nodded and walked a few paces down the road. He stopped and gestured for them to follow.

Scythe took the reins of one of the mares and swung into the saddle of well stitched black leather. It sat on the back of the mare as if she were a regular horse. Scythe had expected to feel the ridge of the spine unbalance the saddle, but it didn't.

Dagger hollered as he climbed onto the other mare. He looked like a knight gone rogue with his black coat atop the Night Mare. The sight of him galloping alone would cause any mortal to perish in terror.

"Let's find that woman," he said, grinning wickedly.

Chip took off down the road at full tilt.

"Ha!" Scythe snapped the reins and the mare took off behind Chip.

Dagger's mare matched hers, and they raced over Ichorisis together. No army could withstand them.

The Night Mares didn't tire or even slow down for a long time. Scythe had peeked behind them and watched the smoke from the beasts' ribcages disappear in wisps. They ran through the forest hills. Bounding over fallen logs with ease.

When the trees thinned out, Scythe unhooked her weapon from her back. She flicked it to the side, elongating it to full size. The rush of battle flooded through her veins. She raised her scythe, blade behind them like a banner, and screamed into the night.

Dagger tied his reins off and pulled out his choice weapons. Raising them in the cold air, he joined her cry.

They rode for hours. They stuck to a generally eastward direction, veering north a bit. They didn't pass many travelers on the road, but there was one walking alone. He couldn't see Chip as he bounded past but the man did stop. Dagger took one side while Scythe took the other, and they raced past, heedless of possibly breaking the shadow trick.

Looking back Scythe saw the cold horror on the man's face as he hugged himself. He looked like he was going to be sick. The tendrils of smoke swirled around him. They hadn't broken the spell, but he felt them.

The trees became sparse, and plains stretched out around them. They passed several villages and a lone cottage. The plains turned to rolling hills, with the road weaving through the valleys and cresting several of the largest ones.

They passed Stymphalia, its gleaming walls bleached a dull white in the night air. Eventually, the ground became jagged. Rocks grew where the trees should have, and the sharp tips of the mountains could be seen cutting off the stars.

Chip reached the crest of a rocky hill and finally stopped. Dagger and Scythe pulled the reins, stopping the mares behind him. The thrill of the ride left Scythe breathless.

Scythe dismounted the Mare. Approaching Chip's side, she saw what had stopped him. A small village lay nestled among the rocky landscape. It was nearly blackened out in the small hours of the night, but Scythe could still see it. There were only about two-dozen houses, smaller than the village she and Dagger had burned together.

She imagined the thatched roofing of the houses ablaze. She could practically see the people scattering in panic in the glorious view of the mountains.

"Maniodes is here?" she asked Chip.

He pointed to a cottage slightly apart from the others on the northern side. It had a large barn that probably required the entire village to put together. A tall fence ringed a large section of empty field beside the barn.

"Do you know this place?" Dagger asked Scythe.

"I don't know every village that crops up," Scythe replied. "Even if I'm one hundred years old."

"We'll have to get its name elsewhere, then. Chip, do you mind waiting here with the horses? I'd rather not risk you being seen by Maniodes."

Chip nodded.

"Dagger, you sneak around front. I'll go around the back, and we'll meet by the barn," Scythe suggested.

"Be careful." Dagger met her eye in earnest. "This isn't a human we're stalking."

"I will be, and you too." Scythe pecked his cheek. "See you by the barn."

Keeping to the shadows of the larger boulders, Scythe crept closer to the house. Glancing over, she saw Dagger's shadow veer right and disappear around the corner.

Scythe found a door and a couple of windows, but they were locked and dark. The second-floor windows were the same. It seemed like a perfectly normal night as whoever lived here slept.

The house was uneventful, but rounding on the barn, staying low behind some bushes, Scythe caught a tiny light coming from a high window. It was little more than a pinprick of yellow flickering light, possibly the flame of a candle. It winked out for a moment then came back.

Movement caught her eye on the ground. A figure melted into the shadow of the house on her side. She'd only seen it for a moment, but she knew the man's form.

"Dagger," she whispered creeping closer to the house.

He broke away from the shadow and joined her by the foliage.

"Did you find anything? There was nothing on the front, just locked doors," he said.

"The back was the same, but come here." Scythe took his hand and led him to where she'd seen the candle.

"Look."

He followed her pointing finger and spotted the flickering light.

"There are two entrances to the barn on the other side. Luckily, they're close together. This way."

They darted to the shadow of the barn and made their way along its side. This close, Scythe heard a horse whinny inside. The smell of them was pungent. A narrow door stood on the east side. The north wall had taller double doors that could open into the fenced area.

They darted to a nearby well and crouched behind the stone. The moon shone in their favor, lighting up both sides of the barn.

"All we do is wait," Scythe said.

"For Chip's sake, I hope it's not too long," Dagger added.

They sat in silence for some time. Scythe was glad she'd chosen to ride in trousers so she didn't have to dirty one of her dresses. Although Dagger scolded her for not wearing shoes again. Over the next hour they watched the barn, but she noted how Dagger's concentration melted into boredom.

"Dagger?" Scythe said quietly, not wanting to risk being caught. "How are you doing about your mother?

The festival was so soon after it, you probably haven't had time to mourn."

His boredom sharpened to curiosity, then changed to sadness.

"I'll be fine," he said, shaking his head as if to clear it. "I knew Mother would go eventually. I didn't know I'd get to be there, but I'm glad I was."

He met her eyes then. "I saw how uncomfortable you were then, actually. Are you alright?"

Her hands balled into fists, but she forced herself to talk. "I may not have felt a mother's love right, but I know what it is supposed to be like."

She realized then that most of her unease stemmed from jealousy. Dagger had a loving mother when her own had loved a plant. She examined her clenched hands, wondering if she was actually mourning Dagger's mother even though they'd never met.

"I wish you could have met her," Dagger said. "In her lucid moments, she was a riot to talk to. She loved riddles."

Scythe stayed quiet, unsure how to unravel her own emotions.

Dagger's hand cupped her cheek, drawing her eye up again. His black eyes in the cold air reminded her of warm coals in a fire.

"Do you miss your own mother?" he asked softly.

Scythe nodded into his hand.

"Have you ever found them in Skiachora?"

"No. I don't think I want to," she admitted.

"That's fine," he said. "We could find my mother. Pay her a visit?"

Dagger was consoling her. Scythe kicked herself for being so selfish.

"If you want," she said.

"I do. I wonder if she's near father."

Dagger let his hand drop, and she uncurled her fists. He glanced over the well. The boredom and sadness vanished as something caught his eye. Scythe followed his gaze.

The narrow door of the barn opened sometime after their talk and two figures came outside. Neither of them held a light source, so Scythe couldn't make out any details, but it was definitely a man and woman. They stayed close to each other in the crisp air. They were certainly two bodies that were accustomed to being close.

The man bent down and kissed the woman. There was no doubt in who the figure was, but he was so short. Maniodes was still taller than the woman, but he only stood about six feet. His hair was the same dark-blue shade in the moonlight. The woman threw her arms around him, holding him close for several moments. The secret lovers parted slowly, still talking about something. The woman stole a final peck before hurrying back into the house. The man kept to the shadows and strode off toward a grove of trees.

"I'll follow him," Dagger whispered. "You follow her."

"Be careful." She gripped his arm.

"I'll be fine." He covered her hand. "I'll meet you by Chip on the hill."

They parted ways, and Dagger followed Maniodes.

The woman had already closed the door of the house. Scythe followed and tried it, but it was locked. Luckily, the lock itself was cheap. Scythe picked the lock easily and closed the door behind her. She headed for the stairs, glad she'd come barefoot. People were still cautions at night. Even in the comfort of their own home, the darkness and the monsters within always crept past their sense of safety. They would investigate strange noises. Scythe left no sounds as she climbed the steps.

Two doors in a hallway waited on the second floor. Scythe opened the left door and peered inside. A wide bed held two sleeping figures. She decided to leave them be for now. The second door creaked slightly, causing Scythe to freeze. There was no movement on the other side, but that didn't mean much. Keeping the door steady, Scythe leaned in and looked inside. This room held a single bed with a feminine figure under the blankets.

Scythe stepped inside and left the door open. The woman didn't stir. Her back was to the door, so Scythe creeped around the bed to see the woman's face.

It was her. Her eyes were closed, and a peaceful smile stayed on her lips as she slept. The same pale hair mixed with a darker shade of lavender spread on the pillow around her.

Scythe felt like a vulture waiting for its moment, and loved it.

# Chapter 40

Scythe returned back to the rocky hill where Chip waited. The Night Mares dug their hooves into the earth, not tethered to anything. She wondered briefly if that was part of their training or nature.

Chip stood from a rock and approached eagerly as she crested the hill.

"It's her house, all right," she told him.

Chip punched the air.

"Has Dagger come back yet?" she asked.

Chip's arm fell to his side as he shook his head.

Scythe looked out over the hills. The small grove of trees was visible from here. Dagger had followed Maniodes in that direction, but there was no way of knowing if their path had changed.

Chip came to her side and tilted his head at her in a questioning manner.

"We saw Maniodes. Dagger followed him," she explained.

Chip looked over the hills with her.

The moon moved the length of half an hour.

The cold bite of steel touched her throat. Scythe instantly went for her weapon on her back, but a hand stopped her. She counted her breath beneath the blade. Rage filled her veins.

"I found him." The voice in her ear was husky.

"What are you doing, Dagger?" she demanded.

"Just a bit of fun." He slid the knife back into his belt as she turned to glare at him. "I came up the side, and you were focused on the valley."

"I should skin you alive. You'd probably survive that."

"Probably would." His eyebrows shot up. "That wouldn't be pleasant."

"It would be for me. Did you really think that little blade would go over well on an espionage run when we're stalking a fucking god?"

He grew more serious, seeing her anger.

"I was trying to lighten the mood," he explained. "Especially after our talk by the well."

That blew the wind out of her sails. "Just read the mood next time. I was worried you wouldn't come back. Anyway, you said it was him?"

"Aye," he said, relaxing again. "There's a dead maple tree in that grove. He went back to Skiachora. It was strange seeing him so short."

"Part of his disguise as Tyndareus, I bet. Walking around at eight feet would draw attention, even at night," Scythe said.

Dagger nodded. "And the woman?"

"It was her," she confirmed.

"Wonderful. You know, we could kidnap her now."

"I thought the same, but I think we should leave her be for now. We can use the tree to get back quickly enough, but let's use the Mares again," Scythe said.

"Right. I'd feel better with a proper plan of attack before we take her. We should talk to Axe too; he might have an idea," Dagger stated.

Dagger and Scythe mounted the Night Mares and rode back home with Chip beside them.

A chasm was waiting for them back at the estate. The path just under the main entrance had cracked open, revealing downward stairs just like back in Chalcis. The foreboding dread poured from it like a thick fog waiting for them. The air was squeezed from Dagger's lungs when he saw it.

Gravel crunched under his boots as he dismounted the Night Mare. Some stones were kicked down the chasm as he approached it with Scythe.

"Dagger, he knows." It sounded like she couldn't breathe properly either.

"We don't know that for sure," he said, not quite believing his own words.

"He didn't know you were following him, right?" Scythe pleaded.

"No, he didn't. At least he didn't react. I even did what you would do and took my boots off. I didn't make a sound."

Dagger scrubbed his hair, trying to remember every detail of Maniodes in the grove. He had walked headlong for the rough center of the grove without pausing or even turning his head. There had been no indication that Maniodes felt anything was amiss. Dagger had even left an extra knife buried into a tree trunk, so they would recognize the place later.

Maybe that had been the indication. What if he let Dagger follow him?

"Dagger?" Scythe's near-panicked voice broke him out of the memory.

"I don't know now," he shrugged. "There was no hint of him knowing I was there."

"Okay." Scythe took a breath. "Chip, can you take the Mares back through the tree?"

Chip nodded, already holding their reins.

"Good." She turned back to Dagger. "We say nothing until he talks first. Just play dumb."

Dagger forced a breath too, hoping he looked calm enough.

"Okay, pinch my hand if I start acting nervous," he said.

"You do the same for me," Scythe agreed.

Dagger held his hand out, and Scythe took it. They descended into Skiachora together as the ground closed above them.

The throne room was full of Incruentus Ferrum and sentries. There were only about thirty in their order, and they were the last to arrive. Everyone had their weapons on hand except for Axe and Maime.

Cross stood among the crowd, looking worried and confused. She twirled a bolt nervously while the crossbow hung on her back. Pitch was there, with his pitchfork, but not in his usual place on the dais. He clutched his weapon like a staff, on the main floor with everyone else.

Maniodes sat on his throne, at his regular eight-foot height. He leaned forward, elbow to knee, not happy about something. His shield leaned against the throne next to him.

Everyone watched Dagger and Scythe enter and stand by Pitch.

"Where have you been?" Maniodes demanded.

"Riding horses in the forest, my lord," Scythe replied.

"I'm sorry to disturb your fun then," Maniodes said sarcastically. "Pitch!"

The boy jumped. He looked terrified.

Dagger squeezed his shoulder, hoping it was reassuring.

Pitch stepped in front of the throne and faced the god.

"What is the one thing in my chamber I ordered you not to disturb?" he asked Pitch.

"The thin box on your nightstand, my lord." His little hands clutched the pitchfork, but his voice was steady. He was probably used to seeing Maniodes in these moods.

"Do you know why?"

Pitch stammered a reply. "I t-thought there were important documents inside."

Dagger's hand gripped tighter in Scythe's.

Maniodes nodded, but it didn't erase the fury. "A good assumption. Did you see any documents inside?"

Pitch blanched. "No, Sire. It's always locked."

"There were scratches on the lock, Pitch. Why?"

Dagger heard Scythe's quick inhale. He squeezed her hand tighter, trying to calm them both.

"It fell over," Pitch said without missing a beat. "I was putting the plate of cheeses you like on the nightstand there and knocked it off by accident."

Maniodes examined his hands, looking morose.

"I just found this in my bootstrap." He held up Chip's finger bone. "Which sentry does it belong to?"

"I don't know, my lord," Pitch claimed. For a child, he was a good liar.

"You are the only one who goes near my boots." Maniodes's voice was murderous. "Why was it there?"

"I don't know," Pitch insisted. "I didn't put it there."

Maniodes sighed, twirling the tiny bone.

"I can't take chances with that box. I'm sorry, Pitch." Maniodes raised a hand without looking at him.

The boy was only able to let out one frightened plea before the color drained from his body. His grey form stood there, frozen, as a green glow sprouted from his chest. He was still solid for a moment but once the green light appeared, he became a transparent husk like the normal dead. The pitchfork clattered to the floor through him.

"No!" Dagger screamed.

Scythe's hand covered her mouth, eyes wide with horror.

The green light of Pitch's soul floated up to Maniodes's hand. The god held it for a moment, watching it pulse as it hovered over his palm. He closed his hand around it, and Pitch winked out of existence. Maniodes picked up his shield then. He slipped his arm through the straps, securing it in place.

Dagger wanted to scream again, but it stuck in his throat.

Maniodes left the dais and approached Pitch's small grey husk. With his shield, Maniodes waved it through the boy like a farmer cutting wheat. The grey image of Pitch dispersed from the impact and dissolved away.

# Chapter 41

"You fucking bastard!"

Maniodes rounded on Dagger. He had been dejected carrying out the sentence before, but now he looked furious.

Dagger stepped forward. Scythe tried to hold him back, but he shook her off.

"He made a mistake, and you kill him for it? You didn't even let him defend himself!"

Maniodes was about to reply but couldn't.

"He was just a boy," Cross cried.

"Your own steward," Axe added. "He admired you!"

"That was rather extreme," Maime put in.

Most of the other Incruentus Ferrum spoke up, all in favor of Pitch. Maniodes watched them all, taken aback by their fury.

"You force Dagger and me to marry for burning a village, but you murder Pitch for dropping a fucking box?" Scythe shouted.

Maniodes's eyes darted over all of the Ferrum, settling on Dagger and Scythe again.

"It does not do to question your betters," he seethed trying to contain himself.

"You are no better," Dagger replied.

"He was a child," Cross said again.

Others began to protest.

"Enough!" Maniodes demanded. "The next one of you to speak ends the same as Pitch."

Everyone stayed quiet then. Dagger's fists shook at his sides. His weapon was in hand now.

Cross stifled a sob.

Silence hung over them all like a patient noose.

"Out, all of you," Maniodes demanded.

Dagger heard the others' footsteps receding, but he couldn't move. Pitch had trusted him. He hadn't heard her approach, but Scythe appeared by his side, weapon at full length. Her frame shook with anger that paralleled his. Pitch had trusted them and ended up dead. The other Incruentus Ferrum stopped to watch.

"Problem, Dagger?" Maniodes challenged. "Scythe?"

The god towered over them, shield still strapped to his arm.

"You murdered him," Scythe said. Her voice was soulless.

"I have that right," Maniodes said. "It was to set an example."

"Of what?" Dagger barked.

"Of those who cross me in my personal life," he growled back. "I don't have to explain myself to you. I am your god."

"You are not my god." The words poured from him like pus from an infected wound. "You are not my master, because we are not dogs you can beat!"

He savored his dagger's weight. Scythe held her weapon at the ready.

"You dare—" Maniodes growled.

"We dare," Scythe interrupted. "I was tired of your dictations a century ago."

"I'll relieve you of them then. I was tired of you undermining me anyway."

Maniodes raised his hand toward Scythe. The scarlet started to drain from her hair, and her skin dulled. The fury in her eyes deepened as she resisted.

Dagger's control broke then. He threw his first knife. The blade stuck in Maniodes's palm, forcing him to lose concentration. Scythe gasped as life returned to her.

Thick, red blood welled past the blade in Maniodes's hand. Dagger was stunned it was a normal color.

Maniodes gripped his wrist and roared at them with a mix of pain and rage.

Scythe struck then, screaming in her crimson fury. She swung perfectly, avoiding the shield, and sliced through Maniodes's tunic and stomach.

Maniodes yelled again, but there were words this time.

"Dogs would have been easier to control!"

He raised his other hand, intending to kill them again. Dagger picked another knife, but his hand went numb. The blade clattered to the floor through grey dead fingers. It had gotten hard to breathe. He heard screams around him, but they were distant, like he was drowning, as the borrowed life drained out of him

Dagger forced his gaze from his graying hand back to Maniodes. He couldn't move. He couldn't fight, but he wanted the god to see his fury.

A bolt sprouted from Maniodes's chest. It was enough to distract him, though he didn't even stagger.

Glorious air rushed back into Dagger's lungs and feeling returned to his hands. He picked up his choice dagger from where it fell, intending to charge rather then throw.

Scythe stood beside him with a maniacal grin.

Before Maniodes could pull the bolt from his chest, a skeleton bounded in front of him. Dagger noticed the chip in its jaw as it raised a spear to ward off Maniodes.

"Chip, No!" Dagger called.

Other skeletons joined Chip. Maniodes was too stunned at the mutiny to retaliate yet.

Chip chanced a look back and waved for them to run.

"No!" Dagger screamed again.

Maniodes reacted then. He didn't give warning as he knocked half of the sentries aside with his shield regardless of their weapons. Chip was among those scattered.

Chip's ribcage broke apart and the spear flew with the dislocated arm. Before his skull could hit the ground, Maniodes snatched it and crushed it into a powder.

Another bolt was shot and struck him. A throwing star imbedded into his shoulder shortly after.

"Traitors!" he screamed.

Cross ran to Dagger's other side, readying another bolt. The grief in her eyes was powerful. He wondered if she had known Pitch well, or if she associated him with her own son.

Scythe charged, weaving through the remaining skeletons. Dagger followed close behind.

With her weapon at full glory, Scythe swung as Maniodes shoved aside another skeleton. She aimed for his arm, probably intending to sheer it off, but Maniodes saw her. He moved in time to catch the blade of her scythe with his shield. The clang of metal pounded in his ears, raising his blood for war. More bolts, arrows, and throwing stars flew to the god. Most of them connected.

Dagger was useless in controlling his rage. He knew he should stay back and attack with a throwing knife. He didn't care. Using the distraction Scythe provided by attacking head-on, Dagger struck from the side.

Aiming low and precise, Dagger cut through Maniodes's boot and the soft tendon of his heel. Before Maniodes could do more than scream, Dagger buried the blade into the knee of the other leg.

The god fell to the side but blocked another blow from Scythe.

Axe ran into view with his weapon. Hammer was beside him, brandishing his hulking war hammer. Now that the god was down, they charged.

Scythe's cackle filled the air. Dagger couldn't stop the laughter bubbling up from his throat either. They wouldn't have to seal Maniodes away or threaten his woman. He could bleed.

Dagger shifted the grip on his weapon while Hammer pinned Maniodes's shield. Axe stood close by, though he looked very uncomfortable.

Scythe swung her weapon around and brought the blade to rest at Maniodes's throat.

He bled from several wounds, but his eyes didn't hold any defeat.

Dagger hoped he could pluck them out.

"Enough!" Maniodes cried.

Dagger was about to scoff. As if they would just stop at his command now. A powerful blast wrenched the air from his lungs. His feet left the floor as he flew back when the force of heat and strength crashed into him.

Ceiling became floor, then wall, then back again. The floor rushed up and didn't catch him gently. When he finally regained his senses, he was on the ground halfway to the main doors.

Maniodes knelt in the center of the carnage. Broken bones and white powder lay closest to the blast while other sentries were scattered in several limbs across the throne room. Most of the Incruentus

Ferrum were scattered through the hall too. Axe must have hit the far wall because he lay unconscious.

Maniodes held Hammer by the throat. The knife Dagger had thrown into it was gone.

Dagger watched as Hammer's life and color drained away. It was a much faster process, apparently, if Maniodes held the victim. Once Hammer was completely transparent, Maniodes closed his fist through the Ferrum's neck. He faded from existence as Pitch had. The green soul didn't even have time to leave his body.

Lace sprinted past Dagger towards the door. Others followed her. Maniodes regained his feet despite the wounds and raised a hand in summoning. Cross skidded to a halt as if caught by a rope and was wrenched backward into his hand. He repeated the process.

"Scythe!" Dagger called, heart pounding, waiting to feel the same pull that got Cross.

"Here."

Following her voice, he spotted her several yards away. She regained her feet quickly. Her weapon was still extended; she had been lucky not to skewer herself on it. Only then did he notice his own hand was empty. Looking around frantically he spotted his dagger stuck in the abandoned ribcage of a sentry. He snatched it up and regained his feet too.

Another Ferrum flew past into Maniodes's hand. A thin man with bronze skin and a large nose. Dagger wondered what his weapon of choice and name had been as he died.

"We have to go," Scythe ran closer to Dagger as he watched in horror while the god picked them off, one by one. She gripped his arm when he didn't reply. "Dagger!"

"But Pitch," he protested, shaking her off. "Chip and Axe."

"We can avenge them later. We have to get out now," Scythe shouted. "Come on, follow me."

She took his hand, and he let her drag him from the castle and chaos.

# Chapter 42

Scythe's cave was cold. The only items left were a table and chairs by a dead fireplace. Around a tight bend in the rock a bed lay abandoned.

There were a few scraps of wood left in the ashes. She lit a meager fire, though it wasn't needed. It took a moment to strike the flint because her fingers were twitching with adrenaline.

Dagger sat at the table behind her. His head was down with his hands buried in his hair.

Scythe stood, brushing ash off her fingers. The light was small and the warmth was non-existent, but it was something.

"You're sure we're safe here?" Dagger asked quietly, as if Maniodes might hear him.

"Yes," Scythe said. "He never came to visit, so I don't think he knows where this place is."

In truth they were still in Skiachora, not far from the hole the Acheron River used to enter Ichorisis. Maniodes would be expecting them to flee as far as they could. She hoped that was the case anyway, so staying hidden but close was their advantage.

Scythe paced, unable to sit still. Her weapon's handle was shortened to two feet, and she wrung her hands over it.

"Did you see what happened to Axe?" Dagger asked, pulling his hands out of his hair. He looked disheveled. "Last I saw, he was unconscious."

"I didn't see him." Scythe paced back behind him toward the little fire.

After a moment, Dagger spoke again. "What the fuck did we do, Scythe?"

"Started a bloody mutiny." It was probably a rhetorical question, but she gave the obvious answer anyway. The words tasted good on her tongue.

"Will you stop pacing, please," he pleaded. "The agitation is not helping anything."

"Well, I'm *sorry*, but I'm a little on edge after that rampage and nearly getting killed." Scythe did stop to face Dagger, though her legs wanted to move.

She wanted to run, scream, and hit something, anything, preferably Maniodes. They had been so close.

"Pitch *was* killed!" Dagger shouted. "And Chip."

Her weapon hand jumped at his outburst.

Pitch was dead, properly dead, because of her. She had scratched that damn box. That little boy trusted them; he loved Dagger like a brother. Chip tried to protect them too. Scythe remembered them both dancing on Nukternios. Chip was wrapped in so much green ribbon it had looked like vines grew from him, and little Pitch having the time of his strange, undead life.

"Why didn't Nyx keep him safe? Pitch said if he did her bidding she would protect him. Where was she?" he continued.

Her scythe suddenly felt heavier as it hung at her side. Her grief didn't match Dagger's, though. He just kept staring at the table surface as if trying to summon both of his dead friends. He looked defeated when she wanted to fight.

She wanted to snap him out of it, but even pacing had annoyed him. She rounded the table and put her scythe on the surface. With free hands, she held his shoulders. He needed that kind of support right now, though she felt cold.

Dagger sighed at the contact and leaned into her.

"We can rest here for now, but carefully," she said. "You go lie down, and I'll guard the door. Then we'll switch."

Dagger just shook his head as if trying to understand.

"You actually want to rest?" he asked, surprised. "I thought you'd want to go charging back and chop Maniodes's limbs off."

"I do; that's why I was pacing," she explained, "but I know when to pull back. He was slaughtering *all* of us. We don't stand a chance in a full attack like that."

"Cross," Dagger said, "and Hammer. Who knows who else he got in that chaos. By Nyx's bone, Axe is probably dead too."

"Some escaped," she said, trying to reassure him.

He didn't reply. Scythe rubbed a hand over his back.

Dagger stood suddenly. He took her weapon and held it out to her. The grief was still in his eyes, but it was sharper.

"I have a plan," he said. "He took Pitch from us, so let's take something from him."

"Does it involve taking his head off?" she asked excitedly, taking the weapon.

"Not quite, but it's just as fun." Even his grin was angry. "Let's get his bitch."

# Chapter 43

The shadows stretched through the tree grove as the sun began to rise and stain the sky. Scythe's eyes hurt in the sunlight, giving her a headache. The dead maple tree closed behind them. She watched Dagger pull the knife he'd left from the tree and put it back in his belt.

"I love your thought process, Dagger, but this couldn't have waited until evening?" she asked. She hadn't known the sun had risen.

Dagger came up behind her, rubbing an eye. Dropping his hand, he said, "You're usually the impulsive one. I thought you'd approve of the blackmail. You did back at the cave, a moment ago. Besides, if we wait, that just gives Maniodes more time to find and kill us."

"I do approve, but the sun is blinding," she countered.

"I know, I know. Let's just get this over with." He set off toward the woman's house.

They could see the building through the gaps in the trees. Horses already roamed the dewy field beside it.

"Wait." She caught his arm. "Let me lure her here."

Dagger was about to protest, then thought better of it. Eventually, he said, "A woman approaching her would seem less intimidating."

"Exactly. You stay here and open the tree. I'll be right back with her, then we take her home."

Scythe patted Dagger's arm and left the tree's shade. She was still dressed in her riding clothes, so the unlucky traveler image would be easy to pull off. Hard to believe her last visit here was just a few hours ago. Scythe froze and looked down at her feet. They were still bare. She cursed and hurried back to Dagger.

"Let me borrow your boots," she said to his confused expression.

He rolled his eyes, then sat on a rock pulling off his boots. They were far too large for her, but once the boots were on Scythe's feet she hurried back to the barn.

The stench of horse was enormous as Scythe approached the barn. It did nothing to help her headache. She approached from the north road, which passed close to the cottage and barn. The woman wasn't anywhere outside at first glance, but the large barn doors were wide open. Scythe caught movement inside.

Scythe walked up to the narrow door, spotting the blond and lavender hair inside one of the horses' stalls. Scythe knocked on the doorframe.

The woman looked up at the noise, tucking a stray hair over an ear. Seeing her awake in the daylight, Scythe realized calling her a woman was generous. The girl couldn't be more than sixteen.

"Can I help you?" she asked, confused, leaning against the stall's gate.

"M-my horse fell," Scythe said frantically. "He got spooked by a snake and ran into the tree grove. His foot got stuck in the roots, I think, and he just toppled over. Gods, his screams wouldn't stop."

"Are you alright?" the girl asked, moving closer. Her desire to help was clear.

"I'm fine. I managed to jump off before he fell."

"What's your name?" the girl asked calmly.

"Skie, and yours?"

"Leda. Your horse is still in the grove?"

"Yes. I-I didn't know what to do."

"Let me get my father," Leda said. "We may be able to bind the horse's ankle, then we can get him here."

"Can't you just come now?" Scythe asked, trying to sound natural and hysterical at the same time. "He's all alone and hurt."

"I know," Leda said, "but my father is better at binding than I am. He's just inside the house."

Leda led the way out of the barn. Scythe wanted to knock Leda out and drag her back herself. She got as far as gripping her weapon on her back under her tunic before an older man, with hair so blond it was almost white, spotted them coming out of the house.

"Leda, who's this?" he asked.

"This is Skie. Her horse broke an ankle in the tree grove. She didn't know what to do so she came here," Leda explained.

"Oh," the man's eyes lit up with concern. "The grove isn't far. We should help the poor beast. Skie, can you lead the way?"

Scythe let go of her weapon and applied the timid persona again. "I can, yes."

"Good, let me just grab my satchel." The man hurried off to the barn.

"Are you sure you're alright?" Leda asked kindly as they waited for her father. "Did you hit your head falling?"

Given her headache, it felt like she'd been trampled by a horse. "I'm fine."

"Does your horse have a name?"

"Dagger," she said instantly. She kicked herself for not coming up with something different.

"Really? He sounds like a tall warhorse."

"He is," Scythe smiled.

"We'll do what we can for him," Leda said. "He'll be okay."

Scythe kept her eyes down and nodded. She kept expecting Maniodes to appear.

"Alright," Leda's father caught up to them with a threadbare satchel slung over his shoulder. "Lead the way, lass."

Scythe took them back up the north road and veered off to the grove. She made sure to keep in the center of the narrow valley, sure Dagger would see the uninvited guest.

The shade of the trees was blessedly kinder on her eyes. The dead maple waited in the center, but Dagger was nowhere to be seen.

Scythe stopped and turned to Leda and her father. Confusion held them as they scanned for the injured horse. Scythe reached under her tunic again for her weapon.

"What's the meaning of this?" her father demanded, growing angry.

"Skie?" Leda asked, uneasy.

Scythe smiled as she extended her weapon behind her back. The two watched in horror as the blade grew and curved over her.

Dagger appeared from behind a tree and bashed the father's temple with the hilt of his weapon.

Leda shrieked as her father dropped like a puppet cut from its strings. She knelt to shake him, crying. A shudder ran through her as she looked from Scythe to Dagger.

"What do you want?" she cried.

Scythe spun her weapon around and brought it down just over Leda's ear. Dagger caught her before her pretty hair could brush the ground.

# Chapter 44

Scythe crept through the cracked opening of the dead tree into Skiachora. Maniodes's castle loomed over her quietly. There were no sentries standing guard, leading her to wonder how many of them had been slaughtered in the chaos. It felt like the stone itself was watching her, making her skin itch. She could see the windows of Maniodes's chamber. If he were inside and looked in the right direction, he would spot her.

The thrill of the chase pulsed through her veins. Only this time, she was the mouse. She couldn't deny: she liked it a little.

Once Dagger had knocked Leda senseless, he picked her up and carried her through the tree to the underworld. As they descended, he noticed her breathing was slowing down considerably and she grew cold. It took a moment for them to realize in the shaded tunnel that color was leaching out of her too.

With several curses they rushed back to the surface and set Leda down in the grass. Her color and breathing returned to normal. They realized then that nothing living could exist in Skiachora. If they took her down, she would die.

Scythe had suggested they take a Night Mare and ride back home. The only way of doing that was to steal one from under Maniodes's nose. Dagger had volunteered to go, but Scythe convinced him to stay. Leda would be more naturally threatened by Dagger. He agreed reluctantly.

Scythe now kept hold of her weapon, shrunk down to the size of a long knife, and made her way up the steps to the courtyard.

She veered left, keeping low, practically hugging the wall. Skiachora was always quiet, no chatter from the ghosts below, no birds calling in the sweet air. Skiachora only held stagnant air of a cave and the occasional screech of a bat. Even The Acheron was silent as it flowed. For one hundred years that silence had been her home; now it frayed at what was left of her sanity.

Scythe found the portcullis she wanted. The iron portcullis in the arch blocked off the stables, but the tall sally port let her in quickly enough after breaking the lock. She didn't have time or patience to pick it open.

The sparse soil gave way to patches of dry grass in the courtyard. Scythe found the stables quickly and snuck inside. She half-expected the creatures to have vanished too, but they were there.

The black fog that came from the beasts pooled around Scythe's feet. The stable was just like any other except for the stink of hay and manure. They didn't have to eat, just like the Ferrum or the sentries. Maniodes probably considered that a useful trait.

Six Mares were housed in this stable, and Scythe picked the closest two. Most of them had their long heads down as if asleep. They didn't have eyes to close, just more thick blackness inside their skulls. The sight was more than a little unnerving.

The first one Scythe approached was awake, or so she assumed because its head was up. She grabbed a random harness and opened the pen's gate. The Mare resisted the harness, but Scythe managed to wrangle it onto its face, cursing quietly. Keeping a tighter hold on the reins than necessary, Scythe went to lead it outside.

Maime stood there, glancing from her to the Mare. His fists hung at his sides, ready to tear something apart. His glare was not kind.

"Thank Nyx you survived, Maime." Scythe pretended to breathe a sigh of relief. She had to keep her guard up.

"What are you and Dagger trying to pull?" he demanded, dropping all pretense of kindness. Not that there had been any to begin with. "Hammer is dead, and Cross, and probably *half* of our numbers. All because of that damn stunt."

"That stunt was us defending ourselves," Scythe bit back.

"Against what? An insult he tossed your way after he killed that pipsqueak?"

Scythe grew her weapon and swung it around. She aimed it at Maime's chest. Maybe she would be able to slash something.

"The pipsqueak was my friend and a child," Scythe defended. "He was practically Dagger's brother."

"Hammer *was* my brother," Maime growled. He stepped forward into the blade. The curve of it was level with him and he leaned into it. Blood spread over his filthy tunic. The man probably only owned the one.

"Wait," Scythe said, distracted for a second. "The one with that giant war hammer was actually your brother? As in the same parents?"

"Yes, that's what brother means."

"How did you two become Incruentus Ferrum together?" She'd never heard of Maniodes choosing a pair deliberately.

"I recommended him," Maime sneered.

"What did the two of you do for a living?" Scythe asked, trying to buy time for a proper plan to surface in her mind but also honestly curious. "I'd love to hear how the two of you became killers under a tyrant together."

Maime's thick eyebrows knit together. "Maniodes isn't a tyrant. He always ran this place well."

"That's rich," Scythe quickly tossed the reins around a post to keep the Mare in place. "I didn't think a man who strangled and beat people to death would appreciate a leash. Hammer clearly didn't. He fought with us rather than run like a coward."

Maime actually growled at that. It sounded like the voice of a bear was lodged in his throat.

"He complained now and then, but he was smart enough not to cause a bloody mutiny," he spat. "Is that what you're trying to do? Change the way things are, bring down the tyrannical king, bring freedom to those oppressed?"

His tone changed to mockery of a noble speech.

"We're dogs to him, Maime. He slaughtered your brother just because he got in the way. He is going to do that to *all* of us."

"No," Maime said. "Once you two ran off, he stopped. He said that any of us still loyal would stand guard at the entrances. He couldn't even trust the sentries anymore because you manipulated them. You tricked Axe too, didn't you? Maniodes took him below for information."

"Axe is alive?" Scythe asked, still on guard but surprised.

"Last I saw. Not that you'd care about the rest of us. You're going to answer for this."

Maime stomped forward, regardless of the blade in his chest.

Scythe planted her feet to keep from moving. Incruentus Ferrum might be stronger than the living, but against their own kind it was balanced out relatively. Maime stood a foot and a half taller than her and twice as wide. He could easily overpower her given the chance, and she wasn't going to give it to him.

"I don't have time for this, Maime." She pushed against the blade with both hands. She'd have to be fast.

"I don't care," he growled. "I'm going to enjoy this."

He grabbed the point of the blade. Blood welled past his fingers. It wasn't natural how he didn't even flinch. If he gained leverage she wouldn't stand a chance.

Scythe pulled up and away from his hand. The point slid through his fingers and the curve cut deep, leaving a long gaping slice in his chest.

Maime lunged forward now that the blade wasn't in his way, as she anticipated.

Scythe ducked under his fist, shrinking her weapon a bit. Sliding under Maime's arm, managing to avoid his other hand groping for her hair, she ended up behind him while slicing his calf.

The bear in his throat came to life again as he made to turn.

Scythe swung her weapon around, striking his face with the butt end of the staff. The roar was cut off with a choke.

Before Maime could regain his balance, Scythe swung the blade back and up, gaining as much momentum as she could. She swung it down again into the back of Maime's neck. She didn't cut through cleanly as she hoped, but she felt the bones grate against her scythe as his spine snapped.

Maime went limp, and the force drove him into the gate of another Mare's stall. All of the Night Mares were awake now, annoyed and stomping at the disturbance.

Scythe pried her weapon out of Maime's spine, and he fell. He wasn't dead by any means, but it did buy her some time.

She pulled the Mare she'd chosen out of the stables. She didn't try getting the portcullis up and managed to get the Mare through the sally port. Once outside the castle, she still didn't feel safe. Maime could have sent a message that would draw the others near.

Scythe ran with the Mare beside her down the castle steps, threw her weapon into the tree roots, and climbed through.

Dagger twirled a knife as he paced, nearly cutting off his own fingers. Scythe had been gone too long. Leda was still unconscious, thankfully. If she were awake and crying for help, he might have cut her throat. The grove was quiet around him, but he twitched at every snap of a branch from some animal.

The sound of wood creaking made him freeze despite his nerves. He ducked behind a tree beside the bushes Leda slept under.

As he watched, knife steady now, the dead maple cracked open.

With a rush of dried leaves at her feet, Scythe came barreling out of the opening. A skittish Night Mare emerged behind her.

Letting go of a held breath, Dagger stepped out from his hiding place. Scythe looked panicked when she spotted him.

"What's wrong?" he asked, dreading the answer.

"Maime was at the stables," she panted. "He was guarding it against us and said other Ferrum were watching other entrances. Also, Axe is alive."

She sucked in a breath after saying all of that in one go.

The new information swirled in his mind. He wanted to ask if Axe was alright, and who else stood against them. He forced those thoughts aside.

"And you only got one horse?" Dagger chose to focus on.

"I was a little pressed for time," she practically shouted.

"Alright, it will have to do." They couldn't afford to bite at each other's throats, too. "We'll get Leda on its back, then you ride to the estate with her."

Dagger went to the bushes and picked up Leda. If she wasn't still breathing, one could easily assume she was dead. She made no noise as he hoisted her over the Mare's back like a sack.

"But how will you get back?" Scythe asked, concerned.

"I'll use the tree and meet you there."

"There could be an ambush waiting down there now," she argued.

"The Mare can't carry three of us," he countered sternly.

She stammered, trying to reply. Before she could, Dagger grasped her shoulders.

"I'll be fine," he said. "You're lighter than I am, so the Mare can run a bit faster. I'll meet you back home."

"Why don't we just set up here? Get Maniodes here to blackmail him," she suggested.

"We don't have a bat to send the message. It will be quicker to get one at the tower back home."

"But— oh fucking hell!" she cursed.

"I'll be fine," he said again to reassure her, though he didn't feel calm.

"Alright, but I'm going to skin you alive if you're not there," Scythe threatened.

"Your concern is touching, my lady," he said, trying to lighten the mood.

Suddenly, Scythe pulled his face down by his collar and touched her lips to his. One hand trailed into his hair.

He leaned into it instantly and stepped forward. Scythe backed into a tree as he pinned her there.

There was a different kind of longing in the embrace. It was stronger, deeper, similar to when they thought they'd die after Marella's death. When they broke apart she admitted, "All things considered, I'm glad I can call you my husband."

"If this doesn't work," he said, still very close to her, "we won't have to worry about it for very long."

# Chapter 45

The daylight stretched as Scythe rode, making her headache worse. It was rather awkward riding bareback while keeping the unconscious girl from falling, but they made it. Scythe slowed the Mare to a walk as they reached the road up the mountain. She had her weapon at full length, anticipating an ambush from the surrounding trees. To her surprise there was none; she had been wishing there would be. The silence was unnerving.

They cleared the broken gate to the courtyard unhindered. The rotted doors stood closed and unguarded. Dagger was nowhere to be seen yet. Scythe stopped the Mare halfway up the courtyard. The dead tree in their yard stood closed as well. She forced a breath against the pressure in her chest. It felt like a boulder was crushing her.

The door creaked open from the inside. Scythe gripped her weapon, instinctively ready.

Dagger stepped out of the estate. Scythe was finally able to breathe as she leapt off of the Mare. He looked disheveled, and his lip had been split open. He hurried down the steps and met her at the bottom.

Before she could ask what happened, he threw his arms around her. Scythe allowed a moment to enjoy his scent of blood and ash as she held him.

"What happened?" she finally asked as he let go.

"Skiachora was empty," he explained, "but Maime and Hatchet were here. They were guarding the place, but I was expecting as much."

"Where are they now?" she asked.

"Tied up and unconscious in the cellar. It took a bit of doing. I was able to surprise Hatchet, but Maime was up for a fight. He said you tried to behead him."

"I broke his neck," Scythe clarified. "Let's get Leda inside."

"Right, right."

Dagger took Leda` off the Mare and hoisted her over his shoulder. Scythe tied it in the garden and followed quickly.

"You're sure Maime and Hatchet are secure?" Scythe asked as they climbed to the second floor.

"Yes," he replied. "And I already wrote the letters to Maniodes and Nyx. I just haven't sent them yet. Did you meet any trouble on the road?"

"No, it was actually a nice ride, rather awkward though." Scythe held the door open to one of the guest rooms.

Dust puffed up from the bed as Dagger laid Leda down. Scythe noticed the letters Dagger had mentioned on the nightstand. Maniodes's had a short and simple statement: "If you want your woman back, come to our home." Nyx's was a kinder request to meet them here, stressing urgency. Scythe picked them both up.

"Let's send these off," she said.

Dagger just sighed and nodded. He looked as tired as she felt.

"What is taking so bloody long?" Scythe asked, whirling her weapon around.

"It's only been ten minutes," Dagger said by the window in the parlor.

"I know the bat will take time to reach Skiachora, but Nyx should be here by now," Scythe argued. She couldn't sit down.

Dagger didn't reply, he just turned back to the window. His arms were crossed as he leaned on the wall watching the trees.

"I'm going to check on the girl," Scythe said, needing something to do. She went to leave the parlor.

"Scythe, I—" Dagger's voice stopped her.

She turned back toward him but he fell silent, looking away from her.

"What?" she asked.

"Nothing," he said taking out a knife and twirling it. "Go check on Leda."

Scythe stayed where she was, hypnotized for a moment by the light glinting off the knife as it spun through his fingers. She tore her gaze back to Dagger's face. He still wasn't looking at her, just continued to study the courtyard below. As if he was expecting the two gods to use the front door. Something was bothering him.

Scythe shook her head to clear it. Of course something was bothering him; they were blackmailing a god, and they had just invited him over for a chat. She turned on her heel and left Dagger with his knife.

Scythe took the stairs two at a time and practically jogged to the guest wing. The only lock they had left was a slightly rusted padlock without a key. They would be able to rip it away when the time came. Dagger had fixed it to the door while Scythe watched the unconscious Leda, but she wasn't confident in it.

Scythe rounded the corner to the guest wing and stopped short.

"That fucking bitch."

The padlock lay broken on the dusty rug, and Leda's door stood wide open.

Scythe came running back through the archway, eyes fearful. Dagger's heart jumped to his throat at the sight.

Before he could ask what was going on, she said, "Leda's gone."

"What? How?" he demanded. He had secured the lock himself. He kicked himself for not guarding the door.

"The rust on the lock was worse than we thought. She must have thrown herself at the door and it just snapped."

Dagger ran both hands through his hair, trying not to panic. Scythe's hands were trembling. He had never seen her this scared before.

"It hasn't been that long," he said. "She must still be here. We can split up and search quickly."

"What about Nyx and Maniodes?" Scythe's voice was both frantic and sarcastic.

"I don't know. Just try to avoid them or stall until one of us finds Leda."

"Okay, okay. You start on this level and I'll run to the tower, we'll trap her in the middle." She became steadier once they had a plan.

"Alright, let's go." He practically jogged out of the parlor. Scythe ran towards the stairs again while he rounded the corner towards the servant's quarters.

"Scythe, what is going on?" Nyx's voice made him freeze. He spun back, heart frantic, and saw Scythe staring into the parlor. From his angle, Nyx couldn't see him, but she saw Scythe. He watched as Scythe went back to the parlor. Before she disappeared through the archway her hand twitched toward him. It was a tiny movement that he almost missed, but she waved at him. She was telling him to go, and she would stall.

"A lot has happened," Scythe said, surprisingly calm.

Dagger thought she was a pretty good actress in front of the goddess. He turned his back on them and ran through the lower level of the estate. He had to be fast, but his mind wouldn't stop whirling with possible horrible outcomes. On top of that, he kept scolding himself for what he'd nearly confessed to Scythe. If he had done that, she probably would have left. She was honest with her emotions now, but part of that was the fear of serious intimacy. They may have made love after Nukternios, but he didn't want to push his luck. Putting words to what he felt might scare her off again. She was a fascinating woman, but so confusing sometimes. That was clear to him on day one, when she'd buried his own dagger in his neck, but then they became more then close friends over the past ten years. He forced those thoughts away; they'd do no good muddying his concentration now. He *had* to find Leda.

She wasn't in the kitchen or servant's quarters, nor was she in any of the secret nooks Dagger knew about. Each empty room causes the personal torment to rise. On several occasions he caught himself turning a corner or opening a door with his dagger raised. Each time he put it back. The girl would be no use to him dead.

On the second floor he scanned the balcony to no avail. Dagger hurried ahead as the anxiety grew. He was hardly discreet about his search anymore. He could only hope he wasn't making so much noise he'd scare her off.

Throwing open the old library's door to the point that it rebounded off the wall wasn't helping his case, but it didn't matter. He froze as he spotted Leda by the missing wall.

She didn't scream. She clutched at herself against the cold, trembling. She spun to stare at him, terror clear in her eyes. Dagger was terrified she'd slip and fall, but she didn't. She stood her ground.

"What did you do to Father?" she demanded. Her pale-grey eyes were filled with tears of anger, but they didn't spill over.

"We left him in the grove," Dagger said as calm as he could manage. "He's alive."

He stepped into the library, one hand extended to Leda as if in peace.

She stepped away from him, closer to the edge.

"I'm not going to hurt you, Leda," he said.

"You did a bloody good job of that already," she jabbed a finger to her temple. A spot of dried blood clung to a strip of lavender.

"Technically, that was my wife. Leda, if you come with me, you will be safe."

He kept using her name to help convince her that he saw her as a living being, not just nameless prey. It was rather easy to manipulate people that way.

"Damn you to Skiachora!" she cursed. She shifted closer to the edge. She glanced down, terrified.

"Leda, if you jump you'll never see that man of yours again."

She looked back to him, shocked.

"Tall man, dark-blue hair?" Dagger said. "Tyndareus?"

Leda blinked, watching Dagger for any lie. "How do you know him?"

"I know who he actually is." He risked a small step closer. "And he's here."

"Liar!"

"I'm not lying, Leda. I'll take you to him right now."

He raised a hand closer to her. He was still too far. If she jumped, he wouldn't catch her.

"Don't touch me."

"Alright," he held both palms out. "Will you step away from the ledge?"

"Did you hurt him too?" she asked.

"No, he's fine. He's in the parlor waiting for us," Dagger lied.

"Does he know I'm here?" Offense joined the fear.

"Well, yes, but through blackmail," Dagger admitted.

"What is happening?" The tears escaped then.

"You'll know everything in a moment. I promise, Leda."

Her arms moved from clutched around her chest to around her stomach. One hand stroked it; she looked like she might be sick.

The entire estate shook then. Dagger had heard of moments of the earth itself shaking, but they were usually accounts from the west. This earthquake was enough to cause part of the floor next to Leda to fall into the air and crumble away. His heart seized, but he was too far to reach her. Luckily, she had clung to the desk and the quake stopped.

"WHERE IS SHE?!"

Maniodes's voice reverberated through the stone shortly after the earthquake.

"What was that?" Leda asked, unsure.

"That was him," he replied.

"You'll take me to him?" she asked after a confused pause.

"Yes."

"You do not touch me again," she demanded.

"Agreed, but we have to move quickly." Scythe was down there with the angry god.

Dagger stepped to the side so as to not block the door any longer. Leda left the edge and skirted around Dagger.

"Follow this corridor to the stairs," Dagger directed.

Leda looked in that direction but didn't move, only shook.

"You're trying my patience, Leda," he growled.

She flinched and started walking. He followed close enough to catch her if she tried anything.

Leda descended the stairs with Dagger close behind, like a lost princess being followed by the evil suitor. Dagger had to give her credit. She held her own in a horrible situation that she didn't understand.

At the bottom of the stairs, she froze again. He caught her eyeing the front door, but he gently nudged her along the proper way. She squeaked but still didn't scream.

The archway provided the perfect tableau for Leda. Maniodes stood in profile to them, framed by the stonework and grimy chandelier. His gaze was murderous under Scythe's blade.

"Tyndareus!" Leda shrieked.

She sprinted down the hall to Maniodes.

Maniodes froze midsentence and turned in time for Leda to latch onto him.

Dagger stood in the archway watching them, surprised that Maniodes had appeared in his shorter height. He had expected the god to tower over them like usual. Scythe strode over to join him proudly in their betrayal.

The shock in Maniodes's eyes made Dagger want to burst out laughing, but he controlled himself. Scythe giggled beside him, hardly able to contain her excitement.

Leda hugged Maniodes, sobbing into his chest. He stood there with his arms slightly raised away from her. His shock descended into cold hatred as he finally held Leda. Dagger realized then that Maniodes had chosen the form Leda was more familiar with.

Nyx stepped away from her son and the stranger, staring in confusion.

"What's wrong with this place?" Leda finally choked out, looking up at Maniodes.

Nyx kept staring at the girl, stunned and betrayed.

"It will be alright," Maniodes said, though he couldn't seem to believe his own words. His eyes kept darting from Leda, to Dagger and Scythe, then to Nyx.

Finally, they rested on the spot of blood in Leda's hair. He touched it, growing furious.

"They hurt you?" His eyes bored into Dagger and Scythe.

"They knocked me unconscious," Leda said.

His fury exploded then. He couldn't even seem to speak for a moment. He shielded Leda from Dagger and Scythe. He thrust one arm downward, and his shield materialized onto it. He stalked toward them with the other hand outstretched, ready to rip their souls out of them.

Dagger planted his feet with his weapon in hand. Scythe already had hers at full length. He loved her grin as the god descended on them.

"Maniodes!"

He stopped. He shook with rage as he looked to Nyx.

Leda screamed then. It was a short shriek before she clasped both hands over her mouth. She stared at the goddess of death standing right beside her. Maniodes, Dagger, and Scythe at least looked human. Nyx's eyes gave her away.

Leda shifted closer to Maniodes, still staring at Nyx. Maniodes shielded her again from the three of them. Not that it could do much good.

"I can explain," Maniodes said to Nyx.

"You disobeyed me. Not only set against you but on Phaos as well," Nyx said. "You took a lover."

"I did," Maniodes said. He didn't sound ashamed or guilty. If anything, he sounded proud now that the secret was out.

"You know how dangerous this is!" Nyx shouted.

Dagger had never seen her this angry. Nyx had always controlled any situation with calm dignity and power, even when it didn't exactly go as planned. Right now, her fists were clenched at her sides. Dagger could only hope that Nyx's anger would stay directed at Maniodes.

"I know, but this sort of thing can't be anticipated," Maniodes said.

"How long?" she demanded.

"Almost a year," he admitted.

Nyx blanched at the news.

"What did she call you?" Leda asked Maniodes quietly.

He bowed his head and answered Leda dejectedly. "My real name."

Leda took a step back from him. Betrayal mixed with her fear. "*The* Maniodes, god of the underworld?"

"Yes." His despair was palpable. Desperately, he added, "I never lied to you about anything, Leda, but this is why I couldn't tell you everything."

He went to touch her, but she moved away. He looked like he had been stabbed.

"I am still the man you know," he pleaded.

Leda clutched at her stomach again. Her eyes softened as she studied Maniodes's sorrow. She took his hand and he sighed.

Nyx moved. She reached into her sleeve and withdrew her bone. It was tiny, but she extended it to its full length and glory.

"No, wait, please." Maniodes shielded Leda again. "Let her drink from the river Lethe. She'll forget all of this."

"The river's power doesn't stretch over a year of memory. You know that," Nyx said.

"She'll forget tonight then, and I'll disappear from her life."

"What?! No!" Leda clutched tighter to Maniodes's arm.

"It's the only way you'll be safe," he protested to her.

"Why can't he be with anyone?" Leda asked Nyx suddenly.

Nyx was taken aback that Leda was brave enough to address her directly. Leda might have been behind Maniodes, but he couldn't protect her.

"He told me in the beginning that our relationship was dangerous, but he wouldn't say why," Leda said.

"Because the last child of a god nearly destroyed the world," Nyx explained.

Leda blanched and broke eye contact. She touched her stomach again, guilt quickly surfacing.

Scythe gasped. "Oh, shit."

Dagger glanced at her, confused, but Scythe was only watching Leda. Maniodes and Nyx looked their way too, as if just remembering they were present.

"She's with child," Scythe said, pointing to Leda.

Dagger had no idea how she had come to that conclusion so quickly. The guilt and fear in Leda's eyes was enough confirmation.

Maniodes turned to Leda with the wild question in his eyes. "Is that true?"

It took a moment for Leda to reply, but she eventually said, "I haven't bled in two months."

Maniodes kept his expression guarded, but fear crept into his eyes.

If Nyx's bone could crack, it would have, based on how hard she was gripping it.

Maniodes looked to Nyx again but couldn't say anything.

Silence filled the parlor. Dagger and Scythe kept their weapons drawn.

"Your Grace?" Scythe said hesitantly.

Nyx turned to Scythe, cold and furious.

"If I may, I think she should drink from Lethe," Scythe said.

Dagger wanted to agree but stayed quiet, not wanting to push the situation too far.

Nyx sighed exhausted. "And the child?"

"It could be watched from a distance," Scythe said. "If it poses a threat, then we do what has to be done."

"*We* do what has to be done," Nyx repeated to herself. "Are you volunteering?"

"I am," Scythe said without missing a beat, though she probably hadn't intended to.

"I will as well," Dagger put in.

They needed Nyx on their side. If their plan shifted from rulers to babysitters, then at least they would be alive.

"You planned this," Nyx accused, stepping closer to them. "That entire festival was to gain my favor, then bring this to light. Why not come to me personally?"

The hurt in her eyes was personal. They had intended to humiliate Maniodes and knew Nyx would get caught in the crossfire. Scythe didn't appear pleased by the situation either. Nyx deserved to know the truth.

"We only learned of the girl recently," Dagger said.

"That's actually why Pitch died," Scythe added quickly. "Dagger and I suspected Maniodes was hiding something, and Pitch remembered the forbidden box. He led us to it and I scratched the lock getting it open."

Maniodes's fists clenched.

"After Pitch was killed," Dagger continued, "I was angry. We both went back for the girl after following Maniodes to learn where she was, and brought her here."

He wanted to ask Nyx why she hadn't protected Pitch. He had done her bidding but ended up dead. Dagger didn't blame her for his death, that was entirely his own fault, but she had promised to protect him. He held the sharp words back. They would do no good here.

"I'm sorry, Your Grace," Scythe said to Nyx, "but you needed to know this was happening. Maniodes certainly wasn't going to confess. And if we confronted him alone about it he'd just kill us to keep it secret. We had to bring you here, hoping you would trust us and, well, protect us from him."

"Nyx," Maniodes tried to interject.

"Shut up," Nyx commanded.

They all fell silent, letting the goddess think. It felt like Dagger's dead heart was trying to strangle him.

"Nyx," Maniodes tried again quietly.

She let him continue this time. Her black and white eyes fumed with anger as she watched him.

"Please, at least let Leda go. She'll forget this whole thing. I'll watch over the babe myself."

"And if it's too dangerous?" Nyx accused. "Phaos's last son nearly scorched all of Ichorisis!"

"I'll do what must be done." His voice was grave.

"What?" Leda stepped away from Maniodes.

He couldn't look at her.

"How do I know you'll hold up to that agreement?" Nyx asked.

"You have my word—"

"You gave that before."

Maniodes fell quiet.

Nyx sighed. "You know what? You never did like being confined. This alone is proof. You will watch this child and kill it if need be."

Maniodes bowed his head in acceptance.

Dagger's heart stuck in his throat. After all of this, Maniodes was still in charge?

"As a human," Nyx finished.

Maniodes blinked. "How do you mean?"

Nyx raised her bone and pointed it at her son. The pain in her eyes matched his as he flinched.

Maniodes grunted and clutched at his chest. He staggered, falling to his knees in front of his mother.

Leda knelt beside him, holding his shoulders, pleading for Nyx to leave him alone.

Maniodes screamed as a golden ball of light escaped from his chest. Once it was out, he was left gasping. Dagger watched, hiding his excitement, as the light drifted from Maniodes and disappeared into Nyx's bone.

Maniodes watched the light go out, then examined his own hands. They looked exactly the same, but he looked scared. The straps of his shield unclasped themselves from around his arm. He watched, dejected, as his shield clattered to the floor. Dagger wasn't entirely sure if Maniodes was just stripped of his divine powers, or completely human now. Given the fear in Maniodes's eyes, he understood what had happened.

"Leave," Nyx commanded.

"Mother—"

"Leave, and if you don't uphold your word, I will do worse."

Maniodes got to his feet, unsteady at first, but Leda helped him. He took her hand, and they left the parlor.

As Maniodes passed between Dagger and Scythe, the cold hatred aimed at them grew tenfold.

"I suppose the two of you want some kind of reward?"

Scythe tore her eyes away from the now-human Maniodes as he and Leda left. Nyx focused on them with crossed arms, her bone now fitted through a loop in her robes. It hung at her hip like a sword.

They weren't completely clear yet. Neither of them could just ask to take Maniodes's place. That wound was too fresh for Nyx to be prodded at.

"Only if you deem it right," Scythe said.

Scythe was already trying to figure out a way to end the night here and now. They could establish themselves as rulers with the Ferrum once Nyx had gone.

Out of the corner of her eye, she saw Dagger about to say something then close his mouth.

Nyx caught Dagger too. "What?"

"I'm just wondering," he said slowly, as a subject, his head bowed. "Who will rule Skiachora now?"

It wasn't as direct as Scythe would have asked, but it could work. Instead of nominating himself, Dagger put voice to the question they were all thinking.

Nyx inhaled, held the breath, and then let it whoosh out. She looked exhausted.

"I suppose you and Scythe want to?" she said bluntly. "That's what all of this was about."

Scythe took hold of Dagger's indirect manner of speaking. "Tonight was meant to bring Maniodes's betrayal to light."

"And avenge Pitch," Dagger added, "but we'll take that responsibility if need be."

Nyx mulled over the idea. She wasn't pleased, but Scythe could see she was honestly considering it. She was rather surprised as well that Nyx had brought it up. Nyx looked tired and worn, as if taking Maniodes's divine essence had drained her. It probably had, now that Scythe thought about it. That, combined with basically losing another son. Nyx probably just wanted the whole situation over with.

Nyx gazed around, surprised and still hurt. "Did you hate Maniodes that much?"

"We didn't *hate* him," Dagger said gently, "but he never understood us. He either ignored or punished us for small things, like Pitch. Though in his defense, some of them were fair and mandated. Our marriage was bizarre, but it worked."

"It did," Nyx nodded. She turned back to Dagger and Scythe, unhooking her bone from her hip. "Kneel."

They did, instantly. Scythe kept her weapon extended; it towered over her like a banner. Dagger placed his weapon on the ground before him, still holding the hilt.

Nyx's bone began to glow gold. The light that had come from Maniodes appeared out of the end and floated toward them. It split into two smaller orbs. Scythe's instinct told her to attack something new and strange, but she stayed still as one ball floated closer to her.

The gold glow disappeared into Scythe's chest, and she clenched back a scream. It felt like lava was being poured into her chest. It spread through her veins, then vanished as quickly as it had come. She was left feeling exactly the same.

Scythe looked to Dagger and saw that he was gasping in the aftermath of the same pain, but he was fine too.

"Stand," Nyx commanded.

They did. Scythe realized her hands were tingling. It was like they had gone to sleep and now the blood was returning to them. It was rather annoying; she hoped it was only a temporary side-effect.

"It takes a lot of power to create a god's essence," Nyx said. "I was able to split Maniodes's in half to give each of you. You'll be able to perform the basic power we can, but in a one-on-one fight, you'll be weaker."

Dagger was examining his hands, probably feeling the same tingling. He met Scythe's eye and beamed. Scythe couldn't stop smiling either.

Turning back to Nyx erased that smile. Nyx's lips were pressed into a thin line. She was still emotional, but she held it well.

She picked up Maniodes's shield and held it to her chest like she was cradling a child. Without warning, she vanished.

# Chapter 46

Scythe weaved through the bowels of Maniodes's castle with Dagger. She corrected the thought quickly; it was their castle now. Skiachora was theirs. The idea hadn't sunk past her skin yet.

The first thing they did after Nyx had vanished was release Maime and Hatchet. Hatchet threw several curses as they untied him. Maime immediately punched Dagger.

Dagger had taken the blow with only a single step back. Maime stared, dumbfounded, probably expecting Dagger's skull to be crushed. The marks of their previous fight had healed shortly after gaining the golden essence of a god. Dagger hadn't even blinked; he hadn't felt a thing. Scythe remembered Maniodes fighting them off, heedless of his wounds. He hadn't felt them. That also explained how he had healed so quickly.

Scythe felt an odd but warm sensation in her stomach, seeing Dagger stare down Maime. He stood his ground and gave Maime a haunting smile.

"Go to the throne room," Dagger told Maime.

"What?" Hatchet started to ask something, but Scythe cut him off.

"We will meet you there with the others. Just go." Now they ran through the cracked corridor, hoping to find Axe quickly in one of the torture chambers. They rounded the last corner, and Dagger threw open the door to the chamber of chains.

Dagger stopped short, sucking air through his teeth. Scythe froze at the sight too.

Axe stood in the center as Dagger had once before. Chains penetrated his body, locking him in place.

Scythe approached Axe but he didn't raise his head. It was bowed, and his eyes were squeezed shut in agony. His breathing was shallow and pained.

"How did Maniodes take them out of you?" Scythe asked Dagger.

"I don't know," he said reaching to touch one chain. He lowered his hand thinking better of it. "They just did after he spoke; it was like he commanded them."

Dagger glanced around, probably looking for some kind of device.

Axe coughed blood.

Scythe followed the chains but they just disappeared into shadows. "He commanded them," she said quietly.

"I have an idea," Scythe took Dagger's arm and guided him to a gap in the chains. "Stand here."

"Why?"

"So they don't hit us," Scythe explained, then commanded, "Retract!"

They did. Their ripped through Axe with a squelch of meat and rattled back into the shadows.

More blood sprouted from Axe's mouth as he shrieked. He fell limp, but Dagger caught him. Axe leaned on him, bleeding, and panting.

Scythe wrung her hands, unable to do more then watch. At least he was free, and Dagger understood his pain.

"You'll be okay," Dagger said, supporting his shoulder. "We won, Axe."

Axe moved then. He pushed away from Dagger, then lunged at him. Surprised by the sudden fury, Dagger let Axe go for his neck. Axe ended up on top of Dagger with his hands locked around Dagger's throat.

Scythe extended her weapon in a second and held it to Axe's neck.

"Scythe, it's alright. I can't feel it," Dagger said quickly and clearly.

Axe's knuckles were white as he squeezed.

She forced herself to relax and lowered the weapon.

"Pitch is dead," Axe growled. "He trusted you!"

"I know," Dagger said gravely.

Dagger didn't fight back as Axe tried to let his fury out. Axe's face contorted in rage and pain, and Dagger just lay there.

Axe tried to lift, then slam, Dagger's head back to the ground, but he was too weak. He slipped and rolled off Dagger, landing on his back beside him. He wheezed through every pant, and blood spread on his clothes.

Scythe shrunk her weapon and pocketed it, but the initial fury towards Axe's attack on Dagger still burned.

Axe coughed again, then said, "How the fuck did you survive that for three days?"

"Not being able to die helped," Dagger admitted, still on his back.

"And now you're bloody gods."

"Yup," Dagger said nonchalantly.

"We could have just locked him in a box."

"I was starting to think that wasn't going to work, actually," Dagger admitted.

"This is a lovely reunion and all," Scythe said, "but I don't appreciate you attacking my husband, Axe."

"He was angry, Scythe," Dagger said, helping Axe sit up. "He has every right to be."

"I know that, but can we get upstairs? The others will want an explanation." She was practically bouncing on her toes.

"What happened after that blast?" Axe asked, leaning on Dagger's shoulder.

Scythe's anger at him cooled. He didn't know how many of them were gone yet; he was unconscious before that happened. Come to think of it, she didn't know who else died because of them either.

"We'll explain in the throne room," Dagger said.

Scythe went to support Axe's other side.

The throne room was empty except for Maime and Hatchet. White powder dusted the floor, along, with the occasional broken bone. Dagger was reminded of Chip suddenly, and his grief returned. Chip had been crushed trying to protect them. There was no sign of Shorty in the room either. All of the sentries were gone.

Hatchet kept the door open as they brought Axe inside and set him down on the dais.

"So what happened?" Maime demanded, close by. His hulking form towered as his arms crossed.

"We'll explain everything when the others arrive," Dagger said. "Where are the sentries?"

"I have no fucking idea, and I'd rather not wait. Just get on with it," he growled.

"We overthrew Maniodes," Scythe said, stepping in front of the brute. "And we'll explain more when the others get here."

Dagger watched as his wife stared down Maime. He glared back, eyebrows knit together, but he only scowled. Pride welled in Dagger's chest as Scythe turned back to him.

While her red eyes held fire a moment ago toward Maime, now they were wide and confused with her back to him. She took Dagger's arm and led him away from the others.

"We have to get the others here now," she said. "They won't wait for bats to send letters."

"Do you know how Maniodes would open the ground to make a path?" Dagger asked, "Like he did for us back in Chalcis?"

"I don't know how he did that. Why would I?"

"You've been here a century, Scythe. He didn't mention any tricks to you?"

"No, we never chatted about ripping holes into the earth leading down here. Pitch might have known something," she said.

Any reply he had died in his throat at the mention of Pitch.

Scythe must have seen his reaction change, because she instantly softened. "Dagger, I—"

"It's alright." He waved those thoughts away. Grieving could wait. "We must have some way to summon them."

Scythe sighed and glanced away, thinking.

Dagger thought about the summons he'd received. The ground in the city had opened right at their feet, but the one at their estate had been waiting for them. Whatever it was that Maniodes could do, there was a limit to it. The second time, he hadn't been able to pinpoint them directly.

"What if it's stronger in the cities?" Dagger speculated.

"But he opened one right outside our house," Scythe countered. "One estate on a mountain is hardly a city."

"But he knew we'd find it."

"Do you think he can sense places better than people?" she asked.

"Maybe, what do you mean by 'sense'?" he asked.

"There was a time I was with him, and he summoned two others for a big job. It was Maime and Hammer, actually. He knew which city they were in. They had some hideout in one of the northern cities. It was like he just thought of them, and in a few minutes they were in his office."

"That's not much of a lead," Dagger said, sighing.

He glanced over to Axe, Maime, and Hatchet. They were waiting awkwardly, occasionally talking. Maime leaned against one of the pillars, staring at the floor.

Something new happened. Nothing physically changed but while thinking of them, Dagger felt the castle they stood in now. It wasn't as if the image of the castle appeared, just the general knowledge of it.

Dagger was about to brush the odd sensation off. It was natural to think of the place they all stood now, but the thought hadn't been his.

"Scythe," he said catching her attention. "Think of Lace."

She blinked, confused, but didn't reply. She glanced away for a moment, then the confusion melted.

"What happened?" he asked eagerly.

"I just thought of the city Potamis after thinking of her. I have no idea why. I haven't been there in years," Scythe shrugged. "It's like I can *see* her, though."

Scythe's eyes widened more, and she jumped suddenly.

"What?" Dagger asked. "What happened?"

Scythe blinked again and focused on Dagger. "I thought of the ground opening, and it did right in front of her. I saw it! Think of one of the others, like Flail. You'll know what I mean."

"Alright," he said, taking a breath.

He brought up Flail in his mind's eye. She was a woman with bronzed skin and brown hair streaked with orange. A flail was always attached to her belt. As he did, the image of Stymphalia appeared. It was so detailed that Dagger was able to pinpoint which crypt Flail was currently sleeping in. He could practically see the woman lounging on top of a coffin. The crypt was small, but Dagger focused on a section of the floor. He envisioned a stairway opening and watched, astonished, as Flail jerked awake at the noise and saw the hole beside her. Dread and fear filled her eyes but she started down the stairs.

Dagger focused on Scythe then. "It worked. All we have to do is *think*, and they'll come. This is amazing," he said taking the moment to relish in the new power. "Go talk to the others. I'll summon the rest of them."

Scythe paused and glanced to the others. "Can't you go talk to them? You're better at diplomacy than I am."

"You'll do fine. You kept Nyx waiting until Maniodes showed up. Besides, I'd like to play with this weird, new summoning power."

"I'd like to experiment too, though," Scythe argued.

"All you have to do is keep them company. It might get chaotic in Ichorisis if we're both opening random holes by people," Dagger said.

"Okay, fine." She threw up her hands in defeat. "I'm their queen now anyway. I have to get used to that."

"I wouldn't use the *queen* word just yet. They might not appreciate that idea. Besides, you were fine around everyone at the ball. What's changed?" he asked, concerned.

"It's different now," Scythe said. "There was no agenda other than becoming allies with Nyx. Now they're going to demand things of us."

"You *had* to see that coming."

"I did. I just…part of me never really thought this would happen. When you were looking for Leda and Maniodes came, I thought we were dead. It's been a long night; I think I'm just tired."

She did look haggard. Dagger was sure he looked the same. He was exhausted, too. He touched her shoulder, then pulled her close. She sighed into his chest and wrapped her arms around him. He took a moment, breathing in the scent of her hair. They both needed rest.

"We won, Scythe," he said gently, not quite believing the words. "We just need to take care of a few things first, and then we can relax. Maybe we can even try out our new bed up in the tower. It's not Maniodes's anymore."

Scythe gave a small chuckle into his chest. She lifted her head and stood on her toes bringing her lips closer to his.

"We'll see where tonight leads," she whispered before kissing him.

The moment ended too quickly when she pulled away. She seemed happier, content at least. He squeezed her hand before she went to talk to the others.

Dagger forced his mind to focus on the summoning trick. Footsteps distracted him for a moment, and Lace and Flail entered the throne room. They approached Scythe and the others, confused. Dagger kept to the side, letting Scythe receive them.

The Incruentus Ferrum order wasn't a large one, and he knew everyone's face, at least. He focused on each one and, in time, their locations were revealed to him. Some of them didn't appear though. He thought of Cross, but he saw only blackness in his mind's eye. Several of them were grouped together discussing previous events, so Dagger was able to summon them all on one go.

There were a couple of times, with Cutlass and Pike, where he couldn't pinpoint a specific city or village. He could feel which direction they were in, but nothing as detailed as before. Pike was on the northern coast heading east, and Cutlass was somewhere in the thick Katesar woods.

This was probably why Maniodes had only opened the ground at their estate after they hunted down Leda.

This summoning power had its limits when it came to the wilderness between the city-states. He opened several holes in the direction each Ferrum was heading and could only hope they would find them.

More footsteps and voices filled the room now. Dagger stayed where he was for one more moment.

He thought of Pitch. The image was detailed and strong. It was as if the twelve-year-old boy stood alive in front of him. But he didn't. No location appeared in his thoughts. Pitch was gone.

He swallowed the sudden lump in his throat. There would be time later to mourn.

He turned toward the others and joined Scythe.

Lace stood by Maime with a hand on his wrist. He still looked furious, but she appeared to be holding him back. Dagger wondered if there was something going on between those two.

The other Ferrum parted to clear a path for him. He felt their confused eyes demanding answers.

Dagger climbed the dais, and Scythe quickly joined him. Dagger stood in front of the black throne beside Scythe. All of the Incruentus Ferrum watched them expectedly, eyes darting from one to the other.

He looked to Scythe for a moment, not sure what to say to them. He was growing more nervous by the second. She seemed at a loss too, but more composed than before.

"What happened?" Flail asked. "Where is Maniodes?"

"He's gone," Scythe replied. "Nyx took his essence and gave it to us."

A murmur ran through them as more questions arose. Dagger saw no point in keeping them in the dark now.

"Scythe and I worked to depose him with Nyx's help," Dagger added. "We uncovered his betrayal to the goddess as well."

"Why, though?" Flail demanded. "That chaos earlier was rather sudden. And you two started it after Pitch died. What does Nyx have to do with this?"

"Maniodes wanted to dispose of us—*all* of us," Dagger emphasized. Twisting the truth a bit simplified things and kept Nyx in a good light. It came rather easy to him as well. "We were only tools to him: weapons. He thought he was losing control. You heard him during the mutiny, saying dogs would have been easier. And we weren't the only ones in the fight."

"My brother died because of that fight!" Maime shouted.

"Exactly," Scythe said. "Dagger and I attacked first, yes, but he didn't hesitate in slaughtering others. Cross was caught in that, and the sentries."

"And Lance, Star, and Blade," another called out. It was a short, dark-skinned man with a longbow on his back.

Dagger hadn't seen their deaths in the confusion but remembered the throwing stars being imbedded into Maniodes's shoulder.

"They are why we took action," Dagger said. "Maniodes never valued us."

The Incruentus Ferrum fell silent. They looked uncomfortable, even a bit scared, as they thought about it. He couldn't blame them for arguing; a lot had happened in one night.

Dagger looked over to Maime, who stood motionless by Lace, and caught his eye.

"So you're in charge now?" Maime asked, clearly not happy.

"Wait, you said Nyx gave you Maniodes's *essence*? What does that even mean?" Lace asked.

"They're the gods now," Maime accused.

"It does," Scythe said, keeping her composure and balance. Dagger was glad she did; he wasn't used to a crowd like this.

More questions rose from the Ferrum in a wave. Dagger was able to catch the words, "that's impossible," but it was Maime who answered.

"It's true," he called. "I hit Dagger, and he didn't even flinch. Just like Maniodes during the mutiny."

"Why did you hit him?" Lace asked, surprised.

"He tied me and Hatchet up in their cellar!" Maime defended.

"I did do that," Dagger admitted, refusing to feel guilty. "We needed our home to be empty for meeting Nyx and Maniodes, and you weren't exactly willing to leave."

"The point is," Scythe rested a hand against Dagger's arm. "Things can be different now."

"Different how?" Flail demanded. "Things were fine before."

"Were they?" Scythe threw back. "Were we ever able to have a civil conversation like this with him before? You saw what he did to Pitch for dropping a damn box."

"And how many of you still have living family you'd like to see again? Maybe not interact with, but watch over even from a distance? Like Axe here. He has a small daughter and Maniodes forbade him from seeing her. Or with Cross; she wanted to go grey to be with her son, but he refused her request," Dagger said.

"And there's something else he did to us. You all remember your past lives, right? I do. I remember my sister, I remember the day my father was killed by thieves, and I remember my mother. She wasn't a sane woman, but that wasn't her fault; it was something in her brain. My point being, I wasn't murderous or bloodthirsty back then. I was a normal person, going about his history studies and learning the family trade. And Scythe here, she fought through a hard life, but she worked through it. When a very hard situation occurred, she wasn't violent. That violence came after death."

He met Scythe's gaze then. Her mouth was pinched, and her eyes were hard.

"I won't go into details," he added. "What I'm trying to say is that when Maniodes picked us to be Incruentus Ferrum he didn't care about our pasts. He gave us a bloodlust that made doing his bidding easier."

"How do we know you're not making this shit up?" Maime accused.

"Ask Axe," Scythe said, gesturing to him.

"Why me?" Axe asked, astonished, still on the dais.

"You told me about your daughter in the library when we met," Scythe said. "Then about the job Maniodes sent you on to kill a little girl. You said you felt different afterward, that you didn't have the taste for murder anymore."

The others were watching Axe intently now. Most of them looked confused, as if they couldn't comprehend another Ferrum not wanting to kill. Dagger felt for the man, making him the center of the attention so unexpectedly, but Scythe made a good point.

Axe exchanged a glance with Dagger. He was still hunched over his wounds, bleeding from all of them. Dagger nodded to him, hoping Axe would speak for them.

"It's true," Axe said after a moment. "After I killed that child, something inside me broke. I don't mean literally. I didn't feel anything change, but *I* changed. If they want to call it bloodlust, then so be it. I do believe Maniodes did something to us. I was just a tutor for hire who had to teach himself to read first. I had never taken a life, nor had I wanted to before becoming this. I'm actually glad that lust is gone."

"But why?" the archer asked. "Why manipulate us like that?"

"Because we were just tools," Dagger emphasized. "Cross was a valuable weapon because of her skill, which he didn't want to lose. She hadn't broken through her bloodlust yet, and he knew that somehow. He knew she would still do his bidding, just as we all did because we liked it. The sentries were the same to him. They couldn't even have their own voices. I think they were taken back by their own leader."

"Maniodes wasn't their leader?" Lace asked.

"He was, but there was another system in place for them. I don't know what, but one of them told me of the original skeleton created by Maniodes, and how that one connects to them all. I don't know where that one is, but I'd suspect the others are with him. Scythe and I will find them either way, and things will basically go back to normal."

They fell silent then; most of them wouldn't meet his gaze.

"You don't need to fear us the way we did him," Dagger said, stepping down from the dais to join them. Scythe quickly followed.

They all stood in an awkward silence, unsure how to continue. Dagger thought of how Maniodes would just dismiss them, but he didn't want to do that.

"I think we should part ways here," he suggested. "It's been a long night for all of us, and day broke a while ago."

"Yes," Scythe agreed beside him. "We can meet again tomorrow night to really discuss everything."

The Ferrum seemed to agree. Most nodded, though some didn't react. Maime just grunted. They left the throne room quietly. The archer even tried to bow, looking uncomfortable, but Dagger reassured him it wasn't needed.

Flail helped Axe stand, and they were the last to leave Dagger and Scythe alone.

Dagger turned toward Scythe and sighed. "That went well, I think."

Scythe gave a slow nod. She looked up to the throne and asked, "What do we do with that?"

He ran a hand through his hair. He wasn't in the mood to deal with the finer details. "Get rid of it, I suppose. It's too big for us. Maybe have two new ones built?"

"Go sit." She pushed his arm a bit.

"Why?"

"Just go." Her grin became more suggestive.

He paused, watching her, and the smile grew. He stepped up to the throne again, watching her from the corner of his eye. He climbed onto the throne and before he could consider how ridiculous he looked with his feet not touching the floor, Scythe was on top of him.

She situated herself on his lap, legs draped over one arm of the throne. Her grin stayed wicked as she played with his collar.

He kissed her eagerly. One hand of his was wrapped around her back, holding her in place. The other caressed her thigh.

Scythe's hand buried itself in his hair, locking him in place. Her lips played along his perfectly.

He reluctantly came to his senses as they broke apart. Scythe kept her forehead on his, regaining her breath.

"Scythe," Dagger said once his voice was steady. "I almost admitted something to you back home."

"I know," she said. "And you don't have to worry about the answer."

If his dead heart could beat it would have stopped again.

He kissed her, taking his time.

"Did you want to head back home?" her voice was husky, as he trialed his lips down her neck.

"You know I do," he said.

Her hand slid down his stomach to his trousers.

"But there's one more thing first," he forced himself to say regretfully while squeezing her thigh.

"What?" she asked, taken out of the moment.

# Epilogue

The moon had only just started to grow soft at the edge, losing its fullness. It peeked low through the branches of the clearing.

Dagger let go of the man's arm, and Scythe let the woman go. The couple instantly went to each other and embraced. Both were covered in clean bandages, and most of their wounds had healed somewhat.

The woman shook as she buried her head into her husband's shoulder. He held her tightly, staring wide-eyed at Dagger and Scythe.

"I know you're terrified," Dagger said to them. "There's nothing we can say to make this better, nothing we could give as compensation."

"Where are we?" the woman asked, shifting to look at them. Her one remaining arm wrapped around the man's waist.

"You're home," Scythe said. "The cottage is just behind you. Bandits had moved in when it was empty, but we took care of them. There's also a bag of gold from them on the table."

The woman looked back to the house. She looked dazed, probably thinking it was some kind of hallucination.

"This a trick?" the man demanded.

"No," Dagger said. "You'll never see us again."

The man probably didn't believe him, but Scythe couldn't tell. Half of his face was hidden in the bandage because of her burning him.

"What are your names?" Dagger asked, curious.

It was the woman who answered, still leaning her head on her husband. "I'm Cilla, and this is Polybius."

"I am sorry about what we did to you." In truth, Scythe wasn't, but they needed to hear that. She was reminded than of her own bloodlust. She still didn't feel a thing for these people. Dagger did, but she didn't. That was something she would have to keep in check.

Before Dagger and Scythe could terrify them anymore, they joined hands and vanished from the clearing.

# Pronunciation Guide

Most names of places and people are based off of the Ancient Greek language in this story. It's not too difficult to pronounce most things actually, mainly because there are hardly any silent letters, all of them are spoken, and there aren't many combinations such as "th," or "ch," making their own sounds. There are exceptions to the rules of course, but this guide should help with the most common names seen in this story.

The names of the Incruentus Ferrum are not in this list, however. They are the names of the weapons they chose written in the English language (Dagger, Scythe, and Axe for a few examples).

Acheron – Ak-e-ron – River running through Skiachora, into Ichorisis
Chalcis – Kal-kis – city-state of Ichorisis
Cilla – Silla
Ichorisis – Ichor-eses – land of the living
Incruentus Ferrum – In-crew-en-tus Fer-rum – undead creatures who deal out mischief and death, ruled over by Maniodes.
Kaliasma – Kali-as-ma – city-state
Limaros – Li-mar-os

Lumeon – Lum-e-on – god of the sea
Maniodes – Mani-o-des – god of the underworld
Marella – Mar-ella
Nereus – Ner-e-us
Nukternios –Nuk-ter-ni-os – end of harvest festival for Nyx
Nyx – Nix – goddess of death, chief deity over all others
Phaos – Fa-os – god of the living
Polybius – Poly-bi-us
Potamis – Po-tam-is
Sappho – Sap-fo
Skiachora – Skia-kora – land of the dead
Stymphalia – Stym-fal-ia – city-state
Tholus – Tho-lus
Tyndareus – Tyn-dar-iu

# Acknowledgments

I'm still bad at these parts but I want to thank my friends, and beta readers. Jessica Pringle, Allesha Bauer, Kelly Marentette, along with Spyroula Manti, you are all awesome. Also to the voices in my head, they still don't shut up.

# About the Author

Emilie Knight studied Ancient Greek and Roman history at the University of Windsor. Using that and her love of Greek Mythology and horror, she ties them together in an amazing dark fantasy combination. Her first novel, *Era of Undying*, does this as well, even being compared to the Odyssey or Beowulf.

CPSIA information can be obtained
at www.ICGtesting.com
Printed in the USA
LVHW090317180619
621511LV00003B/12/P

9 781999 091408